Praise for
ATLANTIS RISING

"Alyssa Day creates an amazing and astonishing world in *Atlantis Rising* [that] you'll want to visit again and again. *Atlantis Rising* is romantic, sexy, and utterly compelling. I loved it!"

—*New York Times* bestselling author Christine Feehan

"An amazing new world you don't want to miss and you won't want to leave. Alyssa Day delivers chills, thrills, and your fill of sexy Poseidon Warriors."

—*USA Today* bestselling author Kerrelyn Sparks

"Wow! Alyssa Day writes marvelous paranormal romance."

—*USA Today* bestselling author Susan Kearney

"Alyssa Day's characters grab you and take you on a whirl-wind adventure. I haven't been so captivated by characters or a story in a long time. Enjoy the ride!"

—*New York Times* bestselling author Susan Squires

"There's nothing more evocative than the world of Atlantis. Alyssa Day has penned a white-hot winner!"

—Gena Showalter, author of *The Nymph King*

Praise for Alyssa Day's previous books
written as Alesia Holliday . . .

"An appealing heroine with a sense of humor and a sexy hero."
　　　　　　　　　　　　　　　　　—*Library Journal*

"Characters that will win your heart!"
　　—*New York Times* bestselling author Suzanne Brockmann

"Holliday does it again! The reader won't be able to put down this . . . story filled with colorful and heartwarming characters."
　　　　　　　　　　　　　　　—*Romantic Times* (4½ stars)

"Excellent . . . fast-paced."　　　—Lori Avocato, award-winning
　　　　　　　　　　　author of The Pauline Sokol Mystery series

"Delightful, delicious, and just plain fun."
　　　　　　　　　　　　　　　　—Susan McBride, author of
　　　　　　　　　　　　　The Debutante Dropout Mystery series

"Fun."　　—Susan Wiggs, author of *The Ocean Between Us*

"Well-written, fast-paced . . . [I] was hooked from page one."
　　　　　　　　　　　　　　　　　　—*The Best Reviews*

"Simply fantastic."　　　　　　　　　—*Affaire de Coeur*

"Charming characters come to life immediately. This is without a doubt in the top ten books of the year."
　　　　　　　　　　　　　　　—*Huntress Book Reviews*

ATLANTIS RISING

The Warriors of Poseidon

ALYSSA DAY

BERKLEY SENSATION, NEW YORK

THE BERKLEY PUBLISHING GROUP
Published by the Penguin Group
Penguin Group (USA) Inc.
375 Hudson Street, New York, New York 10014, USA
Penguin Group (Canada), 90 Eglinton Avenue East, Suite 700, Toronto, Ontario M4P 2Y3, Canada
(a division of Pearson Penguin Canada Inc.)
Penguin Books Ltd., 80 Strand, London WC2R 0RL, England
Penguin Group Ireland, 25 St. Stephen's Green, Dublin 2, Ireland (a division of Penguin Books Ltd.)
Penguin Group (Australia), 250 Camberwell Road, Camberwell, Victoria 3124, Australia
(a division of Pearson Australia Group Pty. Ltd.)
Penguin Books India Pvt. Ltd., 11 Community Centre, Panchsheel Park, New Delhi—110 017, India
Penguin Group (NZ), 67 Apollo Drive, Mairangi Bay, Auckland 1311, New Zealand
(a division of Pearson New Zealand Ltd.)
Penguin Books (South Africa) (Pty.) Ltd., 24 Sturdee Avenue, Rosebank, Johannesburg 2196, South Africa

Penguin Books Ltd., Registered Offices: 80 Strand, London WC2R 0RL, England

This is a work of fiction. Names, characters, places, and incidents either are the product of the author's
imagination or are used fictitiously, and any resemblance to actual persons, living or dead, business es-
tablishments, events, or locales is entirely coincidental. The publisher does not have any control over
and does not assume any responsibility for author or third-party websites or their content.

ATLANTIS RISING

A Berkley Sensation Book / published by arrangement with the author

PRINTING HISTORY
Berkley Sensation mass-market edition / March 2007

ISBN: 978-0-425-21449-7

BERKLEY SENSATION®
Berkley Sensation Books are published by The Berkley Publishing Group,
a division of Penguin Group (USA) Inc.,
375 Hudson Street, New York, New York 10014.
BERKLEY SENSATION is a registered trademark of Penguin Group (USA) Inc.
The "B" design is a trademark belonging to Penguin Group (USA) Inc.

PRINTED IN THE UNITED STATES OF AMERICA

10 9 8 7 6 5 4 3 2

Acknowledgments

Thanks, always, to Steve Axelrod, who makes me laugh, makes great deals for me, and says nice things when I make my once-a-book "aarghhh" phone call.

To my wonderful friends Christine, Cheryl, Kathy, and Val of the Starfish Club for encouragement, and to all my incredible friends who listen, are patient, and offer wonderful advice: Lani Diane Rich, Michelle Cunnah, Barbara Ferrer, Eileen Rendahl, Whitney Gaskell, Beth Kendrick, Cindy Holby, and Marianne Mancusi. To Megan Emish, for the Warriors of Poseidon symbol. To my terrific Web people, Deb and Tara at RomanceDesigns.com, who should have been thanked earlier.

To Suz Brockmann, Ed Gaffney, Eric Ruben, Virginia Kantra, and Cathy Mann, who are brilliant and generous, and to the folks at the *Into the Storm* weekend for sharing their enthusiasm with me and listening to the first-ever reading from this book.

Jenny Crusie and the Cherries, who are funny, cranky, and amazing in exactly the right proportions.

And *always*, of course, to my children, who ate a little too much pizza and watched a little too much TV during the last two weeks of this book, but never once complained. You're the *best*.

Dear Reader,

Thank you for coming along with me on my journey to Atlantis. Be sure to visit me at www.alyssaday.com for free screensavers and to sign up for my members-only mailing list!

Alyssa

In this island, Atlantis, arose a great and marvelous might of kings . . . But in later time, after there had been exceeding great earthquakes and floods, there fell one day and night of destruction; and the warriors . . . were swallowed up by the earth, and in like manner did the island Atlantis sink beneath the sea and vanish away.

—Plato, *Timaeus*, dated at approximately 600 B.C.

One can hardly doubt that significant shifts of the earth's crust have taken place repeatedly . . .

—Albert Einstein, in correspondence to Charles Hapgood, May 8, 1953

Capital City of Atlantis, 9600 B.C.

It was the time before the Cataclysm, forced upon Atlanteans by the greed of humanity. In Poseidon's Temple, in the soul of the seven isles of Atlantis, a group of warriors met with the sea god's high priest. He divided them into seven groups of seven and assigned each a sacred duty and an object of power—a magic-imbued gemstone. Some were to sink to the bottom of the world, shielded from prying eyes and envious lusts by the waters that nurtured them. Others were to join the lands of humans at assigned locations—all high grounds that would protect the lineage in the event of severe flooding.

All would wait. And watch. And protect.

And serve as first warning on the eve of humanity's destruction.

Then, and only then, Atlantis would rise.

For they were the Warriors of Poseidon, and the mark of the Trident they bore served as witness to their sacred duty to safeguard mankind.

Whether they liked it or not.

Chapter 1

Hell is empty
And all the Devils are here.

—William Shakespeare, *The Tempest*

Capital City of Atlantis, Present Day

Conlan waved a hand in front of the portal and briefly wondered whether its magic would even recognize a warrior who hadn't passed through its gateway for more than seven years.

Seven years, three weeks, and eleven days, to be precise.

As he waited, up to his chest in the healing water, death taunted him—flickering at the edges of his vision, shimmering in the deep blue ocean currents surrounding him, pulsing in the scarlet blood that dripped steadily from his side and leg. He laughed without humor, propping himself up with a hand on his knee.

"If that bitch-vamp Anubisa couldn't break me, I'm sure as hell not giving up now," he snarled to the empty darkness surrounding him.

Iridescent aqua lights flashed as if in response to his defiance, and the portal widened for him. Two men—two *warriors*—stood at guard, widened eyes and parted lips mirroring identical expressions of shock as they stared through the transparent membrane of the portal. He shouldered his way through the portal's opening, which enlarged to fit whatever or whoever it deemed worthy of passage.

"Prince Conlan! You're alive," one said.

"Mostly," he replied, then stepped into Atlantis. He drank in the first sight in more than seven years of his beloved homeland, lungs expanding to taste the freshness of sea-filtered air. In the middle distance, the gold-veined white marble pillars fronting Poseidon's Temple glowed with the reflected hues of artificial sunset. Conlan's breath caught in his throat at the sight of it.

A sight he'd been sure he'd never experience again.

Especially when she'd laughingly proposed taking his eyes.

"A high prince with no vision. What a delicious metaphor for the loss of your philosopher-king father, young princeling. Why don't you beg?"

She'd strolled around him, flicking the silver-barb-tipped whip almost leisurely at him, as he stood, helpless, in chains made for creatures borne of deeper hells. Extending one delicate finger, she'd touched the droplets of blood that sprang up so eagerly in the wake of her whip.

Then she'd brought her finger to her mouth, smiling.

"But you will *beg. Just like your father begged when I sliced the flesh off of your mother as she yet lived," she'd purred, evil mixed with a hideous lust in her eyes.*

He'd roared his hatred and defiance for hours.

Days.

He'd even wept, driven to madness from the pain, on seven separate occasions.

Once during each year of his imprisonment.

But he'd never begged.

"But *she* will," he said, voice hoarse with the effort of remaining upright. "She will beg, before I'm done with her."

"Highness?" The guards rushed forward to assist him, yelling out for aid. He whipped his head up, teeth bared, growling like the animal he'd become. They both stopped, midstep. Frozen in place.

Unsure how to react to royalty gone feral.

Conlan staggered forward, determined to take the first steps onto his native soil without aid.

"We must inform Alaric immediately," said the older, more experienced warrior of the two. *Marcus. Marius, maybe?* Conlan focused, certain he must know the man.

It was important that he remember things.

Yes, *Marcus*.

"You're bleeding, Highness."

"Mostly," he repeated, stumbling forward another step. Then the world spiraled down to black.

∾〜∾

Ven stood in the observation chamber, looking down on the hall of healing below, where Poseidon's high priest, clearly exhausted, labored over Ven's brother. It took one hell of a lot to drain the energy out of Alaric. He was rumored to be the most powerful high priest who had ever served the sea god.

Not that warriors knew much about the difference between one priest and another. Or, usually, gave much of a shit. Except, right now, he cared about that distinction.

A lot.

Ven clenched the railing, fingers digging into the soft wood, as he thought about what exactly Anubisa must have done to Conlan. He knew what she'd done to Alexios. One of Conlan's most trusted guards, the Seven, Alexios had spent two years under Anubisa's tender ministrations. Hers and those of her evil apostates of Algolagnia, who drew their only sexual pleasure from pain and torture.

Then she'd left him—naked and near death—to die. In a pile of pig shit on Crete. The vamp goddess of death was big on symbolism. Maybe something she'd inherited from her father-husband, Chaos. And that was seriously twisted right there.

It had taken Alaric nearly six months to retrieve the warrior's memories. That half year had included two cycles of purification in the Temple to cleanse his soul.

Ven didn't want to think it—fucking *hated* to think it—but sometimes he wondered if Alexios had *ever* come all the way back from whatever black pit of hell she'd dragged him into.

Still, Alaric had okayed him. Alexios was back as one of the Seven. It was a matter of honor that Ven trust him.

The Seven served as the most trusted guard to the high prince of all Atlantis. Even when he was gone; presumed dead.

They also led and coordinated the teams of warriors who patrolled the surface lands of the earth. Watching over the damn humans, who'd let themselves be herded like—what did the bloodsuckers call them? Sheep?

While Ven and all of the Warriors of Poseidon had to keep to the shadows. Out of sight. Incog-fucking-nito. Defending the landwalkers from the badasses among the bloodsuckers, the furry monsters, and all the shit that went bump in the night. And, frankly, the badasses seemed to be in the majority in those particular species most of the time.

And they'd done a damn fine job the past eleven thousand years, give or take. Until the day about ten years ago when the freaks that inhabited the night decided to come out of the coffin. First the vamps, then the shape-shifters. The job of Poseidon's warriors got about fifty kajillion times harder when that happened.

For whatever reason, Anubisa hadn't bothered to let her people—her vamp society—in on the secret of Atlantis. But Ven knew that could change any minute. If anybody knew about the capriciousness of gods and goddesses, it was an Atlantean.

Doomed to the bottom of the sea at Poseidon's whim.

Not that he'd ever complain about it. Out *loud*, at least.

Still, it was tough to defend humans when the big, bad, and ugly roamed freely, and the Atlanteans had to stick to the shadows. But Ven had argued the point in the Council until his face turned blue, and then he'd finally given up. The Elders didn't want anybody to know about Atlantis, and until Conlan ascended to the throne, nobody could go against their edict.

Ven looked down at his brother again, barely registering the soothing tones of the harps and flutes being played by temple maidens in the alcoves surrounding his brother. The music was supposed to aid in healing.

Ven laughed. Yeah, except Conlan hated that light, fluffy Debussy shit. When he ascended to the throne, he'd probably ask for Bruce Springsteen or U2 to play at his coronation.

If. *If* Conlan ascended to the throne.

He didn't even want to think about what would happen if Conlan had gone bad. Because guess who was second in line? Yeah. Ven would go from being King's Vengeance to high prince in a royal godsdamned minute, and there was no fucking way he was cut out to lead anything.

He looked down at his brother again, lying so still. Conlan had grown up like royalty, honor and duty and all that happy shit ingrained in his soul. But Ven had grown up pure street fighter. There was a big, ugly part of his soul. The part that had withered and died when he'd been with his mother at the end, before she died. When she'd begged him to save himself. Keep his brother safe.

He'd promised her, sobbing, as she died.

Great fucking job he'd done of keeping his word.

The wood snapped under his clenched fists.

"Tough wood to break with your bare hands," observed a dry voice.

Ven didn't look up at the priest, instead pulling splinters out of his torn and bleeding palms. "Yeah, they don't make these railings like they used to," he muttered.

Alaric walked—more like glided; the man was spooky— up to stand next to him. "I can heal that if you like," he offered, tone dispassionate.

"I think you've done enough healing for one day, don't you?"

Alaric said nothing, merely looked down over the railing at his sleeping prince.

Ven studied Alaric as the priest watched Conlan. Alaric and Conlan had grown up running around the kingdom like the hellions they were, tearing up the streets and fields with their games and pranks. Rarely reined in by their indulgent parents or a community respectful of the royal heir and his cousin.

Later making their way through the taverns and the barmaids with the same verve and boyish charm.

There was nothing of boyishness about the priest now. He wore the power of his office like a shield of armor. Invisible, but unmistakable. The sharp planes of his face and the hawk-like asceticism of his nose reminded all who confronted him that here was a man of faith, stripped to muscle and bone by the demands of his service.

The demands of *power*. If the faintly glowing green eyes hadn't already warned them away, that is.

High priest, dark phantom, instrument of Poseidon's power.

Scary son of a bitch.

"No, there is not a helluva lot of boyish charm left in any of us, is there, Alaric?"

Alaric lifted one eyebrow, but gave no other sign of surprise at the comment. "You want to know if he has been compromised," he said, face gray and used-looking. After a dozen or so hours of healing, it was pretty impressive that he could even stand upright.

"After Alexios—" Ven began, then stopped, unable to go on. If Anubisa had compromised his brother's soul, then the royal family really was doomed. She would have made good, finally, on a five-thousand-year-old promise.

Because Ven would walk into the gates of hell itself to shove his daggers up her bloodsucking ass. And he was honest enough to know he'd never come out of *that* confrontation alive.

Alaric drew a deep breath. "He is whole."

Ven's entire body sagged in a relief so fierce his vision literally went funky; he blinked away little gray spots that floated in front of his eyes. "Thank Poseidon!"

Alaric remained silent, which raised Ven's suspicion. Just a tiny doubt. "Alaric? Is there something you're not telling me? Is it simply coincidence that he gets back here just a few hours after Reisen blasted his way into the Temple and ripped off the Trident?"

The priest clenched his jaw, but said nothing for another minute. He finally spoke. "As to Reisen, I cannot tell. He is yet impossible to scry. For Conlan—"

Alaric hesitated, then seemed to reach a decision, nodding. "The prince is whole. Somehow, in spite of seven years of torture, he is whole. She was unable to compromise his mind or capture his soul to her use. But—"

Ven grasped Alaric's arm in a steel grip. "*But?* But what?"

Alaric said nothing, merely looked down at Ven's hand clenched around his arm. The knowledge that Alaric could incinerate Ven's hand with a single surge of elemental power lay between them.

Right at that moment, Ven didn't give a rat's ass.

But he sighed and released Alaric's arm. "But *what*? He's my brother. I have a right to know."

Nodding imperceptibly, Alaric glanced back down at Conlan's still form. "But simply because she was unable to suborn his soul to her own use does not mean that Conlan retained full possession. No one can survive that duration of torture with his soul intact."

He looked up at Ven, gaze flat. Dead. Promising destruction. Ven saw his own need to kick some vampire ass reflected in the priest's eyes.

"Conlan has returned to us, Ven. But we may not know for a long time exactly how *much* of him returned."

Ven bared his teeth in a fierce parody of a smile. "We'll figure it out. My brother is the strongest warrior I've ever known. And Anubisa is gonna find out exactly what it means that I am the King's Vengeance."

He grasped the handles of his daggers, eyes gleaming. "I'm gonna shoot me some vengeance right up her puckered ass."

Alaric's eyes shone for an instant with a glittering green light so bright that Ven had to squint against it. "Oh, yes. She will learn. And I will gladly assist you with that lesson."

As the two walked out of the observation chamber, Alaric looked back at the railing that Ven had crushed, then at Ven. "Poseidon has some vengeance of his own to offer."

Ven nodded, silently swearing the second formal vow of his life. *If it takes my death to do it, Anubisa will be destroyed. Glory be to Poseidon.*

The bitch is going down.

~~~~~

"Interesting timing."

Conlan tensed, fingers twitching to reach for the hundredth—thousandth—time for the sword that Anubisa had stolen from him. Then the familiarity of the voice penetrated the lethargy of the healing process.

"Alaric," he said, relaxing back down against the pillows.

Poseidon's high priest stared down at him, the suggestion of a smile quirking up the side of his mouth. "It's a little tiresome to be right all of the time. Welcome back, Conlan. Long vacation?"

Conlan sat up on the healers' marble-and-gold table, stretching, staring at flesh knitted whole. Bones unbroken and reset.

Scars that would never heal.

The need to scorch her face clear off her body with a big fucking energy ball consumed him. Ate at his gut. He shook it off and focused on the priest again.

"Right all of the time?" he repeated. "You knew I was alive?"

"I knew," Alaric confirmed, hard lines etched in his face. He folded his arms and leaned back against a white marble column.

Conlan's gaze was drawn to the veins of coppery orichalcum twining around its carved shapes. Dolphins leaping, Nereids laughing at their mermaid play. The scent of delicate green and blue lava-tulips permeated the air.

The images and scents of home he'd been refused for seven damn years.

He wrenched his gaze back to Alaric. "Yet you left me to rot?" Betrayal flared, warring with common sense. Alaric would have had duties to the Temple. To the people.

To Atlantis.

Alaric straightened and slowly unfolded his arms, his restraint only underscoring the enormous power leashed within him, his icy green eyes flashing with fury. "I searched for you. Every day for the past seven years. Even this day, before you arrived, I was preparing to join your brother, who was waiting above for yet another hopeless trip to find and rescue you from wherever they'd imprisoned you."

Conlan clenched his jaw, remembering Anubisa's parting shot, then nodded. "She shielded us. She's more powerful than we ever suspected, then."

Alaric's face hardened, if planes and sculpted lines that already appeared to be cast in marble could be said to harden. "Anubisa," he said flatly. It wasn't a question. "It is unsurprising that the goddess of night can project the void of death to mask her . . . activities."

The word *torture* hung, twisting and pulsing, in the air between them. At least the priest had the decency not to speak it.

Conlan nodded, reaching for the scar at the base of his throat before he realized what he was doing. Forcing his hand down when he did. "She kept me from water. Far away from any water, but for the barest minimum to drink to keep me alive. I had no chance to channel any power—no chance at all."

When he could bear to meet Alaric's eyes, Conlan flinched at the depth of the sorrow and fury there.

"Never once. Never the slightest resonance of your existence," Alaric said, gripping the jade handle of his dagger. He held it out to Conlan, blade down. "If you doubt my loyalty, cousin, end my life now. I deserve it for my failure."

Conlan noted the reference to their family connection in the cynical corner of his mind that calculated the niceties of Atlantean politics. Alaric never spoke a single word that didn't carry at least two meanings. Often polemic, at times pedagogical. Never purposeless.

Conlan accepted the dagger and turned it over in his hands, then flipped it back to its owner. "If you failed in your appointed role, *priest*, Poseidon's justice would be the one kicking your ass. You've no need of mine."

Alaric shook his black hair behind his shoulders, eyes narrowing at the emphasis on his title. Then he nodded once and slid the dagger into its emerald-jeweled sheath. "As you say. We face other problems, *prince*. You have finally returned, only hours after the vehicle of your ascension is lost."

"Tell me," Conlan said, fury scalding the shreds of his self-control.

"Reisen. He killed two of my acolytes." Alaric spat the words out, clenching his fists. "Conlan, he took it. He took the Trident. He's gone above. If the undead get their hands on it . . ."

Alaric's words trailed off. Both of them knew the cost of misused power. Poseidon's former high priest lay rotting in the black abyss of the temple oubliette for overstepping his powers.

Poseidon served deadly reminders to those who betrayed him.

Conlan inhaled sharply, the hairs on his arms standing up in response to the nearly invisible currents of elemental energy Alaric crackled through the room. For his power to leak out like that, the priest must be damn near the edge of his self-control. Or else seven years had seen one hell of a surge in his power.

Conlan didn't know which option should concern him more.

Their friendship had weathered the strain of the demands of politics and power. Conlan trusted Alaric with his life. Didn't he?

It was enough to split a man's skull open.

Clenching the sheets in his fists, he fought for composure. For some semblance of royal countenance to overlay the ragged insanity threatening to eat through his mind.

Through his gut.

To his soul.

His heart was long since gone. Shattered at the end of a whip, while forced to hear silken words whispering of the atrocities they'd heaped upon his lady mother.

Anubisa and her apostates of Algolagnia. They'd murdered his mother an inch at a time, and they'd enjoyed it. Worse, they'd *gotten off* on it. A deep shudder wracked through him, remembering how Anubisa had pleasured herself to orgasm in front of him while she told him stories of torturing his parents.

Again and again and again.

Anubisa was going to die.

They were *all* going to die.

"Conlan?" Alaric's voice almost physically wrenched him out of his memories of death and blood. Alaric. He'd said *hours* later . . .

"Hours? And here I am," Conlan said, remembering. "She let me go. She knew, Alaric. She *knew*."

His final day. His final hour.

"Oh, princeling, you have brought me such pleasure," she murmured in his ear. Then she slid down his naked body and delicately licked at the sweat, the blood, and the other, thicker fluids that pooled to drip down his thighs. *"But I think you must needs return to your people. You have a delightful surprise waiting for you. And, in your current state, you're no longer any fun."*

Standing up, she'd waved one of her attendants over. *"Twelve of my personal guard. Twelve, you understand? Don't be fooled by this temporary weakness. The brat prince of Atlantis has . . . hidden strengths."* She'd run a finger down his cock, laughing as he'd tried to flinch away from her.

Then she'd flicked her gaze back to her attendant. *"Throw him out."*

Still naked, long, curling hair matted with his blood, she'd stalked toward the doorway of the cell that had served as his prison for seven years. Then she'd stopped and looked back at him over her shoulder. "Your bloodline amuses me, princeling. Tell your brother that I come for him next."

He'd cursed, then, finding his voice again. Called her names that he hadn't even known he knew. Until her guards came, and one of them demonstrated that he'd taken offense by way of a club to Conlan's head.

He shook off the image in his head. He was free of Anubisa's hell.

He would *never* be free of the memories.

He might never be entirely sane again.

But he was Conlan of Atlantis, and he had returned. His people wanted a king, not a broken failure of a prince.

Glancing across at Alaric, he saw the concern reflected on the priest's face. Maybe even Alaric wanted a king, too.

Enough of the self-indulgence of dreams of vengeance— and on to the reality.

"We're not boys causing mischief at the running of the bulls festival anymore, are we?" Conlan said, a shadow of re-membered freedom crossing his mind. A time before the de-mands of being his father's son. Before the demands on Alaric as Poseidon's anointed.

Alaric tilted his head, expression wary, and then he slowly shook his head. "Not for many long years, Conlan."

"Too long," Conlan replied. "Far too long." He swung his legs off the healing table and rose to stand.

"Childhood may be outgrown, but loyalty never will be. You are my prince, but—more than that—you are my friend. Never doubt it," Alaric said.

Conlan read the truth in Alaric's eyes and felt better for it. He held out his hand and they clasped arms, an unspoken re-newal of friendship that maybe both of them needed.

Then he stretched, pleased to find his body in working or-der again. He'd need every ounce of energy. "So both my as-cension and my matrimonial obligations to a long-dead virgin are delayed," he said drily. "I find myself unable to summon much concern about the latter."

"Not dead. Merely sleeping, awaiting your need. It is your destiny," Alaric reminded him.

As if he needed reminding. As if he hadn't had that particular duty drummed into his head for hundreds of years. Love didn't figure into the breeding patterns of the Warriors of Poseidon; most especially not into those of royalty.

He scowled at the whimsy. *Love.* A myth to coddle children, at best. "I'm out of here. I'm going after that bastard Reisen. I will retrieve the Trident, Priest. And justice will be meted out to the House of Mycenae."

Alaric grinned at him, giving Conlan a glimpse of the boy he'd once been. "*We* leave now. Ven is preparing for the journey. So much for the welcome-home processional."

Conlan tried to return the smile, but his mouth had lost its memory of how to smile, after so many years of grimacing in agony. Years of howling out his rage and despair.

Alaric raised one eyebrow, his mouth flattening into a grim line. "That's an . . . *interesting* . . . expression. You'll have to tell me one day exactly what they did to you."

"No," Conlan answered. "I won't."

Chapter 2

Virginia Beach

"Dina, think about your baby." Riley Dawson crouched down next to the room's single window, hands loose and open at her sides.

Nonthreatening, nonthreatening, nonthreatening.

Riley forced her facial muscles to relax into an expression of calm, as she watched her massively pregnant sixteen-year-old client jam the lethal end of the very large and very ugly pistol farther down the unconscious man's throat. His skin was pasty white, but she could see his chest move in shallow breaths.

He's not dead. Let's keep him that way, Riley.

"I'm thinking about my baby, Riley. Stay out of it! No way my baby is gonna grow up with a skanky alley cat like this for a daddy." Dina's gaze darted around the room, skittered off Riley's face, then back to Morris, lying still and pale on the edge of the bed.

Riley could see that his chest was moving. He was still breathing, in spite of the force of the gun crashing into the back of his skull that she'd witnessed as she'd walked in the open door for her monthly visit. But she'd been in enough rooms crowded with the noises of EMT personnel and the smell of death to know that a life could end in an instant. And Dina's hand was trembling on that gun.

"Dina, listen to me. I'm sorry you found Morris with another girl. He made a terrible mistake. I'm sure he's very sorry about it. But you have to think about your baby. She needs you, Dina. If you hurt him, you'll go to jail, and then who will raise your baby? You know your mother can't do it." A cramping pain burned through Riley's leg muscles, protesting at squatting on the floor for so long. She shifted a little, careful not to make any sudden or abrupt movements.

Dina barked out a laugh that sounded rusty from disuse. "That crack ho? She ain't no mother. She ain't getting near my baby."

"That's right. You know you're the best person in the world to take care of your baby. Have you thought of a name for her yet?"

Keep them talking. Distract them with more pleasant topics; ones with which they feel a personal connection. The voice of the lecturer from one of Riley's hundreds of hours of training pounded in her head.

Right. Pleasant topics, when she's got a gun jammed down his cheating throat. And how about the fact that I'm going to pee my pants any minute? The manuals never mentioned that little fact.

Dina smiled a little. "I'm going to call her Paris. Like that city in France? With the tower? It's so beautiful. We learned about it in school. I'm gonna take her there someday. Paris Marguerite, after Grandmama."

"That's a beautiful name, Dina. Paris Marguerite. Now please give me the gun. You don't want Paris Marguerite to grow up without her mommy, do you?" Riley slowly straightened up off the floor, ignoring the screaming muscles in her thighs. She stretched her hand out, palm upward.

"Please give me the gun. I'll help you. We'll figure this out together. Please give me the gun, so Paris Marguerite grows up with her mommy to take care of her." She held her breath as Dina wavered, looking back and forth from Riley to Morris.

A man's life balanced on the wavering edge of a teenager's indecision. Nope. That hadn't been in the damn manual, either.

Dina took a huge, shuddering breath, and her shoulders slumped a little. She yanked the gun out of Morris's mouth and held it out toward Riley. Riley felt the breath she'd been holding for the past half hour seep out of her lungs.

Thank you, thank you, thank you, I can't—

Morris's eyes snapped open. He burst up off the bed, blood running down his face from his mouth, and slammed a fist into Dina's jaw. "You hit me over the head, bitch? You pull a gun on *me*? I'll show *you* who pulls a gun on Morris."

As Dina fell to the ground from the force of the blow, Morris aimed a kick at her belly. Riley launched herself out of the corner and toward them, screaming, "No, no! Morris, no! Don't hurt her! Don't hurt your baby!"

The room kaleidoscoped into a fractured image of movement and cacophony of sound. Almost in slow motion, Riley saw the kick land with full force against the side of Dina's huge belly. She heard Dina screaming, Morris screaming, someone else screaming—was that *her*?

She jumped him, not caring that he had to outweigh her by a hundred pounds. "No, no, *no*. Don't hurt her. You have to stop. Morris, you have to stop—"

Morris yanked a handful of her hair viciously, snapping her head back. "Nobody tells me what to do. Especially not some worthless social worker."

He raised his fist. *Move. Gotta move.*

She yanked her head to the left, just as his huge fist slammed into the side of her face. *Just enough. Maybe. Please God, don't let my neck be broken. Room going black. Fight, Riley. Fight to stay conscious.*

Fist coming again. "No, please . . ."

But he ignored her, face twisted with rage beyond hearing, beyond reason. His fist exploded again, except it wasn't his fist.

It wasn't her face.

Thunder? Is it thunder? So black . . .

As Riley fought the blackness, the hand in her hair loosened. Morris's face changed in a caricature of slow motion from a grimace of violent hate to one of surprise. They both looked at the scarlet stain blossoming, blooming, spreading over his shirt. Even as Riley touched a questing finger to the dark stickiness that splattered her face, the room went black.

Conlan opened the portal, focusing on the East Coast of the United States. Virginia, to be precise. Ven had been "collecting intel," according to Alaric.

Translation: beating information out of scumbags for miles in every direction. His brother always had favored the direct approach.

Now Ven was calling the rest of the Seven to him to accompany Conlan to the surface. Except Conlan was in no mood to wait. Not even for his brother. Maybe especially not for his brother. If he saw even a glimmer of pity in Ven's eyes, he'd—

Well. Forget that. Focus on the portal.

Seven years of disuse, and the magic was rusty. Or the portal, temperamental on a good day, was playing with him, Conlan discovered, as he stepped through into water.

Lots of water.

Luckily he'd instinctively heaved in a deep breath before plunging through the shimmering opening. There was another lesson learned the hard way: the portal had its own power, independent of the Atlanteans who had first harnessed it more than eleven thousand years ago.

They ought to hang a "User Beware" sign on the capricious thing. He kicked off and headed for the surface, judging he was about ten meters deep from the looks of the shallow-water flora and fauna that shimmered in the diluted moonlight.

But distances could be tricky in the sea.

And then, there was the problem of where the hell the shore might be. He wouldn't be the first to end up treading water in the middle of the ocean.

The portal's idea of a practical joke. If portals had emotion, this one was packing a vindictive sense of humor.

As he broke the surface and sucked in a lungful of air, an almost-tangible force smashed into him. Agony sliced through his head, then shut off as if by a switch. A bitter taste seared his mouth; a sourness like lemon soaked in brine.

Another wave of pain crashed through him, knocking him off balance. He nearly sank below the waves again, barely noticing the sands of the shores nearby.

He shook his head from side to side, trying to escape the fire inside of his head. He barked out a laugh. He'd had a lot of practice with pain, just lately. *Think, damn you.*

Crazed thoughts swirled in his bruised brain. *If an Atlantean prince's head cracks wide open in the ocean, does it make a sound?*

He almost laughed again, but snorted water up his nose instead. Choking and coughing, he finally forced his limbs to cooperate and headed for the shore, eventually realizing he could touch bottom and walk.

His training kicked in, keeping him upright and coherent. *Analyze. Reason. Use logic.*

A third wave of pain seared through him, driving him to his knees, face caught under the breaking waves. He fought his way back to standing, plunged forward toward the shore.

Vamp mind powers? Doesn't feel like it. They could trap your mind, but not project pain like this. Could it be Reisen? Did the Trident give him some kind of mental power we don't know about?

His boots hit dry sand, and he collapsed, stumbling onto his knees. He sent a mind call out to Ven.

Needed help.

But it wasn't Ven's familiar patterns that answered his call. Instead, a tiny pinprick of awareness deep in his mind sparked, sputtered like a candle in a back draft, and then focused.

An image of beauty sheared by pain. A woman with sun-colored hair.

Something slammed shut in his mind, and the woman and the pain vanished. Almost as if a mental door had closed.

And Conlan wasn't the one who'd shut it.

Chapter 3

Riley blinked at the EMT who was peering into her eyes while his fingers measured out her pulse. She looked away from him and scanned the room, knowing she looked as bleary-eyed as she felt.

He repeated his sentence, slower this time, as if she might not have understood him the first time. "You need to go to the ER and get checked out."

She started to shake her head *no*, but stopped as the movement shot bolts of pain through her skull. "I don't want to go to the ER. It was just a punch."

She brushed his hand off his arm and stood up on unsteady legs, which probably proved his point, but what the hell. "I've had worse. I need to go for a walk. I need air."

She'd already talked to the detective in charge of what was now a murder scene. Her part of it was done. And now the room was closing in on her.

It had been such a surprise to her at first, how many people show up at a murder scene. So many official types convened in a confluence of the mundane—photo taking, fingerprinting, tape measuring.

The profanity of death, obscured by the details of modern police work. It seemed wrong, somehow, as it always did.

She'd seen too much of it. Should have been a secretary, like her baby sister. Quinn never had to face despair. Or fists. Or blood on her clothes.

It was hell on the dry-cleaning bill.

The EMT stepped back and turned off the penlight he'd been shining in her eyes. "I don't think you have a concussion, but you're going to have a helluva shiner. You really should come and get checked out by the doc."

Riley's belly twisted, empty and nauseous. She moved away from him, tuning him out, and scanned the room again. The cheap apartment. The chaos left in the wake of violence.

The stench of death—blood and the body's release of wastes. It had surprised her at her first death scene, that release. The final indignity. A soiled corpse left for the impersonal attentions of the morgue.

Riley heard the moaning sound, low in her throat, and choked it off. She was tougher now. Hardened to it.

Immune to any emotion.

That's what she told herself, at least. Until she saw the bear.

Propped up in the corner of the room, next to a bassinet, a giant teddy bear wearing a pink bow grinned foolishly out at the room, unmoved by the drama that had played out before it.

That damn pink bow sent her over the edge.

"I have to get out of here. Please, just get out of my way. Please." She whirled around and shoved past the EMT, careful to walk around the personnel crouched on the floor taking pictures.

"Hey, Dawson. Where do you think you're going?" The detective she'd spoken with earlier—*Ramsey? Ramirez?*—pulled on a fresh set of gloves, the lines in his face deepening as his gaze traveled to her face. "You look like shit. You should go with them to the ER."

Riley didn't stop; only slowed down a little. "I'm going to be sick. I've got to go get cleaned up and get some rest." She glanced back over her shoulder at him. "I'll call you as soon as I do."

He opened his mouth, probably to protest, but she was beyond caring. What were they going to do, arrest her? They knew who she was and, if only by rep, that her word was good.

He nodded, resigned. Sympathy and something she didn't want to define warmed his expression. *Pity?* He should save his pity for Dina and her baby. They'd need it. She was just doing her job.

This time she did laugh, even though it came out sounding . . . *wrong.* Yeah, doing her job. She was screwing up her job on a royal level.

Another day, another dead body. That made eight murder scenes this year.

He nodded. "All right. You've told us enough for now, anyway. Call me in the morning. You've got my card."

She fingered the card she'd shoved in her pocket and headed for the door. The morning. She'd call him in the morning. Now she had to get to the water. To the beach. Her sanctuary. She felt the power and peace of the ocean calling her.

She needed to feel the caress of the waves, and she'd be fine.

~~~~~

Conlan stood alone in the dark, eyes closed, senses unfurled to seek out the presence of anyone nearby.

Friend or enemy.

Hell, he almost preferred an enemy. He was solidly in the mood to kick somebody's ass. He bared his teeth in what passed for a smile. Then his eyes snapped open.

Because the door holding the emotion out of his mind had smashed open again. He staggered, fought to remain standing under the barrage of anguish. All he could do was try to ride it out and pray his brother or Alaric arrived soon. He closed his eyes again. Fought for focus. Turned to the portion of his training not conducted with swords and daggers.

Compartmentalize. A Warrior of Poseidon cannot countenance emotion. The price of arrogance is your life, Conlan.

He could almost hear Archelaus whispering in his head. *Use all of your senses. Never rely on your mind, alone. To underestimate your enemy's potential to create illusion means death.*

He focused, strained. Achieved detachment. His mind analyzed the problem of his own duality; emotionless calculation studied raging grief.

The evidence supports no internal cause. Seek the external.

So, then. It was outside of him. Somebody—or some *thing*—broadcasted grief powerfully enough to shove through his mental defenses.

The enemy he'd been wishing for, maybe. It was sure as hell no friend. No Atlantean could send emotions to another. "Well, they say be careful what you wish for, right?" he muttered to himself, muscles straining with the effort of managing the flood of anguish.

He spared a thought for the source. Somebody, somewhere, was suffering all nine hells' worth of hurt.

∾⸻⸱∽

Riley trudged away from her old Honda, parked carelessly across a couple of spaces in the deserted parking lot, heading toward the beach. Not many beachgoers at this hour on a chilly October night.

The smell of sea air and salt water reached her, and she took a deep breath, a tendril of calm threading its fragile way through her. Her stomach growled a reminder that it had been more than fourteen hours since she'd eaten. Almost without thinking, she reached into the pocket of her jacket for one of the protein bars she usually carried around.

Regular meals were unpredictable in her line of work.

She started to peel a corner of the wrapper off the bar, and it hit her: Morris would never eat anything again.

The thought smashed into her, doubling her over. What was the magic number? How many times would she have to watch somebody die before she could be blasé about it?

And what the hell kind of person was she that she even wanted to?

Forcing herself to straighten up, she glanced at her watch, then swore under her breath. Nearly curfew. She knew all about curfew; she even had the requisite copy of the 2006 Nonhuman Species Protection Act taped up to a window of her home, as mandated by the new law. "I don't care. I need this walk. Nobody will bust me for a few minutes past human lights out," she muttered. The ocean meant healing. Solace. Her mind desperately needed both.

Talking to myself. Now there's a sign of imminent whacko-dom.

She kicked an empty can out of her way as she finally reached the sand and shoved the unopened protein bar back in her pocket. Maybe later.

The moonlight pirouetted on the surface of the waves, careless in its joy. Unaffected by human concerns. Riley glanced up, judging its phase. She hadn't caught the lunar alert on the radio that morning.

Waxing gibbous. Good. Still a couple of days before the full.

They'd all gotten way better at keeping track of the moon since the shape-shifters had first announced their existence. Funny what a difference a decade made. She probably would have guessed a waxing gibbous had something to do with monkeys, before.

Life had been way easier when the moon was just something cows jumped over in storybooks.

Cows. Storybooks.

That damned bear and its pink ribbon.

Riley sank down on the sand near the water and gave in to the tears.

~~~~~

When a fresh wave of grief flooded his mind, Conlan raised his head, scenting the air.

She's near. She? I don't know how I know, but, yeah, it's a she. Maybe a few miles from here?

He started walking, sped up.

Began to run. Flashed into molecules of pure water with the preternatural speed of his kind.

Must find her.

Need, inexplicable but intense. Primal determination.

Must find her now.

~~~~~

Riley heaved in a shaky breath, trying to surface from the currents of sorrow threatening to drag her under. Dina would go to jail.

Please, God, watch out for Dina.

Riley looked up at the impervious moon again and laughed bitterly. *Although, why do I bother? It's not like the hundreds of prayers I've sent up before have made a difference. The baby is the worst of it. If she even lives, she's going to a foster home.*

Riley thought of a baby she'd just placed with a foster home; one of the better ones. Mrs. Graham loved all of her kids, but had a special affinity for the broken ones. The baby had peered up into Riley's face as she'd handed his twitching, crack-addicted body over to his new caregiver. His tiny fingers had furled and unfurled like sea anemones searching for a sunlight that might never come.

She rubbed her arms, shivering. Mrs. Graham was at max capacity. Riley didn't have anybody available who was as good. Dina's baby probably would be raised in an even worse form of the culture of violence and poverty that had shaped both Dina and Morris.

If the baby even lives.

Riley almost physically shoved the thought to the back of her mind. She couldn't go there. Not now.

Not when she was so close to the edge of sanity.

Put it in the box, Riley. Think about it tomorrow.

Even as she clenched her jaws to stop the scream clawing its way out of her throat, some weird sixth sense picked up the danger. She caught a glimpse of them out of the corner of her eye, creeping across the sand, flickering in and out of sight in the shadows cast by the clouds.

Three of them. She jumped up into a crouch, ready to run, scanning the area for a way to escape.

Stunned that—for the merest split second—she'd felt too hopeless to even try to save herself.

Chapter 4

Conlan swirled through the air faster than he'd ever moved, arrowing his focus to use the droplets of water in the sea air as a prism, until he could see the outline of her shape.

Score a point for Atlantean vision.

Shadows caught at the moonlight, obscuring her face. All he could see was a slender form, huddled on the beach. The impact of her grief magnified—trebled—when he saw her shoulders shudder.

She was definitely the source of the emotional grenade that had smashed into his defenses. No army. No vamp mind-control conspiracy.

One lone human female. And she was projecting *emotion*.

She was *aknasha*. Empath.

Stunned, disbelieving, he sent a tentative mind probe to her. Her mind clamped on to his probe, the energy of her thoughts rearing up, defensive. As if she sensed danger.

She thought he was a predator. He bared his teeth, nearly smiling. He'd been called worse.

He tried to shut down his mental shields, but she lashed out at him. Defense turned to offense—seeking to discern what the hell he was.

Get out of my mind! Defiance. Courage.

Pure, heated emotion.

And, buried way down deep: a tendril of fear.

His logic tried to make sense of the impossible. Not even Atlanteans could project *emotion* into the mind probe anymore. And yet *she* did. On a level so intense, so visceral, that his warrior senses nearly missed the threat to her.

There were three of them. They planned to hurt her. He swore viciously under his breath in the ancient tongue.

They were going to die.

He moved even faster.

~~~~~~~

Riley lifted her head, suddenly aware of a threat far greater than the three who stalked her. Something—someone—she almost *felt* him inside of her.

"Great. Either we've got vamps with new mind-control powers, or that damn sixth sense of mine picks now to go haywire," she muttered, even as she pushed herself up off the beach and started walking. *Fast.*

Maybe she'd been wrong. Maybe they were just three guys out for a walk on the beach.

Yeah, and I'm Goldilocks.

"Hold up there, babe. We want to have a little talk with you," one of them called out in a thick voice. The others laughed, and the menace in their laughter sent a curl of fear shivering up Riley's spine.

The air around her thickened, seemed to swirl with a darker black, as if an opposing force gathered itself, threatened.

But it didn't threaten *her.*

The dark caressed her as it passed, then built into an ominous cloud behind her. She kept walking, faster, nearly jogging now, glancing back over her shoulder. The men had stopped, openmouthed.

"What the hell is that?" one of them said, rubbing his arms. His belly hung low over his belt and his greasy hair was combed over his balding scalp. An angry-looking red scar snaked up out of his collar to the side of his neck. He caught her looking at him and leered at her. "Yeah, you're anxious to get a piece of me, aren't you, chickie? Guess you're not as tough as the other one."

The men put their heads down, driving their way through the shadows of the barrier, and stumbled after her.

She shuddered. Started to run. The unseen threat in the air around her escalated.

Nothing human could do that. It was an intangible presence—but a very tangible threat.

Oh, no. Somebody please help me. It's a damn vampire. Or a shape-shifter. I never should have broken curfew.

The sand seemed to mock her, catching her ankles, making her stumble. She heard her pursuers thundering closer and closer.

She shoved the panic away. *Remember what you tell your clients. It's rape—horrible, soul deadening, but you'll be alive. It's not murder. It's only temporary. Nothing matters but staying alive. You can survive this.*

An inhumanly vicious roar sounded through her head—no, it wasn't just in her head. She *heard* it. She lurched to a stop, glancing behind at her pursuers.

The bastards behind her stopped, too. "What the hell was that, Red? You said none of those fucking werewolves hung out around here," one of them whined.

Riley shook her head, trapped. Bones turned to liquid. She forced herself to keep moving.

Better to risk being lunch for an unseen vampire than victim of a gang bang. Too early for shape-shifters.

"Guess rapists these days aren't up on lunar phases," she said, hysteria threatening to overwhelm her.

The roar came again, stopping her in her tracks. Terror whipped through her. Nothing human made that sound.

She was going to die.

She choked on a laugh. Maybe they'd put her in a drawer at the morgue next to Morris.

A voice—a silken melody of sound—rang inside of her head.

The undead will never have you, little aknasha. *You are too valuable to us. We need to figure out just how you acquired this interesting talent.*

The velvet caress of the voice caught at her mental defenses, trying to insinuate itself into her mind.

Fascinated in spite of the situation, she tried a mental push of her own. *Who are you? How can you talk to me like that? No vampire or shape-shifter has that power, do they?*

She frantically scanned the skies, afraid of an attack from above, then looked behind her at the thugs.

Great. I get trapped in some mind-control games and they catch me. Brilliant, Riley. Why not just give up and lie down now?

The voice sounded in her mind again, gentleness gone, implacable ice in its place. *Do not worry about those fools behind you. I'm in the mood to deliver a little death.*

"Death?" Even as a small, dark corner of Riley's soul stood up and cheered at the idea, her conscience wouldn't go for it.

She'd seen enough death for one night.

She'd seen enough death for one *lifetime*.

"No. Whoever you are, no killing. Please, just help me get away," she said out loud, realizing she was probably bargaining with a freaking bloodsucker.

Stand aside. Now. They're already dead. I don't like vermin who prey on helpless women. His melodic tones wrapped around her senses, raising her nerve endings to heightened alert, even as she bristled at his arrogant presumption.

You picked the wrong woman to order around, bud. And if you are *some kind of preternatural badass, you picked the wrong woman to try to eat, too.*

She whirled around in midstride, dropping into a defensive crouch, wondering how she could possibly defend herself against all four of them.

One of them with enough undead strength to pick up a house.

So fierce! Eat you? *I'm no vamp, fierce one. But I must admit, for some reason the idea of . . . tasting you . . . isn't making me all that unhappy. And I haven't even seen your face yet. So who's using the mind control here?*

His silent laughter insinuated itself into her mind, simmering with . . . sex. A wave of heat washed through her, over her, around her.

"I hope you're not waiting for an answer to that one," she muttered, feeling her face flame and glad for the darkness. "What kind of moron feels sexy when her life is in danger? Next I'll be putting on a slinky nightgown and going down in the basement with the serial-killing hockey players."

She backed away from all of them—mind-control boy's likely direction and the thugs. But one woman didn't have a chance against all four.

Riley watched, fists clenched so hard her nails bit into her palms, as the drunks moved to surround her. The sour reek of their unwashed bodies tripled the nausea she was already fighting, and she gagged as her stomach tried to rebel.

She'd never be able to defeat all three of them, and escape was impossible, now. Not only from them, but from the stranger whispering in her mind. But she could at least punch and kick the crap out of any body part that came in reach.

They wouldn't get her without a fight.

Be still. I'll deal with these criminals. And then, aknasha, *we'll have a little chat about how you transmit emotions through the mind probe. Don't even think about trying to get away from* me.

Riley fell back a step as the stocky, muscle-bound man in front of her reached forward as if to grab her breast. She could smell the fumes on his breath—beer and the sour tang of something stronger.

"Come on, baby, give us a little kiss." He puckered up and made a loud smooching sound, and the other thugs howled with laughter.

The nausea rose again in her throat at the idea of any of them touching her. She feinted back, then swung her foot with every ounce of rage inside of her right for the bastard's crotch.

And it connected, hard.

He howled, clutched at his groin, and dropped to the sand like a big, ugly rock. Riley stumbled back, and the thug behind her grabbed her shoulders, his dirty fingers digging into her skin through her light jacket. She hissed in pain, and an answering hiss of sheer male fury scorched through her brain. From behind her, someone roared his outrage to the skies.

Not someone—*him.*

The man holding her gasped and backed away from her.

She whipped her head from side to side, trying to keep an eye on all three of them at once.

At least the guy on the ground didn't seem to be going anywhere. He lay there, moaning and blubbering in a funny voice. Score one for her, at least.

And then she saw *him*. Black shadow coalesced into a tall figure running toward her so quickly it seemed as though his feet never touched the ground.

Power, raging and furious, swept over her. Her skin iced at the feel of it.

She was either saved, or she was utterly doomed.

Chapter 5

Conlan fought to breathe, nearly blinded by the red haze of rage that seared through him, choking him, threatening to obscure his vision. A berserker rage.

He welcomed it. *Bring it on.*

Raising his arms, he channeled the water from the sea. It funneled up into the air in shards, turning to ice as it rose. He shot the ice daggers at his targets—arrows from Poseidon's bow.

The men fell back, screaming, as razor-edged death sliced into their flesh.

"You don't touch her. *Ever,*" he snarled, as he raised his arms in demand. Poseidon's oceans dominated the world.

Poseidon's Warriors dominated the ocean.

He was high prince and the first of the Warriors, and he would destroy them for daring to touch her.

The surf boiled at the edge of the sand, crests of waves rising to impossible heights, seeming almost to seek their prey. Conlan slashed his arms down, aiming his focus. He commanded the frenzy of waves to rise, higher and higher.

His fury swelled, threatening his control. The red haze

spread further over his vision. To have the ability to strike back again after so many years of powerlessness . . .

Anubisa's mocking laughter sounded in his brain.

He was a fucking head case.

Then a touch—inside him. A touch of courage, of defiance. Light to his dark. Compassion to his mercilessness.

His gaze swung to the woman crouched down in the sand, hands still up to defend herself from the bastards who'd attacked her. In the midst of it all, she'd spared the energy to respond to his madness.

He would smash them for her. Drive the water to strip the flesh from their bones.

Enjoy every last minute of it.

"No! What *are* you? Stop! You'll kill us!" she screamed up at him, defiant still, in spite of the terror she projected.

Beyond reason, beyond compassion, he raised his arms again, then slashed them down, commanding the wall of water to crash down on the shore. To crush the men, where they lay bleeding and groveling.

He drove the wave toward the shore.

Her voice, broken, tentative, sounded in his head. *Stop! Please don't kill me! My sister . . . I'm all she has. And . . . don't kill them. Please. Enough death.*

Conlan marveled at her goodness, her courage.

Her light.

Even as she thought death was crashing toward her, she spared a thought for the garbage who'd tried to attack her.

He followed her thought back along its path to her mind. *I would never hurt you. Trust me.*

Or was he a damn fool? Maybe she was just a talented actress. Nobody that compassionate could be real.

But the red haze lifted, receded. Somehow her mental touch lent him calm. A measure of peace. He was inside her mind—she was projecting emotion. There was no deceit—no evil. Nothing but compassion wrapped up in terror. Sorrow.

Conlan focused his power at the water and the men in its path, speaking a single word. "Abate."

In perfect symmetry, the water pounded the shore in an exact spherical shape around the place where she stood, leaving her untouched by a single drop. He felt her shock and wonder at the spectacle and could almost taste her awe as she reached out to touch the wall of water surrounding her.

She gasped—made a choked sound of laughter. Broadcasted her thoughts: *All I can think of is the parting of the Red Sea, but you're definitely not Moses.*

Conlan crushed the water down on the little pricks, reining it in at the last possible second. He'd *mitigate*.

For her.

They might get a little broken, but they'd live. The wall of ocean pounded them to the sand, but left them with enough oxygen in their lungs to survive it.

Which didn't make him all that happy.

As the waves receded, leaving the men crying, babbling, and damn near shitting themselves, Conlan stepped forward and raised his arms again. The waves eagerly leapt to do his bidding, and the surf boiled in anticipation of another strike.

He got a vicious pleasure out of watching them cower the way they'd wanted to see her cower.

Yeah, I can be a bastard that way.

He spoke with every ounce of rage in his body bubbling to the surface, arm muscles clenching with the strain of holding back the wall of water. "I command you to leave this place and never return. You will not attempt to harm another, or I will track you down and serve up the justice that only this woman's compassion saved you from tonight."

He swept them with his gaze, dropped out of formal speak. "In other words, you'll be dead sons of bitches. We on the same page?"

They babbled their promises in broken voices, then ran off, stinking of fear and piss, when he gestured them away. His gaze only tracked them for a moment, then he turned, inexplicably drawn back to the woman. She had guts, or she had a death wish. Either way, she'd seen him command the ocean, and yet she was unafraid enough to stand her ground.

Trained warriors had cowered in front of him with less cause.

How the hell did one small human have such courage?

A fierce curiosity burned through him. He wanted, no,

needed, to see her face, which was shadowed by her hair and hidden in the darkness. His fury was disproportionate—it didn't make sense. The thugs were buffoons, easily enough cowed.

But for some reason, he'd wanted to slice the flesh off their bodies.

Maybe being tortured for so long would turn anybody into a sick, twisted bastard. Even the so-called next ruler of Atlantis.

A little logic might help. Use some of that much-vaunted Atlantean warrior training.

Yeah, logic. Logic dictated that he study his own reactions. Logic counseled prudence.

She started to edge away from him.

Fuck logic.

He tried on a royal command for size. *Come closer to me, woman. I have a need to see the face of one who bids me not to harm those who threaten her. Are you compassionate or merely a fool?*

She tossed her head, long and tousled hair flying through the air, and something low in his body tightened. She ignored his mental query and his command and stood her ground. "Who are you, and how are you in my mind? You can quit with the ordering me around thing, too, buster. I know self-defense. I would have been fine."

Her voice. It was lyrical, sensuous, music lilting into his ears and resonating through his body. Playing him like delicate fingers on the strings of a harp. His body tightened, straining.

Her body quivered with indignation, yet the emotion she still broadcast confessed the truth. She knew they would have put a big, bad hurt on her.

The *emotion*. Somehow, he kept losing track of the un-expected, unprecedented, unbe-fucking-lievable fact that she was broadcasting *emotion*. She *knew* she would have been se-riously harmed if he hadn't been there—he actually *felt* the knowledge and, with it, her residual fear and sorrow.

She sighed, and her body slumped. "I'm . . . sorry. I should be thanking you. Whoever—or *whatever*—you are, you saved me from those men. Thank you."

Then she raised her head and peered at him. "You're not going to drink my blood or rip my arms off, now, are you?

Because my day has really sucked, and I'm so not up for that," she said, suspicion ringing in her tone.

He blinked, bewildered by her apparent inability to carry on a logical conversation. He figured he'd try using simple sentences and speaking out loud. Maybe terror turned human women into babbling idiots.

Slowly, carefully choosing his words, he tried to explain. "I am not the undead, nor a shifter of shape to animal form. I am . . . other. You are entirely safe with me, *aknasha.*"

She planted her hands on her hips and stared at him. "You keep calling me that. What does it mean? What does 'other' mean? And why do you talk like you walked out of an old-time fairy-tale book?"

As he considered how to answer her, the bank of clouds overhead finally passed beyond the edge of the moon. The shimmer of moonlight on her features plowed a wave of sensation right through his gut. Nobody could be that beautiful.

He almost laughed. *She'd* been talking about fairy tales, and she looked like she'd stepped out of the pages of one. Her face shone with the perfection of a Nereid. The silvery light barely illuminated the red-gold waves that must burn like fire in the sunshine. Her eyes . . .

Not possible. No human has eyes like that.

"They're cerulean," he said aloud, unthinking. "Your eyes."

Cerulean. The color of the royal house of Atlantis.

His color.

"They—my mother had eyes this shade of deep blue," she whispered, one hand reaching up to touch her face.

Conlan caught his breath, feeling her pain. Something about her mother—

"She's gone," he murmured. Somehow he knew it. Felt it. He couldn't understand the pull—as if the magnetic draw of the moon to the tides had infused him. He wanted to touch her.

He *needed* to touch her.

Almost without thought, he reached out to her face with his fingertips. She trembled, but didn't move away, so he dared to caress the curve of her silken cheek with trembling fingers. Longing. Desire surging out of nowhere.

Healthy, clean desire. He hadn't felt desire in more than a century. Certainly not for the past seven years.

Nothing pure. Nothing not twisted.

Damaged goods.

He yanked his hand away from her. "*Aknasha* means 'empath,' " he said roughly. "You're an empath. The first in maybe ten thousand years."

~~~

Riley stared up at the man who had saved her from assault and, probably, rape. Maybe worse. If her mind had conjured up her most erotic fantasy to save her from a grim reality in which she really *was* being attacked, it had done a bang-up job. The man was some kind of superhero come to life.

If they made superheroes who looked like very dangerous Hollywood movie stars, that is. He stood a good eight inches taller than her five foot ten, and his body was a nymphomaniac's wet dream. Heavily muscled shoulders and arms, a broad chest that tapered down to a lean waist. God, his thighs had to be the size of her waist. The man was a mountain of muscle, improbably wearing a black silk shirt that tucked into elegant black pants.

She jerked her gaze up from going any further south and stared fixedly at his chest, her cheeks flaming to know that he'd caught her ogling him.

Although, really, the man must get ogled wherever he goes, so it's not like he isn't used to it.

His silky black hair brushed his shoulders in shining waves, framing a face that defied description. *Beautiful.* For the first time in her life, she used the adjective to describe a man.

He raised her chin with one finger, and she looked up at him again. He was smiling, amusement lighting up his dark eyes, almost as if he'd heard what she . . .

"Oh, God," she muttered. "Empath means you can read my mind?" She stared up past the silky hair, past the perfectly sculpted mouth, and past the cheekbones that seemed carved of granite. Finally, her gaze fixed on the icy black eyes that burned over her. Strange that ice could be so hot, she thought absently, trapped almost mindlessly in his gaze.

"You did hear me, didn't you?" she asked, embarrassment nearly an afterthought.

He touched her cheek with fingers so gentle she nearly shuddered from the sensation, and he spoke inside her mind with a voice that should be outlawed. *I can hear your thoughts, but I can also somehow feel your emotions. It's impossible, but it's true.*

Whiskey wrapped in velvet. His low, purely masculine voice carried a smooth, husky tone that curled around her nerve endings until her skin tightened with desire. Desire that caressed every erogenous zone she'd never even known she had.

Desire that he would *touch* her. Desire that he would keep talking to her on the mental path that no other person had ever shared with her.

Desire.

His voice echoed in her mind, rough. Strained. *I hear you, and maybe you should think other thoughts. Because something about you is burning me up inside, and I don't know if I'm up to the challenge of controlling it.*

She sensed his puzzlement, almost as if he were seeking the answer to an unanswerable problem. He stepped closer to her and wrapped one hand gently around the nape of her neck. *I need to touch you. I don't want to frighten you, but please let me touch you. Just my forehead to yours.*

His eyes held a stark plea. *Please.*

Trembling, sure she was out of her mind to agree to it, she nodded. She couldn't help herself. Something inside of her wouldn't let her run away. Maybe insanity, or maybe just the adrenaline high from surviving two near-death experiences in a single evening.

But every protective instinct that had served her well in her job—that should have been shouting *caution, caution, back away from the superhunk*—was screaming *yes, yes, yes, touch me, touch me.*

Riley snapped out of her mental ramble, realizing that the hottest man she'd ever seen was bending toward her. Slowly, ever so slowly, he lowered his face toward hers, as if to kiss her.

Oh, if he'd only kiss her.

A mere breath away from her, he smiled a slow smile of sheer male satisfaction. It made him look even more the predator he clearly was.

I'm down with that, aknasha. *But first, I want to feel the touch of your mind.* With that, he lowered his forehead to hers.

For the second time that night, Riley's world exploded.

Her body stiffened, and she jerked backward so hard she'd have fallen if he hadn't captured her with strong hands on her arms. He. Him. *Conlan.* His name was Conlan and he was . . . some sort of leader. Thoughts and impressions leapt from his mind to her own, drowning her in sensations and colors. His . . . thoughts? . . . aura? . . . *soul?* . . . a vivid blue-green, like a pool of the clearest water or the depths of the sea. But blackness—a boiling blackness swirled in the middle of it.

Torture. Pain. A name—a face—dark beauty ruined by evil and madness.

Anubisa?

She twisted in his arms, trying to escape from the intensity of his mind's capture of hers, but he held her with arms like steel bands.

Just as the pain branded in his memories held her in its thrall. *Torture, pain, burning—slicing, shredding, searing agony . . . How could he have borne so much pain for so long?*

She gasped, trying to breathe, trying for distance. No longer trying to pull away, but seeking to understand.

How? How was he inside of her mind? She felt him—she knew him—she *understood* him on some fundamental level. She could read his fierce determination to discover her, to explore her, to . . . *have* her? The intensity of his mind scan changed, with all the subtlety of the tidal wave he'd called earlier, into an outpouring of sexual longing.

A violent hunger, tinged with his shock at his reaction to her. She yanked her head away from his in a desperate attempt to protect herself and thought, for an instant, that she saw blue-green fire raging in the depths of his black pupils.

She shook her head to clear it, and spoke out loud to try to dampen the hunger rising between them. "Conlan. Your name is Conlan, right? I don't know how I know that, but . . . mine is Riley."

Then, in spite of her fear, she laughed a little. "Wow. Talk about a 'me, Tarzan, you, Jane' moment."

Then the memories banished the smile from her face. "How could you bear it? So much pain for so long . . ."

She shook her head, aching for him. Aching for this man she didn't even know. "It would have driven me insane."

He finally spoke, voice flat. "Don't jump to any conclusions. I never claimed to be sane."

Chapter 6

Conlan threw his head back, gulping in a lungful of air, the ugly reality of his memories stark in the silence between them. She had more courage than he'd even guessed, this small human. With his mind thrust into hers, he'd touched the fundamental core of her—their thoughts nearly melded. The purity of her soul shocked him; his cynicism was centuries old.

One touch and he knew her, somehow.

Intellectually.

Emotionally.

"Again. I need to touch you again," he said roughly, pulling her closer. "Please."

He gazed down at her, willing her not to deny him. She stared back at him, fear subsiding into acceptance, and then she nodded and closed her eyes, lifting her forehead to his.

But he didn't want a mere innocent touch this time. He needed just a taste of her. Just a small taste. He knew he was lying to himself about the *small* part even as he thought it.

He didn't care.

He swept down to capture her lips with his own. At the first touch of his mouth, her eyes snapped open, and she gasped just enough for his tongue to sweep inside of her mouth and complete his possession. The taste of her sent all sane thoughts out of his head. He felt the energy bursting from him, seeking the elements.

He didn't even try to stop it. The sea boiled up over the edge of the sand and underneath them, and the wind whipped itself into a frenzy around them.

Cyclone force.

Her body trembled and she arched into him, the softness of her curves enticing, but it was the touch of her mind that drove him toward madness. His body hardened beyond any need he'd ever known, aggressive, dominating, until his clothing was surely going to burst from the pressure.

He drove his tongue in and out of her mouth, thrusting and retreating in a cadence older than time. Wanting to climb inside of the warmth of her mouth and the haven of her body all at once.

Sanity tried to rise in his mind and push past his fierce need. *Riley. Her name is Riley. She's human.*

This is wrong.

She touched his face.

Sanity never had a fucking chance.

Even as he pulled her against the hardness of his body, Riley knew he must be dreaming. Nothing, *nothing*, had ever felt like this. Power surged through her, heat melding her to him.

She wanted to climb on him, climb inside of him, feel his body rubbing against her, pounding inside of her. The intensity of it shocked her even as she moaned for *more, more, more*, all reason lost in the tempest of wanting.

Needing.

She clutched at his rock-hard biceps, trying to hold herself upright. Maybe trying to pull him closer. She mindlessly moved her hands, put them on his chest, down to his hard, flat, stomach, up to his neck. Drove her fingers into his hair. Closer, closer. She heard a moaning sound, and it was her, *her*. She was whimpering. If his tongue hadn't been in her mouth, she'd be begging him to pull her even closer.

She stopped breathing, focused on his emotions, pulled the colors of them inside her. The blues and greens and the sparkling crystalline passion swirling around, and she was lost in it, lost in him.

Lost.

The idea of losing herself snapped her to a brief rationality. She fought to push back from him, reaching for sanity, battling with ravenous desire.

Sanity surrendered.

She made a tiny moaning sound inside of his mouth, and Conlan was lost, too, wanting, craving, needing. *Only* her. Only *her*. Now.

He tried to concentrate on her thoughts to keep from tearing at her clothes like an animal. He sent his mind inside of hers—inside of her soul—and was captivated by her innate goodness, selflessness, and light.

The epiphany of her purity slammed into him with a force beyond reason. He was paralyzed.

He was *destroyed*.

She wanted *him*, too.

Consumed by the twin revelations of her spirit and desire, flaming heat flashed to volcanic intensity inside of him. The passion and elemental energy in the air snapped and crackled around their bodies, incinerating him from the inside out.

His body went up in flames, and he wanted *more*.

His need turned voracious. Just one touch. A single taste.

A taste that went on forever.

His hands caressed her spine, pulled her hips closer to his heat—his need. His mind and body screamed for this one moment when passion, not obligation or duty, was allowed to rule his actions.

Her scent, the silk of her hair, the warmth of her skin next to the sea-spray chill of his own all combined to blast duty out of his mind.

He wanted, no, *needed* to carry her down to the sand and take her body, over and over, pounding into her warmth with the relentless fury of the surf. His heightened senses scented her desire, rising to match his own, even as she clutched at his shoulders. His hands shaped her curves, touched her softness, molded her body to his own so tightly that she must surrender to his claim.

Something primitive—feral—raised its head inside of him and demanded that he do just that.

Stake his claim.

Leave his mark on her.

His *mark*. The flames. Suddenly, he realized the mark of Poseidon on his chest was burning into his flesh almost as it had the day he'd sworn his oath. A reminder? He tried to think, to study the sensation, but his body was drowning in raw need.

Lost in the miracle of her mind and her body, he kissed her, claiming her with his mouth. His hands tightened on her until she cried out a little. The tiny whimper wrenched him out of his mindlessness and he stilled, sanity trying to resurface.

She pulled her head back, eyes dazed and lips swollen. "You're hurting me," she whispered.

He released her instantly, hands trembling, cursing himself for having caused her pain. "I'm sorry—*damn* it. I'm—there is no excuse."

He bowed his head, breathing hard. Self-loathing iced over any remnants of passion. He bowed deeply and then raised his gaze to hers. "Please accept my apologies. I have never—*no*. I'm as much of a brutish asshole as the scum that just ran away from here."

She smiled a little, the edge of fear receding from her eyes but still present in her mind. She was trembling. Maybe as much from fear as passion, now.

He was *lower* than scum.

She tried to speak, breath coming rapidly and clearly trying for calm. "I don't . . . I can't . . . you can't . . ."

She heaved in a deep breath and backed away from him. "What the hell *was* that? I don't do things like that. I mean, I just did, so you must think—but I don't. Oh, stop babbling, Riley."

She gave him another shaky smile, still breathing hard. "Since you probably saved my life and all, you're forgiven for, well, practically assaulting me right here on the beach. Not that I wasn't cooperative, or whatever. But I have to leave." Riley backed carefully away from him, seeming not to realize that he lingered in her mind.

Honesty. Even embarrassed by what she thought of as her own wanton behavior, she was honest enough to admit to him that she'd felt the same raging desire. His respect for her bravery increased, even as he had to fight his body's demands that he sweep her back to his palace and hold her captive for a year.

Or two.

Preferably naked at all times.

Conlan felt the fierce smile spread across his face. She was courageous, and beautiful beyond belief, and she was *aknasha*.

It was his *duty* to study her. To spend a great deal of time with her.

To rationalize the hell out of the fact that I want to get her naked and underneath me. In my bed. Here on the sand. Anywhere. Just soon.

Now.

He sucked in a deep breath, fighting for control. The Trident. He had to find the Trident. He'd tuck her safely away in Atlantis in the meantime.

He thought of the warriors standing guard, training—hell, just the thought of other males walking around anywhere *near* Riley—and his breathing tightened in his chest.

Okay, so she could stay in the temple.

With the priests. The *celibate* priests.

Away from Alaric, oath of celibacy or no.

Riley took another step back, and he still could sense her confusion. She doubted her sanity. Exhaustion was overwhelming her. The night's events had battered her—*he'd* battered her.

He couldn't regret touching her. Kissing her. But he regretted pushing her already stretched resources even further. An alien sense of tenderness washed through him. He wanted to protect her.

Even from himself.

He smiled down at her, but it wasn't enough to reassure her. Riley nearly stumbled in her haste to get away from him. "I have to go home. It's late. The curfew and all. I have to—good-bye."

As he moved to follow her, he sensed that Ven and the Seven had finally broken through the waves, and that Alaric was close behind. He knew that he could track her from a distance. He'd scanned the area to confirm that the attackers were long gone.

But it took everything in him to stand still and let her go.

Just long enough for her to reach her home. She'd want to pack some of her things.

He didn't know how long he'd keep her in Atlantis.

Something deep inside him protested at ever letting her go. *Not for long, this time at least. I'll be at her side in less than an hour. The rest—the rest I'll have to figure out later.*

He refused to think of his duty. Of his intended queen he'd never met.

As he watched her run from him, his mind supplied her name, almost caressing the syllables. He whispered it aloud. "Riley."

When his body hardened even further at the mere sound of her name, a stark truth slammed into him. She was no mere empath.

She was *his.*

Conlan shook his head. Stupid. Futile. His duty was clear. Noble lineage. Destined royal breeding program.

His lip curled. *Royal stud farm.*

His gaze went back to Riley, spotlighted on the edge of the beach where she'd turned to stare back at him. Tentatively, her mind reached out to his. *Good-bye, Conlan. Thank you.*

You're welcome, Riley. But there's no way that it's good-bye.

As she disappeared into the night, he raised his arms and hurled a wave of fierce joy into the sea, and a family of passing dolphins threw themselves into the air in celebration—an arabesque of shared delight. The air resonated with the vibrations of Poseidon's power.

Then, without warning, weakness and dizziness crashed through him. Conlan stumbled backward and then fell to the sand.

And fear for Riley shot through him.

He shook his head back and forth, trying to clear it. He hated the idea, but he had to do it.

He had to call for aid.

Ven! I need . . . I need your help.

Chapter 7

Some hundreds of miles away, the Lord High Vampire Barrabas raised his head, scenting the air. Something—*what*? Just for an instant, he'd felt a disturbance in the elements beyond anything . : .

"But, Senator Barnes, as leader of the Primus, you must—" the human said, cringing.

Barrabas hissed at him, hating the false name. *Barnes*. A pathetic excuse for a name.

He knew, however, the ill-advised nature of claiming his legacy. Many still remembered his history-cursed name, and the events that Pontius Pilate had set in motion that day.

Soon. Soon he would come into his own, and then the name of Barrabas would be hated and feared with such magnitude as to make what went before seem as nothing to these sheep.

The sheep in front of him prostrated himself right there on the concrete floor of the Primus's central underground chamber.

"As leader of the Primus, I *must* do whatever I *want* to do," he sneered. "The other two houses of Congress will do exactly what I tell them, won't they?"

The human groveled and crawled backward out of the room, probably considering himself lucky, given what he'd witnessed.

The vampire's gaze flicked to the congressman from Iowa and the senator from Michigan who had been causing such problems. They dangled, feet off the floor, arms threaded through the shackles bolted into the wall.

The females of his blood pride flitted around them, slicing delicately into the skin of the chained men and sucking at the blood running down their naked forms. The Iowan still moaned, though the other had long since gone silent.

Barrabas considered and discarded conclusions regarding the relative strength of their party affiliations based upon their stamina, and then he flung himself into his thronelike chair. Eyes narrowing, he focused on the disturbance he'd felt in the elements.

"What could have such power?" he muttered, fingers drumming on the arm of the chair.

The door to the chamber slammed open and his second, Drakos, soared into the room. "Did you feel it, Barrabas?"

Barrabas nodded, a nearly imperceptible movement of his head. "I felt it. What was it?"

Drakos floated down to the ground, silvery hair settling around his shoulders. Barrabas was not unaware of more than a few of his women sneaking avid gazes at his general.

Something will have to be done about Drakos. He grows nearly powerful enough to challenge me. Perhaps it is time for a new second.

But aloud he only replied to the spoken question. "Maybe nothing. Maybe everything. Send out the vanguard. We cannot afford to be distracted now."

"Anubisa?"

Barely, just barely, Barrabas contained the shudder. "She has been . . . *unavailable* as of late. Not that she ever tells us anything of what she knows."

"Still, if we defy her—" Drakos clenched his jaw.

"Enough," Barrabas roared. "Do as I say."

"As you command, so it will be done," Drakos responded, averting his gaze and bowing low. "I will lead them."

"No. I need you here," Barrabas said. "Send another. Send Terminus."

Drakos raised one eyebrow, but otherwise his face was entirely unreadable. Unsurprising for a more than nine-hundred-year-old vampire, but inconvenient nonetheless.

Barrabas stood up in a movement of pure blurred speed that might have terrified the chained Iowan, if one of the women hadn't just sliced through his jugular.

"Good politicians are so hard to find these days," Barrabas observed. "They all lack a certain endurance."

Stepping around the spray of blood and inhaling the thick, coppery smell with pleasure, Barrabas waved a hand to his general. "I have a more important task for you, my second. I need another telepath. I was, perhaps, oversolicitous in my affections with my last one."

He thought back to the lump of inanimate flesh he'd left on the floor of his bedchamber, with more than a little regret.

Drakos spoke emotionlessly. "Telepaths are few and far between, my lord, and growing ever more difficult to locate. I had hoped this one would—"

Barrabas cut him off. "You question me, Drakos?"

Though he *had* been unusually hard on telepaths this past year. His lusts for blood and flesh were rising, not abating, as he grew older and stronger, and something about hearing his victim's tormented thoughts through the telepathic link was unbearably succulent.

If only empaths still existed. To actually *feel* the sheep's pain as he inflicted it . . . he shuddered in simple ecstasy at the thought.

No other had survived as long as he—there was none Barrabas could ask to learn if he would face even more ravenous hungers as more time passed. Perhaps he was destined to become more of an animal than the shape-shifters he planned to destroy.

Shaking off his black thoughts, he led Drakos out of the chamber, glancing back at his women, who were frantically lapping at the congressional fountain of blood. "And get my secretary. I have a new proposal to make in regard to that last bill that got filibustered. I think the rest of the Congress may find it more . . . palatable . . . now."

He stopped at the door and jerked his head toward the remains of his most determined opponents on the Hill. "Then get someone to take out the trash."

Chapter 8

Conlan inhaled a deep breath, sure that Riley's scent lingered in the air surrounding him. He could taste her in his mouth—her warmth and sweetness. Still feel the imprint of her silken skin on his hands, on his hardened and aching body. He could still sense the emotions she was broadcasting so loudly.

Everything in him demanded that he go after her. Need bordering on obsession swamped him, but centuries of training rose to override his instincts. He must face and analyze the threat. He'd never experienced anything like that wave of weakness. It had passed in minutes, but who knew if it could come back?

Also, what the hells had caused it? Was it from sharing her emotions?

By Poseidon's balls, it was like nothing he'd ever heard about in all of the histories of his people. Nothing he'd ever been warned against.

He needed to identify the cause of the weakness, so that he could prevent it. Defeat it. As Alaric loved to proclaim, *knowledge is power*.

He reached out for his brother on their shared mind path.
Ven?

The voice came immediately in his head, ringing with fury and—better hidden but still evident—concern. *Nearly there, my brother.*

The duty ingrained in him after so many years battled to regain control of his mind. His duty was to recover the Trident. Finally ascend to the throne that he'd avoided thinking about for the past two centuries. Lead his people.

A future king didn't abandon his duty to follow a woman.

He laughed, humorless. *Yeah, duty. Because just what Atlantis needs sitting on the throne after my father's half millennium of perfect rule is a fucked-up head case who couldn't even escape from a vamp.*

His jaw tightened, and he paced circles in the sand. Not that Riley—or any woman—deserved to be burdened with him, either.

His thoughts flashed to Anubisa. What if pain had ruined him? What if sex for him would now always be tainted, twisted?

Wrong?

What did he have to offer any woman? He must be rational.

Right. Except rationality was fucking impossible. His body tightened further, painfully, just at the thought of Riley's hair slipping through his hands like the finest Atlantean silk. She hadn't felt *wrong.* Nothing about her, about them together, had felt anything but right.

Too right. How could it be so right to hold a woman he'd just met?

A *human?*

Closing his eyes, Conlan breathed slowly in through his nose and called on the discipline of his training to dampen his raging need. He was high prince, and he knew his duty.

Yeah, well, screw *duty. Ven has five minutes, and then I'm going after her. I'm going to make sure she's safe before I go recover the Trident.*

A swirling fountain of water shot up into the air, carrying Alaric to the sand. Dramatic as always.

The priest's midnight-black hair swirled around his shoulders, reminding Conlan of the stories told about him. Alaric as the dark guardian of Poseidon's rages. The people invoked the high priest's name to terrify children into minding their parents.

Conlan scowled, for the first time wondering how Alaric felt about being made into the stuff of nightmares. The glimmer of sympathy vanished, though, when the priest started laughing.

"My patience is damn near at an end, so laugh at your own risk," he snarled, feeling like a fool, trying for dignity when he'd recently been sprawled in the dirt.

Knowing that Alaric knew it.

Alaric grinned at him. "You don't appreciate my fun, Conlan? I spend so little time on land, I deserve to enjoy it, don't I?" He strode forward and held out a hand. Wearing form-fitting black pants and a black silk shirt nearly identical to Conlan's own, Alaric could have been his twin.

His *evil* twin.

Still, Conlan didn't have time for childish sulking. He grasped the outstretched hand, knowing Alaric would read him more easily through touch.

Needing to know what had happened to him, even as he resented the intrusion into his head.

"A fountain of water? Your childish games bring unwanted attention to us, priest. Be advised that I prefer it that you stop," he growled, resorting to formal speak.

Alaric grinned again, clearly unrepentant, and released his hand. "Uh-oh. You're calling me *priest*, instead of Alaric. That must mean you're trying on your kingly ways, old friend."

Then the grin faded, and the illusion of amiability vanished with it. A dark and lethal predator remained, ice-green eyes glowing with power. "Be *advised* that I do what I wish. Poseidon's high priest answers to none but the sea god himself."

Before Conlan could frame a retort, he felt, rather than heard, his brother shoot up through the water, barely breaking the surface. He turned to watch Ven stride through the sand, the coppery blades of his orichalcum daggers unsheathed and held at the ready.

Ven held the title of King's Vengeance by heredity and by battle right. No warrior was more skilled. Nobody could kick vamp or shape-shifter ass better. Which was a handy trait in the man whose sworn duty it was to protect his brother the high prince.

Except for those times when Conlan sped off for the surface without waiting for either his brother or his elite guard.

As he'd never done before. Something to prove, much?

Conlan dismissed the idea of arguing with Alaric and turned to his brother. Ven was going to be pissed.

He had a *right* to be.

Ven stormed up the beach toward him. "What in the name of the nine hells were you thinking? Are you out of your damn mind? We're facing a threat that we don't even understand, and you pick *now* to go all Rambo?"

Conlan strained to keep the snarl out of his own voice, and almost succeeded.

Almost.

"Do you offer battle challenge, my brother?" He got right up in Ven's face, in spite of the fact that his baby brother had a couple of inches and maybe fifty pounds on him.

Ven bared his teeth. "Look, you idiot—"

Conlan very deliberately swept one arm out, a ball of turquoise and silver light flashing in his upturned palm. Then he swept his gaze over Ven and the rest of the Seven and drew what shred of dignity he still possessed around him. "I think you overstep the role of King's Vengeance, my brother. I answer to no one."

Even as the words left his mouth, he realized their similarity to those Alaric had just uttered.

Evidently, so did Alaric, whose eyes gleamed with amusement. But at least *he* had the sense to keep his mouth shut.

Not so with Ven. He gaped, staring at the ball of pure energy crackling in Conlan's hand. "Overstep? I over*step* the *role*? I *am* the King's Vengeance, you overgrown excuse for a pigheaded princeling."

Conlan glared at his brother, the two of them toe to toe, Ven giving as good as he got. Then the sound of applause broke through his focus. He jerked his head around to sear Alaric with a glare. The priest continued to clap his hands together.

"Lovely. Very impressive," the priest drawled. "We have Reisen on the loose with the Trident and some unknown threat who has drained our prince's power, and yet we have time to play 'whose dick is bigger?' between the Brothers Grimace."

Conlan opened his mouth, then closed it again, anger draining away. He waved his fingers and the energy ball vanished, then he stepped back from his brother.

"You suck at respect for royalty, don't you?" he said to Alaric. "But, as much as I hate it, you're right."

Conlan glanced at his guard, all clad like his brother in the black leather pants and long coats Ven had demanded they wear on any trips to the surface. Ven figured badass biker dude was as good a cover as any for men who towered over most human males.

Conlan's warriors—*Poseidon's* Warriors—stood at battle alert, hands fisted on blade handles, all constantly scanning their surroundings for imminent threat to their liege.

And here he stood wasting their time with a pissing contest.

Ven shoved a hand through his hair. "Yeah, yeah, whatever. Anyway, what happened? We all felt the disturbance in the elements when you were attacked. What kind of creature could have done that? Was it a vamp?"

"No—"

Ven continued, talking right over him. "And why in the nine hells did you face it without us? Why *leave* without us?"

Conlan glanced at his men, his brothers in arms, before responding. Denal wore an expression of keen reproach, but immediately schooled his expression to implacability when he realized Conlan was watching him.

Ven followed Conlan's gaze through the line. His warriors. Sworn to the service of Poseidon and to the throne, they faced lives of grim purpose. They fought any who threatened humankind. Many died. Those who lived got patched up and returned to fight again.

And their reward? Bound into loveless marriages with females they were ordered to wed. As he himself would do in two weeks' time.

Conlan measured the tenor of his men, realizing anew how lucky he was. There was nobody he'd rather have at his back.

Alexios, fierce, scarred face grim.

Brennan, emotionless but for the whitened knuckles on his blades.

Justice, blue-tinged hair in a braid to his waist, the handle of his sword rising from its sheath behind one shoulder. The member of his Seven who Conlan understood least—trusted least. But a warrior to be reckoned with, by anyone's measure.

Bastien, towering over the others. Nearly seven feet of pure muscle and honed battle instincts.

Christophe, skin glimmering faintly with the residue of barely controlled power.

Finally back to Denal, the youngest of the Seven and newest to the role. He'd still been training at the academy when Conlan had . . . gone away.

Before Conlan could speak, Ven's voice rang out again. "Are you going to clue me in on what you were thinking? Were you even thinking at all? These men are sworn to protect you, even to die for you. But you have to go play action hero?" Ven snorted, disgust written all over his face. "'Cause that worked out so well for you the last time, right?"

Somebody gasped. Conlan inclined his head, acknowledging the solid body blow. If he'd waited for sufficient warriors when he'd chased Anubisa back into her lair, maybe he'd . . .

No. Hindsight was for losers.

He fought for calm in his voice. "Still don't hesitate to fight dirty, do you, brother?"

Ven shook his head, brows drawn together. Disgust plain on his face. "A good ruler allows his subjects to do their jobs, Conlan. Maybe it's about time you learned that."

Conlan whipped around to face his brother, fists clenching. Then he took a deep breath and considered. "Maybe you're right."

He heard another gasp from behind him. Even before his capture, they'd never heard much in the way of backing down from their prince.

Maybe it was time. Reason should temper rage. Maybe the philosopher had to rise to stand hand in hand with the warrior.

Conlan nodded at his brother. "You're pissing me off, but you make a lot of sense."

Ven blinked, apparently speechless. Conlan kept talking while *that* happy state continued. "But I'd consider it a personal favor if you'd forgive and forget, and we could get on with finding the Trident."

Ven blinked again, then swept a brief bow, a grin quirking up the edges of his lips. "Consider it done, Your Highness."

"Call me 'Your Highness' again, and I *will* kick your ass,"

Conlan said, a rueful grin spreading over his face, then fading. "I should have waited, I admit it. But that's not all I need to admit. We've got to talk. Consider it a matter of the utmost urgency."

Ven raised a single eyebrow. His body, if possible, stiffened into an even more heightened state of wariness, as he whipped his head from side to side, scanning the beach and darkness beyond. "What is it? Reisen? Did you encounter any of the vamps or were-folk? Give me something to *fight*, damnit."

Alaric glided noiselessly across the sand, coming closer, reminding Conlan of a shark preparing to strike.

"What was the threat?" Alaric demanded. "Did you encounter some new form of magic that can control even the elements?"

Conlan shook his head, weighing his words. "I'm almost certainly going to regret telling you this. But you have a right to know. Especially when it concerns a potential weakness."

Except now he was talking about a personal weakness. A weakness in the heir to the throne. Atlantean political strategy would demand he keep silent.

Atlantean battle strategy would demand that he reveal all.

He measured Ven and Alaric with his gaze. Ven was family, and Alaric had been Conlan's friend since childhood. Conlan had never concealed any truth from either of them. Yet, as he gazed into the fierce green glow of power shining in the priest's eyes, Conlan came to an unpleasant realization: *he wasn't entirely sure Alaric could say the same.*

Conlan called his guard to approach, then spoke clearly and in the formal tones of his office. Never mind that formality felt false after so many years.

Hell, maybe if he *sounded* like a king, he'd feel like one. "My haste in departing was unseemly and wrong in this matter. My brother reminds me that a good king allows his warriors to do what they have trained to do."

He measured the face of each warrior in turn, and then continued, voice somber. "However, be advised of this. I will be king, and I am even now high prince. I will act as I consider warranted at all times."

He paused, flashed a grin at Ven. "Just try to keep up, little brother."

Humor fading from his face, Conlan lifted his head and scented the wind for any change in the elements, scanning for any of the living or undead nearby. Then he sent out a mental casting to touch Riley again, gritting his teeth at the realization that even their brief separation was making him tense.

Edgy.

Damnit. Who was she? More, what *was she?*

She didn't even realize that he'd stayed in her mind, unnoticed, as she'd driven the short distance to her small home. He'd broken the connection during the discussion with his warriors and Alaric.

He sent out a gentle touch. *I'm here, Riley. Are you safe?*

He sensed her startled gasp and could almost see her. Her touch returned to him, her emotions fluttering like tiny sea anemones in his mind.

Conlan? You can still talk to me? But I'm almost ten miles from the beach and—somehow I know you're still there.

I can feel you, aknasha. I'm going to protect you, too. You have great value to . . . my people.

She sent a slight hint of amusement—that, and an overwhelming sense of her exhaustion. *That is a very pretty thought, but I'm not very valuable to anyone. I just need to take a bubble bath and go to sleep now. Good-bye.*

With that, the feel of mental doors crashing down snapped off his connection to her. He flinched back from the sensation, mouth dry, fighting to keep his body from hardening anew at the idea of her naked body glistening in a tub of scented bubbles.

He clenched his eyes shut and groaned.

Ven's eyes narrowed. "What is it? The threat?"

Conlan's eyes snapped open, and he saw Ven and the rest of the Seven crouch into battle readiness, blades at the ready. Alaric threw his arms into the air as if to command power, the ocean waves instantly responding with a crashing symphony of percussion against the shore.

Conlan held up one hand. "No, it's okay. There is no threat."

He grinned. "Or, to be more accurate, the threat is going to take a bubble bath."

Chapter 9

"What is it, Lord Reisen?"

Reisen sliced his hand through the air, commanding his warrior to desist. Stop making noise while Reisen opened his mind and senses to any disturbance in the elements.

For a minute, he'd almost thought—

But, no. Conlan was long dead. The royal house in chaos. Nobody willing to step up and admit that Anubisa had murdered the heir to the Seven Isles.

Until now.

Reisen glanced down at the long shape wrapped in scarlet velvet on the table. The Trident. He almost couldn't believe that he'd actually taken it. That it now lay on a table in one of his safe houses, right under the noses of the sleeping landwalkers in the buildings around him.

Snatched out from under Alaric's nose.

The thought of that last gave him a great deal of satisfaction. Arrogant prick. Their final confrontation, nine days ago, flashed into his mind.

"You know he's not coming back, Alaric," Reisen said, pacing the marble floor of the priest's private receiving chamber. "It's been seven years. Even if he does come back, he won't be Conlan."

He stopped, fixing the priest with his gaze. "He'll be— wrong."

Alaric folded his arms across his chest, looking more like a street thug than Poseidon's chosen, until you saw the power burning in his eyes. "Conlan is stronger than any of the rest of you. Stronger than any warrior in Atlantean history. Poseidon has given me no indication that he is dead. Or changed."

Alaric's eyes narrowed. "Do you tell me that you doubt the sea god?"

Reisen smacked his fist into his palm. "I have never blasphemed, and I'm not starting now, so don't go there, priest. I merely wonder if you're really hearing what Poseidon is telling you. Or are you just channeling your own hopes for your boyhood friend?"

"Never dare to challenge me, Reisen. The house of Mycenae will regret it." Alaric didn't raise his voice, but the walls of the temple shuddered.

Reisen never blinked. "Perhaps it is you who will regret this day, Alaric."

Then he strode from the temple, never looking back.

Already formulating his plan.

～～∽

Reisen reached out to touch the folds of velvet covering the Trident. He'd been more than half prepared to be killed for the sacrilege of touching it. Poseidon's Trident. The vehicle of ascension for Atlantean kings for millennia.

Yet, when he'd grasped it that day in the temple, it had remained quiescent. Inanimate. Merely a pretty artifact, melded gold, silver, and orichalcum shaped in the same design he wore branded into his chest.

But with seven open spaces that showed where its seven jewels had nestled before the Cataclysm.

Before they were scattered to the surface lands for protection and safekeeping.

"My lord—" the warrior began again. Pulled from his musings, Reisen glanced at him. Micah, first of his Seven.

"We need to move on. They will surely be after us soon," Micah said, hands fisted on the handles of his daggers.

Brother warriors of Poseidon. Further bonded by the enormity of the act they committed now.

"Is it justice, Micah?" Reisen wondered aloud. "Is it justice that we do for our homeland? Or is it treason, as Alaric will surely name it?"

Micah's eyes shone with the fervor of their cause. "It is justice to seek the jewels that have been lost. To restore Atlantis to its former glory, my lord. After more than eleven thousand years, it is surely time."

Reisen nodded slowly. "Yes, it is time. We were tasked to serve as first warning on the eve of humanity's destruction," he said, quoting the ancient words.

"The brazenness of the denizens of the night is surely more than a first warning," Micah growled.

A smile fleetingly crossed Reisen's face. The *denizens of the night*. The archaic language reminded him that Micah hadn't spent much time out of Atlantis. And yet, it was chillingly accurate.

"To Atlantis, then, Micah," he said, holding his own dagger high in the air. "To restoring the glory and supremacy of Atlantis."

The rest of his warriors, who'd entered the room as he and Micah spoke, raised their daggers above their heads in unison.

"To Atlantis!" they shouted in unison. "To Mycenae!"

Reisen smiled. Yes, to Atlantis and Mycenae. And to his own ascension to the throne of a newly restored Atlantis.

"To Mycenae," he roared.

Then he glanced yet again at the bundle on the table, struck by a glimpse of motion and flickering light.

"I must have imagined it," he muttered, words drowned out by his warriors' thundering shouts.

Because, just for a split second, the velvet had seemed to glow.

"Are you out of your royal mind?" Taking a break from pacing and swearing viciously in ancient Atlantean, Latin, and a little-used dialect once heard near Constantinople, Ven stopped in front of his brother, hands fisted on his hips.

Conlan sighed, not knowing whether to award his brother battle medals for creativity, or order Justice to arrest the King's Vengeance for treason.

I could flip a coin . . .

Conlan stepped in close to Ven, invading the nine hells out of what Ven liked to call his personal space. "I did not ask for your judgment upon my actions. I merely described a possible threat to our warriors. If more humans have the capacity to incapacitate us with emotional telepathy—"

He didn't mention that he'd left out a hell of a lot in the telling. There was no threat to Atlantean security regarding his fierce attraction to her.

Admit it, attraction is a tame word. Try overwhelming, ball-breaking lust.

He blew out a breath. Even princes were allowed some privacy, right?

Ven shook his head in disgust, then resumed pacing and cursing. Conlan tuned him out after he heard something about "spawn of a dung beetle" in early Portugese and turned to Alaric, who had remained uncharacteristically silent during Conlan's explanation of the evening's events.

Alaric speaking was dangerous enough.

Alaric silent was deadly.

The priest stared at him, unblinking, seeming almost inhuman in his stillness. If ever a man had seemed unsuited to the priesthood, Conlan would have named Alaric. Matching Conlan in height, Alaric's heavily muscled form suited the lethal menace in his eyes.

No schoolboy would ever seek him out to tell tales of childish mischief in the confessional, for certain. And yet it was rumored that more than one woman, seduced by Alaric's dark beauty, had harbored hopes of convincing the dark priest to . . . *bend* . . . his vow of celibacy.

Conlan nearly laughed at the thought. It was well known that Poseidon would strip the powers from a priest who breached his celibacy vow. Power was Alaric's only mistress;

no female could come between him and his quest for ever more of it.

As if reading his prince's mind, Alaric bared his teeth in a cold pretense of a smile. "I agree with Conlan."

"Look, I—*what*?" The agreement threw him off.

"You heard me," Alaric returned, face expressionless. "You want to follow this human to her home to ensure her safety. You demand we transport her to Atlantis as your . . . *guest*. I agree with you."

Ven exploded. "Great. Now I have two of you out of your freaking minds. I'd have expected better of you, Temple Rat."

Alaric's gaze shifted smoothly to Ven, and something whispering of deadly danger shimmered in his eyes. "I am high priest to the sea god now, Lord Vengeance. It is time we put away childish . . . endearments."

Conlan shifted to stand between the two men. The last thing he needed was his two most trusted advisors bashing each other's brains out. "Calm down, Ven. You've gotta be a role model for my warriors, right?"

Ven snorted. "I *am* a role model in all things that matter. But standing emotionless and icy in the face of seriously deep trouble is not my style. I'm more a 'take names and kick ass' kind of guy."

He paused for a moment, slamming his daggers back in their sheaths. "And agreeing that we take a human to Atlantis? Especially *now*, when the Trident is in the hands of the enemy? I repeat, you're both out of your *fucking* minds."

Shaking his head, Ven nonetheless stepped back and away, sweeping an arm out as if to urge Alaric to continue.

Alaric shrugged. "Knowledge is power. The human has powers that are unknown to us. If she truly can convey emotion over the mind path, then she must be studied and analyzed for the source of that ability."

Ven started to interrupt, but Alaric held up a hand. "Not to mention the potential enormity of a weapon with the power to bring a warrior of such strength and mental shielding as Conlan to his knees," he said, his tone clinically dispassionate.

Conlan made a growling sound low in his throat, surprising himself and, from the looks of it, everyone around him. "You would dissect Riley in a laboratory, if you believed that was the only way to understand her gifts, wouldn't you?"

Alaric raised one eyebrow. "*Riley?* You know her name?"

Fury rising, Conlan clenched his fists until his knuckles turned white, fighting to regain enough composure to speak. "You. Will. Not. Touch. Her," he gritted out.

Alaric immediately held his hands out, palms facing down, as if to show that he intended no harm. He lapsed back into formal speak, perhaps realizing the threat from Conlan. "I sense a disturbance in the elements surrounding us, and yet you showed no outward sign until now. As I am unlike your human, and cannot sense emotions, you must explain your reaction to my words."

Conlan forced his hands to unclench and took cleansing breaths. "I don't even know if I *can* explain. Or, if I could, that I would want to."

He shook his head, trying to clear it. His mind involuntarily reached out to touch Riley's restlessly sleeping consciousness. That simple touch calmed him a little.

Just enough to piss him off. What the *hell* was going on?

"I need time to understand it, myself," he admitted.

Ven broke in. "Alaric, surely you must see that our most important job is to retrieve the Trident, not play babysitter to some human female. I like humans myself, Conlan, and have enjoyed many a happy hour with them."

Conlan's brother flashed a wolfish grin. "Hell, sometimes with two of 'em at a time. I've even defended thousands of them from the vamps and the damn shape-shifters over the centuries. But you don't see me going around staking out their houses."

Someone barked out a laugh. Conlan's gaze whipped down the line of his warriors. Bastien. Of course. He was too damn big to be afraid of anything. Even the wrath of two Atlantean princes.

Damn. He had to admire the sheer balls of the man.

Conlan turned back to Ven, nodded. "You're right. But this one is different. She may have the ability to be used as a weapon against me—against *any* of us—and how can that be good?"

The part of his brain where duty gave way to need shouted out at him. *And I want* her. *I will* have her.

Duty be damned.

"Agreed," Alaric replied, startling Conlan. But of course Alaric was responding to his words, not his thoughts.

Or so Conlan hoped. If the priest had mastered thought-mining, the politics of Atlantis were headed for a big pile of reeking whale shit.

Alaric's gaze never flickered. "She could distract us at a critical point and cost us the object of our quest. We contain the female, and then we retrieve the Trident. It is the wisest course of action, as you say, Conlan. It is also true that I need time and a quiet place in which to scry for its location."

Ven grumbled a little then rolled his eyes. "Well, when you put it that way . . . Let's do this thing."

He jerked his head toward the left, and Bastien, Denal, and the rest ranged themselves around Conlan, Alaric, and Ven. Black coats billowing out behind them, nine of the deadliest predators ever to travel the earth and its oceans shimmered into watery mist and headed for a tiny house holding a sleeping human female.

And once I see her again, I'll realize that this insane attraction was a momentary thing. We'll secure her for later study, and then we'll retrieve the Trident.

Nothing has changed.

Except Conlan's years of training in self-awareness mocked him.

Fool. Everything has changed.

She changed it.

But even with his discipline, his training, and his dagger-sharp logic all brought to bear on the issue, he didn't know which *she* he meant.

Chapter 10

Riley looked at the clock again, for the third time in an hour. She'd slept for what? Maybe twenty minutes? After leaving two practically incoherent voice mail messages on Quinn's cell phone, that is.

She rolled over and sat up. Not really surprising that she wasn't sailing through fluffy dreamland, considering. Her thoughts flashed to Dina and the baby, then to Morris. She shuddered as the delayed reaction finally hit her.

"That could have been me. He was trying to kill *me*," she whispered, then clasped her arms around her knees and rocked back and forth. A shudder worked its way down her body till she sat trembling, tears sliding down her cheeks.

"And he wasn't the only one. Those men tonight—if *he* hadn't been there . . ."

Conlan.

Just thinking his name conjured his face in her mind. Elegant, aristocratic cheekbones. A strong jaw. Lips that must have been sculpted by the most artistic of angels.

A frisson of heat curled through her abdomen. *That kiss. That was . . . something.*

Oh, get over yourself, Riley. Angels, *sheesh. It's not like you haven't seen beautiful men before.*

"Nobody like him," she whispered to the darkness of her bedroom. "Never any like him. Never anybody who could step inside my mind."

Except Quinn. She and her sister had always been able to share an almost telepathic form of communication. They'd never thought much of it; everybody knew about twin speak. Ten months apart was close enough to be almost twins.

But never with anybody else. Never a stranger. Never an incredibly gorgeous man who had saved her life—or at the very least, saved her from a hideous assault.

Conlan.

Then a voice, gentle but insistent, inside of her mind.

Yes, I am here.

Then came his concern, sharp and ferocious. *Do you need me? Are you in danger?*

She held a hand up, almost as if she could touch the color-ful emotions swirling inside of her. Not *her* emotions.

His.

"Since it's a dream, I may as well answer you. Because this has to be a dream, doesn't it? Just a little PTSD to round off my day." Riley scrubbed tears off her face.

Yeah. That had to be it. None of it had really happened. Nobody could cause the ocean to act like that. Not even vamps.

What is PTSD? And why are you lying to yourself? You know I'm real, aknasha. *You hear me in your mind. You feel my emotions, although I have no idea how that is even possible.*

Riley laughed. She couldn't help it. His voice was like cool ocean waves caressing her nerve endings and soothing jagged edges.

And spiking her calm to excitement in ten seconds flat.

How was that even possible?

"Okay, Mr. Figment of My Imagination. What the hell. I'll go with it. PTSD means post-traumatic stress disorder. Which is what I've got going on after Morris nearly shot me to death."

She laughed again. "One hell of a case, from the looks of it. I mean, no pink elephants for me. I have to conjure up a drop-dead gorgeous man who can share his thoughts and emotions with me."

She stood up and headed for the bathroom. "I've gotta have some drugs somewhere. Maybe just a small Valium?"

Then the fire again, as his emotions darkened. *Someone shot at you?*

Low, dangerous. A different kind of shiver caressed her at the stark male command in his voice.

Not that she was the type to go all tingly over some hunky alpha male. "I'm fine. He's dead, so get over your 'I'm the law' thing."

But his voice came again, freezing her in her tracks, something smug and purely masculine in the words.

You think I'm gorgeous, hmm?

Riley rolled her eyes. Evidently, even in Hallucination Land men had enormous egos. She wondered idly what else about him was enormous, then caught herself when her face got hot. *Don't go there, Riley.*

Perhaps I am *simply a figment of your imagination,* he said, shades of reasonableness and amusement tinging his words in her mind. *Perhaps you should not look out your window.*

"What?" She ran to the window and yanked her blinds up, staring wildly down at her tiny garden. Four, no five, men stood below, standing in a loose ring around Conlan. She noticed that they were all the size of Conlan, and all dressed in black, before she wrenched her attention to the figure standing alone in the midst of them.

Looking up at her.

"Oh, holy crap, it's you," she whispered, placing her palms on the window, trapped in his gaze.

Yes, it is definitely me. If I'm only a figment of your imagination, can the figment say that I'd really appreciate it if you'd . . . rethink . . . your clothing before you show up in front of my men?

His voice in her mind took on a husky tone. *Not that I don't appreciate your choice of nightwear.*

Glancing down at herself, Riley's cheeks burned. She wore only an old and worn green tank top—that had Smart Girls Rock traced on it in faded gold thread—over a pair of lacy underwear.

A rather teensy pair of underwear.

Face flaming, she backed away from the window, uncertain of whether to be afraid, embarrassed, or excited that he was real.

Real and standing outside of her house.

She settled on a combination of all three, her breathing suddenly shallow and fast. But she'd seen *inside* his heart, his memories, even his soul, somehow, and there had been honor and integrity—no hint of serial-killer tendencies.

Well, if she wasn't going with Option A: Figment of Her Imagination. Damn, this was confusing.

Either way, she had some questions for him. She was a social worker, for Pete's sake. She put herself in danger as a matter of course. And she'd been inside this man's mind. She knew he had no intention to hurt her. She wasn't sure *how* she knew, but she knew.

As she dragged on a pair of jeans, she laughed without much humor. "Danger is my middle name."

The voice sounded in her mind, amused again. Glad she could provide so much entertainment for him.

She could literally *feel* his laughter curling inside her as he spoke. Or sent her thought waves. Or whatever.

Really? I would have guessed Trouble.

She grinned before she realized she was doing it. Her first smile in a long time. "You'd better be prepared for trouble, Conlan, if you can't give me a good explanation for what you're doing in my front yard."

The smile faded from her face. Great, there was an Option C. He was some kind of freakish stalker. Like she hadn't had enough to deal with, for one night.

For one *lifetime*.

But she wasn't a coward. Or stupid, either. Riley yanked a sweatshirt over her head then grabbed a phone, the better to dial a quick 911 with. Then she ran down the stairs and peered through the peephole. Yes, he was still there. Conlan and some men who were clearly also from the Land of Hunks.

Taking a deep breath, she pulled open her front door. And that's when all hell broke loose.

Vampires. It was raining materializing vampires.

She'd seen them before, sure, everybody had. Not just on

CNN either. She'd seen them up close and personal, prowling the alleys and the backways of the city. Looking for victims who were all too willing, dangling the elusive promise of immortality, luring the young, the weak, the hopeless.

But she'd never seen a full two dozen of them, swooping down from the air, arrowing in on the tiny patch of lawn in front of her house.

The same lawn where Conlan stood with his men.

She snapped out of her shock; shouted a warning. "Watch out, Conlan! Vampires!"

But he and his men were already looking up, unsheathing daggers of some sort. The blades flashed like copper fused with diamonds, beautiful and deadly.

Sort of like the man himself.

Riley, get back! Conlan thundered in her mind. *Close that damn door and hide.*

But she stood there, frozen, the phone forgotten in her hand. The silence was surreal—battle scenes in the movies were always full of clashing armor and shouting.

The battle scene before her was all the more terrifying because of the near cessation of sound.

The largest of the vamps landed in front of Conlan, sword drawn. Conlan crossed his daggers to block the blow, then sliced down viciously, striking the vamp's left arm. With an upswing, he drove his dagger into the attacker's heart, and the vamp slumped to the ground.

More men came running from around the corner of her house. They were dressed in black leather and long coats, like some terrifying biker gang. One of them, hair in a long, blue braid to his waist, broke the silence. He roared—a name, a challenge—something that sounded like *"Poseidon!"* then flew into the air in a wild leap, a sword and dagger held up and out in front of him. He landed on top of a vamp who'd tried, but failed, to twist out of the way.

Blue-hair thrust both his weapons into the vampire's neck, twisted his clearly powerful arms, still yelling fiercely, and then yanked the blades back out.

Riley stood, unblinking, hand-to-hand combat and sword-play crashing through the night around her.

Focused only on the vampire's head.

The head that fell off his body and rolled to a stop a few feet away, right next to her dormant azalea bushes.

She clutched at the door frame with one hand, slowly shaking her head back and forth, swirling fog threatening to obscure her line of sight . . .

Well, that didn't happen, did it? Because nobody decapitates vampires on my lawn, right? Can't be good for the grass. Or the azaleas.

She recognized the symptoms, objectively. She was going into shock. Numbness, graying vision, a spreading cold—

Then she looked up and met Conlan's gaze. He'd felt her terror. It must have distracted him, because she could tell he didn't notice the vampire who leapt at him from behind, aiming his sword at his back.

Her numbness shattered.

"Nooo!" she screamed, hurling herself off the porch and toward the two of them. Unthinking. Urgency driving her. She had to help him. Had to protect him.

Must protect him.

"Leave him alone!" she shouted. She jumped on the vampire's back, reaching around his neck to grab at his throat. Throttle him.

But it was too late. The vampire hissed at her as he pulled his sword back, dripping with Conlan's blood.

"You leave him alone *now*!" she repeated, mindless with rage. Her self-defense classes kicked in, fingers reaching, digging, in a barely remembered tactic.

Go for the eyes, Riley. No matter how big they are, you can always go for the eyes.

She dug her fingers in, gagging against the feel as her nails dug into squishiness. The vampire screamed with agony and twisted, heaving her arms away from him.

Smashing her to the ground.

He turned, clawing at his streaming eyes, and Riley tried to crawl backward to escape. Then the vamp roared out his anguish again, spittle flying from his cracked and twisted fangs, and focused on Conlan, lying so still next to her. The vampire reared back one booted foot, clearly planning to kick Conlan in the head.

Riley sucked in a torrent of air and screamed with everything she had in her. She launched herself in front of the vampire to somehow block his foot from crushing Conlan's skull.

And a hailstorm of coppery blades sliced through the air above her to land in the vampire's chest and throat. His foot wavered, and he staggered.

An arc of blue fire—or electrical current—or *something* not human, no, *never* human, not even vampires had blue fireballs, what the *hell*?—shot from the hands of one of Conlan's men and incinerated the vampire's head.

Incinerated.

Demolished.

As Riley collapsed back onto Conlan's still form, she started to laugh.

Then she couldn't stop.

She laughed and laughed, not registering when the laughter turned to sobs, finally looking up and seeing the ring of men looking down at her, blades drawn. Her head throbbed, ached, seemed as if it would split open from the reverberations of . . . *what*, exactly?

The one standing a little apart from the others tilted his head and pinned her with his icy green gaze. He was beautiful, like the rest of them, and yet his eyes were flat. Dead. In her job, she'd seen hardened recidivist criminals with more emotion in their eyes than his had.

"Conlan is not seriously harmed. The blade was coated in poison—the dose would have been fatal to a human," he stated, imperiously looking down his nose at her. "It will be little trouble to clear it from his blood."

She hiccupped a little, caught her breath, and then glared her defiance up at him. "You look like a serial killer, buddy. But whoever you are, unless you really *can* help Conlan, you'll have to come through me to get to him."

A collective gasp went up from the others, all six, no, all *seven* of them—she'd almost missed the one lying on the ground, blood dripping from his head as he raised it to look at her.

"She seeks to protect him where we have failed," he gritted out, wiping blood out of his eyes with one hand. "And we, sworn to his service."

Another one of them who looked an awful lot like Conlan

nodded his head, face grim, then barked out a laugh. "She sure pegged you, Temple Rat."

Laughing Guy dropped to a crouch on one knee before her, smile fading to somberness, and bowed his head. "Your courage is unknown to us in humans, lady. You offered yourself to protect my brother. But you must let our healer help him."

She clutched at her head, trying to keep it from cracking open, shocked into silence as she recognized the source of the driving pain. It was *him*. The one kneeling in front of her.

No, not exactly. She looked at them all, wonder drowning out fear. It was *all* of them. Their emotions. Their rage and pain.

Riley reached out one hand to the huge man who claimed to be Conlan's brother, gently touched his arm, and then flinched back. "Pain," she whispered. "Fear for your brother. Fury and vengeance . . . who is *Terminus*? . . ."

As the man's eyes widened, mirroring her own shock, she scanned the rest of the group. Colors, too many colors, pain, the percussion, the drums of their fury pounding in her brain.

Pounding in her heart.

Pounding in her *soul*.

Too much. Too much. *Toomuchtoomuchtoomuch*—

She smiled her best, most professional "Hello, I'm your new social worker" smile and primly clasped her hands together. "I've had enough now, thank you," she whispered.

Then she closed her eyes and, for the second time that night—the second time in her *entire life*—she slipped into unconsciousness.

But she heard him—Conlan's brother—as she fell down the dark well of silence into the black. She heard the shock in his voice.

"She read me, Alaric. My emotions. And she may have been thought-mining me. She was reading us *all*."

∞～∞

Barrabas lifted his head, hissing. Drakos raised his gaze from the maps on the table of Barrabas's private chamber. "My lord? What is it?"

"It's Terminus," Barrabas snarled, smashing the lamp off the table and to the floor. "He is dead."

"But—"

"*Permanently* dead. His connection to me snapped. I felt his violence and rage, as a master vampire will feel all of his bloodline." It was an unsubtle reminder. Drakos was not of Barrabas's bloodline, and so Barrabas always faced a twinge of doubt about him.

"Something—something new, Drakos. We're facing something new, and whatever it is—*who*ever it is—has the power to manipulate the elements."

Drakos turned his head to regard the steel vault door built into the wall. "Is it Anubisa? Are you still convinced that she seeks a return to Ragnarok?"

"The Doom of the Gods. Maybe. She is daughter-wife to Chaos. What else would she seek? She feeds not on blood, but on terror and despair."

As I would if only I could, and more and more as the years pass.

Drakos interrupted his master's thoughts. "Is it time to consult the scrolls?"

Staring at his most brilliant general, Barrabas pondered for a moment. *Is he loyal? Can I trust him? Or, does it matter? If he helps me discover the answers I need, he can meet with an accident easily enough.*

Barrabas crossed to the vault. "I think, perhaps, that it is."

Chapter 11

Conlan's nerve endings burned, pain searing through his body. He came awake with a roar, clutching the throat of the figure in front of him. "Death to the apostates of Algolagnia!"

And looked into Alaric's pitying eyes.

He released his viselike grip on the priest's throat, looking away. Pity was the one thing he'd never stand for—not now, not ever.

He needed—he *needed*—

"Riley?" he asked, voice hoarse. The healing process always burned the body, left the throat sore as if parched. Glancing down at his torn and bloodied shirt and the smooth, unbroken skin where he'd last seen a sword point piercing through, he knew he'd required a little help from Alaric.

Another debt to pay.

Alaric exchanged a glance with Ven, who stood on Conlan's other side, then looked back at Conlan. "She is unharmed," he said.

Conlan dragged himself up to sit on the edge of the bed, scanning the familiar room that he recognized as part of one of Ven's safe houses. It hadn't changed much in the years since he'd last seen it. Same utilitarian furniture. Same movie posters on the walls.

A couple of predators snarled down at him from the *Komodo vs. Cobra* film poster opposite the bed. Conlan looked from the giant beasts to his advisors and nearly laughed. He'd give even odds if the K or the C came up against his brother or Alaric.

On second thought, the reptiles wouldn't stand a chance.

"Yeah, she's all right *physically*," Ven added cryptically.

Conlan stood, swung around to face his brother. "What do you mean, 'yeah, physically'? Is she hurt? Did one of the vamp bastards get to her with some kind of mind trick?"

He was breathing hard with the effort of remaining upright, but damned if he wanted them to know. It was bad enough that Alaric got a free pass to his mind with every healing.

Ven shook his head. "No, in spite of the part where she threw her body in front of a vamp's foot to protect your thick skull. Or—hey, *this* is good—the part where she jumped on the back of the bloodsucker who skewered you."

Conlan's blood rushed out of his face, and the weakness in his knees doubled. "She put herself in danger for me? Where is she? I must see her now. I've got to—"

Alaric smoothly interrupted. "Perhaps you might say a word to young Denal, who believes, in spite of being outnumbered three to one—"

"Yeah, and in spite of his *head wound*," Ven interjected.

"That he has failed his prince," Alaric continued, his eyes snapping green fire at Conlan. "Perhaps you might consider the well-being of your men above that of a *human*."

Conlan clenched his fists, a berserker rage spiking inside him. He forced it down. "Perhaps," he mocked, "*perhaps* you might tell me where they all are, so I can go see for myself."

Ven motioned with his hand toward the doorway of the room, and Conlan headed toward it, first stumbling, then gaining strength as he walked. When he reached the doorway, he paused and looked around at Alaric. Remembering his duty, no matter how much the words stuck in his throat. "My thanks for the healing. And maybe, instead of berating me, you can

figure out why my mind is full of nothing but this *human female* I just met."

Ven laughed. "Hell, Conlan, I can tell you that. She's
freaking hot—"

Conlan whirled around, his hand rising without his volition
to grasp the front of Ven's shirt. "You'd better stop right there,
brother," he snarled. "Compare her to your whores at your
own peril."

Ven whistled, clearly unimpressed, then peeled Conlan's fingers off his shirt. "*At my own peril*, huh? If she's got you using
formal speak on *me*, big brother, I guess she really is special."

"Special, definitely. I'd say dangerous, as well," Alaric said
quietly.

Conlan ignored him and headed out the door, finally clearing the fuzz out of his brain long enough to remember that he
could reach out to Riley's mind. But when he tried, he got
nothing.

Which didn't help with his peace of mind, by a long shot.

Ven led him down a short hallway to one of the house's
several bedrooms and pushed open the door. Conlan could see
a form huddled under the quilt, unmoving.

Fear pierced him. He clutched Ven's arm in a steel grip, as
much to keep from running to her as for support. "You told
me she was unharmed."

"Relax. She just seemed to shut down, mentally. Processing
overload or something. And no wonder, after what she did."
Ven sketched in the details of the battle, including Riley's part
in it.

Conlan stood there and listened to how a fragile human
had put her life on the line for him, and pain stabbed into his
chest. Right in the vicinity of the heart he thought he'd lost.

When Ven got to the moment when Riley had stood up to
Alaric, Conlan's eyes gleamed. "That must have put a sword-
fish up his ass. A 'mere human' standing up to Poseidon's
high priest? Damn, but she's brave."

Then he shuddered, self-loathing crashing through him.
"Of course, I should have been protecting her. And the rest of
you, too."

Ven put a hand on his shoulder. "Relax, bro. We had no
way of knowing the vamps were sheathing their blades in poi-

son these days. That sword wound wouldn't have even slowed you down without it."

Dragging his gaze away from Riley, Conlan looked at his brother. "And the rest of the Seven? Is anybody hurt?"

"Come on, I'll show you while Riley sleeps for a while. Mostly nicks and bruises, nothing they wouldn't get in a good game of *Tlachtli*," he said.

Conlan almost laughed. Trust Ven to compare a deadly battle to the ancient Atlantean game of court ball. Well, the Aztecs had sacrificed the losers when *they'd* played it, right?

They headed back down the hallway toward the room Ven had turned into a games and TV room. "Denal got bashed pretty hard in the head. Luckily, his skull is damn near as thick as yours. Plus, he's got a big-ass case of 'I failed my liege lord' going on. You may want to say something."

Conlan clenched his jaw. "I'm a big boy. I don't care about me. But you—all of you—need to protect Riley for me."

Ven's mouth dropped open, then he snapped it shut. "So. I'm gonna wanna know how this chick brought you to this state in—what?—a few *hours*?"

Conlan blew out a breath as they rounded the corner. "Yeah. I'd like to know that, too."

The six warriors lounging in the room came to various forms of attention when Conlan and Ven walked in. Justice, his ever-present sword sheathed on his back, leaned against the far wall against the *Godzilla* movie poster. He paused from studying the view outside the room's single window, flicked a mocking two-fingered salute Conlan's way, then turned to look outside again.

Bastien and Christophe were doing battle on the air hockey table in the corner. Bastien's huge hand swallowed the mallet he used to strike the puck. They looked up at him, but didn't stop knocking the yellow disc back and forth across the table.

Brennan muted the sound on the television, then slowly rose from the couch to stand. He gazed at Conlan, dispassionate as ever. Poseidon had cursed Brennan for a minor transgression involving a Roman senator's daughter by removing his emotions.

Except maybe having no emotions wasn't a curse, but a blessing.

Conlan wasn't entirely sure. Especially with his mind continually trying to reach out to Riley, who still lay unresponsive.

Alexios ducked his head, a new habit. Then he defiantly raised it and shook his hair away from his face. The terrible scarring caught the glow of the lamps; the light shadowing twisted ridges and valleys of flesh.

Conlan remembered how Alexios, with his dark blue eyes and long mane of brown and gold hair, had always been forced to fight off the women. His eyes returned to the scarred left side of the warrior's face. Would a woman be repelled by it or drawn to the pain haunting his eyes?

It wasn't a question Conlan would have thought to ask. Not before—not now—but for the awareness of Riley sheltered in his mind.

Conlan met Alexios's gaze. "Never be ashamed of scars you earned defending me from Anubisa and her plague of vampire guards, my brother."

Alexios made a sound, nearly a growl, low in his throat. "Scars earned *failing* to defend you, you mean, my lord. As we failed to protect you again, tonight."

A small sound, abruptly cut off, swung Conlan's attention around to the far corner of the large room, where he saw Denal half sitting, half reclining against the back of another couch.

"Denal, are you healed?" Conlan asked, striding over to talk to the youngest of his guard.

Denal grimaced. "I am healed. Tired, but healed. Except for my heart, my prince. My heart is desolate for having failed you."

Placing his hand over his heart, Denal looked up at Conlan. "Please take my life now."

Conlan blinked. "Do *what*?"

Ven snorted, standing just to the right and behind Conlan. "He's read too many old scrolls. Plus, this is his first trip topside."

Ven dropped into an easy crouch beside the younger man. "Dude, you've got to haul your vocab into the twenty-first century."

"*Dude*," the warrior bit off. "However you phrase it, the truth remains the same. I was nearest to Conlan when that vampire attacked him. I should have taken the blade."

Conlan reached out to lay his hand gently on Denal's head for an instant. "However, from Ven's account, you were battling three vampires on your own, including another one who'd tried to gut me, right? And you took an axe to the side of your head?"

Denal dropped his eyes, but nodded. "It was only the flat end of the axe, my lord."

Bastien interrupted, his low voice a rumble. "Yeah, at least it was his *head*. Nothing important in there to damage. We're golden."

Conlan felt the laughter rising in him at Bastien's familiar teasing, but knew Denal was far too earnest to understand that his prince wasn't laughing at him. He bit back his humor and turned a serious face to his youngest warrior. "Thank Poseidon that it was the flat end of the axe, or your head would be split in two. And enough with the 'my lord' and 'my prince' stuff. Call me Conlan."

He turned in time to see Justice snort and roll his eyes. "Do you have something to say to me, Justice?"

The warrior pushed himself away from the wall, uncoiling like a leopard preparing to strike. Strange that he'd always reminded Conlan of a jungle animal. Even with the blue hair.

"Conlan, *prince*, whatever we call you, the fact remains— you still haven't told us what happened to you. What Anubisa *did* to you."

Justice flicked his gaze down and then back up Conlan's body, his expression only the slightest fraction away from being a grave insult. "We don't know that you haven't been . . . compromised. Do we?"

As one, Ven and Christophe headed for Justice. "I'm going to kick your ass for that, blue boy," Ven snarled.

Christophe said nothing, just raised a hand, scowling. A shimmering ball of energy coalesced in his palm.

Conlan held up a hand to stop the confrontation. "Enough!" he commanded. "Leave him alone. He has a point."

Alaric's voice sounded from the doorway. "He *would* have a point, if I hadn't been the one who healed you. Both now and before."

Stalking into the room, Alaric came to a halt in the middle. "Do any of you doubt Poseidon's powers?"

Not even Justice dared blasphemy. As one, seven heads shook from side to side.

No doubt here.

Alaric smiled that terrifying smile of his—the one that kept even the greediest Atlantean lord kicking in his full tithe to Poseidon's Temple. "As you should not. The healing process is not simply physical. I see inside of the true intentions and darkest memories of the one being healed."

His gaze shot to Conlan. "Our prince is not corrupted, though any of the rest of you would have been. He is stronger than even *he* knows."

Conlan broke his gaze away. The idea of Alaric sharing his memories of torture and fire wasn't exactly comforting.

"Damaged goods."

"Warped beyond redemption."

Anubisa was the queen of lies, and yet maybe there was the edge of truth in what she'd told him so many times.

Alaric continued. "Left to Anubisa's delicate touch, most of you would have broken. Conlan came back to us whole. Stronger than he was before. Do not question his rule in front of me again, Lord Justice."

Justice bowed his head. Either he agreed, or he was biding his time for challenge.

Conlan decided to worry about the latter at another time.

Alaric almost casually waved one hand, and the energy ball still glowing in Christophe's hand winked out. The warrior snatched his hand to his mouth, hissing.

"Don't play with power in front of me, *little boy*," Alaric said to him. "You refused the strictures of the Temple."

Christophe, a good two centuries past being a boy, little or otherwise, stepped toward Alaric. Defiance outlined every inch of the tightened cords of muscle in his neck and throat.

"Poseidon's power isn't limited to those of you who let the Temple cut your balls off, priest. The power of calling water and the other elements is free to those of us who dare."

Alaric's eyes gleamed so brightly it was as if a piercing green searchlight flashed over Christophe's face. "I don't think you want to have a discussion about *balls* with one who faced the Rite of Oblivion and lived. There are no eunuchs in my temple, *little boy*."

Christophe didn't back down. "Yeah, well, the rite of acceptance as a Warrior of Poseidon is no solstice picnic. Perhaps you ought to remember *that, old man.*"

Conlan stepped between the two of them, even though Christophe had shown enough sense to step the hell back. "That's enough. We need to focus on the Trident, as you keep reminding me, Alaric. Not settle old scores—or start new ones—right here in front of the hockey table."

He turned to Christophe. "And not *all* elements, Christophe. You know that fire is forbidden to the Warriors of Poseidon—to all Atlanteans."

Bastien slammed the air hockey puck into its goal with a flourish. "Yeah, nobody would be stupid enough to play with fire, my pr—er, *Conlan*. We're golden. Why don't you and Alaric get some rest so we can get an early start in the morning? We have some Mycenaean ass to kick."

Alaric nodded. "I admit to needing rest after performing two healings. That poison took more than a little effort to disperse."

Conlan noticed for the first time that Alaric's face was almost gray and cursed under his breath. A ruler should be aware of the health and needs of all of his subjects. Even those who were strongest.

Yeah, well, I suck at being a ruler. No argument there.

"Rest," he ordered. "I'll be in with Riley. Ven, set up shifts to watch. You can—"

Ven rolled his eyes. "I know what to do, Conlan. This isn't my first day on the job."

Conlan inclined his head, returning to formal speak to underscore his demand. "I cede the task to the King's Vengeance. All of you—remember your early training and shield your emotions."

There was no other way to say it but baldly. "Riley is *aknasha.*"

He heard the indrawn breaths, saw Alaric's eyes narrow, and waited.

Brennan spoke for the first time since Conlan had walked into the room. "That would explain her reaction after the battle. If she needs guarding, perhaps I would be the appropriate choice, since I have no emotions with which to overwhelm her senses," he said in his quiet voice. "It would make my curse bear some merit, for once."

Conlan narrowed his eyes, searching the warrior's face for signs of bitterness, but there was only the patient calm with which Brennan always faced the world. A curl of anger stirred in his gut at the idea of Brennan—of *any* male—spending time with Riley.

All righty, then. I need to get a fucking grip.

"Thanks, Brennan. We will discuss our plans in the morning, but I appreciate your offer," he said, inclining his head toward his emotionless warrior.

Then he turned toward Ven. "I need some rest, to complete the healing. Give me until dawn, unless there's some new crisis."

With a last narrow-eyed glance at Justice, Conlan left the room. Heading for Riley, who was sending out flutters of awakening consciousness.

As he walked down the hallway, he heard Bastien. "Ven, what's the deal with this Riley? An emotional empath after so many thousands of years? What the hell is going on?"

Conlan shook his head, pulled by an almost magnetic compulsion toward her room. *I wish I knew.*

Chapter 12

Alaric waited until he heard Conlan's footsteps reach Riley's room, then turned to face the Seven. "We need to discuss this human—this potential *aknasha*—and what we shall do about her."

Ven leaned back against a well-stocked bookcase. "You planning to hold this discussion behind my brother's back?"

His voice was calm. The look in his eyes was not. "Skirting perilously close to treason, my man."

"He may not be receptive to reason right now," Alaric returned. "He's not exactly acting rationally about her. Did any of you notice that he never questioned the presence of those vampires?"

Justice turned from the window to cast a sardonic look at Alaric. "Yet, somehow, when *I* mentioned that he might not be rational, you jumped down my throat."

Alaric shook his head once, dismissive. "This is not a question of whether or not Anubisa compromised him. I told you that she had not, and I stand by my pronouncement. However, his actions in regard to this human female are not entirely logical."

Alexios made a noise in his throat, just short of a growl.

"You, of all people, would deny him a distraction from his nightmares? From the torment that no doubt haunts him, day and night?"

Alaric wondered whether Alexios was talking about Conlan's torment or his own. Wondered if Alexios knew, himself.

Then dismissed the question as irrelevant.

"I would deny him nothing, especially not the vehicle of his ascension. However, every hour that Reisen holds the Trident, Conlan is one hour closer to losing the throne of Atlantis."

Slamming his game piece down on the table, Bastien clenched his hands into fists, enormous arm muscles bunching. "I will reach down into Reisen's throat and rip his kidneys out. I will slice his balls off and use them for earrings. I will personally turn every warrior in the House of Mycenae into a eunuch."

Ven pulled one of his daggers out of its sheath and examined the blade. "Oh, I'm sure you'll have a little help with that, my friend. And, speaking of vamps, what the hell *was* that about? We've encountered enough of them on our patrols, but we try never to leave witnesses. Why are we suddenly getting attacked by a group of bloodsuckers?"

He stopped, the blood draining out of his face, the lines bracketing his mouth whitening. "Anubisa. She's finally broken the curse that kept her from telling the vamps about us, hasn't she?"

Ven slammed his dagger back into its sheath. "We're fucking doomed."

Brennan, unruffled as ever, stood utterly still. "But were the vampires after us, or is the female the target? That was Terminus leading the pack. He is one of Barrabas's most trusted generals. What use would Barrabas have for Riley? Does he recognize her empathic powers?"

He put his hands together in front of him, steepling his fingers. "We have hunted Barrabas for more than two thousand years, with no success, and the humans elect him to their government. Senator *Barnes*. You must admit, the irony is delicious."

Justice smashed his fist into the back of the couch. "You've got a fucked-up sense of *delicious*, warrior. All that means to me is that he's more visible these days. The better for me to find him, catch him, and cut his ugly head from his ugly damned body."

Brennan moved his head a fraction of an inch and pinned Alaric with his gaze, ignoring Justice entirely. "Further, the question remains, Alaric. Do you yet lack the energy to scry for the Trident?"

Closing his eyes, Alaric sent his senses reaching out into the night. But the energy required to remove the poison from Conlan's bloodstream had drained his resources. He felt nothing—not even the slightest resonance from the Trident.

And the loss of it was like a gaping wound in his soul.

My duty. Mine as high priest to safeguard the sea god's Trident.

My failure.

He opened his eyes, feeling the weight of everyone's gaze upon him. "I must rest. I can feel nothing of the Trident's power. Reisen and his warriors are certainly shielding themselves from me, but I should be able to sense the location of the Trident when I have recovered from the healing."

Further considering, Alaric finally shook his head. "I have no idea what to think about this attack. But know this: if Reisen has somehow allied himself with the undead, Poseidon's vengeance will be vicious beyond the meaning of the word."

From the couch, where he huddled on one side, Denal laughed bitterly, then pounded his fist against his leg. "Vamps, Reisen. A human who shows more courage than I. I'm utterly useless. First, I failed to protect my prince, and then I allow our priest to waste his energy healing my worthless head."

Justice leaned forward and smacked Denal in the side of his now-healed head. "Yeah. Good job on your first mission, Junior."

Denal leapt off the couch at Justice, but Alaric had endured enough of them both. Almost negligently, he waved one hand, causing Denal to hang mid-leap, frozen in the air.

Justice whistled, but stepped back from Denal. "Nice trick, man. Can you teach me how to do that?"

Alaric's view of the room shimmered to emerald green, and he knew the limits of his self-control had finally been breached.

Brennan stepped forward. "The sea god's power is shining fiercely from your eyes in warning, high priest. Perhaps I may intervene and escort you to your rest?"

Christophe grinned. "Yeah, catch a chill wave, dude. Don't go all 'power of the gods' on us."

Brennan's lack of any emotion, combined with Christophe's irreverence, returned a measure of calm to Alaric. The green glow receded from his vision. He stared at each of the Warriors in turn, and each bowed to him.

All but Ven, who simply quirked a smile. "Yeah, yeah, you're the big bad—you're the dark bogeyman. But we still haven't figured out what we're going to do about this female. Plus, Barrabas is going to get his panties in a serious twist once he finds out we sliced and diced his general."

Alaric released Denal, who thumped to the floor.

"We'll take the female to Atlantis, to the Temple. We will study her and find out if she truly is *aknasha*. Moreover, we will research the ancient scrolls for talk of the soul-meld," Alaric replied, suddenly touched by the icy fingers of fear.

"The what?" Bastien asked, brows drawing together.

Alaric studied them, weighing how much to disclose. If Conlan had found soul-melding—last written of more than ten thousand years ago—with a *human*, Atlantean tradition would be rocked to its very foundation.

Everything would change.

Everything.

He fought off the premonition, squared his shoulders. "It is nothing to worry about at this juncture. As to the vamps, we will continue to defeat them, as we have done for millennia."

He paused, then slowly nodded his head. "And the female? If she poses any threat to Conlan, we will kill her."

~~~~~

Riley woke from an uneasy sleep in which harsh-faced men with glowing eyes tried to murder her. She twisted to look at her alarm clock to see how long she'd managed to rest *this* time. Except her alarm clock wasn't on her nightstand.

Come to think of it, *that* wasn't her nightstand.

She jerked up, suddenly entirely awake, and wrestled with the quilt that pinned her to the bed.

Not her quilt. Not her bed.

Where the hell am I?

When the door started to open, she let out a little cry and rolled off the bed, quilt and all, immediately raising her head to stare across the bed at the intruder.

"It's you," she gasped, as Conlan filled the doorway. Every muscled inch of him, standing there in nothing but his pants and his unbuttoned shirt. She couldn't help it; she stared. The man was pure muscle from the vicious-looking scar at his throat, to his chest, all the way to his chiseled abdomen, and further down to his . . .

She jerked her gaze back to his face, her cheeks burning, and tried for a little "I wasn't checking you out" bravado. "This stalking thing has got to stop."

His lips quirked in a half smile, then his face arranged itself back into seriousness. "I'm here to offer my thanks, my lady."

Completely aware of how ridiculous she looked, sitting on the floor trapped in a quilt, Riley tried for dignity. "What's with the Camelot speech? One minute you sound normal, and the next you sound like Sir Lancelot or something."

She pushed her hair back away from her face, wondering just how bad she looked. Not that this was exactly the time to go all girly, but she was feeling a little insecure in front of Adonis or whoever the hell he was.

He laughed a little, and the sound of it stilled her whirling thoughts—stole inside her, wrapping itself around empty spaces.

It didn't make sense—*none* of it made sense.

How could someone she'd just met fit like a puzzle piece matched to her own jagged edges? She'd never believed in love at first sight, or destiny, or pretty much anything to do with romance.

She saw the results of so-called love every day at her job. Saw, and tried to pick up the pieces. It was enough to send Cupid to the gin bottle.

But there was something about this man . . .

"You're right," he said, walking farther into the room, pushing the door shut behind him. "We forget, sometimes, the modern speech we've learned over the years. Especially in times of duress, when we revert to formality as a matter of protocol."

He bowed his head. "I offer my apologies, nonetheless. You deserve more from me than I have words to give."

She could feel a torrent of emotion from him, as if a door opened and his feelings poured through. Remorse. Sorrow.

Aching, biting pain.

She lifted a hand to her head, expecting the barrage of emotions from the others to thunder through her head any minute, but, thankfully, the emotions of everyone else seemed to be muted, subdued. Her mind was packed with cotton wool, shut down. In self-defense?

Why couldn't she remember what had happened? She'd seen Conlan through the window, and then . . . "Where am I? Why has my head gone all fuzzy? Why are you—oh, heck, will you turn around for just a moment?"

He raised one of those elegant, dark eyebrows, then nodded once and complied.

"You are in a safe place. Your head is no doubt recovering from the barrage of emotions thrust into it earlier," Conlan answered. "I asked my warriors to shield their emotions from you. I should have realized it would be painful for you to be subjected to so many of us at once. I'm sorry for that."

She fought her way out of the quilt and stood up. "You don't have to keep apologizing, Conlan. Just maybe tell me what the hell is going on."

Much less embarrassing to face him eye to eye, rather than looking up all six and a half feet of him.

"Okay, Conlan, you can turn around now. And I'd really like some answers. First, are you—"

Midsentence, the gauze over her mind lifted and her memory returned in full. The battle. The sword. Conlan falling—lying so still.

Her eyes widened, and she started walking, then running, around the bed toward him. "Oh, holy crap! You—you were dead! Or almost dead! Why are you standing up? You should be in a hospital!"

She reached him and grabbed the edges of his shirt, yanking them back to look for the hideous sword wound that must be . . .

Had to be . . .

Wasn't there.

"It's not there," she said slowly. "How is that possible?"

Almost dazed, she placed her palm over his heart, waiting. Then she felt it. The thump of his heartbeat. The muscles of his chest tightened under her hand, and she looked up at his clenched jaw, then jerked her hand back.

"You're not a vampire, because you've got a heartbeat," she said. "Are you a shape-shifter? What kind of furry are you going to get?"

Backing away, she looked for windows, another door, maybe a zookeeper.

Any kind of help.

He laughed again. "I'm not going to turn furry, brave one. I am nothing you know."

"You can say that again," she muttered.

Suddenly, shockingly, he knelt in front of her. Even kneeling, his head came to her chest, reminding her again of his size and strength.

Not exactly the kind of stranger you wanted to be alone in a room with.

Except—except she'd been inside of his mind. And there was nothing but integrity in what she'd felt of his emotions. She didn't know *how* she knew that, but she did.

He looked up at her, his black eyes intent. He was the most beautiful man she'd ever seen—more handsome than she'd ever imagined a man could be. Maybe she *was* dreaming.

The tiny flame of blue-green she'd thought she'd imagined before flickered in the center of his pupils. "I am sworn to be a protector of all humankind, and—but for one brief lapse of time—have fulfilled this role for centuries. Yet tonight, in one moment, you showed more courage and bravery than I have ever known."

She started to speak, but he stopped her by taking her hands in his own. "You have my gratitude, and you will be under my protection for now and until the waves no longer touch the shore."

It had the feeling of a promise—the feeling of a vow.

Suddenly, Riley was having a hard time remembering *any* reason why she shouldn't want to hear promises or vows from this man. Except . . . except . . . something he'd said—

"*Humankind?* Well, it was pretty clear out there that you weren't human, what with the balls of vamp-incinerating energy. So just what the hell *are* you?" she said, breaking out of the trance his words had put her in and backing away.

Conlan smiled and rose gracefully to his feet. "I'm not of any of the nine hells," he said. "I am Conlan of Atlantis."

Riley burst out laughing. "Oh. Right. Of course you are. And I'm Alice of Wonderland."

She shook her head. Old Alice had it right. *Curiouser and curiouser.*

Chapter 13

Conlan put his hands behind his back, clasping them together. He couldn't let her know the self-control it was costing him to stand in this room with her.

Alone.

With a giant bed taking up most of the floor. Every part of his body tensed at the thought of wrapping her back up in that quilt.

Wrapping her up in his arms.

What in the nine hells was wrong with him? He was worse than a randy recruit coming out of training. He'd never re-acted this way to a woman.

Any woman. Especially not a human. Even one who looked flushed and sleepy and exactly as she would look in the morning after a night of pleasure in his arms.

Focus.

His thoughts flickered to the Atlantean maiden who had been selected for him.

The woman he'd never met—who'd never met him.

More archaic Atlantean politics, cold and dead.

Unlike the woman who stood in front of him, warm and alive.

"Hot, even," he murmured.

Riley only stopped moving away from him when she backed into the bed. His gaze was drawn down to her legs. Miles of legs. Endless legs wrapped in snug, faded denim.

He wanted her legs wrapped around his waist.

Breasts tempting even under that oversized shirt, generous enough that he could see them press against the fabric when she moved in certain ways. He'd felt them against his chest on the beach. Her waist curved in perfectly. Just the right size for his hands.

She was lush and luscious. Not a stick figure of a woman like the type popular this decade. He could hold her under him, drive into her without the worry of breaking her, fill his hands with her—

"Atlantis. Right," she said again, jerking him out of his fantasies and maybe even stopping him from coming right there in his pants.

He cursed under his breath in ancient Atlantean.

"And you can stop that right now," she continued, cheeks pink again. As pink as they'd been when she looked at his chest. The thought of it sent heat crashing back through him, and he took a step toward her.

"Stop what?" He took another step.

Her voice was breathless, husky. "Stop staring at my legs. Stop looking at me like I'm on the menu. Stop coming closer. Stop being so . . . so . . . so over the top."

"Over the top?" Another step.

She held her hands up as if to ward him off, though he was easily another five steps away from her. "And stop repeating everything I say," she said, stomping her foot.

It made him smile. So fierce! No wonder he couldn't shake her from his thoughts.

He was in trouble.

He didn't care.

"If I promise to stop repeating your words, may I take another step?" he asked, drinking in the sight of her. In the golden glow of the bedside lamps, her hair was firelight on amber. Sunshine on the golden dome of Poseidon's Temple. Eyes as blue as the ocean surface at twilight.

Damn, suddenly he was a poet. He was losing his mind.

Maybe another step closer wasn't such a good idea. He stopped walking.

She shook her head, then nodded. "I don't think—yes, no, *aargh*! Why is it so hard to think around you?"

Conlan folded his arms over his chest, reason suddenly returning. "That's a good question," he said, eyes narrowing. "Why do *you* have such an effect on *me*? What *are* you? How can you access the Atlantean mental paths and—more to the point—how can you feel our emotions? How can I feel yours? Are you a weapon sent to test my defenses?"

"Weapon, yeah, right, you idiot. I'm not a weapon, I'm a social worker." Stepping sideways, Riley began to edge around the bed. "And I see we're back to the Atlantis thing. You're from the lost continent. The figment of Plato's imagination that supposedly disappeared more than eleven thousand years ago. *That* Atlantis?"

He unfolded his arms and took another step toward her. He couldn't help himself.

He didn't *want* to help himself.

"Plato was disciplined for his talkativeness in the *Critias* and *Timaeus*. The poet Solon knew no better than to share with Plato the secrets he'd gained from that Egyptian priest. But our descendants know to keep the secrets of Atlantis."

Another step. Her tantalizing scent reached him. Fresh. Slightly floral, with a touch of green. Ocean ferns, perhaps.

He inhaled deeply, knowing he could find her by scent alone from that moment. Loving her scent in his nostrils.

Wanting her taste in his mouth. His hands actually ached to feel her skin.

She was looking at him. Oh, *right*. Something about continents. "Not so much a *lost* continent. *We* always knew where we were," he said. "We've simply developed shields to hide the Seven Isles from your technology."

He smiled. "Your invention of submarines was almost a problem for a while."

She backed clear around to the other side of the bed. "Okay, show me your gills."

Completely caught off guard, Conlan stared at her for a moment, then threw his head back and roared with laughter.

Riley looked at him as if he were insane.

Of course, she wasn't that far off. He probably *was* insane.

Catching his breath, he shook his head. "Thank you for that, *aknasha*. I needed to laugh, after the events of this evening."

His smile disappeared. "After the past seven years, in fact."

Making a decision, he backed away from her and dropped into the chair in the corner of the room. "If I sit here, far away from you, would you feel safe enough with me to listen to what I have to say?"

Trembling, seemingly poised for flight, Riley stood for the space of several heartbeats looking at him. Finally, she seemed to reach a decision of her own. She nodded and sat, cross-legged, on the bed. "Yes, I'll listen. It's the strangest thing, but I already feel safe with you. Or maybe it's not strange, considering what happened on the beach earlier."

Conlan wanted truth between them. "You've been inside my mind, Riley. Unwanted or not, you know me now on a deeper level than most people do. Maybe on a deeper level than anyone, barring our healer."

She stared at him, hesitating, then nodded.

"You must realize by now that I've been inside your mind as well," he said, almost afraid to admit it. "I've seen your goodness and your self-sacrifice. I *know* you."

Unless her deception was hidden behind some mental trickery, his mind mocked him. Who knew what a true empath was capable of?

Jumping up off the bed, Riley began to pace back and forth in front of him. "You don't know anything," she said bitterly. "Goodness? Yeah, right. I'm just somebody who tries to do her job the best she can. And usually fails miserably at it."

She stopped in front of him, so close he could reach out and touch her. He had to clench his hands on the arms of the chair to keep from doing so.

To keep from touching her. *Damn*, he wanted to touch her.

"Tell me," he said, instead.

"Right. You're from mythical *Atlantis*, and you want to hear about a day in the life of a social worker?"

"Tell me," he repeated, opening his mind to her so she could feel the truth of it. Feel how he wanted to know all about her.

A look of wonder came over her face. "You really do want to know, don't you?"

"I do."

She paused for a moment, then sank down onto the carpet near him and—almost in a trance—recounted the events of her day. As she related the story of the girl with the gun, Conlan had to fight with every ounce of his self-control to keep her from seeing his rage. He wanted to kill. He wanted to rend, tear, and put his fist through the wall.

He did none of those things, but sat with a mask of calm on his face, reaching desperately for his training, for his objectivity. How could he be affected so much by this woman?

He looked at her, sitting on the floor in front of him, anguish on her face as she told of the children she tried so hard to rescue. Babies having babies. The hopeless struggle against poverty and a society that didn't have time for the lost ones.

As she talked, as he felt the emotions underlying her words, the question in his mind changed.

How could he *not* be affected so much by this woman?

Her words trailed off. "So that's when you showed up, and I guess you know the rest. Maybe now you can tell me exactly who and what you are, and why you followed me to my house."

She looked around, blinking, at the room, then scrambled to her feet, wary again. "While you're at it, you can let me know where the hell I am."

He stood, slowly, so as not to startle her. "You humble me, Riley. I must match your honesty with my own. I am chief among the Warriors of Poseidon, sworn to safeguard humankind."

Grasping the edge of his shirt, he pulled it aside to show the mark of Poseidon he bore. High on the right side of his chest, where the sea god himself had burned the symbol of the Warriors of Poseidon into Conlan's flesh.

The circle representing all the peoples of the world, intersected by the pyramid of knowledge deeded to them by the ancients. The silhouette of Poseidon's Trident bisecting them both.

"This mark I wear offers testimony to my vow. And yet, from what I hear between the words in your retelling, this night you deserve to wear it more than do I."

She lifted her hand, almost as if to trace the symbol with her fingertips. Then she pulled her hand back and grinned. "You're doing that formal talking thing again," she said. "Somehow, it reminds me of my mother, yelling for me when I was in trouble. *Riley Elisabeth Dawson* meant I was in big trouble."

"Riley Elisabeth," he repeated, savoring the sound of it. "It fits you. Strong and feminine, both."

Somehow, unknowing, he'd moved closer to her. The heat of her, the seduction in the curves of her body, in the line of her neck, drew him in. She looked up at him, flickers of alarm changing to awareness in her eyes.

He could still *feel* her inside him. Her thoughts, her emotions.

He wanted to feel himself inside *her*.

Conlan lifted his hands to her arms, pulling her forward. Slowly. Gently. Giving her time to deny him.

Praying she wouldn't.

He stepped forward to meet her halfway. Drinking in her scent. Wanting to bury his face in the silky hair that tumbled past her shoulders.

Wanting to bury his body in her heat.

By Poseidon's balls, he needed to touch her again. Needed to kiss her again. "Riley," he groaned. "Please."

She knew exactly what he meant. He could see it as the awareness in her eyes changed to expectation.

Anticipation.

She lifted her face and touched her lips gently to his. And he was lost.

Lost in the sensation, in the colors sparkling in her mind— in his mind—in *their* minds together. Lost in the feel of her softness pressed against his hardness. The kiss deepened.

He deepened it. He swept his tongue inside of her warmth, her sweet, welcoming mouth, and his knees nearly buckled when she put her arms around his neck and pulled him even closer to her.

Heat, colors, and a torrent of need. Caught in a maelstrom, a cyclone, a full-on, balls-to-the-wall ocean gale of wanting, he tightened his arms around her and lifted her until her feet were off the floor. Her breasts rubbed against his bare chest. He groaned deep in his throat, in *her* throat, in the space trapped between their mouths.

She lifted her legs and wrapped them around his hips, wiggling to gain purchase on his body, and the heat between her legs was suddenly right up against his cock. Impossibly, he hardened even further, sure he was going to split his pants—rip her shirt open—tear her jeans off. Find out if the colors in his head would intensify into a starburst when he drove into her.

The passion swallowing his senses rocketed through him with a bang.

Or no, *damnit.* That was the door slamming open.

Conlan whirled around to face the threat, snarling, pushing Riley down and behind him as he did so.

Mine. Mine to protect. Mine!

Ven stood at the door, mouth hanging open for the second time that night. "Er, yeah. Well. Ah, sorry to interrupt, but Alaric figures you need your rest and you're, well, you're broadcasting a sex vibe that is so slamming loud you're making every man in the house horn— ah, *uncomfortable.*"

From behind him, Riley made a choked sound. Conlan felt the waves of embarrassment pulsing from her. He fought for rationality, sucking in a deep breath.

Ven. My brother. Not a threat.

"I—yeah. Rest." He took another deep, steadying breath. Alaric. The Trident. "Has he been able to scry the location of the Trident?"

Ven shook his head, amusement stamped on his face. "No, he needs to recuperate from the healing. But he used a few unflattering words to describe how you're, ah, keeping him from his rest."

Conlan could imagine how his brother was editing Alaric's language. If Riley were broadcasting this furnace of sexual desire to every warrior in the house—and to the priest, who'd taken a vow of celibacy—well, damn.

Damn.

"Point taken," he said, still breathing hard. "Riley also needs to rest." He waited for his brother to take the hint and leave, but Ven wasn't much for subtlety.

"Aren't you going to introduce me, brother?" Ven stood there, no sign of movement, grinning at him like a fool.

Conlan opened his mouth to smack him down, but Riley surprised him by stepping out from behind his back. "Look, Tarzan, I may be embarrassed, but it's not like you need to protect me from your own brother, right?"

She walked toward Ven, who'd snorted out a laugh at "Tarzan." She walked to him, shoulders squared, as if trying to act nonchalant. "I'm Riley."

When she held out her hand toward his brother, Conlan took an involuntary step forward, a growl starting low in his throat, before he caught himself.

He snapped his head up and stared at Ven, shocked by his own reaction. From the look on Ven's face, Conlan had surprised his brother, too.

Conlan dug his fingers into his thighs, fighting for control. What was *happening* to him?

Expression wary, Ven glanced away from Conlan and took Riley's hand and gently shook it. "You can call me Ven."

Then Ven did something that surprised the hell out of Conlan. He bowed deeply, unsheathing his daggers in a flowing motion and crossing them over his chest. "My service and my honor are yours, Lady Sunlight, for your defense of my brother and prince."

Riley snapped her head around to stare at Conlan, horror in her eyes. "Prince? Did he say *prince*?"

Ven straightened. "Oops. I thought you told her, Conlan, since we're taking her home to study."

The sparkle of Riley's emotions sharpened and then snapped shut inside of Conlan's head.

She fisted her hands on her hips. "Prince?" she repeated, voice going dangerously low. "Taking *who* home to Atlantis? And study *what*, exactly?"

Ven's lips quivered, as he evidently tried to keep from laughing. Conlan grimly vowed to make him pay, in a large and serious way. The King's Vengeance wasn't above getting his ass kicked by his brother, even now.

"Oops again," Ven repeated. "Later, dude. I can see you two have things to talk about."

As Ven backed out of the room and closed the door behind him, Conlan sighed with real regret. "Any chance we can go back to the kissing part?" he asked, trying for his best innocent expression.

She narrowed her eyes. "Start. Talking."

He sighed again. "Yeah. I didn't think so."

Chapter 14

Riley backed around the bed again, needing to put space between herself and Conlan. Or, should she say, *Prince* Conlan.

Prince Conlan. Holy Atlantean royalty. What had she gotten herself into this time? And why did he have to smell so good? Like spices and ocean and pure, unadulterated man?

Between his delicious scent, that unbelievable body, and his sensual voice, she should have known he was too good to be human. Heck, her last date had been a lawyer who had way more brains than muscles.

Not that she didn't think Conlan had brains. She'd been inside his mind and caught a glimpse of fierce intelligence. Most of what he said demonstrated logic and an analytical aptitude. But when he touched her, well, logic went right out the window. Right out *both* of their windows, to stretch a metaphor clear out of shape.

"After a decade of living with shape-shifters and vampires who pretty much walked right out of the myths and legends and into the streets—heck, into *Congress*—the idea of Atlantis isn't as hard to believe as it might have been," she admitted. "Plus, there's that nifty trick you did with the water. Makes sense that an Atlantean would have power over water, right?"

He smiled that slow, dangerous smile, and she rushed on before she could get distracted. "So, do you talk to fish? And what about the gills? Got 'em? If yes, where? I mean, are you . . . um, do you have . . . *normal* parts?"

He blinked, then started laughing again as the burn climbed up her chest to her face. "You never say the expected, do you?" he asked.

Then he smiled and raised his hands, palms up. A glowy blue-green light emanated from both of them and sparkled up and out, around and around, spiraling in a cascade of light around the room and then through the door into the bathroom.

In seconds, the leading edge of the spiral of light returned to the bedroom, but with one startling difference. The light swirled in a whirling tunnel of water. The tube of liquid—maybe three or four inches thick—curved and swooped around the room. Around her, where she stood, frozen, her mouth hanging open.

Then it returned to Conlan and surrounded him, seeming to caress his body for a moment and then vanish into his skin.

Except he wasn't wet at all.

She snapped her mouth shut, sure she looked like an idiot, especially when his smile turned into a laugh.

Damn, but he was *seriously* hot when he laughed. Her nerves, frayed already from the overdose of testosterone and, okay, the sheer sexual tension in the room, shredded even further.

She leaned back against the wall and rubbed her arms with her hands, trying to get rid of the goose bumps. "No, I don't usually do the expected," she said, trying to return to the normality of their previous conversation. "You should hear the things my sister used to do to me to keep me from blurting out her secrets in front of boys. Neat trick with the water, by the way."

He eased himself back down in the chair, keeping his distance, clearly trying to put her at ease. "Thanks. I can do balloon animals, too."

"I just bet you can."

He grinned at her. "I never had a sister. It was just me and Ven. Do you have any other sisters? Or brothers?"

"No, just the two of us. Mom and Dad died when we were

young, and we developed an 'us against the world' mentality. The foster homes . . ." She bit her lip. "We learned not to love people. You love somebody and they leave."

She shook off the melancholy. It's not like he wanted to hear this stuff. Except, he looked interested. He *felt* like he was interested.

"Quinn is—well, she's kind of fragile. I always took care of her, even though she was a little older." It didn't really make sense to share her family history while backed against the wall, so she cautiously took a step forward and perched on the edge of the bed.

Ready to jump away from him if he came near her.

Or was that ready to jump *on* him if he came near her?

She ruthlessly shoved the thought out of her mind. *No thinking about sex, no thinking about sex, no—*

"Thinking about sex," he said.

"What?" she gasped, stunned to hear him speak her thoughts. Except maybe she shouldn't be surprised, given how they'd shared each other's emotions. Still, she could feel her face flaming again. One of the joys of being a redhead was the tendency to blush like a house on fire. Didn't exactly make for a poker face.

He clasped his hands, resting them on his lap, then looked up to meet her gaze. "We need to talk about this. The intensity. Of the attraction between us, which is intense. It's really . . ." He paused, cleared his throat. "Intense."

She laughed a little. "Yeah. I get that you think it's intense. Well, it's not like I go around jumping every hunky foreign prince who comes my way. Not that any royalty hangs around my neighborhood, but you know what I mean. Intense."

That smug, all-male smile returned to his face, which, in spite of every feminist principle she'd ever known, somehow made her want to put her mouth on him.

All over him.

A wave of heat washed over her, and she groaned. "Conlan, I don't *know* what this is about. Could it be—could it be some kind of side effect of reading your emotions? Maybe I'll react this way to every Atlantean I meet."

He immediately tensed in his chair, leaning forward, the hands clasped in his lap going white-knuckled. "For whatever reason, Riley," he ground out through gritted teeth, "I don't seem to be able to handle the thought of you *reacting* this way to *any* other male, Atlantean or otherwise."

She watched him as he visibly fought for control, his nostrils flaring as he breathed deeply, white lines deepening at the corners of his mouth. The thought that *she* did that to him— made him lose control, even a little—was, oddly enough, turning her on.

A *lot*.

Especially since she had the feeling he wasn't the type to lose control all that much. She'd seen inside his mind, after all. Rigid control, duty, and honor. Not a lot of spontaneity or footloose happiness.

And the pain. Oh, she'd never forget the pain.

"Conlan, not that I encourage this tree swinging and chest beating, but I think—I think it's not a problem," she ventured. "After all, I kinda forgot that your brother was just in the room. He even *looks* like you, and he must have a lot of the same superpowered Atlantean DNA, right?"

Conlan smiled a little and nodded, still clenching his hands together.

"Well, there was nothing. Zip," she said, shrugging. "I mean, he's great-looking and all—"

Conlan made that strange growling noise low in his throat again, and she held up her hands, palms out. "I meant to say that he's *okay*-looking and all, but I didn't have any urge to strip his clothes off and lick him all over or anything," she finished, smiling.

Then she realized what she'd just said, by implication.

Oh, crap.

Conlan hadn't missed it, either, if the expression on his face was anything to go by. The look that said he wanted to lick her right back.

Heat spiked through her center, making her actually clench her legs together against the wetness that threatened to spill out.

Okay, this is bad. Thoughts of hunky prince licking anybody—er, anything—are off-limits.

He shoved a hand through that delicious black hair of his and shot up out of the chair. Then he started doing a little pacing of his own. "Riley, until we understand why we're reacting like this to each other, it's perhaps better if we stay away from each other."

"Yeah, okay, that's fine. In fact, why don't you take me back to my house—or just call me a cab, a cab would be good, and I'll get out of your hair," she said, inexplicably hurt by his having voiced the same thing she'd been thinking only moments before.

He stopped pacing and turned to stare down at her. "I'm sorry, but you're not going anywhere."

Hurt changed in a flash to pissed off. "What do you mean? Look, buddy, you may have the right to order your Atlantean flunkies around, but I'm an American citizen. You've got zero rights where I'm concerned."

He strode over to the bed and sat next to her before she could move. "It's not about rights, *aknasha*. It's about your own protection. The vampires who attacked us at your house— why were they there? Were they after us? I suspect so, given the nature of the attack."

Taking her hands in his, he continued. "But now they know you live in that house. They're going to be wondering what connection you have to us. You won't be safe there anymore."

She looked down at their hands, wondering if he even realized that his thumb was caressing the back of her hand. Wondering how such a small gesture could make her bones turn to liquid.

Suddenly afraid that he was using some sort of Atlantean version of mind control on her.

She yanked her hands away from his. "So what you're saying is that you've ruined my life."

"No," he said softly. "I think what I'm saying is that you've complicated mine."

Scooting back from him on the bed, she tried to be rational. "All right. Let's back up. Tell me what I need to know about Atlantis. Tell me why these vampires are after you. Tell me what *aknasha* means, and why you're so freaked out that I might be one. I work better with information, so give me some already."

Conlan smiled, and some of the tension seemed to leave his shoulders. "Information is definitely something I can give you. You deserve it. First, my homeland. *Atlantis*. It would take years for me to tell you about Atlantis. Much of the myth, some of the legend, and even some of the fantasy is true."

"But no gills?" Riley couldn't help but return his smile, her own a little mischievous.

"Definitely no gills. We are much like you."

"So, human, then, with special powers?"

He shook his head. "No, not human. A cousin to your species, certainly. Closer to humankind than to the shape-shifters. Far different from the undead. We lived in harmony with your kind for many thousands of years."

"And then you sank below the water, and now you live in a bubble, right?" Riley knew she was being flippant, but a girl had limits as to how much she could absorb in one night.

That unbelievably sensuous smile quirked the edges of his lips, and he leaned back against the headboard of the bed. "No, no bubbles. No mermaids, either, before you ask. Holly-wood movies aren't really a source of historical fact, Riley, in spite of what my brother might think."

"Hey! I loved mermaids when I was a little girl. I wanted to grow up and have a dolphin for a pet and swim with my fish tail and the whole thing," she said indignantly.

He leaned forward, suddenly intent. "You were at the beach tonight, after experiencing traumatic events, instead of retreating to your home. Why was that?"

Suddenly uncomfortable, Riley shifted on the bed, looking anywhere but at him. "I don't know," she admitted. "I've al-ways been that way. I go to the ocean for solace, for solitude. For healing."

The starkness of her words hung in the silence between them for a long moment, and then he leaned back against the head-board again. "That may be important, Riley. I don't know why, but it feels like something important. Maybe Alaric will know."

The name sounded familiar, and she squirmed a bit. "Alaric? Is he the scary one who looked at me like I was a bug stuck to the end of a pin? I kinda threatened to hurt him."

His eyes widened, and then he grinned. "Oh, I'd give half the royal treasury to have seen that."

Riley laughed, trying not to freak out about a guy who calmly said things like "half the royal treasury." Holy *crap*.

He raised one eyebrow, and seemed to get tense all over again. "You're not going to tell me that you thought *he* was great-looking, too?"

"He looked like a convicted felon," she said flatly. "He made me want to call for backup. So, no worries, not even the slightest hint of an attraction there."

He leaned forward so quickly she almost didn't see him move and lifted one of her hands to his mouth, kissed it briefly, and released it. "Thank you for that, Riley. I don't understand why—and I have to be honest, I don't like it one bit—but I seem to have a need to know that you're not attracted to any of my warriors. To any other males at all."

She rolled her eyes. "Look, Conlan, I know you might think otherwise, because of the way I reacted to you, but it's not like I'm some kind of nymphomaniac."

"And that would be bad because . . ." he drawled, the gleam coming back to his eyes, and the intriguing blue-green flame in his pupils flashing at her.

"Don't be a pervert," she said, laughing. "Okay, and that's another thing. Why do your eyes get that blue-green flicker in the middle of them, like right now?"

He sat up fast, ramrod straight. "My eyes do what, exactly?"

"Sorry, didn't mean to upset you. It's just that your pupils are so black, until you get that blue-green flame in them. I was a little bit curious."

Conlan shot up off the bed. When he turned around to face her, she noticed that his eyes had gone black again. When he spoke, his voice was icy. "It's very late, Riley. I need to discuss strategy with Alaric before I rest. You should also get some rest, because we'll undoubtedly be leaving early in the morning."

He strode toward the door, leaving her gaping in his wake. "What the hell just happened? Do you Atlanteans have split personalities or something? And why do you think I'm going *anywhere* with you in the morning? You still haven't explained anything to me, *Prince* Conlan, or whoever you are," she said, temper rising.

He stopped at the doorway, looked back at her. "I am Conlan, high prince of Atlantis," he said, voice flat. "I need explain myself to no one. The Warriors of Poseidon have been the defenders of humanity for more than eleven thousand years, and I have been their leader for centuries."

He yanked the door open, took a step, then stopped. "My reaction to a human female, *aknasha* or no, changes nothing."

Before she could even begin to think of a response blistering enough to peel strips off his hide, he was gone, slamming the door shut behind him.

"You—you *jackass!*" she yelled, jumping up to run for the door. But before she could reach it, she heard the unmistakable click of a lock. Momentum carried her the rest of the way and she yanked on the handle, but only confirmed what she'd known when she heard the noise.

That arrogant, overbearing, dictatorial scumbag of a prince had *locked her in the room.*

Oh, he was so totally going to pay.

Chapter 15

Conlan leaned back against the door to Riley's room, shaken more than he wanted to admit, even to himself. *His eyes got a blue-green flame in them?*

When he wasn't channeling the elements—or any power at all?

Oh, he was screwed.

Something was seriously wrong with this scenario. Eyes didn't display the flame of Poseidon except when the person whose skull the eyes happened to be stuck in channeled power. Called the elements.

Not when sitting around chatting with a female.

A human female.

Unless . . . The thought that had driven ice through his veins flashed back into his head, refusing to be ignored. His mother's bedtime stories about ancient Atlantean lords and their ladies. Stories of fierce battles and enduring love.

Tales of the legendary gift of the soul-meld between an Atlantean and his mate, which branded a warrior's heart and soul as surely as Poseidon's mark branded his body.

It was impossible. The soul-meld was a legend, a fable. A

fanciful bedtime story. Nothing more. Soul-melding did not exist.

Like empaths don't exist, right?

Oh, *damn*. He needed Alaric to figure this one out. Soon. As soon as the Trident was retrieved. After they'd figured out why the hell those vamps had attacked, and how to find the Trident in the first place.

Or even what to do about Reisen.

Yeah. All the subjects he'd forgotten to raise with Alaric and the Seven earlier.

He was *screwed*.

~~~~

At dawn the next morning, Conlan woke from a fractured sleep to the smell of coffee and the sound of low, male laughter. For a minute or two, before he moved from the bed he'd fallen into, exhausted, late the night before, he lay completely still, examining what he was feeling. Actually, what he *wasn't* feeling. It was a kind of absence. The *lack* of something—*what*?

His eyes snapped open as the truth came to him. What he'd felt—what was missing—was rage.

Fury.

He'd needed the flames of anger to defeat helplessness. To goad him into living for the long years that he'd been Anubisa's captive. He'd fed those flames with memories of his parents and thoughts of his brother and Atlantis when despair or pain threatened to overpower the rage.

But now, in spite of the vampire threat, and even in spite of Reisen's treason, he'd let loose of some inner core of fury that had shored up his foundation for so long. His thoughts turned inward, examining, focusing on the building blocks of his psyche.

Of what Alaric had called his *uncompromised soul*.

It had been close. *Damn*, but it had been close. There had been so many times when he'd wondered why he bothered to try to stay alive. Why he kept fighting her.

Why he didn't let death take him.

Conlan thought back to the concrete floors and the ten-inch-by-ten-inch metal grate in the floor.

"The better for the blood to drain into," she'd said, fangs

flashing in the light of the dozens of candles that ringed the room. *"It's not like I'm going to drink it all, princeling. There will be much to tempt my blood pride down below."*

Her blood pride. More like her coven of minions from hell. He'd heard them wailing and gnashing their fangs in the cavern below his cell every hour of every day.

Every hour of every night.

Until the day she released him.

"And that's what pisses me off the most, isn't it?" he snarled, sitting up and swinging his feet off the bed. "That she *released* me. That I didn't escape on my own. In the end, I turned out to be no better than any of the rest of her pets, didn't I?"

Just like that, it was back. The empty, barren landscapes inside his soul were filled with wrath.

He welcomed it. Hell, he and rage were old buddies.

Conlan? A delicate touch in his mind. *Are you okay?*

Riley.

For a heartbeat, the lyricism of her voice and the sparkling blues and golds of her emotions combined to drive the flames from his mind. He closed his eyes and drew in a deep breath, sure that he could smell her clean, fresh scent. Flowers and the ocean.

Surer now—definitely louder, her voice pounded through his head: *Conlan! If you're okay, get your ass over here and unlock this door, or I will pound on your head!*

He started laughing at the contradiction. Ah, his delicate flower. Never one to say the expected, was she?

Nope. And she wasn't *his* anything, either. Better for both of them if he didn't forget it.

Sobering, he sent his reply back to her: *On my way. Try not to chew through the wall, okay?*

He felt a slight trace of her amusement sparkle through him in colors of warm honey and gold. Then that peculiar slamming sensation in his head, which cut off any trace of her.

Oh, yeah. She was pissed. This ought to be fun.

Not.

~~~~~

Reisen looked up from his contemplation of the object in his hands, eyes still dazzled, when the thud of heavy-soled boots thundered down the hall toward him. Micah strode into the room, followed closely by several more warriors.

"My lord," Micah said, breathing harshly. "While patrolling, we discovered a nest of shape-shifters based in a tattoo parlor in Virginia Beach."

Reisen laughed. "That seems a little odd, doesn't it? Do you think the tattoos come back after they take animal form and then return to human?"

Micah folded his arms over his chest, staring at Reisen with his usual implacable expression. "My lord?"

Shaking off both the whimsy and the near-trancelike state he'd gone into while staring at the hen's-egg-sized emerald in his hands for the past hour, Reisen stood up. "And? What did you do about it?"

Micah shrugged. "We returned here to tell you about it. I wasn't sure if our quest allowed time for battling a bunch of furballs. Especially after the Council's decree that we only destroy shape-shifters proven of wrongdoing."

Reisen carefully replaced the emerald in its silk pouch and gently tucked the pouch back inside its small wooden box. The leaders of the East Coast cell of the Platoists had been only too anxious to give him the emerald, when they'd learned the truth of their organization's central tenet.

Atlantis was real.

Moreover, Reisen was an Atlantean prince. They'd treated him like a god. He hadn't exactly hated it.

He'd thought the human was going to piss in his pants. Luckily for all concerned, the man had managed to contain his excitement long enough to retrieve the emerald and gift it to Reisen.

Who now had to figure out how to use it. Unfortunately, that was easier said than done. But some things were easy. "We all swore a sacred vow to protect humanity. It gains us nothing to restore Atlantis to its rightful place in the world, if that world is overrun with bloodsuckers and shape-shifters. In this, as in so much else, the Council is wrong."

Micah nodded, smiling. "I was hoping you'd say that," he said, with his hands on the handle of his battle-axe. "All this tension has me in the mood to kick some shape-shifter ass."

The warriors ringing Micah nodded and growled their

agreement. Reisen carefully packed the small wooden box and the fabric-wrapped bundle of the Trident into a leather carrying bag. One of the warriors stepped forward. "May I carry that for you, my lord?"

"Thank you, but this is one burden that I'm honored to carry myself." With that, Reisen led them to the main room of the house to do some planning. He still had more than a day before the scheduled meeting with the Platoists.

Plenty of time to kick some shape-shifter ass.

Chapter 16

Riley was still grumbling under her breath a good ten minutes after Conlan had shown up and unlocked the door to her room. She'd read him the riot act. Just when she'd started to trust him and believe in all his crazy Atlantean royalty stuff, he'd pulled a prison warden act on her.

But after he'd sketched out the bare-bones truth about the vampire threat, some crook named Reisen who'd stolen a precious artifact, and apologized five or six times, she'd calmed down.

It was insane, but she knew she could trust him. Amazing how being able to feel a man's emotions cut through the doubt. This was mainly about protecting *her*.

She'd switched to subverbal grumbling after tasting the coffee he'd brought as a peace offering. It was hot, sweet, and delicious.

Words that could also describe Conlan. She peeked up at him through her lashes. How unfair was it that the man looked even better in the morning? All that muscle hadn't diminished one bit in the light of day. Worse, she noticed new things about him. Like the faint blue highlight to his black hair. It didn't look like a salon job, so it must be an Atlantis thing.

She tightened her hands on her coffee cup, mostly to keep from reaching out to touch his hair.

It was a compulsion. A craving. It felt the way her addict clients had described the need for their drug of choice.

Conlan paced back and forth in the room, mostly ignoring her. Or at least not looking at her. Considering the tension in his massive shoulders, she'd bet big money that he wasn't unaware of her.

She was clean, at least. The small bathroom attached to her room—her prison cell—was well stocked with an assortment of soaps, shampoos, and conditioners. Brand-new toothbrushes wrapped in plastic lay in rows in a drawer under the sink.

The thought of it pissed her off all over again. "So, bring a lot of women here, do you?"

He stopped pacing and whirled around to face her. "What? What are you talking about? I haven't been to this house in more than a decade. It belongs to my brother."

She nodded. "It figures. Like brother, like brother, right? You're just a couple of good old boys who kidnap women and drag them to your evil lair."

"Are you on some sort of medication? Or are all human females as completely illogical as you are?" He looked genuinely puzzled, which almost made her smile.

"So you spend a lot of time protecting humanity, just not much time having conversations with it. Us. Am I getting the gist of this?" She drained her coffee cup, placed it on the small table next to the wall, and nodded at the door. "Also, are you going to let me out of here anytime soon? Not that being abducted hasn't been great fun, but I have a date with Detective Ramirez."

She flinched at the sound of the low rumbling growl that started in his chest and worked his way up out of his throat. "You're not going anywhere, Riley," he said. "And if you like this Ramirez at all, you'll forget about going on any dates with him. I seem to be somewhat unstable even hearing of the idea."

The look on his face was possessive and predatory all at once. He suddenly resembled a feral jungle animal defending its territory.

She *so* hadn't had enough coffee for that. "Are you going

to start peeing on the walls next, to mark your territory?" she asked, all sweetness and light. "Because we had a tomcat who did that when I was a kid."

She smiled up at him. "My dad had him neutered."

One moment, he was standing across the room from her, and the next he was right up against her body, crowding her backward until her butt hit the dresser. "I've already faced one female who wanted to neuter me," he whispered in her ear. "Trust me on this. If I could survive *her*, my balls are infinitely safe with you."

She bit her lip, flustered. The scent of him, oddly like sunlight on seawater, clean and bracing, filled the bare inch or two of space between them. She had the oddest urge to bury her nose in his neck and simply stand there, inhaling him.

She raised her hands to his chest, instead, blocking him. "I didn't—I mean—your balls are safe—oh, heck. All I meant was that I have to go to the police station and make a statement. Detective Ramirez is the lead on the case."

Conlan's shoulders relaxed, and the aggression he'd been radiating went down a notch. Cautiously, Riley lifted the mental shields she'd placed around her emotions earlier. She and Quinn had practiced for hours as kids, at first building pretend brick walls and then, as they grew older and more sophisticated, pretend titanium doors in their minds.

Quinn had claimed all her doors were made of kryptonite, but Riley had just laughed. "It's not like we're ever going to face any superheroes, Quinn," she'd said one day when they were on opposite ends of their twelfth year.

"You never know," Quinn had replied, dark and dramatic as always.

"What is kryptonite?" Conlan asked, fingers twining around a strand of her hair.

"What? How did you . . . oh, right. I opened the door," Riley said, at first startled and then resigned. "Well, since it's already open, let's go for broke."

With that, she lifted her hands to his face, braced herself, and for the first time in her life sent her emotions, her thoughts, and her curiosity winging inside of another person.

And was nearly brought to her knees.

Strength. Courage. Honor. Duty.

Glimpses of the past.

A man, graying, with Conlan's eyes, stood next to a woman so beautiful that Riley gasped.

Mother. Father.

Shift: *A boy, it had to be Ven, and another, the scary healer guy, maybe? She wasn't sure, since the boy with the green eyes so like Alaric's was smiling.*

She didn't think the healer had ever smiled.

All of them riding horses, laughing.

Shift: *Rows of men, all huge, muscled, gorgeous, naked to the waist, sparring with swords and daggers in some kind of arena.*

Shift: *Fires. Knives. Teeth, no, fangs. Pain. Searing, agonizing, ripping pain. She was dying—no, he, he, it was Conlan, they were torturing him, they were killing him . . .*

"No!" she screamed, her hands falling away from his face as she fell backward into the strength of his arms. "No, no, no, no, no."

As he lifted her gently, held her in his arms, all she could do was sob.

~~~⁂~~~

Conlan stared down at the woman crying in his arms and felt the walls he'd built around his heart start to crumble. He literally heard the crashing sounds of the bricks and mortar, and all he could think of was how badly he needed to get away from her.

As he started to release her, she clutched at his arms and looked up at him through pain-drenched eyes. "*Damn* them for what they did to you. I hope you track them down and rip their bloody guts out. I'm so sorry, Conlan. I should—I should never have intruded on your privacy."

She slowly reached up to touch the scar at his throat. "I'm so sorry," she repeated, whispering. Then her eyes narrowed and she met his gaze again, her expression ferocious. "I hope I get a chance to run into any of the ones who hurt you. They won't hurt anybody else, ever again."

He blinked, unable to remember when words had touched him the way hers did. She wanted to *protect* him. She wanted to *avenge* him.

The cracking sound of those walls he'd built up inside himself turned into an avalanche.

He tightened his arms around her again, burying his face in her hair. "Never apologize to me for your grace and your light, *mi amara aknasha.*"

She pulled away a little and looked up at him through the tears running down her face. "What does that mean?"

He shook his head, the lump lodged in his throat rendering him unable to form the words in English. She'd *really* think he was insane if he let her know he'd called her his beloved empath.

Speaking of insane, he probably had about ten seconds before Ven came pounding on the door. He sucked in a huge breath and pressed a kiss to her forehead, then dropped his arms and stepped back. "Riley, I know this must feel like you got dropped into the middle of one of those horror movies Ven loves so much, but you have to trust me—"

Riley flashed a brilliant smile at him, wiping the tears off her face. "Trust you? Are you kidding? After what I just saw, I'd trust you with my life."

Relief washed over him, loosening the clenched muscles in his neck and shoulders. "Good," he said, trying to smile. "Because you may have to."

Chapter 17

Riley followed Conlan down a long hallway lined with classic horror movie posters. She stopped, laughing, in front of the toothy tomato decorating the *Attack of the Killer Tomatoes* poster and then turned her gaze to *The Blob.*

"Steve McQueen," she mused, tracing the edge of the frame with one finger. "I *loved* this movie."

Conlan held his hand out to her and grinned. "You and my brother are going to get along just fine."

As they rounded the corner into some kind of large games room, she jerked to a stop at the sight of the crowd of enormous men who sat, stood, leaned, and basically filled up every ounce of space. Well, the men and the cartons, boxes, and trays of food that covered every spare inch of surface. The room looked like an invading army had stopped by for breakfast.

God, they were huge. No wonder they needed to eat all that food. It probably took a zillion calories a day to feed each one of them. She closed her eyes for a moment, reaching inward to be sure her titanium-door emotional shields were firmly in place. She didn't want a repeat of the night before.

Almost to a man, they all shot up to attention and stared at her, most of them grasping the handles of the daggers they wore.

Would you like some coffee with your instruments of death? She covered her mouth to try to stop it, but she had an insane urge to laugh. Stress giggles, Quinn called it. Except Quinn rarely got them.

Riley always did.

She tightened her hold on Conlan's hand and lifted her chin to face them, the flash of hysteria draining away at the sight of the deadly intent on their faces.

"This is Riley Elisabeth Dawson," Conlan said. "She is *aknasha*, and she is welcome among us. Please accord her all courtesy."

"Riley, let me introduce my warriors. These are the Seven, my most trusted comrades. You know Ven, of course," Conlan said, gesturing to his brother.

"Ah, yes, the classic movie buff," she said, smiling. "Steve McQueen *rocks*."

Ven grinned at her from across the room, holding up a half-eaten bagel in salute. "You are clearly a superior judge of films, Lady Sunshine."

Conlan continued. "Lord Justice."

The one with the long braid of blue hair and the sword, still strapped to his back, nodded, unsmiling. She nodded in return. The man would be drop-dead gorgeous if he ever smiled. She glanced at the sword. Maybe he preferred just being drop-dead.

"Bastien."

The giant leaning against the far wall, a doughnut box clutched in his huge hand, smiled at her. "My pleasure, Lady Riley. Anybody brave enough to jump on top of a bloodsucker, unarmed, to defend my prince is golden with me."

She felt her cheeks heat up again, all the way to the tips of her ears. "Just Riley, please. And thank you. It was maybe more stupid than brave, though."

Another warrior, with an easy smile and a mischievous look to him, bowed. "Christophe, my lady. And most of battle is more stupid than brave, is it not? 'Tis why men wage it, not women."

His bright blue eyes gleamed with humor. "I'd be honored to share my breakfast with you, lovely one, *aknasha* or no."

Conlan growled, low in his throat, but with such resonance

that it reverberated through the room. "Stay away from her, Christophe. You'll play none of your wooing games with her."

Riley rolled her eyes and yanked her hand out of his. "Wooing games? You're talking like Lancelot again. And I never liked Lancelot. Smarmy, underhanded guy."

Ven started laughing. "Oh, that did it. You're a Steve McQueen fan, and you just smacked high prince big britches down. My heart is yours forever."

Riley grinned, inexplicably feeling incredibly safe surrounded by a couple thousand pounds of Atlantean warriors.

Conlan growled again and took her hand back. "As I was *saying*, the one who thinks he's a ladies' man is Christophe, and this is Alexios."

A man who stood in the corner, half behind a bookcase, nodded his head to her and bowed slightly, but didn't speak. When he lifted his head, she caught sight of ferocious scarring on his face, but he quickly ducked his head so that his amazing golden hair covered it. The morning light from the window lit up his mane of hair like a crown.

She blurted out what she was thinking. "Wow. Movie stars would pay a fortune to have hair like that. You are so lucky."

Alexios lifted his head again, eyes narrowed, mouth flattened in a grimace. His scars showed up in harsh relief in the sunlight. "Lucky? Perhaps once, long ago. You'd do well to remain far from me and my version of luck."

She recognized the pain in his eyes and, almost without thinking, dropped her shields a fraction and reached out to him.

Then jerked back so hard she slammed her back into the wall. "No, *no*, I'm . . . I'm so sorry," she whispered.

She crashed her mental shields back down. "I am sorry for your pain and your loss, Alexios," she said, her voice gaining strength. "Please don't give up hope, though. There is always a chance of a better tomorrow."

"Stay out of my emotions, *empath*," the warrior growled. "You invade my privacy."

Conlan tried to pull away from her, body tensing, but she stopped him with pressure on his hand. She considered telling Alexios it had been accidental, discarded the idea for truth, and held her head high. "You are completely right. And I apologize for that, as well."

Alexios paused for a moment, surprise widening his eyes, and then he bowed to her. "Your apology is accepted. As Bastien stated so elegantly, your courage yesterday has purchased you so much forgiveness with me."

Conlan squeezed her hand. She sensed the pride and relief he felt, wondered at the strength of the feelings.

Even through her shields.

Another warrior stood up from a wing chair and walked toward her, then stopped and bowed. His face was all sharp planes and hard lines, and waves of black hair swept back from all that hard masculinity to his shoulders.

He had the palest green eyes she'd ever seen—a color that made her think of springtime. "I am Brennan, Lady Riley. You have my gratitude, as well, for your courage last night. I would ask a favor from you, if I may."

Conlan asked before Riley could get the words out. "What kind of favor, Brennan?"

Brennan inclined his head toward Conlan, then turned back toward Riley, eyes intent, yet oddly devoid of any emotion. The guy had to be a great poker player.

"Contrary to Alexios, I would ask that you scan me and let me know what you might learn of my emotions," he asked in a perfectly flat, perfectly calm tone of voice.

It sparked her curiosity. "Why would you ask that? Is this some kind of a test?"

He tilted his head to one side. "Perhaps. But a test only of myself and not of you. Will you grant me this small favor?"

Riley looked up at Conlan, who nodded, jaw tightening. "Only if you want to do it, Riley."

She hesitated, then nodded. Pulling her hand from Conlan's, she held both hands out at her sides, closed her eyes, and opened her mental door. An odd buzzing assailed her senses, as if the mental currents of the Atlanteans in the room were being broadcast in stereo at her, but from a distant location.

She focused on Brennan and shut out the feedback noise. As she'd done with Conlan, she sent her senses winging inside of the warrior who stood so still before her, though she flinched a little, anticipating the force of his emotions.

Then gasped at what she found. Or, rather, at what she *didn't*. Her eyes snapped open in shock. "How are you doing that?

How are you shielding your emotions so completely that I can't feel the slightest glimmer of them?"

The warrior looked down at her, eyes still calm. "I shield nothing. Would you try again?"

She blinked, not understanding. "Would you mind if I touch you?"

From beside her, Conlan made that strange growling noise again. Then he wrapped an arm around her waist and pulled her tightly to him.

"Honestly! I've had enough of this territory-marking crap from you," she said, elbowing Conlan in the side and pulling away from him. "Get over yourself. This is *interesting*."

Brennan raised one eyebrow, and somebody in the room barked out a laugh. Riley ignored them both. "May I?" she asked again.

Brennan nodded once and closed his eyes. Riley took a step closer to him, close enough that she could reach his face with her hands, but not so close that Conlan would have another Tarzan moment. She lifted her hands and placed them on Brennan's cheeks.

Closing her eyes, she sent her senses probing inside of him, more forcefully than before. Searching, seeking, delving for the slightest hint of color—the tiniest trace of emotion.

There was nothing. The depths and shallows of his soul were as clear as crystalline mountain water. As transparent as melted glacier ice.

There was nothing. No feelings. No emotions. "It's as if your soul has died—your *humanity* has died—but your body doesn't know it yet," she whispered, regretting the words as soon as they'd slipped out.

She lowered her hands, backing away from him. "What *are* you? How can your soul be empty of all but your intellect?"

Brennan smiled, but not the slightest touch of it reached his eyes. "I am cursed. I had hoped that one who is *aknasha* would find some trace of the emotions that I'd prayed one day to regain. But if it is not so, then you are correct. I am merely a dead man imitating the actions of the living."

The utter absence of feeling behind the words, which should have been screamed in agony and sorrow, underscored what he'd told her.

Impulsively, she placed a hand on his arm. "I don't understand much about this *aknasha* business. But if anything about this ability I have—well, if in any way I can figure out how to use it to help you, I promise to do my best."

Behind her, Conlan inhaled sharply, and she turned to him, ready to argue. But the look in his eyes had nothing to do with possession, and everything to do with awe. "You honor us, Riley. We bring vampires to your home, abduct you in the middle of the night, and treat you like a prisoner, and yet you have the grace to offer your help to my warrior brother."

She blushed and rolled her eyes. "It's not that big a deal. I just—"

"You *just* offered your help, again, after you may well have saved my life last night. Believe me, it is a very big deal."

Brennan bowed deeply to her. "And to me, a great honor indeed that you would offer."

Before she could think of a reply, she heard the sound of a throat clearing behind her. She turned back toward the room, and the man she'd seen lying injured on the ground the night before stood in front of her, daggers unsheathed and crossed before him.

"I am Denal, Lady Riley. And your courage and selflessness shall be the source of the songs of poets for centuries to come," he said, voice fervent.

Then he dropped to one knee before her. "I hereby declare myself to be Lady Riley's champion and defender, if she will have me."

She watched, speechless, as he held his daggers out to her, handles first, and bowed his head. She swung her head to look at Conlan, hoping for advice on how to handle the situation, but he merely lifted his shoulders briefly and said nothing.

Taking a deep breath, she opened her mental shields again and fought that curious feedback buzzing, then took the measure of the man kneeling in front of her. He was the polar opposite to Brennan—Denal was all flashing emotion and eager notions of honor, duty, and chivalry.

She smiled a little, wondering if she'd ever been so very young. Then the smile faded, as she realized that he might in fact be a *lot* older than she was.

This Atlantean stuff was complicated.

But he was still kneeling, still waiting. The sense of anticipation was thick in the room. As she looked around the room, she realized every one of them was waiting to see how she would handle Denal's declaration.

Taking a deep breath, she took the proffered daggers. "I, well, thank you, Denal. In dangerous times like these, I can't think of a more valuable offer than protection. You—"

She glanced around again, trying to think of the proper words. These guys seemed big on formality and ritual. Finally, she settled on simplicity. "You honor me."

Denal looked up at her, eyes shining, then rose to his feet. She handed his daggers back to him, hoping that was the right thing to do. He took them and put them back in their sheaths on the sides of his massive thighs.

The other Warriors started clapping and cheering and stomping their feet. She smiled and started to say something, when an icy voice broke in from behind her. "Isn't this touching? Perhaps next we can all have a group hug."

Chapter 18

Conlan swung around to face Alaric. "I don't appreciate your tone, priest," he said, folding his arms over his chest.

Alaric raised one eyebrow and shrugged. It wasn't like Conlan had expected him to be intimidated, but a little respect might be nice.

"You'll get respect when you earn it," Alaric replied, eerily imitating Conlan's thoughts again.

Conlan filed the detail for future consideration and then, before the gasp even finished leaving Riley's lips, he slammed Alaric up against the wall. "Either you serve me, or you do not. Poseidon gave you the rank of high priest, but the role of royal adviser is mine to bestow."

He stared into the priest's eyes. "If all this attitude is your way of saying you want out of the job, consider it done."

Releasing Alaric's shirt, he turned to Riley. "You must be starving. Hopefully, one of these bottomless pits saved us a muffin or two."

She gaped up at him, mouth opening to speak. But he shook his head and, surprisingly, she went along with him and remained silent.

As they started to walk across the room toward the low

coffee table covered with food, he heard Alaric's voice behind him. "No, I don't want *out of the job*, you idi— my *prince*. I'm trying to *do* my job, which includes reclaiming the Trident, so you can ascend to the throne."

Conlan had never heard such anguish in the priest's voice. With a hand under her elbow, he urged Riley toward Ven. Then he turned to face Alaric. "The fault is not yours. If anything, it's my fault because I wasn't there to protect the Temple."

Bastien slammed his coffee mug down on a table. "The fault is mine. I had many friends among the House of Mycenae. The gods know I should have suspected their plan."

Justice laughed. "Yeah, it's everybody's fault. It's nobody's fault. Does it really fucking matter? While we sit around here eating toast and assigning blame, Reisen gets farther and farther away."

Conlan held up a hand. "Enough. Justice is right. Alaric, have you been able to scry for the Trident?"

"No. I get flashes, and then it's gone. Almost as if they've discovered some magic shielding for it. Or the Trident hides itself from a failed priest."

Ven spoke up, voice heavy. "Then we're doomed. We can search the old-fashioned way, but he could be a thousand miles or more away by now, in any direction."

"He's got a band of warriors with him," Christophe ventured. "Unless they've split up. It would be tough to hide ten or more warriors traveling together."

Conlan took a deep breath, trying to remain calm. "Then we will also divide to follow them. Alaric, is there any way you can magnify the scrying?"

Before Alaric could respond, Riley interrupted. "By any chance, are you talking about a bunch of guys who give off the same emotional vibe as you all do, except with a lot of 'rah, rah, quest, quest' crap thrown in?"

Nine heads whipped around to face her. She blinked, then continued, gaze turned inward. "If yes, they can't be more than twenty miles from here. I've had to work hard to shield from their emotions for the past half hour or so. I thought it was some kind of feedback loop from all of you, but I'm figuring out how to sort and separate, and they're definitely different."

She closed her eyes, and Conlan could feel her concentration. Then she jumped up from the couch, nearly dropping her muffin on Ven's head. "And we need to get going. Because they're heading out to attack some shape-shifters. *Now*."

~~~~~

Ven jerked his head toward the door, and the Warriors strode out of the room behind him, leaving Conlan and Riley arguing over somebody named Ramirez. It was almost funny, the way Conlan was suddenly worried about the feelings of a human female. If that's what soul-melding did to a man, thank Poseidon that it had never happened to him. He liked his women brainless and forgettable, and he had the feeling Lady Sunshine was neither of those things.

Not his problem. At least, not yet. If she caused a problem, well, he'd take care of it. That was his job, right?

He reached the entryway closet and threw open the door. Reaching in between a few of the jackets and coats, he grasped the hanging rod with one hand, and twisted it three-quarters of the way forward, and then a half-turn back.

There was a click and a whirring sound, and the rod—coats and all—retracted into the opening made by a panel that slid open on the right side of the closet. A second panel, in the back of the closet, opened noiselessly to a small room filled with a lot of shiny toys.

"That's a sweet arsenal, Ven," said Christophe, crowding close behind him. "What have you got in there?"

Ven flicked on a light switch, and spotlights shone on the contents of the room. "Let me give you a tour, my man," he said, moving past a rack of submachine guns to lift down a shotgun exclusively designed for him.

"This baby is a Franchi SPAS-12. A combat shotgun designed with loving care by the Italians, who are brilliant with cars, guns, and any kind of exquisite machinery. And it's specially modified to hold these."

He held up a bullet-shaped glass vial, filled with a viscous liquid. "Extremely high-dose Special K. The one thing nearly guaranteed to bring down a shape-shifter."

Denal shouldered his way in, eyes wide. "Special K?"

"Ketamine. Animal tranquilizer. Hold this." Ven slapped the gun into Denal's hands.

"Guns. Poison. Explosives. We've got it all, ladies," Ven said, a grim smile curling the edges of his mouth.

"The power to control the elements is no longer enough for you, Vengeance?" Alaric asked.

"Save the scorn for somebody who gives a shit. Not all of us have your level of access to Poseidon's power," Ven said.

"I'll stick with my sword," Justice drawled. "She and I have killed more bloodsuckers and shape-shifters than all of your toys put together."

"Suit yourself. That's more for me to play with," Ven returned, loading up. "There's plenty here for anybody who wants some. As they say in the movies, boys—"

"Lock and load!" Christophe shouted, grinning.

Ven nodded. "Lock and load."

Conlan's fingers clenched on the steering wheel of the Mercedes as he listened to Riley's phone calls. First she'd called into her office and asked for some time off. From what he'd gleaned of the one-sided conversation, they were more than happy to grant her the time. It sounded like she hadn't taken much time off in the past few years.

Why didn't *that* surprise him? She had a sense of duty as ingrained as any warrior's.

"Hey, Detective Ramirez, it's Riley Dawson," she said into her cell phone, quite pointedly not looking in Conlan's direction. He was amused by her defiance.

Not just amused, to be honest with himself. It made him hot. Although, for some reason, all the woman had to do was *breathe*, and it made him hot.

Definitely not a good sign.

She was quiet for a moment, nodding at something the detective was saying on the line. Then she spoke again. "Thank God."

She glanced at Conlan. "The baby's going to be okay." Then she spoke into the phone again. "Yeah, I can come in and give you a statement, but pretty much what I told you last night is all I know.

"Okay, then. You have my cell number. Just call me."

As she flipped her phone shut, Conlan debated and then

decided against telling her that her cell phone was not going to be getting any signal when she was deep beneath the ocean.

She'd figure it out. Why borrow trouble?

Alaric leaned over the seat from his spot in the back, directly behind Riley. "I hate cars, Conlan. Tell me why you believed it was so important for us to use cars?"

Conlan flicked a glance at him. "Traveling via mist is easy enough for you and me, and even Ven, but not as easy for some of the Seven, especially over long distances. And it would definitely freak Riley out. Since she's the only one who can sense Reisen and his men, I wanted her to feel comfortable."

Ven spoke up. "I'm good with this. My toys don't travel well. No metal without orichalcum in it, remember? Hey, we've got fine engineering, a smooth ride, and an excellent sound system. I've got some killer CDs loaded, if you want to click on the tunes."

Conlan looked in the rearview mirror, making sure that Justice and the others were behind him in the Hummer. "Not exactly inconspicuous vehicles you picked, are they, Ven?" he said drily.

Riley made a small sound in her throat, and her hands clenched around her tiny telephone. "We need to get there, fast. They're close now. I—they must be in the park. This is the road to First Landing State Park. I'd heard that the local Shape-shifter Appreciation League had a forum there."

Ven snorted. "Great. Now the bastards have an appreciation league? When they spend most of their time finding ways to eat you people?"

Riley turned her head to look at him, eyes troubled. "I don't think that's entirely true. Both shape-shifters and vampires have made a considerable effort to integrate peacefully into society."

It was Conlan's turn to be disgusted. "Are you all fools? For thousands of years, both races have considered humans as sheep—their personal food supply. Suddenly, they come out into the daylight—metaphorically speaking—and the first thing they do is try to take over. How is that integrating? Peacefully or otherwise?"

"I, well, I sort of agree with you." She sighed. "I always

thought it was a little freaky that only a few years after we even knew vampires existed, suddenly they're running their own house of Congress. I mean, how did that happen without some sort of mind control?" she said.

"Mind control or physical threat," Alaric said smoothly. "It seems that many of your dissenting voices have met with untimely accidents or disappeared. Did none of you notice the pattern in that?"

"I don't know what you're talking about," Riley said. "There hasn't been anything about that in the news."

"You mean the shape-shifter-controlled media? I wonder how *that* could be possible," Alaric returned, sarcasm heavy in his voice.

Conlan pulled into the park's entrance and found a spot for the car, vicious thoughts whirling around in his brain. As he slammed the car into park and shut down the ignition, he shifted in the seat and stared at Alaric. "Do you suspect that they could be teaming up? After so many centuries of blood feud, do you really believe that the shape-shifters would help the bloodsuckers?"

Alaric returned his stare calmly, although Conlan noticed that the priest's eyes had begun to glow. "You've been gone for most of the decade, Conlan. There does seem to be a spirit of cooperation between them that was never there before. It worries the Council a great deal."

"Hell, it worries me a great big fucking deal," Ven snarled. "If we—

Riley shrieked, in a high-pitched, shrill tone that Conlan had never heard before. She clutched her head and screamed. He pulled her into his arms, trying to comfort her. Needing to comfort her.

Needing to make that inhuman sound stop. "Riley! Riley, what is it?"

She abruptly stopped shrieking and stared up at him, eyes vacant and turned inward. "They're here. They're here and they're killing. Murdering. Violence and death and pain . . . *No!* No, that's not possible!"

She started to scream so loudly Conlan thought his eardrums would rupture. He took her by the shoulders and shook her a little to try to pull her out of the hell she was clearly experiencing.

"Riley! You're safe. You're here with us. You have to shield from those emotions," he said roughly.

She shook her head back and forth. "No, no, no, you don't understand," she moaned. "It's Quinn. Somehow, they've got my sister. I can feel her—I can feel her, and she's *dying*."

Ven and Alaric jumped out of the car and slammed their doors shut, then Ven yanked Conlan's open. Conlan lifted Riley onto his lap and pulled her out of the car with him. He helped her to stand, arm firmly around her waist. "Tell us. Point us to where they are, Riley. You know we can help her if you do."

She looked up at him, still clutching her head, still dazed. "What? Pain, Quinn, *nooooo*!"

Alaric's head snapped up, and he pointed down a path. "There. I can sense the Trident now. It's blazing with power. And—I don't know how, but I can sense her sister, too," he said, lips drawn back in a snarl. "I can *feel* her inside my skin. Riley is correct. If we don't get there fast, she's going to die."

The Hummer pulled into the parking space next to them, and the warriors piled out. "Hey, cool place. So, what's the scoop?" Christophe called, then he stopped, frozen, as he caught sight of Riley. His face hardened, and he headed toward them, followed by Bastien and the others.

"We go after them now," Conlan commanded. "Riley, you stay here out of danger, and—"

"No! She's my sister!" she snapped at him, seeming to come briefly out of her daze. "I'm coming with you."

"We don't have time to argue about this," Alaric said. "And we're attracting unwelcome attention." He nodded to a group of campers who were openly staring at the leather-clad group of warriors. Then his entire body jerked, as if he'd taken a blow.

"Now. We go *now*," he ground out, green eyes glowing more brightly than Conlan had ever seen them. Walking, then running, Alaric took off down the trail into the woods.

Ven looked to Conlan, who nodded. "Follow him. All of you. I'll be right behind you."

As the warriors pounded down the trail after Alaric, he looked down at Riley, who still leaned against him. "You remain behind, where it's safe, or I swear I'll stay here and sit on you," he growled.

She blinked. "Yes, okay. I'm feeling very weak, suddenly. But will you bring Quinn back to me right away?"

"I promise," he said, then opened the car door and helped her back inside. She leaned back against the seat, clearly exhausted, and he felt a wave of concern for what the empathy must cost her.

He bent down to her and pressed a kiss on her forehead. "I'll bring her right back to you."

She looked up at him, eyes huge in her pale face. "Then *go*. Go now."

As she closed her eyes again, he gently shut the car door, looked around to see that the tourists had moved behind their large camping vehicle, and then he shimmered into mist. He'd get there more quickly—and unseen. And may the gods forgive anyone who had dared to harm Riley's sister.

Because Conlan had no mercy in him.

Chapter 19

Riley waited a few seconds, then peeked under her lashes in time to catch the sight of one massive Atlantean prince dissolving into a shower of mist.

"What the *hell*?" She blinked, then rubbed her eyes. "Great. The Atlantis version of Houdini."

But she didn't have time to worry about him and his stupid tricks—Quinn's pain was scorching through her. She shoved the car door open and jumped out, then took off down the path in the direction the Warriors had run just minutes before.

"As if some stupid man could keep me from Quinn when she needs me. Not now, not ever." She started to run, sending up a prayer of thanks for the old running shoes she'd thrown on the night before and still wore.

Another bolt of pain from Quinn shot through her. She doubled over for a moment, then straightened and ran even faster, sending reassurance to Quinn the only way she knew how.

I'm coming, Quinn. I'm coming. Don't you dare die on me—you're all I've got.

Conlan had just passed Ven and the Seven running down the trail when the path widened and turned to the left. As he rounded the corner, body still in the form of translucent mist, he came upon a scene of violent death.

The shock of it destroyed his concentration, and he transformed back into his body with a nauseating jolt. Roughly a dozen bodies, bloody, mutilated, and torn, littered the path. He felt the bile rising in his throat as the Warriors thundered up behind him. The peaceful, sunlit forest trees served as a mocking contrast to the grisly sight.

"This is wrong," Ven snarled from beside him. "This is way beyond wrong."

Justice shouldered his way up on Conlan's other side, sword drawn and lips curled back from his teeth. "Do you see Reisen? Is he one of the dead?"

Alexios walked past, then, and he and Conlan started to examine the fallen bodies. The others followed, daggers and guns at the ready, eyes scanning the forest constantly for a hint of returning danger.

"This one is a shape-shifter," Conlan called out, seeing the telltale eyes. A shape-shifter's eyes reverted to animal shape and color in death. The one lying in hacked-up pieces at his feet had been some kind of wolf.

Then he jerked his head up and looked around for the one who should have been there before him. "Alaric, where are you?"

"I am here, and I need your assistance," Alaric replied from behind him. Conlan swung around to see the priest, emerging from behind a fallen tree, and started toward him, then stopped, midstride.

Alaric's face was cast in harsh, feral planes, his eyes wild and fiery green. He spoke again, his voice promising brutal death to the architects of this destruction. "She is beyond my help. She will die."

A frantic pounding of feet interrupted whatever response Conlan might have been able to think of, and he and Alaric both turned to see Riley running full speed around the corner.

She saw the scene and screeched to a halt, shaking, and began to scream. "Quinn! Where are you?"

Conlan ran to her, but it was Justice who caught her as she

went down. He swept her up in his arms and handed her carefully to Conlan, then made a slight bow. "Your human, my prince."

Conlan ignored the trace of mockery in the warrior and bent his head to Riley. "Shh. She's not gone yet. You have time to say good-bye."

She gasped in heaving breaths and started screaming again, pushing and clawing at him to try to get down. "No! Not my sister. Let me down. Let me down now!"

Instead, he pulled her closer, turning her face toward his chest, so she wouldn't have to look at the carnage surrounding them. Then he strode over and around the bodies toward Alaric.

When he reached the deadfall of trees, he relaxed his hold on Riley and set her gently on the ground. Alaric was kneeling in front of the body of a woman. A wound in her shoulder was pulsing blood. Conlan scented the air. The sulfur smell of gunpowder.

She'd been shot.

Quinn had short dark hair, instead of Riley's gold, but her silken white skin and delicate facial features were stamped with Riley's strength and beauty.

Riley threw herself on the ground and put her arms around her sister, sobbing. For an instant—a split second that passed so quickly Conlan wasn't sure he'd actually seen it—Alaric tensed, fingers curling into claws, as if he were going to attack Riley.

Even as Conlan moved to place himself between the two, the moment faded. The green flames in Alaric's eyes muted slightly.

"Help her!" Riley lifted her sister's head carefully onto her lap and stared at Alaric. "Help her! I know you can do it. You healed poison and sword wounds and broken heads. You can surely heal a little—oh, my God, it's a gunshot wound. Please, *please*," she begged, somehow sobbing and issuing a command all at once.

Alaric shook his head back and forth, a dazed expression on his face. His eyes were wild, almost rolling around in his head. Conlan had never seen him like this.

"I can't," he muttered brokenly. "I can't reach her. I can only feel the pain she's sending out. I can't get past it."

Conlan dropped to one knee beside Riley and put his arms around her, hoping to give some comfort. She elbowed him viciously and shook him off, never for a moment looking away from Alaric. She curled her lips back from her teeth and snarled so ferociously she almost looked like a shape-shifter herself.

"You can, and you will, because I will *push* you past it." With that, she grabbed Alaric's forearm in a viselike grip and forced his hand down to her sister's shoulder. "I've seen healings on TV. Witch healings. They need to touch in order to do it. I'm guessing it's the same with you."

As Conlan watched, somehow Riley managed to win the struggle with Alaric, combating his reluctance with sheer desperation. As the priest's hand passed through the last inch of space separating it from Quinn's shoulder, Conlan saw an aquamarine glow pass from Alaric's palm into Riley's sister.

When Alaric's fingers finally touched Quinn, her body, resting in Riley's lap, jumped at the contact, and her feet drummed into the red-and-gold pile of fallen leaves in which they lay. Riley, still holding tightly to Alaric's arm, closed her eyes.

Alaric threw his head back, flinching, the cords in his neck standing out in stark relief as every muscle in his body seemed to tighten.

Conlan lifted his hands to Riley's shoulders, but an electric shock slammed him back away from her. For the space of several seconds, the three—Alaric, Quinn, and Riley— were frozen in a painful tableau, limned in a luminous blue-green light.

Then, as one, Riley and Alaric slumped forward, gasping for breath. Conlan caught Riley before she could fall forward onto her sister, gently taking her chin in his hand and searching her face for signs that she had been harmed.

Alaric caught himself, one hand on his knee, the other still in place on Quinn's shoulder. "I do not know why you were caught up in the healing process, Riley. I have never channeled the healing powers like that before. Are you harmed?"

Before Riley could respond, a quiet, slightly husky feminine voice cut across the sound of rasping breaths. "If you move that hand one inch closer to my boob, I'm going to cut it off."

~~~~~~

Alaric took one look into Quinn's eyes as they opened and fell back away from her. Shooting to his feet with such speed that Conlan almost wasn't able to track him, Alaric backed away from them, shaking his head and muttering something to himself.

Conlan was unable to make out the words, but he heard the cadence of ancient Atlantean and wondered at it. He stroked Riley's hair, a brief touch more for his comfort than hers, and stood to follow Alaric.

He caught the priest on the other side of the path as Alaric began to shimmer into mist. "Stop," he commanded. "Where in the nine hells do you think you're going? What just happened?"

Alaric reverted to corporeal form and whirled around to face him. "You want to know what happened?" he asked, wild fury in his voice, desperation dark in the harsh lines of his face.

"You want to know what *happened*?" With two steps, he was right up in Conlan's face.

"I'll tell you what *happened*, my prince," Alaric continued, rasping out the words. "What happened was I sent my healing energy inside Quinn. Inside that *human*. And she grabbed hold of me."

He shoved a hand through his hair and laughed a little wildly, eyes flaring green and hot.

Savage.

"She dug her mental claws into my *balls*, is what happened. I healed her, and she destroyed something in me. Shredded it."

"What—" Conlan never got the question out.

"My control," Alaric snarled. "The absolutely rock-hard control that I've spent centuries perfecting. Your little girlfriend's sister reached out with her emotions, or her witchy empath nature, or what the hell ever, and all I wanted to do was *fuck* her."

Conlan moved back half a step at the ferocity in the priest's voice and dropped his hands to his dagger handles. For an instant, icy death menaced in the air between them.

Alaric laughed, bitter again. "Oh, you don't need your blades. In spite of the fact that I wanted her more than I've wanted anything in my life, I won't touch her. Although, even now, my mind tortures me with images of pounding into her body, right there on the ground in the mess of her own blood, fucking and *fucking* her until I drive myself into her soul." Alaric viciously kicked at a tree and shards of bark flew into the air, then disintegrated in the green energy bolts he shot at them.

This was new and dangerous territory, and Conlan attempted to proceed with caution. "Alaric, you must—"

"Yes. I *must*. I must never succumb to any lusts, or my power is ended. Certainly, I would be of no further use to you or to Atlantis. No use to the jealous bastard of a sea god whom I serve," the priest said flatly, his voice suddenly devoid of the rage and passion that had infused it moments before.

"I *must* get away from her," he continued. "Now. From this place. I am ruined for this day, in any event. This . . . this energy drain has voided any hope I had of re-scrying for the Trident until I recover. I will meet you back at Ven's safe house tonight."

Conlan grasped his friend's shoulders, shaken by the blasphemy he'd never heard from him before. "Alaric, know that your use to me and to Atlantis goes far beyond the powers you gained from Poseidon. Your wise counsel has served me well for centuries, and I will need you when I ascend to the throne."

Alaric stared over Conlan's shoulder toward Riley and her sister. "These empaths. They signal a treacherous difference in our ways, Conlan. I can sense it. Change is coming. Peril that comes from within our very souls."

With that, he took two running steps and leapt into the air, transforming into sparkling mist that quickly vanished.

Conlan watched the air into which Alaric had disappeared for a long moment, considering his parting words.

But Alaric had been wrong. Change wasn't coming.

It's already here.

Chapter 20

Twenty minutes later, Conlan stood with Ven, grimly contemplating the pile of bodies they and the rest of the Seven had pulled behind the deadfall of trees. Centuries of serving as a warrior had yet to inure him to the foul stink of death, and his stomach growled an urge to reject its contents. He scrubbed at his hands with leaves, then realized the futility of the effort and called water from the surrounding leaves and a tiny stream some hundred yards away to cleanse his hands.

The mist became fluid in the cupped bowl of his hands and he washed the blood from hands and forearms, wondering how Reisen and his remaining warriors had escaped undetected after surviving this carnage. They must have been spattered with gore.

Except, of course, when they traveled as mist. Which may have explained why Riley no longer detected them. He'd have to test his theory with her sometime. Sometime when a dozen dead men weren't lying at his feet.

Almost involuntarily, his mind reached out to hers, but she'd slammed those damned shields of hers down so tightly he wouldn't know she was there if he hadn't just left her. It was better that way, though. There was only so much that she could be expected to endure.

Justice and Bastien were roaming through the woods on either side of them, searching for any sign of Reisen and his remaining warriors, while Christophe and the others stood guard.

Emotionless Brennan stood with Riley and her sister.

Riley had told him they were wasting their time. "They're gone. Or they've magically learned how to mask their emotions in the past half an hour. Because I can't feel a thing."

Conlan was unsure of how far he could rely on her ability to sense the Mycenaean warriors, given the extent of the terror she'd just experienced. But her senses, however compromised, were all he had.

Alaric was gone.

"We've got to get rid of the bodies. We can't leave this mess for the human authorities," Ven growled, wiping sweat off his forehead with his arm. "It's a nightmare."

Conlan nodded. They'd tallied seven dead shape-shifters and five Atlanteans. The evidence of the battle needed to be destroyed. "We're not exactly going to dig a big hole," he replied. "There is one way, but it will take both of us to do it to so many."

Ven shot a look at him. "You're not thinking—"

"What else could I be thinking? We must employ the final solution."

Ven whistled. "*Mortus desicana.* I didn't even know you knew how to channel that kind of power. Have you ever—"

Conlan cut him off. "No. Not that I wouldn't have tried it on Anubisa, if I'd had a fraction of a chance. But this is different. These men are already dead. The penance would not be tasked against us."

"Are you sure about that? What does the temple rat say?"

Conlan hesitated, unsure of how much to divulge. Alaric would hate to be exposed in any weakness.

In any event, there was no time. "He's gone. The healing— he returned to the safe house."

"What? He went all girly after healing a simple bullet wound? I'm going to give him so much grief—"

Conlan heard rustling in the trees approximately fifty yards away and concentrated. It was Justice. But the sound underscored their need for haste. "Ven. Focus. Will you help me channel the *mortus desicana* to destroy these bodies, or do I do it myself?"

"I'll help you. Poseidon help us both if you're wrong about the penance. Twelve bodies . . . we might not survive it."

Looking around quickly to make sure that Brennan still kept Riley away from the bloody pile of the slain, Conlan took a deep breath and held his hands up, sending his call into the wind.

If she saw this, she'd think he was the same kind of monster who'd created this bloody nightmare.

Beside him, Ven did the same, and they both began to chant.

"Poseidon, Father of Water,

"Lord of elements, avatar of justice for all Atlanteans,

"Hear our plea, feel our need,

"Lend us your power for the *mortus desicana*,

"Hear our plea, feel our need."

"For a moment, nothing. Despair surged through Conlan. Had Poseidon truly abandoned him as unworthy after what Anubisa had done to him?

Damaged goods. Damaged goods. Damaged—

Then a surge of electric power stormed into his body. From the air, from the water in the ground, from the wind itself. Up through his feet, through his skin, down into his skull from the cloudless sky. The power of the elements ripped through his flesh, screamed through nerve endings, tore at his control.

He fought with it, contained it, channelled it. Not even realizing he was doing it, he roared out his dominance over the power. "I am Conlan of Atlantis, and I command you to the *mortus desicana*!"

With that, he flung the power out of his body through his hands at the pile of bodies and watched, gloated, *gloried* in the *power.* The roaring rush of the elements covered and surrounded the bodies of the dead, rushing into every pore in their skin, into every orifice, and did their terrifying work.

Sucking, *draining* every ounce of water—every drop of fluid—out of the bodies. Sucking it out and returning the fluid to nature, from whence it came. Drying, *desiccating* the bodies of the dead.

Whispering to Conlan with fury, with frenzy, with the sly Siren call of unadulterated power. The *mortus desicana*.

The power with the potential to suck the fluids from the tissue and bones of those who were *still alive*.

The sheer seduction in the thought choked him, stopped him. His horror at what he could become, at what wielding such power might do to his mind—to his *soul*—cut him off from the source of the elements instantly.

As he lost control, he fell back, gasping harshly, against the nearest tree. When his vision cleared of the power and the haze and dust from the dried-out bodies, he saw Ven, collapsed on the ground, trying to raise up on one arm.

As Conlan attempted to stand, to recover enough of his strength to proceed, a sharp voice cut through his exhaustion.

Justice. "Interesting, my prince. I did not know you had mastered the calling of forbidden death." Justice bowed slightly and walked around the pile of dust and bone fragments that lay where the bodies of twelve men had been only minutes earlier. He kicked at a skull that had rolled away from the rest, and it exploded into a shower of fine, dry dust.

Justice cocked his head and stared at Conlan and Ven, eyes narrowed. "Very interesting, indeed."

<center>~~~~</center>

Barrabas leaned back in his carved wooden seat in the center of the Primus main gallery, hours after everyone else had gone home to their meaningless lives. He was well contented by the day's work. Yet another codicil to the 2006 Nonhuman Species Protection Act he'd authored—one of his proudest accomplishments—was now only a single signature from becoming law.

He'd shoved the codicil through with persuasion, charm, and brute force. The disappearance of two key members of the human houses of Congress hadn't hurt, either.

He smiled, a baring of teeth that would have terrified the weak man who probably sat, quivering, in the Oval Office at that very minute. His advisors were begging the president to veto the bill.

Barrabas knew the weakling didn't have the spine for it.

"Lame duck" took on a whole new meaning when a politician was dealing with a master vampire.

"You must be very pleased with yourself, Lord Bar— . . . Lord *Barnes*." Drakos had entered, unnoticed, and now strode down the aisle toward him.

Barrabas didn't particularly care for a general who could sneak up on him, which reminded him yet again that he'd have to decide soon about finding Drakos's replacement.

Perhaps Caligula. The thought gave him a perverse pleasure, and he smiled again. "Yes, Drakos, I am very, very pleased. The consolidation of power is simply a matter of acquiring and honing knowledge."

Barrabas stood, then levitated from his position down to the floor of the chamber. "If you know both your enemy and yourself, you will come out of one hundred battles with one hundred victories. Know neither your enemy nor yourself, and you will lose all."

Drakos raised one eyebrow. "Sun Tzu?"

Barrabas inclined his head. "A true master strategist."

"Was he, too, one of us?"

"No, although it is astonishing that he was not. If only I'd had the opportunity . . . Well. No matter. What have you to report?"

"Our spies report a complete failure in determining what may have happened to Terminus and his vanguard, my lord. We—"

But before Drakos could finish his thought, a chill swept through the chamber. Though colorless, it destroyed the light. Though odorless, it reeked of bile and death.

Though soundless, it deafened them, driving both to their knees.

Choking, suffocating, Barrabas barely had time to form the name in his mind before she spoke.

Anubisa. Goddess of the night.

Her voice rang with the chimes heralding the hangman's noose, the headsman's axe. The sound of ground glass shredding the vocal cords of screaming humans shrieked in her tone.

Yet, somehow, her words were quiet and still. Death stealing the breath of an infant in its cradle.

As he'd seen *her* do. Not merely breath, but blood.

As he'd *helped* her do.

He wondered at the broken shards of his long-murdered conscience as they poked at his liver.

Twisted in his brain.

He was screaming with the agony of it before she'd completed her first sentence. And then he was unable to make any sound at all.

He collapsed on his face next to the unconscious form of his general.

"You grow stronger, Barrabas," she crooned in her poisonous lilt. "When last I saw you, you were sodden with your own piss long before I formed words."

He wrenched his head to the side, tried to gaze into her face, and the ice in the air intensified. Turned his bowels to water.

He'd pray not to soil himself, but to whom did dark lords pray?

To the bitch goddess in front of him, of course. And she had nothing of mercy or compassion in her.

He clenched his buttocks together and listened.

She laughed. At the sound of her laughter, living things died. He'd seen *that*, too.

A tiny blood clot in his brain burst, shooting blood out of his nose. He lay still while it trickled down the side of his face to pool on the floor underneath his cheek.

"Is that your offering to me, Lord *Barnes*? And, yes, of course I know about your pitiful attempt to disguise your true self from these sheep."

The tips of her fingers and the bottom of her silken gown were all he could see. She wore white. A travesty, virginal white on the goddess of all lusts.

Which is why it amused her so.

She'd told him that once. Then she'd broken him.

Again and again.

He cringed to remember. Cringed to remember how, at the very end, he'd begged her for the pain. For the humiliation.

Groveled for the twisted perversions.

She gestured with one hand and released him. Suddenly able to move, he was afraid to do so.

He was no stranger to her games.

"Rise, my Barrabas. I hear from your cesspool of a mind that you remember our fun with . . . *yearning*. Shall I pleasure you again with my toys?"

He stood, struggling to contain the shudder that threatened to devour his body. Her toys. Iron-clawed whips. Steel manacles that fit many more things than only arms and legs.

Braving a glance at her, he saw that she was unchanged. If anything, more beautiful than she'd been three hundred years ago when he'd last seen her.

Last *felt* her.

Almost died the true death from it.

Silken waves of midnight black hair caressed curves of such perfection that they would drive a human male to drooling madness. Piercing eyes the black of damned souls gazed at him, a spark of red in their exact centers.

She must be in a good mood.

Maybe he wouldn't die.

Maybe not this time.

"Afraid to answer me, *Lord* Barrabas?" She infused the word with sarcasm sharp enough to flay flesh from bones.

He'd done *that* with her, too. More of her "toys."

"I . . . forgive me, my lady goddess. I have no words, before your beauty." He stammered out the words, knowing that flattery might have a chance to distract her. She was Death personified, but she was an ancient *female* death. Pretty words drew her attention like shiny things to the eyes of a crow.

"Yes. Yes, I am beautiful, Barrabas," she preened. "And I have been constrained from playing my favorite games for far too long, due to Poseidon's curse. But this day and yester eve bring me great joy, my young one. Do you wish to know why?"

Though nearly three thousand years old, the "young one" was afraid to do more than nod.

She caressed his cheek with a fingertip, and his skin burned and sizzled in the wake of her touch. He fought to keep from flinching.

"The princeling himself broke Poseidon's curse. He has revealed the existence of Atlantis to one of the sheep, thus breaking the ancient stricture laid upon me by that prick of a sea god," she said, skirts whirling around her with the force of her anger.

Barrabas gasped. "Atlantis? The lost continent of legend truly exists?"

She smiled again, and her mouth was crowded with far too many teeth. Shiny, dagger-sharp teeth. He leaned toward her, hypnotized at the sight, but she laughed and turned away.

"No, Barrabas. I am in no mood to sample your wares again. First, I will tell you of Atlantis, and how you will serve me in my plans. Then." She smiled again and prodded the motionless form of Drakos with one slippered foot. "Then I will teach your general how to play."

Chapter 21

Riley planted one hand on her hip, the other still supporting Quinn, and stared up at the walking mountain of muscle who was barring her path. "Look, Bastien, I appreciate your loyalty to Conlan. Really I do. But Brennan already let us go, and I need to get my sister to a doctor."

A trace of warm sympathy crossed Bastien's handsome face, but he shook his head and folded his arms across his enormous chest. "I am sorry, Lady Riley, but I am unable to allow you to pass."

Riley heard a sharp *snick* sound, and suddenly a lethal-looking knife blade was pressed up against Bastien's neck. And Quinn was the one holding the nonpointy end of it.

Riley gasped, but Bastien merely sighed, as if he were totally unconcerned with the six inches or so of steel pointing at his throat.

Quinn moved away from Riley and pushed her a little way back with the arm not holding the knife. "Here's the deal, buddy. You let me and my sister go, or I'll slice your carotid artery into little pieces before you can say 'not-so-jolly giant.'"

Bastien actually smiled. "I am unsurprised that you would have the courage of a warrior five times your size, small one.

Your sister's blood is strong in you. Were you suckled with tiger's milk?"

Riley snapped out of her shock and grabbed her sister's arm. "Quinn, stop! These men are . . . well, they . . . they're the good guys."

Quinn turned to look Riley in the eye, hand holding the knife never wavering. "Riley, there are things here you don't understand. Those men who were dead—they were—"

"They were shape-shifters and Atlantean warriors," Conlan said, stepping onto the path next to Riley. "What will be interesting to learn is how you came to be lying, injured, in the midst of them."

Brennan silently appeared beside Quinn. "I sensed that you had finished the *mortus desicana*, and that it would be safe to let Lady Riley and her sister walk toward you," he said, bowing slightly toward Conlan.

Quinn's eyes narrowed, but she finally put the knife down and stepped back from Bastien, who winked at her. "Outnumbered by Atlantean warriors. That would actually explain a lot about the way they . . . Well. Do you have any proof of this ridiculous story? And what are you doing here?"

She swept out a hand at the path. "Were those your men who attacked my wolves?"

Riley's heart, which had finally begun to slow down, started racing again. "What? *Your* wolves? What are you doing hanging out with a pack of shape-shifters?"

Quinn gently patted her arm, with the air of a parent comforting a toddler. "Shh, sis. It's okay. I'll tell you about it later."

Oh, that was *so* not happening. Riley yanked her arm away from Quinn's hand. "You can stow the condescending attitude, Quinn, and tell me what the hell you're doing here and why you had a . . . a *gunshot* wound that you nearly died from?"

Quinn had the audacity to roll her eyes. "A little dramatic, don't you think? It was only my shoulder. I've had worse." Her face softened, and she pulled Riley close in a fierce hug. "I'm sorry, baby sister. I love you so much—I never wanted for you to see any of this world." Quinn pulled away suddenly, and she scanned the area.

"Speaking of which, where is that other man? I had the strangest feeling that he crawled into my skin to heal me from the inside out . . ." Her voice trailed off, and her hand reached up to touch her shredded shirt and the unbroken skin underneath it. "I know I didn't imagine that gunshot."

"We can share our stories back at the house," Conlan said. "I think it's past time we got away from here."

"The scene of the crime," Quinn added, lines of sorrow and exhaustion on her face. "Where are they? What did you do with . . . their bodies?"

Ven stumbled up to them, looking like he'd been on a three-week bender. His skin was gray, and the dark circles under his eyes went on for miles. Riley looked from him to Conlan, whose face was also drawn and pale, though less so than Ven's.

"What exactly happened to you two?" she asked, opening her mind and emotions for the first time since she'd seen the bodies.

But Conlan's mental shields were down in a big and serious way. She couldn't feel anything from him.

Ven, though, either wasn't as strong or else he was too tired to care. She felt it from him—the sorrow, the weariness, the horror at what they'd done.

But she didn't understand the emotions. "What did you do to the bodies?" she asked, echoing Quinn.

"We had to dispose of them. We can't leave that kind of mess for the human authorities," Conlan said, jaw clenching.

"But—no! You can't do that! We have to call 911 and—"

"He's right, Riley," Quinn said wearily, head drooping. "This is something beyond even the P Ops. Especially if they really are from Atlantis."

Conlan held a hand out to Riley, and she blinked at him in utter disbelief. "But, that can't be right. Paranormal Ops guys deal with this kind of stuff all the time, right? I mean—"

"Riley," Conlan said, voice gentle. "There is nothing left for them to find. Please. We need to get your sister out of danger."

Riley hesitated another minute, then nodded, squaring her shoulders. "Sure. Fine. You're right. Atlantis exists, vampires attack me, I nearly get killed by my client's boyfriend, and my sister is in league with werewolves. What's abnormal about that?"

She tightened her arm around Quinn, and they headed down the path toward the cars and, hopefully, toward some answers.

Conlan stared out the window into the fading sunlight, pondering how the world could go mad in a matter of hours. Neither Quinn nor Riley would speak to him on the drive back to the house, and Quinn had fallen asleep almost immediately upon their arrival. Riley sat, unmoving, in a chair near her sister's bed, as she had all afternoon.

Alaric was still missing.

He'd sent Bastien on patrol, to see what he could sniff out, while Christophe used his freakishly genius ways on the internet to hack into any local media networks he could find.

Ven had gone to track down a contact in the local shape-shifter population, Alexios with him. Maybe there would be news of what exactly a local pack of wolves was doing messing with Reisen and his men.

Although, knowing Reisen, it was the other way around. The House of Mycenae wasn't exactly subtle about their feelings that the only good shape-shifter was a dead one.

Brennan paced by on the grass outside the window, standing guard, and sketched a salute toward him, then pointed up. So Justice had taken up a position on the roof. Good.

Denal sat on the floor outside Riley and Quinn's room, daggers at the ready. He was taking his duty as Riley's self-professed champion and defender very seriously.

Even, to Conlan's amusement and consternation, as regarded his prince.

"She doesn't want to speak to you now, my lord," Denal had said, white-faced—probably at his own audacity—but firm, standing in front of the door to the bedroom.

Conlan had nodded his head, acquiescing.

For the moment.

But he'd leaned close to his young warrior and spoken quietly. "You serve her well, Denal. But know this. If I wanted to go to her now, neither you nor any force of nature itself would stop me. Remember that in the future."

Denal, to his credit, hadn't backed down. But Conlan had heard the explosive exhalation of breath as he'd walked away from the room and its guard.

Conlan closed his eyes and tried to reach out to Riley, but

her mental shields were still locked into place. Then he sent a summoning on the shared Atlantean mental path.

Alaric, where are you? We need you, priest.

~~~~~

It was nearly nine-thirty by the time Quinn woke up. Denal, camped out at her door, had tried to persuade Riley to eat something several times, but the sight of Quinn lying near death in the middle of some kind of supernatural über-battle had ruined her appetite.

Quinn lay sprawled out on her back, arms flung wide, the same way she'd always slept. As Riley stared at her, Quinn's eyes fluttered open.

"Riley?" she whispered, voice hoarse. "Where are we?"

"You fell asleep in the car, Quinn," Riley said, leaning forward to grasp her sister's hand. "We're in a house that belongs to Conlan's brother, Ven."

Quinn squeezed her hand—a brief pressure—and struggled to sit up. She looked down at her shoulder. She still wore the ruined shirt she'd had on when she'd been shot. "What happened, Riley? Who was that man, and how did he heal my shoulder?"

"I'm not exactly sure how he heals, Quinn. His name is Alaric, and he—"

"Alaric," Quinn broke in, eyes widening. "I knew it. Somehow, I knew that was his name. It's almost as if he talked to me when he was inside me."

"Inside you?"

"Yes. I could feel him working inside me to heal my shoulder. It was the strangest thing. Almost as if a ball of energy—blues and greens and silver, but with darkness shadowing it—was literally traveling inside my skin."

Quinn shook her head, then shoved dark curls out of her eyes. "Or am I just losing my mind?" she asked, anguish clear in her eyes.

"You're not losing your mind. I've been through almost the same experience with Conlan. There is something amazingly different about these Atlanteans. I can reach into their emotions on a level far deeper than I've ever done with anyone except you, Quinn."

Riley jumped up and started pacing the length of the small room. "And they can feel my emotions, as well, to a certain extent. This is almost unbelievable, but Conlan can read my mind, at times. He . . . I don't know how to describe it. It's beyond anything I've ever felt."

Riley turned toward Quinn at the sound of her low whistle. Quinn stared at her, searching her face with her gaze. "What's that tone in your voice, Riley? I haven't heard that tone from you since college. No, maybe never. Do you have feelings for this guy?"

Riley's face burned, and she ducked her head, but not before Quinn had seen it. "I don't know. I don't know what I feel, except that I've been inside his mind, Quinn. And I've never seen anything like it—I've never *felt* anything like it."

She crossed the room to sit on the edge of the bed next to her sister. "He saved me. He saved me from some thugs on the beach who would have raped me or worse. Then he saved me—well, we sort of saved each other—from a band of vampires who went batshit on my front lawn."

Riley grabbed Quinn's hand again, held on as if to a lifeline. "I've seen inside him. The pain—I don't know how anyone could have survived the torture I saw in his memories."

"Another stray animal you want to bring home?"

"Want to bring home," Riley mused. "The *want* part is certainly true. I—I can't believe I'm admitting this, but we have this amazing animal attraction thing going on. I want him more than I've ever wanted anything or anyone in my life."

She shook her head. "It's completely nuts."

Quinn pulled her hand out of Riley's and grabbed her sister by the shoulders, then gave her a little shake. "Are you—and I ask this in the nicest possible way—out of your tiny little mind? How long have you known this guy? It seems like I would've heard from you a little earlier, if you'd been dating Mr. Hotshot Atlantis Dude for very long."

Riley shook her head. "We're not even dating. I only met him last night. And yet I know him more than I've ever known anyone. Except for you. And when we're together, well—"

Quinn whistled again. "You don't even have to say it, little sister. I can tell by the color your face just turned that you and he set off some serious heat. Did you sleep with him?"

"No! I didn't! I just met him. But, well." Riley bit her lip, considering. "Okay, here it is. If I'd had a chance, I probably would have. I've never felt that kind of attraction to any man. Ever."

She stopped midthought. "Wait a minute! Forget my non-existent sex life. We're talking about *you* here. What on earth were you doing with a band of shape-shifters? And what is this tough-guy act? It's not like you're . . . I mean—"

"I know what you mean. Poor, fragile Quinn, who every-body always has to protect," Quinn said bitterly. "Well, some-times you have to grow up. And I didn't bother to let anybody know that I'd changed, because being weak and useless is a good cover. Think Zorro or the Scarlet Pimpernel."

"But when . . . what . . ." Riley's voice trailed off. She wasn't sure how to ask her sister what needed to be asked.

She wasn't sure she wanted to hear the answer.

"Later. I'll tell you about it later. Maybe." Quinn stared at her for a long moment, then swung her legs off the bed and bent to pull on her boots. "You're better than I ever was at measuring the character of a person by their emotions, Riley. So I guess I'll take your word about this Conlan. But only on the condition that I get to test him myself."

A knock on the door saved Riley from responding. "Go away, Denal. I told you I don't want any food," she called.

The door swung open, framing Conlan in the doorway. "It's not Denal, and as much as I think you *should* eat some-thing, it's more important that we talk. I need to know what your sister knows."

Riley tried to see behind him to the hallway. "Where is Denal? I thought he'd never leave."

Conlan shrugged. "I think Ven might be holding him up-side down out a window right about now. He seems to have forgotten that I'm his high prince, in his zeal to serve you."

Only the hint of the smile at the corners of his lips gave away Conlan's reluctant amusement at his warrior's defection.

Before Riley could respond, Quinn stood up and strode over to stand toe to toe with Conlan. "Prince, huh? If you've pulled a fast one on my baby sister, you will answer to me. And I'm the type of girl who will kick your Atlantean ass."

With that, faster than Riley had ever seen her move, Quinn

placed her hands on Conlan's temples. "Let me in, let me in, little fishy," she said in a singsong voice.

Conlan, staring at Riley over Quinn's head, never moved. Riley knew how fast he could move. He could have snapped Quinn's hold in a heartbeat. Heck, he could have snapped Quinn's *arms* in a heartbeat.

But, instead, he smiled at Riley, then closed his eyes. There was utter silence in the room for nearly a minute. Then Quinn dropped her hands and stumbled back and away from Conlan.

"Who are you? How could you possibly survive that kind of torture?" She kept backing away from him, until she reached the bed and dropped down onto it next to Riley.

"Quinn, are you all right?" Riley reached out to her sister with her emotions. But, for once, she couldn't reach her. She jumped up to face Conlan. "What did you do to her?"

"No, it's what did *you* do to *him*?" Quinn said from behind her. Riley turned to look at her sister, but Quinn's attention was focused on Conlan like a laser beam. "Somehow, Riley, you're inside his soul."

Heat swirled through Riley. She looked into Conlan's eyes, opening her emotions to him. Feeling the truth of her sister's words.

Not quite ready to let him see that he was inside *her* as well.

Footsteps thudded down the hall toward them. Ven's voice preceded his entrance. "Conlan, we've got a problem. Or maybe I should rephrase that. Hell, we've got a buttload of problems. This one is new though."

"Consider me to be another problem, Atlantean," Quinn snarled. "Because until I find out why your people attacked mine, I'm going to be all over your ass."

Ven looked Quinn up and down and grinned. "Honey, I'd consider that the best part of my week. Hell, maybe my entire fucking year."

An icy voice swept into the room an instant before Alaric shimmered into a hard, menacing presence between Quinn and Ven. "I bid you fair warning, Vengeance. If you touch her, I will destroy you."

Riley jumped up, with some thought of protecting her sister from Alaric, who was the scariest man she'd ever seen.

A man who just happened to have magic powers of death going for him.

Inexplicably, Quinn started to laugh. The sound shivered through the room, high and wild. "Welcome to the tea party, fish face. I have a strange feeling that you and I need to talk, especially after you practically had your hand on my boob," she said, still smiling that eerie smile. "At the very least, it seems like you owe me dinner."

Riley looked at them all—Conlan, Ven, Alaric, and her sister—and slowly shook her head. "Has the whole world gone insane?"

Chapter 22

Reisen limped down the stairs of the abandoned warehouse Micah had located for them. Thank Poseidon that the Trident was safe, still strapped to his back under his coat.

He'd been lucky.

Luckier than five of his men. Five warriors slain, and for what? To protect a human population stupid enough to welcome the shape-shifters and the bloodsuckers with bared necks?

The only possible glimmer of light in the black fucking tunnel of his day was that there hadn't been any mention of the battle in the media. Of course, the furry-assed controlled the media since they'd taken over CNN and the broadcast networks, so he guessed it wasn't enormously surprising.

Still, he decided to take it as a point for his side. After all, Alaric couldn't follow a news story that he never heard.

The priest would be tracking the news. Alaric would make it his life's mission to find a way to track Reisen down and separate his balls from his body.

Slowly.

He glanced at the glowing numbers on the face of his father's silver pocket watch. It was ironic that the only remembrance he carried of his father was the one rendered unstable by the powers he channeled.

Watches didn't like the powers of the elements, much. He pulled his cell phone out of his pants pocket, grimacing at the blank screen.

Not much machinery did, come to think of it.

But he wouldn't need to confirm his appointment with the Platoist Society. It wasn't a meeting they were likely to forget.

And when the Trident was whole and in his control, the five he'd lost today would be avenged.

His father, too.

The landwalkers would burn.

~~~

Conlan positioned the players in his impromptu meeting quite deliberately. Alaric leaned against the wall on one side of the room.

Riley sat with Quinn on a couch directly across the room from Alaric.

He and Ven took the other two walls, so it looked like some weird game of four-player Atlantean chess, using real game pieces.

Come to think of it, he'd felt a hell of a lot like a pawn ever since his return.

That shit was over.

Quinn stretched her legs out and crossed one boot over the other, in a clear display of studied nonchalance. She was every bit as tough as her sister but—unlike Riley—Quinn knew she was a hard-ass. She *owned* it.

And for a few seconds, when he'd allowed her inside his mind, he'd felt the black stain on her own soul. She had secrets, Quinn Dawson did.

Dangerous ones.

"Are we talking or just staring at each other all night?" Quinn drawled. "Not that you aren't all a fine bunch of eye candy, but I've got things to do, people to kill."

Riley stared at her sister in disbelief. Conlan sent a light touch to Riley's emotions, checking for any false note.

No, nothing. She was completely bewildered by Quinn's presence in this disaster.

Conlan folded his arms over his chest. "Interesting choice of words. Perhaps you're ready to tell us what you were doing with those shape-shifters you call 'your' wolves."

Alaric said nothing, merely stared at Quinn, unblinking, eyes glowing a hot green.

Quinn laughed. "Yeah. Right. Well, you show me yours and I'll show you mine, as they say."

"Hey, what exactly do you want to see? I'm game," Ven said.

At the words, the room trembled, as if an undersea fault line threatened. Conlan felt the icy wind shear past his face toward his brother, and knew what caused the temblor.

Or, rather, *who*.

"Cut it out, priest," he growled. "Whatever you're playing at, we don't have time for this shit. We need to put our respective cards on the table, now."

It was as if he hadn't spoken.

"You want me to show you mine?" Alaric stalked across the room toward Quinn and Riley, but stopped a half dozen paces away, before Conlan or Ven had a chance to move. "Well, how about this?"

Eyes glowing hotter than Conlan had ever seen, Alaric casually lifted first one, then the second, of his hands into the air. In tandem with the motions, Quinn and Riley were lifted off the couch until they were levitating inches from the ceiling, still in seated positions, resting on glowing balls of blue-green light.

"How's that?" Alaric demanded. "Or how about this?"

He sliced both hands in a downward motion, then raised then, palms up, muttering something under his breath. The women plunged down toward the floor, then a fountain of water caught them and gracefully lifted them both back onto the couch.

With another abrupt hand movement, the water disappeared. Neither Riley nor Quinn had a drop on them.

Riley gasped a little. "Wow, that was pretty . . . that was—"

"Cute parlor trick, fish face," Quinn said. Then she feigned an enormous yawn. "Are we done with the smoke and mirrors? Or, excuse me, that was *water* and mirrors, right?"

In the space of a single heartbeat, Alaric was lifting her off the couch and up against him. "Don't push me, female. We would both regret it."

But it wasn't anger that Conlan heard in Alaric's voice. It was an almost-pleading desperation.

When Quinn answered, her voice was so quiet that Conlan could barely make out her words. When he did, they didn't make any sense.

"Forget whatever you think you saw in me, beautiful one," she murmured. "I am ruined."

What she did next sent both Conlan and Ven rushing across the room to protect her. Because she lifted her hands and put them on Alaric's face.

A sound Conlan had never heard before issued from the priest's throat, a hard, choked sound filled with soul-destroying pain. A shock wave of a sound that literally smashed Conlan and his brother backward, landing them hard on the floor.

In the seconds it took for him to catch his breath and look up, Alaric was gone. Quinn stood alone, hands still frozen in place where Alaric's face had been.

Tears running down her own.

Riley jumped up and put her arms around her sister. "Maybe we should put this off until the morning," she said, glaring at Conlan. "I think Quinn has been through enough today. We've both been through enough. I need to take her home, Conlan."

Before Conlan could utter a word of protest, support came from an unexpected source. Quinn wiped the tears from her cheeks with the backs of her hands, then cleared her throat.

"No," she said. "I think you should stay with them."

∼∽

The four of them sat around the kitchen table, Riley and Quinn holding mugs of hot, sweet tea. Conlan and Ven each had a beer. Conlan sat near enough to Riley that she could reach out and touch him if she wanted to.

It's not like she *needed* to touch him.

Much.

Most of the other men had all stopped by, trailing in by ones and twos, some bringing food and beer, some bringing news.

None bringing results. Reisen had vanished.

Riley had tried to smile at each of them, especially Denal,

who'd kneeled in front of her and presented an armload of flowers, then backed out of the room, careful to maintain a safe distance from Conlan and Ven.

Ven had made some crack about Denal's schoolboy crush, but nobody'd even mustered up a smile.

Now they sat, each of them lost in his or her own private thoughts. When Justice appeared, it was almost a relief.

"So, the gang's all here," he said in that smart-ass way he had. Of course, anybody who could carry off a waist-length blue braid worn over a sword strapped to his back probably could be as much of a smart-ass as he wanted.

She'd seen what he could do with that sword.

"My lawn will never be the same," she muttered.

Quinn looked up from contemplating her mug and caught sight of Justice. "You!" she gasped. "I thought you were an urban legend."

Ven leaned back in his chair, balancing it on two legs. "Right. The nutball axe murderer who hangs out at Lover's Lane, and Justice. Makes sense, really, when you think about it. Both of them give you a case of the ugly creepies, right?"

Justice ignored the ribbing and focused in on Quinn. "What exactly have you heard?"

"Oh, defender of the weak, modern-day Robin Hood, blah blah blah. You're a little hard to miss," Quinn returned, sweeping her gaze from his boots all the way up the six and a half feet or so to the top of his blue-plaited head.

Justice bowed slightly. "You, too, would be difficult to miss. Your fury and grief burn brightly enough to light up the city. You might wish to learn from your sister the technique of shielding your emotions."

With that, he left the room, long strides eating up the floor, leaving Quinn scowling at his back.

Riley thought it was past time for her to intervene. "What is going on, Quinn? I'm getting the feeling that you're not an administrative assistant for an insurance company, after all."

Quinn's laugh sounded rusty, as if it had been a long time since she'd found anything funny. "No, not for an insurance company. Like I said before, I need to know what the deal is with the Atlanteans before I tell you anything."

She pinned Conlan with a stare. "What side are you coming down on?"

"Side of what?" Riley asked. "What are you talking about?"

"Side of the revolution, baby sister."

Riley sucked in a breath. Sure, she'd heard rumors of a revolution against the rapid encroachment of the supernatural species into human society and government. But she'd stayed out of it. She wasn't political—she had enough to do just trying to keep her clients healthy and fed.

And alive.

Conlan nodded slightly. "Okay. Here's as much of the truth as I'm willing to tell you right now, and I do it on the condition that neither of you share this information with anyone."

Ven's chair came down on all four legs with a bang. "You can't do this, Conlan. You can't—"

"Riley has a right to know, since we are taking her home with us. And her sister must therefore know, as well."

Riley felt the nerves in her neck go board rigid. "You said that before. Funny, I don't seem to remember being asked to go anywhere."

Conlan took her hand in his and squeezed it. "Do you trust me?"

"I—" She paused, thought back to the glimpses she'd had into his memories; into his soul. "Yes. I trust you. This *aknasha* thing we have between us—it may be overwhelming my common sense, but I do know that I can trust you. But where is home? Are you really talking about the lost continent of Atlantis?"

Ven snorted. "We were never lost. Just hiding from you fools."

Quinn leaned forward, resting her folded arms on the table. "I'd watch who you called fools if I were you, fish boy."

He grinned. "Wanna check me for gills?"

"Enough! Can we quit with the bickering and just get on with it?" Riley asked.

Conlan nodded. "Yes. We're from the continent of Atlantis. More than eleven thousand years ago, the Seven Isles rode the surface of the waters as do your own lands. Our civilization and technology were far superior to that of the humans of the time, but we shared such knowledge of the sciences and the arts as we deemed appropriate."

"So you condescended to help out us poor lowly humans?" Quinn sneered.

"Quinn. Not helping," Riley murmured, and her sister rolled her eyes, but subsided.

"As often happens, the humans with whom Atlantis had always enjoyed a peaceful coexistence became greedy," Conlan continued. "Not all; not even most. But a few corrupt ones in power. Enough to push the idea of conquering our lands and taking for themselves what was ours."

"Yeah, like especially the gold and anything of value," Ven growled.

"We could have worked it out. According to the ancient scrolls, we were on the verge of working it out. But that's when the vamps decided to get involved," Conlan said.

Riley shuddered. "You had vampires even back then?"

"The bloodsuckers have been around since the beginning, when the god Chaos bedded his twisted daughter Anubisa and began the whole foul—" Ven lapsed into a lyrical-sounding language that wasn't the least bit recognizable to Riley.

"They may be *aknasha*, but they don't understand ancient Atlantean, Ven," Conlan observed, a wry grin quirking up the edges of his lips. Then the humor faded from his face and an expression so terrifyingly haunted took its place that Riley squeezed his hand, hard, to try to pull him out of whatever hell he saw in his mind.

It seemed to help, a little, but Riley still saw the stamp of a predator on the fierce cast of his face. She was careful not to reach out and touch his emotions.

She knew she didn't want to visit whatever he saw in his mind.

"Anubisa," he ground out. "The unholy union of Chaos and Anubisa, the goddess of death. Their offspring were the ancestors of all bloodsuckers. Anubisa is a vamp herself but, as near as we can figure out, she feeds on negative emotion more than blood. The more passionate, the better."

"Like the pain of torture," Riley whispered, suddenly understanding what she'd seen and felt in Conlan's memories.

He pulled his hand away from hers and smoothed his expression to a mask of calm.

A *false* mask of calm, most likely. How could he have survived that? How could anyone?

With the thought came despair. "How can we defeat somebody who thinks she's a goddess?"

"She *is* a goddess," Ven said.

Riley shook her head. "Not to me. I'm monotheistic and only recognize one God. Not that I'm disagreeing with your beliefs in any way, but I have to have faith that she's not all-powerful. In any event, if she has godlike powers, we're in trouble."

"You forget, we are also led by a god. Poseidon's power exceeds that of Anubisa," Ven pointed out.

Rage tore through her. "Well, where the hell was he when his own prince was being tortured nearly to death?" Riley shouted, shoving her chair back to stand. "Where was your stupid sea god then?"

Conlan pulled her into his arms for a brief hug, then smoothly pulled her to a seat on his lap, as if he'd been doing so for years.

"I am honored that you would defy Poseidon himself in your defense of me, *mi amara aknasha*," he murmured into her hair.

The feel of his breath on her ear stirred something down low in her abdomen, and her thigh muscles clenched. If Quinn and Ven hadn't been sitting right there, both of them staring with openmouthed disbelief, she would have turned in his lap and planted some major lip-lock on Conlan.

She might do it, anyway.

Quinn's eyes narrowed. "Fine. So big problems with the humans, and then what?"

Ven answered this time. "Then the gods got into a big stink of a fight, and the Cataclysm happened. Big, 'earth itself might be destroyed' kind of catastrophic shit that happens when a bunch of children start fighting over their toys."

Conlan's voice was a rumble in his chest against Riley's back. "Though my brother edges close to blasphemy, he is essentially correct. Atlantis was forced under the sea to protect itself, both from the humans who threatened and from the battle between the gods. First magic, then a mix of magic and technology have shielded us from discovery for these many years."

Riley, suddenly feeling shy, slid off Conlan's lap and back onto her own chair. "But you've been coming up to the surface all this time?"

"No, not always. It took time to learn the secrets of travel between our land and the surface. But we had sworn the oath as Warriors of Poseidon. The warriors of that time would stop at nothing to find a way to return to guard humans from the increasing vampire and shape-shifter threat."

Conlan drained his beer, put the bottle back on the table with some force. "It's our job to keep you safe, even when you do your best to hinder us."

Quinn toyed with her mug and then seemed to reach a decision. Shoving her curls out of her eyes with one hand, she started to speak. "Okay. I've been scanning you both and, for what it's worth, your emotions tell me that you're giving us the truth. I say for what it's worth because, if you really are Atlantean and an entirely separate species—"

She looked up for confirmation and Conlan nodded.

"Then it's possible that my much-prized abilities to scan emotion are worth precisely nothing when it comes to you. Are your emotions even remotely similar to ours?"

Ven started to respond, but she held up a hand. "No, don't bother. It feels true to me, and I have to go with my gut instinct, or I have nothing. And if I start doubting my gut now, the game, as they say, is up."

Riley put a hand on her sister's arm to confirm what her senses were telling her. Quinn was telling a truth that was very painful for her. Riley's nerve endings flinched back from the anguish underlying Quinn's words.

"It's okay, Quinn. Whatever you need to say. I'm right here," she murmured, sending waves of reassurance and love through their personal sister link.

"Well, tall, dark, and ugly over there called us fools. He's right. Not all of us, but enough of us hid under a rock and let change happen without trying to fight it," Quinn began, voice flat.

Riley winced at the echo of her earlier thoughts. Maybe Quinn thought she was a fool, too. "Not being political or marching on Washington doesn't make a person a fool, Quinn," she said. "Some of us try to make a difference on a local level."

Quinn grabbed her in a brief hug. "I wasn't talking about you, honey. You give twenty-four-seven to those losers you work so desperately to save. I'm talking about the people who sit on their fat asses and do nothing while vamps take over our government."

"They're not losers," Riley said quietly. "They're people who never had the basics to improve their lives. I try to help with that."

"I'm sorry. I know you do. You're right, they're not losers. And you're pretty much a fucking saint to do what you do. But my path is a little different."

Ven suddenly whistled, staring at Quinn with admiration evident in his gaze. "Takes a street fighter to recognize another one. You're in the rebellion."

Quinn inclined her head, unsmiling. "Yeah. And telling you this could get me dead in a hurry, so consider it an even trade for what you told us about Atlantis."

She paused, sucked in a deep breath. "I'm not just *in* the rebellion. I'm one of its leaders. And those wolves your pals killed? They were on my team. So I'm responsible for their deaths."

Quinn snapped her mouth closed when Brennan walked into the room, staring at him with suspicion.

"It's okay, Quinn, this is Brennan," Riley reassured her sister. "He—"

"He has a nifty trick of burying his emotions way, *way* down, doesn't he?" Quinn said, eyes narrowing. "I almost didn't feel them at all, dude. Nice hostility, by the way. How'd you manage the emotional block?"

Chapter 23

Riley stared through the window into the night. "I can't believe she left. I can't believe my sister, the *rebel leader*, just
took off into the night on an *urgent mission*. I keep thinking
I'm trapped in a B movie, and I'm going to wake up any
minute."

Conlan couldn't stay away from her any longer. He'd
watched her courage as she'd learned and accepted everything
he and her sister had thrown at her that day.

It had been far too long since he'd touched her, and his
hands craved the feel of her skin. In two strides, he crossed the
bedroom and wrapped his arms around her. "I'm so sorry, *mi
amara*. I hate that you were forced into this rude awakening to
the ugly reality of what's going on now."

She pulled away and turned to face him, hands fisted on
her hips. "Ugly reality? You want to talk to me about ugly reality? My clients routinely kill each other in their homes.
Their babies are born addicted to crack and then sometimes
starve to death before I can get them any help at all, thanks to
Senator 'I'm a master vampire' Barnes and his slash-and-burn
job on social services for humans. So don't tell *me* about ugly
reality."

He leaned against the wall, forcing himself to stay back from her, in spite of his body's demands that he pull her close again. "Children are often the first casualties of war."

She spun on her heel and walked away from him, then sank down to sit on the bed. Putting her head in her hands, she moaned. Then she looked him in the eyes. "When did it become a war? Nobody declared a war, not that I know of, and yet suddenly I'm on the front lines."

He crossed to her, sat next to her. Everything in him rebelled against the words that he forced out, but she'd earned his respect with her courage.

She deserved her freedom.

"If you want out, just say the word. I believe that your empath power may be enormously helpful to us in our battle to protect your people. That is the truth."

She said nothing, merely gazed at him, unmoving. Her emotions shielded from him.

"But this is also the truth," he rasped. "Somehow, I have feelings for you beyond anything I ever dreamed possible. Even now, my body is raging at me to take you. To strip you bare and have you underneath me on this bed."

She gasped a little, but didn't move away. Conlan chose to take that as a hopeful sign.

"I need you, Riley. Yes, Atlantis needs you. We need to study this power you have and see if we can duplicate it. If Quinn hadn't convinced us that her mission was so urgent, I would have tried to persuade her to come with us, too."

"She felt emotions from Brennan, Conlan. That has to give him hope."

"May it not be false hope. Brennan deserves better than what life has doled out to him."

He tried to focus. Tried not to be distracted by the scent of her. By the desire swamping him. "The *aknasha* ability—we hope to discover if it can be used against us. Or maybe used *for* us. But, in spite of this need—*both* of these needs—in spite of my duty as future king of the Seven Isles, I would let you go."

He clenched his hands together to keep from forcibly keeping her with him, prayed that he'd keep it together until she left. He was a man and had enough dignity to want that.

Not that he wasn't close to begging.

"Once I would have taken. Now, knowing you, I ask. But you need to tell me now. You need to stand up and walk out of this room right now. I'll ask Ven to take you anywhere you want—somewhere safe. But it has to be *now*."

He finally turned to look at her, his body clenched so tightly he thought he might snap. Burning with need, yet icy with fear that she would go. "Because if you stay, I'll take it as a yes. Yes to Atlantis, to our cause, but—most of all—yes to me."

She reached up to touch his face with one trembling hand. "Conlan—"

He yanked his head away from her. "Don't you get it? My self-control is gone," he snarled. "All I've got left is a bare shred of dignity over a furnace of *want*. You have to get the hell away from me *now*."

He jumped up off the bed, away from temptation. Away from the woman who was, somehow, everything he'd ever wanted. He closed his eyes and stood, head bent, shoulders heaving with the effort it cost him to keep from stretching her out on the bed and taking her mouth with his own.

Taking her body.

Finally, *finally*, he heard her light footsteps as she began to walk across the floor. The footsteps that would carry her away from him. He flinched as a pain greater than any Anubisa had ever administered washed through him, searing the heart he'd thought gone forever.

Then the footsteps stopped.

And she stood in front of him, her eyes enormous in her pale face.

"I'm not going anywhere, Conlan. My answer is yes."

Riley looked up at Conlan, aware deep in her heart that she'd just made the most important choice of her life. He stared down at her, eyes widening, then threw his head back, muscles in his neck straining, as he gulped in air like a drowning man.

Then he exploded into motion. He wrapped his arms around her and yanked her into his body so quickly she let out a little sound when her breasts pressed into his chest. He tightened one arm around her waist and lifted the other to wrap his palm around the back of her head.

"Thank you, *mi amara*," he whispered, his lips inches from her own. "Thank you for this gift."

She almost had time to worry—it had been so *long*, she didn't really *know* him—and then his mouth came down on hers. And, as his emotions opened to her, she realized that she'd never known *any* man so well as she knew this one.

She wanted him with every ounce of her being. His lips were soft and firm and exactly right, and he kissed with the passion of a man who was starving for her. She pressed closer to him, desperate to feel all of him against her, wanting more and more and more.

Conlan pulled back from her a little, his breathing harsh. He'd known that she tasted like warmth and sunlight and sweet, clean passion. But now she tasted like something even better.

She tasted like she was *his*.

He crushed his mouth to hers again, needing to feel her compliance. Her surrender. Her acceptance of his desire and his need. "Now," he said, hearing the pleading in his own voice, not caring. "Please. Now."

"Yes," she said, curling her arms around his neck. "Yes, please. Now."

He swept her up off the ground and carried her to the bed, kissing her the entire time. In seconds, he was locking the door and then back at the bed. He stripped off his shirt on the way, desperate to feel her skin on his.

She lay there, her hair spread across the pillows, his fantasy come true. He wanted to weep from the joy of it.

Wanted to roar out his possession to the world.

He did neither. Simply touched her. Finally, *finally*, touched her.

Riley trembled when Conlan eased his body down on the bed next to hers. Somehow his chest and shoulders seemed even bigger without his shirt. He was a wall of muscle, but she'd seen past the proud warrior exterior to the man inside.

When he touched her, fingers gently stroking her cheek, then her neck, she noticed that she wasn't the only one trembling.

The realization sent her reeling that final step over the edge of any remaining inhibition. This big, tough warrior who could stand and battle vampires and shape-shifters and anything else that went bump in the night wanted her so badly his hands were shaking.

She pulled his head down to hers and smiled. "Kiss me. Kiss me and make me feel safe again," she whispered.

The heat of the blue-green flame burning in his eyes scorched her nerve endings, sending warmth and wetness straight to her center. Her breasts felt fuller, tighter, as though they wanted the weight of him against them.

She arched up against him and, before he had a chance to obey her request, she took control.

She kissed *him*. Softly, gently.

His scent surrounded her. Spicy and warm and *male*, and suddenly gentle was *not* on the agenda.

She moaned and kissed him, lips capturing his, tongue diving into his mouth. She wrapped one leg around his legs and pulled him down to her, wanting, *craving*, needing to feel his hardness against her.

Conlan thought he might possibly have died and gone to the mountain of the gods. Riley was setting him on fire, pulling him into her and kissing him like she was starving and he was dessert.

Which gave him ideas.

Really, really great ideas.

He pulled away from her lips and kissed a path across her cheek and down to her neck, where he bit and suckled at her, reveling in her throaty moans. With one hand, he pushed at her shirt, moving it up to bare her warm belly, sliding his fingers further up until he cupped the underside of her breast.

She gasped at the touch and arched into his hand. "Touch me, please touch me, Conlan."

He rolled over and pulled her up, yanking her shirt over her head, then kissed her again, his tongue plunging inside to claim her mouth. It was a hard kiss, a branding kiss.

Mine. Mine. Always mine.

The thought came from so far inside him he didn't recognize the source. A primal urge to mark her, to claim her, to carry her off to his palace and never let her go shook his body with the force of it. He knew she could feel it, because her emotions suddenly registered shock through her empathic connection to him.

Then she smiled beneath his lips and sent waves of acceptance to him. She was feeling strong, sure in her uniquely feminine power over him, and she let him know it.

His body tightened at the feeling and the colors of her arousal in his body, in his brain. His cock hardened to the point of pain inside his suddenly too-tight pants. Pulling away from her mouth, he looked at the round and perfect breasts filling out the bits of lace that covered them. He wanted his mouth on them.

With one hand, he worked at the tiny clasp, groaning in frustration when it didn't come undone immediately. She laughed and captured his hand in her own.

"What's the matter? The big, bad warrior can't figure out a simple bra clasp?" she teased, voice husky and warmth shining from her eyes, her happiness sparkling like fairy dust in his mind.

"The big, bad warrior is going to bite it off with his teeth if you don't help," he replied. Then he bent down and took her nipple in his mouth, right through the fabric, and she arched up off the bed, moaning.

With his other hand, he caressed her other breast, cupping and squeezing it. Rubbing his thumb over her nipple in rhythm with suckling its twin. Her moans grew more frantic, and she clutched at his back while her head whipped back and forth on the pillow. "Oh, please, oh, please."

He released her nipple from his mouth, blew warm air on it, and watched the shudder rip through her body. "Please what, Riley? Say it."

"Please. I need you." She put her hands on his head and urged him up toward her mouth. But he wasn't done yet. He moved his mouth to her other breast and replaced his thumb with his mouth. Hardened even more when her body jerked up against his and she rubbed her core against him, wordlessly pleading. He gently bit her nipple and she gasped, then moaned out his name.

"Now, damn you, now. I need you inside me now," she said, breathing harshly, eddies of passion and sharp, spiking desire flowing from her emotions and through him.

"Yes," he ground out. "Yes, I'm going to take you now."

Riley stared up at the man who'd driven her nearly insane

with wanting, almost not recognizing him beneath the ferocious and primal need stamped on his face.

Maybe she wasn't the only one going out of her mind, here.

He rolled over and bent to throw off his boots and socks, then stood and stripped his pants off in one violent motion. When he stood before her, proud and tall and gloriously naked, she caught her breath. "You're beautiful," she whispered, reaching out to touch one muscled thigh. His erection, as big as the rest of him, strained, jerking a little, at her touch so near to it.

She wanted to taste it.

He laughed a little. "I am a warrior. Scarred and worn, definitely not beautiful. But *you* . . . you make the gods themselves weep with envy at your beauty."

He reached for her hands, pulled her to stand next to him. Then his fingers were at her waist, unfastening her jeans, and she was suddenly as naked as he.

For an instant, she was shy. Then he put his hands on her, and she was frantic with need. "Touch me, Conlan. Kiss me and touch me everywhere. I want your hands on me."

It was his turn to groan, and he captured her head in both hands and swooped down to kiss her with such possession and fire that her heart seemed to skip a beat or two. She caught at his shoulders, trying to hold herself up on knees gone weak.

He ran his hands down her body, lightly touching her arms, then her hips, then stroking up the plane of her back. She trembled and pushed against him, loving the feeling of his hardness against her. Wanting it inside her.

As if he could hear her, he ran his hands down the front of her body, cupping her breasts on the way. She moaned again, wanting him to stop torturing her.

Wanting him never to stop.

Wanting *more*.

His hands continued their path, now stroking down her belly and then, finally, one traced a path through the curls between her legs and lightly across the heat of her.

He raised his face to look at her, fierce triumph in his smile. "You're wet for me, Riley. You're *drenched* for me."

"I . . . *oh*—" Before she could form the words to answer

him, he drove two fingers inside her, and she lost the ability to speak.

She clenched around his fingers and nearly cried out at the pleasure of it. "Oh, yes, Conlan. Yes, please, more."

Conlan sent a prayer of thanks to whatever gods would hear him. She was so responsive to him, so hot, so wet. As she tightened around his fingers, he thought he might lose all control and ejaculate before he ever entered the sweet wetness of her body.

He'd never felt passion with this crashing force before.

Damaged goods, princeling. The hated voice whispered through him, stopping him, freezing him—but only for an instant.

Then Riley opened her eyes and stared straight into his soul. "No. *No.* She's not here—she'll never hurt you again. Don't let her in, Conlan."

She kissed him, deliberately clenched her warmth around his fingers again. "Feel *me*. I'm real. I'm here. Don't let her win."

Something burst in his heart. "Yes, yes, *mi amara*. You are here for me. You are mine. She is less than nothing," he rasped out, words fervent as a prayer.

He withdrew his fingers, and Riley whimpered a little, but then he swept her up into his arms and dropped her on the bed. She blinked, seemed to come back from some far distance, and shook her head a little. "We . . . I . . . protection. I'm safe, but—"

He understood instantly, since her feelings were open to him. "No, we are immune. I can't even catch a cold from you, nor you from me, my beautiful one. And we cannot produce children without the ritual of fertility being blessed by Poseidon."

She nodded, feeling the truth of his words in his emotions. Then she held her arms up to him and smiled with such sensuous promise that his knees turned to water.

As he dove down to cover her body with his own, he opened his heart to her. Threw off any remaining emotional shields, so she could feel the great gift she'd given him.

Then he pulled her knees up on either side of his hips and drove into her all the way to the hilt in one stroke, roaring out his pleasure.

Gasping out her name.

Resting his forehead against hers, he labored for breath. "Mine, Riley. Say it. You're mine."

She caught his face in her hands and drew him down to her mouth. "I'm yours, Conlan."

She kissed him with all the passion he could feel in her soul. She looked up at him, blue eyes warm and glowing, and smiled at him again. "And you're mine, too."

Riley's body arched to meet him. The emotion that washed through him and into her was a revelation. Awe . . . astonishment. Simple gratitude.

He had never belonged to anyone. Had never been wanted just for himself since he was a child.

His gratitude transformed into a tsunami of passion, tempered with warmth, and he shared it all with her through their bond. She shuddered underneath him, and something in him seemed to snap.

"I'm sorry, Riley, but I don't have any more control," he managed, grinding out the words. "I'm going to take you now, and it's going to be hard and fast. I promise I'll try for finesse later, but—"

She held a finger up to his lips and smiled, feminine power shining in her eyes. "Less talking. More action."

With a shout of joy, he pulled back and thrust into her again, his body catching the rhythm that was older than even Atlantis. Older than the gods themselves.

She arched into him in time with his thrusts and he rode her, stroked her, thrust into her again and again while he felt her body tightening around him and the tension building and building inside her.

Riley had never felt anything like it before. The heat and slick tension, the coiling electricity of his body pumping inside her, the hard muscles working under her fingers, the glow in his eyes showing her that he was loving every minute of it as much as she did.

It was all driving her over the edge. Every nerve ending in her body sang. The pressure climbed in a starburst crescendo until she exploded, free-falling into space, fingers digging into his shoulders to keep from cartwheeling off the edge of the world.

He tensed, muscles straining for control as she shuddered beneath him. As she came back to solid ground, she opened her eyes and stared up at him. "Conlan?"

He bent to press a gentle kiss on her lips, the stark outline of the muscles in his neck and shoulders telling her how much his restraint cost him.

"Riley, know this. As the ancient stories foretold, so it is true. I have waited for you, unknowing, all my life."

She stared at him, dazed by what his words and his emotions were telling her. "Are you saying—"

"I love you, Riley. You have captured my heart." With the words, something in his control seemed to break. He plunged into her once, twice, three times more, then drove into her with one final thrust that took him so deep she felt him against her womb. He threw his head back and yelled her name, exploding inside her. His mind, his heart, even his soul opened up to her more fully than they ever had before, and she felt herself dancing, twirling, reveling in his emotions.

In his passion.

And she exploded again, spiraling up and up into a place she'd never been before. Exploding again around him. Falling and falling . . .

Into *love*. Somehow, incredibly, she loved this man she'd only just met. This man she'd known forever.

Before she could catch her breath from the realization, she seamlessly wove her shields into place. It wasn't knowledge she was quite ready to share. Not even with Conlan.

Not yet. It was too soon. If you loved people, they left. She wasn't ready for him to leave.

Maybe not ever.

Conlan collapsed on top of her, holding himself up with his arms so he didn't crush her with his weight. The only sound in the room was panting. From both of them. After a minute or so, he stirred himself to move, rolling to the side, still holding her in his arms.

"Forget the mountain of the gods," he murmured. "I'd give that up for *this* in an instant."

Chapter 24

Riley woke up, warm, content, and deliciously sore in places that hadn't been sore in a very long time. For a moment she didn't open her eyes, perfectly happy to just lie there with Conlan's arms around her, her head nestled on his shoulder. Sunlight warming the room. Peace, even the illusory peace that she knew it was, warming her heart.

"I wondered when you might wake up, sleepy one."

She turned a little to smile up at him. "Sleepy one? It was after four when you finally let me rest."

The smile on his face was smug and undeniably male. She laughed, then pinched him.

"Hey!" He rolled over and caught her underneath him. "Do you know what the penalty is for assaulting the person of Atlantean royalty?"

She rolled her eyes. "Oh, poor baby. That tiny pinch? Surely the dungeon."

Conlan's eyes gleamed with mischief and something decidedly lascivious. "Oh, no. No dungeon for you. The penalty is hard labor. In my bedchambers."

Riley giggled. She couldn't help it. The sight of her proud

warrior, for once lighthearted and teasing, simply made her happy.

Conlan's heart stuttered at the sound of Riley's carefree laughter. He'd never stayed around after bedding a female. He'd always known he must avoid entanglements.

But Riley. *Riley.* Laughing, cheeks flushed with happiness and the aftermath of the night's passion. He'd felt her desire deepen—known when her emotions capitulated.

Still, she had not admitted it.

Not in words.

He grinned. "Maybe we'll have to work on that."

"Work on the idea of me doing hard labor? I think not," she said, squirming in an attempt to get away.

He lifted his arm, let her pull up on her elbows. Which put him exactly where he wanted to be, with his face level with her adorable little belly button.

He pounced, trapping her again, and licked across her warm skin.

"Hey! No fair," she said, still laughing.

"Be still," he murmured, then slid farther down in the bed, until he was staring at an intriguing triangle of red-gold curls.

"Conlan? What are you—"

Her voice cut off with a gasp as he moved his hand and traced through the curls with one finger. "I think your penalty is about to begin, *mi amara*. Lie still and accept your punishment."

He moved her thighs apart, trapping them in his hands.

"But—"

He swept his tongue along the path his finger had taken, and she moaned. He smiled. "I think the prisoner must behave, or the penalty will be extended."

Riley caught her breath as Conlan's tongue swept across her again. Nerve endings she didn't even know she had sizzled and flashed fire through her veins, sending an arc of electricity blasting straight from his tongue to every inch of her body.

She moaned as he kissed and licked and suckled her, paying the same attention that he had to her breasts. Except this time, she was going to come in his mouth if he didn't stop.

She whipped her head back and forth on the pillow, drowning

in the sensation. Surrendering to the primal heat that sparkled from him, from her, from them both. Who knew where one ended and the other began? Oh, his lips, his tongue, his *mouth*. She was going to explode. If only, if only . . .

He slid one finger inside her and pressed down.

"Conlan!" somebody—was that *her*?—screamed.

He added a second finger and thrust them in and out of her wetness in time with what his tongue was doing, and she gasped, begging, pleading.

And then he stopped.

Her eyes flew open and she stared down at him, trying to breathe, trying to focus. He smiled up at her, pupils nearly consumed with that dancing blue-green fire. "Come for me, Riley. Let me taste your sweetness in my throat."

Then he bent his head again and she shattered at the first touch of his mouth. Coming and coming and coming until she thought she would pass out from the sensation.

When he finally released her, he pulled her down beside him and touched her cheeks. "You're crying. Did I hurt you?"

She gazed up at him through the tears tangled in her lashes. "No. Far from it. I think . . . I think you may have healed something in me."

She wrapped her arms around his neck and pulled his head down to her. "I need you inside me, Conlan. Please."

Satisfaction and pure possessiveness shone in his eyes. "Then you will have me."

He pulled her legs up and centered his thick erection over her, nudging at her sensitive core. "Now?" he asked, teasing.

"Now."

With one thrust, he seated himself in her to the hilt, his heavy sac slapping against her bottom. She screamed and clenched around him, convulsing again and again.

He pulled back and thrust again, groaning, as her body tightened around his thickness. In fewer than a dozen strokes he yelled out his own release and shuddered in her arms, spasming inside her for a long time.

When she could form words, she laughed. "Okay, I'm totally pleading guilty if that's the punishment."

He rolled over, pulling her with him. "I'm not sure we could call that a punishment," he said, still breathing heavily.

"Although maybe for you. My control is as bad as an untried lad in his early days at the Academy."

She snuggled into his arms. "Tell me."

"About my lack of control?"

"About Atlantis. It must be incredible."

He caught her lips in a kiss. "It is more amazing than you could ever imagine. I cannot wait to show you my home. But first, a shower. Then food. Then I'll tell you anything you want to know."

Riley shook her head. "Food. At a time like this. Is food all men think about?"

He sat up with her still in his arms, then stood, carrying her, as if she weighed nothing. "I'm not sure you can ask me that after this night, little empath. At least not with any credibility."

"I'm not little! Put me down," she said, holding on to his neck tightly and laughing.

"I will. In the shower." He waggled his eyebrows in a fake leer. "Did I mention I'm from Atlantis? I'm really great with water."

She laughed all the way into the bathroom, where she discovered that he wasn't great with water at all.

He was spectacular.

~~~~

Ven walked out of the shower and realized what was niggling at the edge of his brain. He hadn't heard anything from Riley's room all night. And he'd definitely seen Conlan go in there after unceremoniously dumping Denal on him. He'd expected an explosion.

Of one kind or another.

Not that he'd planned to stick around if anything like those vibes of pure sex had started pumping through the walls, like they had the other day. Something about an empath and an Atlantean set sexual tension to *loud* on the broadcast frequency.

Might be something to consider.

He thought about Riley's sister while he pulled on clean pants and a T-shirt. Nah. Chick was too dark and complicated for him. He liked them simple and welcoming.

Easy to leave.

The gods knew he was destined for the same unwelcome fate

as Conlan. Married off to some ancient maiden they'd pick out for him at the time.

It was the royal duty to carry out the Council's plan for the Atlantean lineage.

Sucked to be a prince.

Not that any of Poseidon's warriors escaped *that* exciting chore. Forced marriage to an eleven-thousand-year-old virgin. Woo-hoo, could he control the excitement?

At least he had another fifty or so years before it was his dick on the block. So to speak.

He grabbed the bag he'd tossed by the door when he'd come back in the middle of the night. Figured Riley would be wanting it about now.

Grinned at what he might discover in her room.

He pulled open the door and walked into the corridor and nearly ran into Alaric. The priest wore all black again, which only highlighted the extreme pallor of his face.

Somebody didn't get his beauty sleep.

"Watch your step, Vengeance." The snarl on the priest's face would have scared most people.

Ven just laughed. "What's got your panties in a bunch? Couldn't sleep after making a fool of yourself in front of Riley's sister last night?"

Alaric froze, then slowly turned his head to stare at Ven. Power glowed a fierce green in his eyes. "You may wish to learn to watch your step in more ways than one. I am nearly at the limit of my patience."

Ven started to give it right back to him, but something in the priest's eyes stopped him. If he didn't know better, he would have sworn Alaric was in some kind of pain.

If he didn't know better.

"Hell, why ruin the day before I've even had any coffee? Let's hit the caffeine, Alaric. Oh, and I have to give this stuff to Riley, if she and Conlan didn't kill each other last night. I didn't feel anything at all from her room last night."

Alaric's lips thinned, but he started walking toward the kitchen. "I shielded their room. If I'd had to feel any of their—well. I shielded the room. Leave it at that."

Ven blinked as Alaric strode off down the hall. Something

was definitely wrong, beyond even the obvious guilt that tore at the priest for the loss of the Trident.

"Which reminds me, we need to get our asses in gear," he muttered, then crossed the hall to knock on Riley's door. "Rise and shine, sleepyhead."

He didn't hear a response and wondered if the shield kept her from hearing his knock. Cautiously, he opened the door. "Riley?"

And was treated to the glorious sight of Riley's beautifully bare backside as she stood, stretching, beside the bed.

She let out a little scream and dove into the bed, yanking the covers up over her body.

"Oh, man," he said, looking down at the floor, at his boots, anywhere but at her. He could feel his face heat up in a slow flush.

Not that seeing a woman naked had ever bothered him before but, hell, this was Riley. Lady Sunshine. She was as brave as any warrior, and she deserved better than some idiot walking in on her.

Plus, from the scent of sex in the room, Conlan was going to try to kick his ass.

"It's okay, Ven, you can look up now," she said drily. "I'm decent. Thanks for *knocking*."

He grinned at her. "Hey, don't blame me. I did knock. Alaric put some sort of spell on the room to shield it so we didn't have to put up with . . . er, I mean, oh, *crap*."

Her face flamed red all the way down her throat and the enticing part of her chest he could see above the sheet she was clutching. "Oh, God. Oh, I never, we never . . . *ohhhhhh*."

Naturally, that was the moment Conlan chose to walk out of the bathroom, damp from the shower and wearing nothing but a towel. "What? Ven! What are you doing in here?"

He stepped between Riley and Ven, blocking Ven's view. "What are you doing in here when Riley is undressed?" he repeated, an ominous threat in his voice.

"Oh, chill out, bro. That's exactly why I'm here."

Riley made an interesting squeaking noise from behind Conlan. *"What?"*

He held up the bag so she could see it over Conlan's

shoulder. "I couldn't sleep last night. Thought you might be tired of wearing the same clothes. Stopped by your place to see if anybody unfriendly was hanging out there and brought you some stuff to wear, some of your girly crap, whatever."

Conlan started to smile and took the bag from him. "So I see Riley has the same effect on you that she does on Denal, baby brother."

Ven narrowed his eyes. "Yeah, well, don't forget I can kick your ass twice a day and three times on Fridays, *old man*."

Riley jumped out of the bed, wrapped in the sheet, and rushed over to them. "Thank you, thank you, thank you! I was *desperate* to get my hands on some clean clothes. You're the best!"

She slipped between Conlan and Ven and stood on tiptoes to press a quick kiss to Ven's cheek, then snatched the bag out of Conlan's hand. "Thank you so much! Now if you two will excuse me, I'm going to get dressed so we can figure out how to recover the Trident and save the world."

Ven and Conlan both stood there, gaping, as she hurried to the bathroom, wrapped up like a mummy and trailing the end of the sheet behind her.

"A little pillow talk?" Ven asked, grinning at his flustered brother. "By the way, I didn't see any signs of vamps posted at Riley's house. They must have been after us."

"Thanks, Ven. I don't know what I'd do if . . ." He paused, eyes narrowing, then shook his head. "Riley is the most amazing woman—no, the most amazing *human*—no, not even that. She's the most amazing *person* I have ever encountered. She accepts whatever is thrown at her and moves to conquer it."

Ven shoved his hands in his pockets, a tendril of concern snaking through him. "So, she's pretty amazing. And she also seems to have conquered *you*, brother. Have you told her about your destined queen yet?"

Conlan clenched his jaw. "No. I don't— No. But I need to talk to Alaric, Ven. Things are going to have to change."

Ven said nothing, not sure of what words would accomplish. Things were going to change, that was for damn sure. He just wasn't sure whether or not that was a *good* thing.

Riley dug into the bag, thrilled to see that Ven had known enough about women to bring an assortment of her toiletries. Now for clothes.

She pulled out a handful of silk and leather.

He had to be kidding.

This was what Atlantean warriors considered useful battle gear for empaths? Silk camisoles and her one and only miniskirt?

She rolled her eyes. The skirt was the only leather in her closet, so biker-look man must have thought it was the thing to wear. At least he'd shoved her favorite pair of boots and a blue sweater in there, too, so she wouldn't freeze to death.

By the time she dressed, Conlan was gone. She spent about five seconds thinking about how she *so* didn't want to face the warriors, when everybody would know what she and Conlan had been up to all night, but the scent of coffee overrode any shyness and she wandered down to the kitchen, chin raised.

Only to find the room empty. But a full pot of coffee—fresh, from the smell of it—sat there tempting her. She selected a muffin from the enormous, half-empty box on the table to go with it and sat down at the table, prepared to enjoy a quiet breakfast before she saved the world.

Heh. Social worker takes on the Primus. Film at eleven.

"Of my detached body parts, most likely," she muttered.

Somebody cleared his throat behind her, and she nearly dropped her coffee mug.

"I beg your pardon, Lady Riley?"

She turned to find Denal standing in the doorway to the hall. "Nothing. Just mumbling to myself, which is never a good sign. Come in. Do you want some coffee?"

He bowed to her and, oddly enough, it didn't faze her. She must be getting used to it. *Great.*

Add swelled head to the list of things she needed to worry about.

"No, thank you, but I would avail myself of another of those blueberry muffins, if I may?"

She laughed. "Denal, seriously, we have to work on your language. Bring it into this century. And, sure, avail away. Pull up a chair."

He bowed again and took a seat across the table from her, back to the wall. Then he took a muffin and sank his teeth into it, a look of bliss spreading over his face.

She grinned; she couldn't help it. He looked like a nine-year-old kid like that. Which made her wonder. "Denal, exactly how old are you? You guys keep throwing out words like 'centuries' when you're talking about stuff, but I had too much to wrap my brain around to go there before."

He swallowed and wiped his mouth with a napkin, then looked at her seriously. "I am soon to celebrate the anniversary of my birth, Lady Riley. Do you celebrate such times?"

"Yes, with cake and ice cream and balloons. And, please, just Riley, okay? So how many candles will be on your cake?"

He looked puzzled. "Candles?"

"One candle per year. So my next cake will have twenty-eight candles, which is way too close to thirty for my liking," she said, shuddering at the thought. "And you?"

He grinned at her. "I am afraid my cake would give rise to a conflagration, Lady . . . *Riley*. My candles would number two and twenty."

She laughed. "Right, junior. Twenty-two is hardly enough for a conflagration. You couldn't even roast a marshmallow with twenty-two candles."

Denal finished his muffin and selected another, then shook his head. "Two *hundred* and twenty. Perhaps enough to roast a chicken or two."

She blinked. "Oh. Well. You look great for your age," she said weakly.

Two hundred twenty years old? And he was the *young* one? But . . .

"Denal, how old is Conlan?"

He looked surprised. "He has not shared that with you? But I thought you and he . . . Um, rather—"

It was her turn to smile, even though she could feel her cheeks turning pink. "It's okay, Denal. We're still . . . feeling our way through things."

He looked down at the table, which suddenly must have become fascinating, since he wouldn't raise his gaze to meet hers. "I offer my apologies. I did not mean to cause you discomfort."

"Trust me, this is nothing. You should have been around for

some of the things my sister did to embarrass me when we were kids."

He finally looked up, mischief gleaming in his eyes. "I was the youngest of eight, and have seven older sisters. I can imagine full well how things must have been between you. Mine used to dress me up like a doll and make me sit through interminable tea parties."

"Oh, I am so gonna use that against you, kid," Bastien's good-natured rumble of a voice cut through the room. "Maybe we can set up a tea party for you on our next mission?"

Denal jumped to his feet, crumbs dropping to the floor. "If you ever tell anyone that story, I'll—I'll—"

Bastien laughed. "Might want to stop there, until you grow a little bit, youngling. Besides, I'm tired from being out on patrol all night. Wouldn't be a fair fight, would it?"

Riley fought to keep from grinning at the idea of Denal going up against Bastien. The older warrior towered over him by nearly a foot and was as broad as the side of a small hill.

But the conversation brought her back to her earlier point. "Good morning, Bastien. So, if Denal is a youngling, how old are you?"

"Good morn, my lady. I have nearly four hundred years, praise be to Poseidon." Bastien ambled over to the coffee and poured the rest of the pot into an enormous mug that looked like a doll cup in his hand.

"And Conlan?" she asked, not sure she even wanted to know the answer.

Bastien cocked his head and gave her a quizzical grin. "Prince Conlan is merely a few weeks away from the age of his ascension to the throne, of course. He will celebrate five hundred years on that day, when he meets his lady wife and becomes king of all Atlantis."

Riley dropped her coffee mug and stared, unseeing, as coffee ran in rivulets across the table. "When he meets *who*?"

Chapter 25

Riley shoved her chair back from the table and stormed down the hall in search of one lying, deceitful, soon-to-be-neutered Atlantean prince.

She found him in the dining room with Alaric, both of them bent over a large map spread over the table. Her treacherous body tingled a little at the sight of him, dark hair pulled back from his face with a leather tie, muscled legs just wide enough apart that she could imagine fitting right in between them, lying back on the table—

—and turning into human bimbo of the week while his fiancée waited back home at Atlantis.

"You're a dead man," she began, then faltered when Alaric lifted his head and pinned her with that scary green glowing gaze of his.

But not even facing Alaric at full steam would stop her. Not this time. "Back. Off. Alaric." She bit off the words. "You and I are going to go around about whatever it is you did to my sister, but I need to talk to your *prince* for a minute."

Alaric's lips curled back from his teeth and the flashlight behind his eyes strobed up about a thousand degrees, but Conlan held up a hand. "Enough. What is this about, Riley?" He held a hand out to her, sending warmth and confusion through their emotional bond.

She slammed down her shields. Hard. Enjoyed the sight of his flinch.

"Forget to tell me anything when you were *undressing* me last night, *Prince* Conlan?"

He drew his eyebrows together, confusion clear in his eyes. "What—"

"You. Half a millennium old. Which is way, *way* too old for me, anyway, by the way. The throne. And, hmmm, what was it?" She tapped a fingernail on her teeth, looked up at the ceiling.

"Oh, right. Your *queen*. Ring any bells, asshole?"

She heard somebody gasp behind her, but was way beyond being embarrassed. Humiliated, sure. But it wasn't like everybody in the house didn't already know she was the prince's slut du jour.

Riley's face burned at the thought, and she was glad that Quinn was gone. Conlan took a step toward her, and she pulled one hand back in a fist. "I've never punched anybody in my life, but if you take one more step, you can be the first. Did you know that it has been *years* for me? Years since I trusted any man enough to take that step with him?"

Tears ran down her face, and she brushed them away with one hand, hating her weakness. Her stupidity.

"Riley, I swear to you—"

"Oh, yeah. This should be good," she said bitterly. "Tell me all about how it's not what I think. That you weren't cheating on your fiancée with me last night. That the feelings you showed me weren't a pile of astonishingly putrid *lies*."

With that, the pain finally worked its way through her anger. Seared through her defenses and scorched its way through the center of her being. She faltered, nearly collapsed from the intensity of the pain.

"How could you?" she cried. "How are you able to lie to me with your heart?"

Conlan blurred into motion and caught her, his arms steel bands around her. "Everyone leave us," he barked out, eyes feral with rage.

She shoved at his chest, tried to get away from him, crying now. Hard, wrenching sobs that felt like they'd rip out her throat.

He'd already ripped out her heart.

She dropped in his arms, dead weight, hoping he'd let her go. Unable to force her legs to hold her up. He went to the ground with her, falling to his knees in front of her, still holding her. She felt the waves of his anguish buffeting her. The waves of his emotion pushing at her, peddling their false claims of honesty and truth.

She screamed. "Get out of my head! It's all lies. You are going to marry . . . what's her name?"

"I don't—"

She snarled in his face, driven to jealous anguish beyond anything she'd thought she had in her. "Tell me her *name*!"

Conlan dropped her arms, released her. Shoulders slumping, he looked her right in the eyes. "I don't know her name. We've never met."

She fell backward, mouth falling open. "What? I don't understand. Why—"

"Why, indeed?" Conlan said, visibly drawing power into his body. His skin glowed with a faint blue-green iridescence and the flame was back in his eyes. "If I'm fit to be the king, then I should act as king, should I not?"

With that, he took Riley's hands in his and looked back over his shoulder at Alaric, who'd never left the room. "As king, I should have the right to choose. Because the ancient breeding program has been the way of the Seven Isles since the beginning does not mean it must continue as such."

Conlan looked at Riley, who sat, tears still streaming down her face, wondering what he was talking about.

Wondering why she cared.

Though she told herself she hated him, she could see the royalty in him, even kneeling on the floor. A position that would have rendered any other man subservient did nothing to diminish the kingliness in him.

The command.

She tried to breathe through the weight pressing on her chest—through the knot lodged inside her throat.

His next words knocked any remaining breath out of her.

"I, Conlan of Atlantis, high prince of the Seven Isles, therefore decree that the ceremony of mate-choosing shall no longer apply to any who do not wish it. And I renounce it. As king, I will choose for myself."

The gasps from behind her were louder this time, and her own echoed them. Alaric went dead white and clutched the edge of the table with both hands. Riley noticed it all only on the periphery of her senses; Conlan's face filled her vision.

She couldn't form a single word.

He stood, drawing her up with him, and put one arm around her waist. "I make my choice now. I choose her. I choose Riley Elisabeth Dawson, *aknasha*, human, to be my lady wife and queen."

He turned to Riley, joy fierce in his gaze. "If she will have me."

Before Riley could say a word, Alaric cut in. "No, you do not. You renounce nothing. Or else you doom Atlantis and the human world to a second Cataclysm."

Alaric smiled bitterly at her, then swung his gaze back to Conlan. "And your human will die."

As if to echo his proclamation of doom, the crashing sound of thunder ripped through the room and a lightning bolt of energy smashed into Alaric.

Conlan gasped and dove on reflex across the room toward Alaric as another bolt of energy scorched through the air at the priest.

"What in the nine hells?" he shouted, but he wasn't fast enough.

The pure green burst of fire smashed into Alaric dead center. The priest lit up as though electrified, arms jerking like some demonically possessed marionette.

Conlan heard Riley screaming behind him, but he was trapped in the elemental current driving through the air and into Alaric.

It lasted for hours, or for mere seconds. There was no way to tell. Time suspended itself on the cusp of energy gone rampant.

Then, as suddenly as it had come, the paralyzing beam of power vanished. Ven and Justice ran into the room, shouting, as Conlan leapt forward and caught Alaric as he fell.

He lay the unconscious form of the priest on the table and turned, breathing harshly, to help Riley.

She stood, trapped, between Ven and Justice, who each held one of her arms and whose grim expressions signaled a major need to hurt somebody.

Conlan was all *over* that idea.

He started toward Riley. "Take your hand off her or the next thing you'll feel will be my boot up your ass," he snarled at his brother.

"Yeah? And what exactly are you protecting? The woman—the *empath* who had the power to shut you down on the beach and now took Alaric out?"

Riley gasped. "What? Are you kidding? How could I do that?"

Denal spoke up from the hallway. "Lady Riley would never—"

Bastien cut him off. "Shut up, boy. This is a matter beyond your knowledge."

Conlan's steps faltered. He *knew* her. He'd been inside her *soul*, godsdamn it. But, it was true that she'd been so furious, and then Alaric—

"What are you thinking?" she cried out. "Why are you looking at me like that? You can't possibly think that I—"

A hoarse voice from behind Conlan cut into her plea. "She is telling the truth, Conlan. She had nothing to do with this."

Conlan swung around to see Alaric pulling himself to a sitting position on the table, face drawn and pale. "That was a sign from the Trident. It is ready to be found."

The breath left Conlan in a rush, relief nearly making him dizzy. "Riley, I—"

"No," she said, voice devoid of any feeling. "You can keep your pretty speeches. You've just proven that I'm nothing to you."

She pulled her arm free of Ven and, head held high, turned to leave the room. At the doorway, she stopped and spoke without looking at him. "I can feel Reisen again. If I can help you locate him, I will. For Quinn's sake. For the rebellion."

Conlan tried to reach her emotions, but—worse by far than the locked shields—all he encountered in her mind was desolation.

"And stay out of my mind, Conlan. We're through."

Denal looked around at all of them, dared to speak. "What do we do now?"

Alaric answered. "Now we wait for another surge, so that I can locate the Trident."

Bastien slammed his fist into the wall. "And then we go open a can of whup ass on the House of Mycenae."

Conlan stood there with his guts bleeding on the floor, and the woman who'd caused it walked down the hall and out of his life. He bared his teeth in a snarl. "Exactly right, Bastien.

"Exactly right."

～～◇～◇

Anubisa lifted her head from the limp and bloody form of Barrabas's pathetic excuse for a general and hissed. The disturbance in the elements had blown through her mind like a clean wind driving the acrid stink of death off a battlefield.

She *despised* clean winds.

It was time to put Barrabas to work.

Chapter 26

Riley sat on the couch in the games room, emptiness washing through her, an island of quiet in the midst of the rushing preparations for battle. She and Alaric had spent the entire day working together to try to locate Reisen and the Trident. She'd intermittently received frustratingly brief connections to their emotions, even as the Trident played a dangerous game of cat and mouse with the priest.

Finally, with the sunset, the flashes of power had become more powerful. Alaric had been able to track them, and the stronger emotional broadcasting she was feeling from Reisen and his warriors had helped triangulate a location.

Now, it was all about waiting. She was unable to process so many frantic emotional ups and downs, so she'd decided to quit trying.

After she'd steadfastly ignored Conlan all afternoon, he'd finally gone away to help prepare to hunt down Reisen and the Trident.

She'd help them find their Trident they needed so badly, and then she'd never have to deal with any of these bastards again.

She nearly reached out to touch Conlan's mind before she caught herself and slammed her mental shields shut.

The Trident. Yeah, the thing that *he* needed so badly, so he could go become the *king* and marry his precious *queen*. Well, bully for him. The look of doubt on his face when Ven had accused her of harming Alaric was something she'd never forget.

Could never forgive. He'd been inside her—mind and body—inside her *heart*. But he'd still doubted her.

Thank God she'd never told him that she loved him.

"Not that I do," she muttered bitterly. "Fleeting moment of lust-induced insanity, right?"

A shard of pain lodged somewhere deep in her chest twinged a protest at the thought, but she crushed it.

Ruthlessly.

Just like he'd been. *Ruthless.* Crushing her stupid fantasies of finally finding someone who would understand who she really was—and love her. Not abandon her.

"Riley?"

Great. Now she was even imagining his *voice*. She squeezed her eyes closed more tightly and ignored the wetness that pooled on her lashes.

A finger stroked her cheek, and her eyes flew open. She hadn't conjured him. He was here.

He knelt in front of her, took her hands in spite of her attempt to avoid his grasp. The room was suddenly empty, too. No warriors, no weapons. Just the two of them.

And the pain.

"Riley, you can't let a second of doubt destroy what we found between us," he said. "Alaric and his doomsaying can rot in the nine hells, for all I care. I *need* you."

Even with her shields clamped shut on her emotions and blocking his, she could see the anguish in his face. The lines bracketing his mouth seemed to have deepened a decade's worth in the space of the past half hour.

She probably didn't look so hot herself.

Not that she cared. She closed her eyes again, determined to shut him out.

Weakening when she felt his breath on her face—felt his kiss on her forehead.

"I've only survived for five hundred years by never trusting anyone, Riley. Never believing in anyone. Never loving anyone."

She opened her eyes, needing to see his face.

Then she opened her shields, needing to feel his heart.

Both told her the same thing. Conlan—this proud warrior—was humbling himself before her. Desperate for her forgiveness.

The pain in his eyes rivaled anything she'd felt in his memories from the time of Anubisa's torture. And suddenly she couldn't bear it.

Couldn't bear to be the one who caused him pain.

"Conlan, I—"

The sound of boots striding down the hallway interrupted her. It was Ven, and he had his battle face on.

"Alaric says we go now. The Trident is screaming inside his head, and there's a new level of power to it." He stared down at Conlan and Riley, clearly not happy with what he saw, but didn't say another word. Just turned on his heel and stalked off.

"I have to go now, *mi amara aknasha*."

"I know. Be safe."

"You *will* be here when I return?" Conlan's voice was fierce, desperation making it hoarse. "We can work this out then. Promise me."

"Yes. I promise. Now go. The quicker you go, the quicker you'll come back."

He crushed her to him in a fierce hug, then claimed her lips with a searing kiss. "I'll leave Denal and Brennan to stand guard with you. Stay safe for me, Riley. I need you to be safe."

Moments later, he was gone, the front door slamming behind him. She sank down on the couch, wondering if he would survive the confrontation with his enemy.

Wondering how she could survive if he did not.

⁓⁓⁓

Reisen stared with no little satisfaction at the blue-robed, kneeling forms of the twenty members of the Platoist Society who had come to offer their service and their worship to a prince of Atlantis.

Not yet *high* prince, but that would come.

The main floor of the warehouse made a perfect impromptu meeting place. He stood on a wooden pallet, the table before him bare but for one cloth-wrapped bundle. Candles lit the table, though floodlights were on in the building.

Soon the Trident would light up the night.

He put one hand in his jacket pocket, fondled the gem contained there. Now was the time for a little display of power.

"Rise and watch the fulfillment of the prophecy," he shouted. "Watch the first step in the Warriors of Poseidon taking their rightful place among the society of earth again."

He gently pushed the folds of fabric away from the object they'd all come to see, and lifted the gleaming golden Trident high above his head. "The Trident of Poseidon! Instrument of power for the ruler of Atlantis for untold millennia!"

Roaring cheers shook the walls and stamping feet thundered through the echoing cavern of the room. "Atlantis! Atlantis! Atlantis!"

Reisen pulled the emerald from his pocket and lowered the Trident to eye level. Closing his eyes briefly, he uttered a brief prayer.

"Poseidon, Father of Water,

"Lord of elements, avatar of justice for all Atlanteans,

"Hear our plea, feel our need.

"Restore Atlantis to its former glory.

"Hear our plea, feel our need."

He opened his eyes and, before he could think about the horrible death that awaited him if he'd guessed wrong, plunged the emerald into the uppermost of the seven empty openings on the staff of the Trident.

Power surged as soon as the emerald snapped into place, sizzling through the Trident and nearly burning his hand. He clenched his fist even more tightly around the staff, thundering out his joy and triumph with everyone else.

Blinding green and silver light shot out from the Trident and lit the darkened room with the intensity of the desert sun at noon. The elements themselves answered the siren call of the Trident and wind whipped into a frenzy around him, raising the cloaks and hair of the humans.

Ribbons of water surged into the room from the walls, from the ceiling, from rusty pipes that hadn't carried water for many years. They twirled and twisted around the room, dancing with the light, waltzing in a sparkling display of power.

The power, oh, the *power*. Reisen's voice was nearly gone, his throat raw, but he continued to shout out his victory.

Atlantis will be mine, and these weak humans will fall soon after. Once again, the world will tremble at our footsteps.

At my *footsteps.*

"I am Reisen of Atlantis, and I decree that it will be so."

The Trident spiked a surge of blistering heat through his hand at the words, and he laughed even as it burned his flesh.

Laughed at the pain.

Began to plan for the battle.

Chapter 27

"May I sit with you?" Denal hovered at the doorway, looking a lot like a gunslinger from the Old West. In addition to the daggers strapped to his thighs, a complicated series of leather straps hung in some kind of double holster across his chest.

"Going to the O.K. Corral?" Riley asked, mustering up a smile.

His eyebrows drew together. "I beg your pardon?"

"Nothing. Never mind. It's a Wild West thing, probably before your time. Not that anything is before your time, practically. Oh, forget it."

He strode to the window. Moved the blinds aside to peer out. "Brennan is taking first outside watch. We don't really expect any problems. Nobody knows where we are."

"That's what Reisen and his bunch thought. What if they have an empath on hand, too?"

She watched his eyes widen as horror slid across his face. "We never thought of that! But, but Alaric said you are the first in ten thousand years to be *aknasha*."

She stood, paced. "Right. And then there's my sister. And who knows how many more that you've all missed in your arrogance?"

"Do you know of more such as yourself and Lady Quinn?"

Lady Quinn. How she'd laugh at the sound of that.

Or maybe she wouldn't. Riley didn't really know this new Quinn. The one who led werewolves into battle.

She opened her mind. Sent her emotions out into the night, seeking for her sister.

Felt nothing. As if Quinn really *had* died in that bloody forest. Or shut her out, once again. Hiding the things she'd done and the person she'd become.

She saddened at the thought.

"Lady Riley?"

She blinked. Focused on his face. "No. No, I have never met anyone other than Quinn who can send and pick up on emotion the way we do. I think my mother may have had the talent. Something about my memories of her . . ."

Closing her eyes, she sent her senses down a different path. Seeking the second person who'd moved into her heart and staked out a camping spot.

Conlan.

She felt his reaction; the blues and golds of warmth and caring flooded her.

Riley? You have need of me?

No. I . . . no. Be safe. Find your Trident and return quickly. Please.

His amusement shimmered through her, touched strongly with relief. *Even at a distance, you order me about. We must discuss this penchant you have for disrespect toward royalty.*

Hey, I'm part of a democracy, buddy. We kicked one royal ass for our freedom, don't think we can't do it again.

Before he could respond to her teasing, the connection between them wavered. Ice shot through her veins.

Conlan?

I'm fine. Need to—need to focus. See you soon.

And his mental barriers slammed shut, throwing her forcibly out of their emotional bond.

Denal stood in front of her, fists clenched on the hilts of his daggers. "What is it?"

"I don't know. I think it's nothing. I hope it's nothing." She sank down on the couch. "Now what do we do?"

"We wait," he said, grim. "Though I should be fighting with the rest of the Seven to recover the Trident."

He was so young. Young enough to be angry when left out of a battle and bloodshed.

Or maybe it was the *male* in him, not the youth.

She smiled, rueful. "I'm sorry you drew babysitting duty."

It took him a beat. "What—oh, no. I am honored to serve and protect you, my lady. It is merely—"

"Don't worry about it. If I had a couple of those daggers and knew how to use them, I'd want to be in on the action, too, I guess. At least helping to protect—"

"The prince." Denal nodded. "It is true what the legends say of *aknasha*, then? That you can form the soul-meld so quickly?"

"The what?" Riley felt her cheeks heating up that she was so easy to read but she was curious. "What's a soul-meld?"

"It is said that when one who is *aknasha* truly loves, she will open to her beloved, so that he can travel inside the corridors of her heart and soul."

"Very poetic," Brennan said, entering the room. "The disadvantage of this 'hiding in plain sight' that Ven prefers with his safe houses is that the neighbors are wary of one such as myself patrolling the night."

"Drawing unwelcome attention here in suburbia, are you?" Riley asked, trying for a light tone. Denal's words had shaken her more than she wanted to admit.

Truth had a way of doing that. *One who truly loves.*

"Hard to be inconspicuous when you're six and a half feet of hottie, Brennan. Do they have some kind of gorgeous potion in the water in Atlantis?"

She looked at the two of them, standing there all muscle and cheekbones in leather and a cascade of steel. Like they'd flashed in from some weird parallel universe where runway models wore weapons.

Denal was shaking his head. "We do not live in water in Atlantis. The dome protects us."

She blinked, then laughed so hard her sides ached, tried to explain when he got all huffy. "No, no, I'm not laughing at you, Denal. Only at myself. Dropped down the rabbit hole with Hot Models Gone Wild."

That set her off again with the worst case of the stress giggles she'd ever had, and Denal shaking his head at her only made it worse. Even Brennan smiled, though it never reached his eyes.

When she could catch her breath again, she wiped her eyes. "Okay. Sorry. Really. Sometimes it hits me like that. No doubt I'll be laughing on my deathbed. How about pizza? Two or three?"

She studied them, upgraded her plans for the order. Distraction. That's what they needed. "No, *five* pizzas loaded with the works. And we can pop in one of these movies. Ven may have the finest collection of classics I've ever seen. Anybody for the original *King Kong*?"

Conlan followed Alaric as they flew across town, bodies transformed into shimmering mist. Ven and the others followed in two of Ven's collection of cars. They'd discovered early on that modern weapons—indeed, any that didn't contain at least a trace of orichalcum—failed to be changed by the magic of the transformation process.

Ven did love to have his toys with him. Man had more weapons than an armory.

And they'd surely need them. Though five of Reisen's warriors were slain, they might still be outnumbered. The House of Mycenae might have brought many, many more to guard the stolen Trident.

Why? He sent the thought to Alaric.

He believed you dead. Wanted Atlantis to take what he considered its rightful place among the landwalkers. Grew impatient with the timid ways of the Council. Saw himself as king, no doubt.

Conlan heard the underlying note. *You believe as he does?*

Though he was no empath, he had no trouble reading the disgust in the priest's thoughts.

If not now, when, Conlan? We are charged to protect mankind. Do we fulfill that vow by hiding like women? No, that is inapt. For your woman and her warrior sister have no thought of hiding, more's the pity.

Alaric put on a burst of more speed, as if trying to outrun

thoughts of Quinn. Conlan needed to understand more about that reaction, to be sure. But there was a matter far more urgent.

Alaric, what is this doom you spoke of? A second Cataclysm?

But instead of answering, Alaric plunged down through the trees sparsely surrounding a vacant lot that abutted a large, ruined-looking building.

A building filled with light and sound and surrounded by cars.

As the priest shimmered back into his body, he threw his head and arms back, tension in every straining muscle. "The Trident is here. It calls me—taunts me. Send for the others. We have found it."

Conlan, who'd been communicating their direction to Ven throughout the journey, sent the final directions through their mind link. *Ven. Hurry.*

Ven's thoughts shot back to him like an arrow. *Five minutes, tops. Then we're going to make the lord of the House of Mycenae regret the day he was born.*

"Five minutes, Alaric. We need to wait for the others. From the sign of the parking lot, we're seriously outnumbered."

Alaric started forward, eyes gleaming in the dark. "Mostly humans," he snarled. "I can feel them. Anyway, no matter. None of them are any match for me. I will wreak Poseidon's justice upon their flesh."

Conlan flashed in front of Alaric, blocking him. Barring his way. "You will wait. As your prince, I command it. If you are destroyed through a fluke of superior numbers, what hope is left for Atlantis?"

Alaric's face was savage. No trace of Conlan's boyhood friend shone through the vicious intent on his face. "Out of my way, *prince*. This is the work of a god, and you may not countermand me in my goal."

"Not as prince, perhaps. But as your friend?" Conlan put out a hand to grasp the priest's arm.

The light from Alaric's eyes burned where it touched Conlan's face, but he held his ground.

Alaric yanked his arm away, lifted his hands to call power, and bands of wind jerked Conlan off his feet and onto the ground. He battled with the element of wind to try to rise.

Alaric merely stared down at him, face like stone. "I have no friends."

And then he strode across the field toward the blazing windows of the warehouse.

Chapter 28

Anubisa sneered at the bowed head of the so-called master vamp. Her father-husband would writhe in shame were he to see the diluted blood of their race.

Lucky for all that she'd killed Chaos when she had. She thought back to his death with sorrow.

Sorrow that it could never be repeated.

The sheer, soul-destroying ecstasy of ripping out her incestuous lover's jugular as he climaxed inside of her. His impotent rage as his seed and his blood flowed out of his cock and his neck into her.

He'd made her a goddess of death, and she'd eaten his soul. So fitting, somehow.

But now she was left with this pale imitation of greatness who dared to try to lead.

"The fissure in the natural fabric of the elements? Did you not feel it, fool?"

He cringed at her feet, not man enough to face her. "I did feel it, Exalted One. What would you have me do?"

She almost gently swung out one silk-shod foot and kicked him with enough force to hurl his body through the air. He smashed into the wall of his chamber and slid down to the floor. Nearly boneless.

Useless.

"Rise, you pathetic sack of worm dung. What I would have you *do* is track it down and find these Atlanteans who dare to disturb the elements." Rage fired her eyes to a flaming red and she barely felt the blood trickling down her face from her retinas.

"And take Drakos with you. I think he may have some of the sense that you so clearly lack."

"But—"

She stilled, and the air in the chamber dropped to a temperature frigid enough to freeze human blood. So. This was what rage felt like. It had been centuries since she'd elevated her mood beyond lethargy.

"You question *me*?" she asked, her voice a whisper of torrid death.

"Never," he gasped, pulling himself off the floor.

"Find the Atlanteans. Now. And I may yet let you live."

~~~~~~

Ven drove the last hundred yards or so with the lights off, burning up the street. Atlantean night vision was an asset sometimes.

Justice was out the door before Ven could shove the gearshift into park. Bastien and Alexios were out of the backseat on his heels.

Ven jumped out, looked up at the sound of wind rushing over his head. It was Christophe, determined to travel via mist, though his strength and speed were no match for Conlan and Alaric.

Ven nodded. He understood pride.

"Conlan!" Justice's voice rang out, and Ven started running.

Damn it. Not his brother. Not again.

He pounded up to the group of warriors as Justice pulled Conlan to his feet.

"Are you harmed?"

Conlan glanced at him, shook his head, sucking in air. "No, but I'm going to kick Alaric's glowy green ass for him when I get my hands on him. Bastard magicked me out of his way to get to the Trident. Wouldn't wait for backup."

Christophe shimmered into form beside them, face rapt, staring toward the ugly steel-and-block building on the other side of the field. "It's the Trident," he breathed. "It's singing. I've never felt such power."

Face transfixed, Christophe stumbled off in the direction of the building, unheeding of Ven's call to stop. Bastien stepped in front of him and casually popped him in the jaw, nearly knocking the warrior off his feet.

Blinking, eyes beginning to register his surroundings, Christophe rubbed his jaw and scowled up at Bastien. "What in the nine hells did you do that for?"

Bastien grinned. "You've had that coming for a while. Oh, yeah, and you were in some kind of trance, too."

Conlan strode forward. "Enough. We need to fan out and figure out what we're getting ourselves into. What Alaric is likely in the middle of already. If there are any sentries, take care of them. Quietly."

Bastien drew his daggers. "Quiet is my middle name, my lord. We're golden."

Christophe snorted. "Ugly is your middle name."

Alexios started forward, rammed his shoulder against Christophe as he passed him. "Another word, and you will discover an entirely new meaning of ugly, shit for brains," he growled.

With hand gestures, Conlan motioned Justice to take point toward the left and Alexios to do the same toward the right. He went straight up the middle, muttering a quick prayer to Poseidon that Alaric would hold off another damn minute.

That was when the windows of the building shattered.

~~~~~

Brennan's head jerked up. "Someone approaches." His hands went to the weapons that were never far from his hands.

Riley had noticed they were all like that. Even in bed with her, Conlan's daggers had been on a table within reach.

Her cheeks turned pink as she realized she was, for about the fiftieth time in the past hour, thinking about Conlan naked. Sheesh, she was turning into a guy, with sex, sex, sex on her brain. Next she'd start scratching her crotch and develop a driving need to play fantasy football.

"It's probably the pizza guy," she said. "Yippee for on-time delivery. Let me grab my wallet."

Brennan and Denal both stood to accompany her. She planted her fists on her hips. "It's the pizza guy. Who is probably some skinny high school kid who will pee in his pants if you two come to the door looking like Conan the Atlantean. Okay?"

The doorbell rang, and Brennan shook his head. "You will not go alone."

She appealed to his logic. "Look, if you scare the guy, he'll have some big story to tell back at the pizza place, right? Do you really want the address and phone number of your so-called safe house to be stored in the computer system of people who think a drug-dealing biker gang lives here?"

Denal drew his sword, all "I'm the warrior, and you're the poor defenseless maiden" attitude.

Riley rolled her eyes. "Brennan? You're the older and wiser, right? Don't I make sense?"

The doorbell rang again.

Finally Brennan nodded. "You may go. I will stand behind the door as you effect the transaction."

"Fine. Let's go before my pepperoni gets cold."

She paused the movie—you had to love Fay Wray—and pulled her wallet out of her jacket on the way. Brennan handed her some folded bills.

"You will not pay for our food, Lady Riley. Although we thank you for the offer."

She shrugged, let him put the money in her hand. "Okay. Maybe being a royal warrior pays better than being a social worker?"

Brennan positioned himself behind the door, moving an umbrella out of the way. "Do Atlanteans really need umbrellas? I thought you guys *liked* water," she teased, hoping Denal would start talking about the dome again.

But Denal merely grinned and shook his head, lurking behind the closet door. She glanced down at the wad of bills. "Sheesh, we don't actually need a couple of hundred dollars for pizza. The guy would get a heck of a tip!"

Laughing, she pulled open the door, still separating the bills. "Come on in, dude, how much is—"

And was knocked backward onto the floor by the first of a swarm of hissing vampires.

~~~~~

Alaric faced Reisen across the heads of the cowering humans, wanting to vomit at the sacrilege of seeing the Trident in this dismal place.

With this thieving bastard.

The concussion of his first blast of energy had bounced off a circle of power surrounding the Trident and its bearer. Yet even as the Trident protected Reisen, its siren call sang ever more urgent in his head.

Rescue me, priest. Take me back to the temple of my god.

The power in it, amped up beyond any he'd known before, scorched him even while it seduced. Power beyond imagining.

And Reisen had only added the first jewel.

Yes, only the first. Restore me to my glory, Alaric, and glory and power will be yours beyond measure.

For the span of a mere whisper of thought, Alaric's thoughts turned to Quinn. But she could never be his. If power would be his only mistress, he would ride its heat.

He raised his arms, levitated into the air, and floated over the bodies of the warriors who'd fallen at his first blast.

"I'm coming for what is rightfully mine, Mycenaean," he called, his voice deep and resonating with the power he channeled.

"Yours? You claim much for yourself, priest. The Trident belongs to Poseidon. You are merely his servant," Reisen sneered. "Or do you aspire to godhood now that Conlan is dead?"

"Conlan lives, fool. He is even now on his way to defeat your pathetic force—what is left of you after the shapeshifters defeated you yesterday."

"You lie!" Reisen roared. "You would lie about your dead prince in pursuit of your own power?"

Conlan's voice cut through the hum of gathering power. "It seems the rumors of my death have been greatly exaggerated."

Reisen jerked his head toward his very alive prince. Shock must have loosened his grasp, for his hands trembled on the Trident, and he nearly lost his grip on it.

Even as Reisen's warriors stirred and started to rise from where they'd fallen during the first blast, Ven, Justice, and the rest flowed in through the building's windows and a back door. Surrounded the room.

Reisen stood, gaping. "Conlan! How are you alive after seven years?"

Conlan took a step toward him, menace shadowing his features, royal command in every line of his body. "Oh, we'll talk, Mycenaean. Or rather, I'll talk, and you'll listen. But for now, you'll return the Trident to Poseidon's priest."

Reisen held the shining staff in the air. "I think not. We have decided that Atlantis shall take a new path. Even if you are not compromised by so many years with Anubisa, you are stuck in the past. I am the way of the future. With this, I am unstoppable."

Alaric drew on the elements, formed a ball of shining power and hurled it at Reisen. The Trident only deflected a part of its force, and the energy sphere smashed Reisen back a few steps. Around him, warriors of the House of Mycenae drew steel and began their approach.

Conlan turned his gaze to Alaric, nodded. "Let's play."

～～～

Riley stared up into the red and glaring eyes of the vampire whose hands crushed her throat. She heard voices; the sound of battle. Denal and Brennan roaring out the name of Atlantis and Poseidon. Yet somehow it all sounded far, far away.

And seemed to be happening in slow motion.

All she could focus on was the drop of saliva gathering at the corner of the vamp's mouth as it killed her. As it drew back its lips over yellowed and cracked fangs and reared its head back to strike.

She was going to die at the fangs of a vamp with bad teeth.

I never told Conlan that I love him.

Despair gave her power. She thrust her arms up, then out, in the tactic she'd learned to break the grip of an attacker.

Of course, that had been with attackers who couldn't lift her house with one hand, like a damn vampire would be able to do.

But still, it weakened his grip for a split second. Enough for her to slam her knee up into its crotch, wondering as she did it if vamps even had testicles.

Its hideous shriek told her they did.

She rolled out from under the screaming creature, and she was screaming herself. Shattering the night with an ear-splitting, wordless scream.

Sending her thoughts and terror out to Conlan, more powerfully than she'd ever broadcast.

Vampires! Too many! Denal—oh, God, no.

She froze for a moment, overwhelmed with horror. Too many, too many, *too many.*

And I'm not going to die like this.

She grabbed the umbrella that still, improbably, leaned against the closet door and ran for the four vamps that were attacking Denal.

"Get your lousy hands off my friend!" she screamed, even as Denal stabbed the point of his sword through the chest of the vamp in front of him. It must have hit the heart, because the vamp exploded into a nasty mess of blood and bone onto the carpet.

Even as Riley forced herself to run through it, the pointy end of the umbrella aimed at another vamp, the mess began to dissolve.

Brennan shouted at her from the corner, where he battled three more. He must have already killed some of them, because there had been far more than seven pouring through the door.

"Riley! The one who attacked you! You must take its head!"

She stopped, stared at Denal, then Brennan, then back at the vamp, now trying to stand.

"With a freaking umbrella?" she yelled.

"Behind you! The closet!"

She yanked open the closet door and saw a roomful of weapons. "What—"

She grabbed the closest thing, something that looked like a battle-axe from an old movie. "What the hell. I always wanted to be a Viking."

Stop babbling, Riley, she told herself, scared nearly out of her last wit.

"Riley! Now!"

She jerked and whirled around, axe held out in front of her.

And sliced off the top of the head of the vamp crawling up behind her. Blood and brains cascaded out of its skull, splashing gore on her legs and boots.

Which drove the last ounce of sanity out of her mind. "There are brains on my legs!" she screamed, hacking and slashing at the dying vamp, one stroke taking the head off at the neck.

"I can't stand this! I. Can. Not. Stand. This."

She ran from the room, slid in the blood and brains on the floor, nearly fell. Sobbed in terror and sheer, spiking adrenaline.

Ran for the vamps surrounding Denal, still hacking and slicing with the axe. "No, no, no! Leave him alone!" she sobbed, screamed, roared. Not making any sense. Not caring.

It was way past time for sense. "There are *brains* on my *legs*! I am a *social worker*! I will cut off your head *in triplicate*!"

Blind rage overcame her, and she swung from right to left, putting all the fury and uncertainty of the day into her stroke. The axe sliced into the shoulder of the vamp in front of her and sliced all the way down into the center of its chest.

As it fell to the ground, shrieking, the axe went with it. She couldn't pull it out. It was wedged in the vamp's bones, in its rib cage.

"Riley!" Brennan's voice thundered at her. "Get out of here now! Get out—run to safety. *Now!*"

Denal, still battling fiercely, sword in one hand and dagger in the other, stared at Riley over the shoulder of the vamp attacking him. "Lady Riley! Please! Away to safety! Let me fulfill my role as your protector."

She stood there sobbing, frozen between the two battling groups. Brennan brought down another vamp, and only one stood against him. Denal still fought two.

"Must get another weapon. Must help," she cried out. "Conlan! Where are you?"

But when she tried to reach him, all she felt was that curious blankness that Reisen had surrounded himself and his men with earlier.

She turned around, forced legs covered in gore and dripping with blood to carry her back to the weapons room. Had almost made it when she heard the loud thud and Denal's anguished bellow.

Turned around to see. Screamed again and fell to her knees.

Brennan stood, gasping, over the now-headless body of the final vampire.

Denal lay on the floor, impaled by a sword that the vamp had driven through his stomach before it died.

As she watched, tears nearly blinding her, the life and the light in Denal's eyes dimmed and went dark. His head fell to the side, and he died.

Chapter 29

Conlan stood with the points of his daggers pressing against two different throats. The warriors he'd disarmed held their breath, backed against the wall, no doubt reading their deaths in his eyes.

The whooshing noise of steel through air warned him to the danger seconds before yet another of Reisen's men fell dead next to Conlan's feet. He turned to see Justice wiping his sword on the fallen man's clothes. "Just watching your back, Conlan."

Conlan nodded. "Literally, I see. I owe you one."

Justice raised an eyebrow. "Oh, I think we shouldn't start keeping track, my lord. Because the 'you owe mes' are up to the double digits, now."

Ven and the others held the rest of the Mycenaean warriors at bay behind the barrels of semiautomatic shotguns. The problem with Ven's toys was that the reliability of machinery was chancy at best around anyone channeling the elements.

Dangerous at worst.

Ven always said he liked to live on the edge.

Alexios moved among the humans, checking on their well-being. They all wore odd robes and expressions of terror mixed with awe. Conlan caught the murmurs of "Atlantis, Atlantis."

Another problem to add to his ever-growing list.

On the makeshift stage, Alaric faced Reisen, who still held the Trident. A shimmering wall of energy flared up and between them, wavering toward first one, then the other.

Reisen had no training in using objects of power, but Alaric had once told Conlan that the Trident seemed to have a mind of its own. "More fickle than a beautiful woman" had been his expression.

But Alaric seemed to be winning this battle.

The men on the other ends of his blades twitched, and Conlan pressed the daggers a fraction of an inch deeper into the tender skin of their throats. "Do you think I'm distracted? Do you plan to make your move now?"

They stood silent, eyes widening in denial. Afraid to speak, probably.

Terrified of a prince come back from the grave and turned savage killer.

Good.

"Who knows what Anubisa did to me while I was gone?" he asked, mocking them. "Maybe I'm secretly a vampire, too."

He leaned closer to them, pulled his lips back over his teeth, and hissed.

The man on his right made a squeaking noise, then his eyes rolled back in his head and he dropped like a stone. Conlan barely had time to jerk the blade away before the damn fool impaled himself on it.

The warrior on Conlan's left wasn't the slightest bit intimidated. "Maybe you are worse than a vampire, if you play childish games like that with men who deserve better, my lord."

The words stirred a distant shame. Then anger followed it. "You dare to chastise me? Remember anything about treason? Blaspheming against the Temple of Poseidon by stealing one of its icons? Daring to attack your high prince?"

The man's defiance never lessened. "I am Micah, first of Reisen's Seven. We believed you were dead, and that Atlantis had no leader. You—"

"Ven was heir to the throne, and everybody knew it. Nice try at rationalizing, though."

Micah sneered. "Ven? How many times has he made it clear that he wants no part of rule? He's more at home in a tavern than in the palace. Reisen also has the blood of kings in him, and he would serve our people well."

Conlan stepped back, sheathed his daggers. Flicked a contemptuous glance down and back up the warrior. "So you think to lecture me on the demands of the throne? Go back to your mother's skirts, boy, and leave the thinking to the men."

Micah roared out his defiance and charged, exactly as Conlan had expected. He snapped out his fist and smashed Micah in the face.

Micah blinked, then fell forward and landed on the floor on the nose that was probably already broken.

"You picked a bad day to land on my shit list, warrior," Conlan said, almost to himself. Then he swung around to head for the magical battle of wills still raging in the front of the room.

Alaric had fought his way to the Trident, and he was inches away from laying a hand on it. The shock wave of power that blasted out in concussive circles had driven everyone else in the room to their knees.

Conlan started toward them, and another blast of power poured out of the Trident, waves of blue-green and silvery light sparkling with heat and thunderously loud. He ducked, and most of the energy passed over his head.

The second it was past, he dashed toward Alaric and Reisen, determined to bring an end to the standoff.

"For Atlantis! For Poseidon!" The words ripped out of his throat, no less powerful for being involuntary.

He was *back*. By the gods, he was back.

Anubisa hadn't won, after all.

He'd nearly reached them when Riley's voice, her *emotions*, pounded into his head with driving rage and pain.

Conlan!! Death anger sorrow death death death noooooooooooo!!

The shock wave of her emotion knocked him off his feet, and he fell to his knees, choking on her pain, a few paces away from Alaric and Reisen.

Come to me now!! I need you need need need powerrrrr!!

Riley had no voice left for screaming. Had no strength left for sobbing. She fell, dragged herself, crawling, through the unspeakable residue of vampire guts and blood and death coating the floor with its filth.

Somehow made it to Denal just as Brennan reached them both. She tried to focus through eyes drenched with tears, realized Brennan was wounded. Badly.

He limped. So many cuts and bites and blood covered him, she didn't know how he was still standing.

Bites. Oh, no.

"Brennan? Can Atlanteans turn into vampires?"

He shook his head, fell to his knees beside Denal's body. "No," he ground out, shuddering. "Virus. Not—not vampire. Kills us or we shake it off."

He gasped and clutched at his neck as his body arched back in the throes of a terrible convulsive spasm.

She reached out to hold his hand, not knowing what else to do to help.

"Might be bad this time," he gasped. "Must get you to safety."

"I tried to reach out to Conlan. Nothing—only blank, dead space where his emotions should be," she said, fighting back more tears.

Then letting them fall. What did it matter now?

Denal deserved at least her tears.

"Take it out! Brennan, we have to take it out," she begged, knowing she didn't have the strength left to pull the sword from Denal's body.

Brennan nodded, silent and grim, his skin already shriveling back into the bones of his face. His skull clearly visible under the flesh of his face.

He took a deep breath, and rose to grasp the hilt of the sword. Used it to pull himself up, then gathered his last energy. With one powerful jerk, he pulled it out of Denal's body and flung it away from them down the hall.

Then he collapsed next to Riley, strength spent. "I can no longer protect you, my lady. I have failed you. I am sorry."

She shook her head, tears still falling. Then she bent over Denal and lifted his head and shoulders into her lap. When she'd managed that, stroking Denal's lifeless face with one hand, she reached out to twine her other in Brennan's hair, trying to give some comfort.

"No. You never failed me, neither of you did. It was your stupid worthless excuse of a sea god. Where was your precious Poseidon when we needed him?"

She realized she was shouting at their god, didn't care. "Where were you when your *prince* needed you, you selfish bastard? Swimming around and frolicking with a fucking Nereid?"

Brennan tried to raise his hand, but it fell back against his side, shriveled and ancient. He was wasting away in front of her eyes.

"Where are you now, huh? You prick! I challenge you!! Heal these men, your warriors, if you're so all-powerful!" She screamed her rage until her throat burned and her skin caught fire from the inside.

An inferno of pain seared, burned, roared through her and into the room, scorching her breath as it came out of her lungs. She laughed, wild and savage.

"Yeah? Is that all you got? Come on and smack me down in person, you rotten coward! What kind of god are you, anyway? Come on! I dare you! *Come heal these men!*"

A cascading torrent of flames twined with water burst out of the ceiling and flooded the room. Surrounded Riley and the two fallen warriors. Branded her flesh with its searing intensity. In the midst of the pain, Riley found an oasis of calm inside herself. A moment of reflection cast upon her by desperate need.

So this is how I'll die. Mocking a god.

A voice resonating with power beyond anything she'd ever imagined thundered through the room, through her head, through the fabric of her reality:

MAGIC COMES ONLY AT A PRICE, AND LOVE COSTS ALL. DO YOU OFFER YOURSELF FOR THESE MEN?

The pain stopped. All that she knew was light and color and the cool mists of an ocean breeze. She was wrapped in the sea and filled by the voice of the sea god.

She'd dared to love a prince, and now his god would kill her for her temerity.

The voice blasted through her again, resonating in her bones, her teeth, her blood.

DO YOU OFFER YOURSELF FOR THESE MEN?

She hesitated, knew the answer must be utter truth. Looked down at their faces and into her memories. Joyous Denal, shy behind a bouquet of flowers. Emotionless Brennan, hungering for the feelings that were stolen from him.

And now their *lives*. This was her cost.

Will you let Conlan know that I loved him?

YOU DO NOT BARGAIN WITH A GOD.

She bowed her head, ignored the tears streaming down her face. The pain that shredded her heart.

She nodded.

Said the words out loud, needed to hear them. A promise. An offering. A solemn oath. "Yes. I offer myself for these men."

SO BE IT.

The water spiraled up from the floor, out from the walls, and down from the ceiling. Cushioned Riley and the two warriors in its curling caress.

Somehow, she knew to hold out her hands.

Somehow, she knew what appeared in them.

Shining with the glare of a dozen suns, the image of the Trident coalesced across her palms an instant before she felt the weight of it.

SO BE IT! THIS I COMMAND!

A fierce luminosity spread from the Trident across Riley's body to encompass first Denal, then Brennan. Quickly it grew so bright that she was unable to see them, had to shut her eyes against the glare. But she felt their still forms next to her.

The water turned to fire, and it seared across her back like the lash of a flame-tipped whip, driving her down, screaming, falling, burning.

As the blackness came, she welcomed it. Her life for theirs. Her final thought was of her sister.

Hey, Quinn. You'd be proud of me. Took me dying to do it, but I'm finally part of your revolution.

～～

Even as Conlan fought to raise his head, the Trident had disappeared in a blaze of color and light. Reisen and Alaric had screamed as they were thrown back by an explosion of power that blew out every light in the building.

By the time Ven and the others had gotten their wits back enough to pull out the flashlights they carried, Conlan had jumped up on the wooden stage to find Alaric.

He knelt beside his friend, relieved beyond measure when he heard the priest still breathing. In the light shining from Ven's flashlight, Alaric was dead white. Alaric's eyes opened, and the fiery green glow in them burned up at Conlan. "The Trident?"

A rasping voice came from behind him. Reisen. He whirled to protect himself from the danger he'd ignored like a fool in his fear for Alaric.

But Reisen was no threat. If anything, he looked worse than Alaric. Blood trickled from the corners of his eyes and from his nostrils. "It's gone," he gasped. "That voice—in my head—talking of death. Then the Trident blew up in my hands."

Reisen dropped his head in his hands, not paying the slightest attention to the half dozen swords, daggers, and guns aimed at him from close range. "It's gone. What have I done?"

"You heard her, too? You heard Riley in your head?" Conlan grabbed Reisen's arm, shook him. "You heard her call?"

"We all heard her, brother," Ven said. Conlan scanned the group, registered the nodding heads.

Leapt to his feet, then took to the air. "Then she needs us. Denal, Brennan—they all need us *now.*"

And he transformed to mist, soaring across the room to the window that would lead him to the outdoor air and back to Riley.

Calling out to her with his emotions as he did.

Praying, when he felt only blankness, that it wasn't too late.

~~~~~~

Reisen opened his eyes. The power drain had taken him under, probably for a while, if the stiffness of the arm bent under his body was any indication. He struggled to sit up, looking around the dim room. The moonlight through the windows shone the only light on the devastation.

Bodies, both human and Atlantean, lay scattered on the floor. Many were stirring even as he watched; not dead, then, but caught in the blast.

Then he realized what was missing. Conlan and the Trident were gone.

He'd failed.

Reisen closed his eyes as the impact of his failure crashed over him. He was out of options and should end his own life. His death would be marked as the passing of the traitor who had destroyed the honor of the House of Mycenae.

The shouts snapped him out of his indulgence of self-pity. Wave after wave of vampires flew in through the windows to land on his warriors and the defenseless Platoists.

A full dozen headed for him.

He smiled, unsheathed his daggers. At least he'd die as a warrior and take some of the infernal bloodsuckers with him.

"Bring it on."

Chapter 30

Conlan thought he'd known torture before.

That was nothing compared to the pain that ripped through him at the sight of Riley's nude and bloody body lying on the floor, Denal and Brennan sprawled out next to her. A sword, daggers, and an axe lay near them.

All of the weapons were coated in blood.

He flashed through the open door, transforming back into his body, anguish roaring up through his throat.

"Riley, no, no, no." He fell to his knees beside her, ripping his shirt off to cover her nakedness. Then he pulled her warm body into his arms.

Her *warm* body. Afraid to believe, he held his palm over her mouth and nose, nearly touching her.

And felt her breath.

She was alive.

"She's alive! By the gods, she's alive." He dropped his forehead against hers, breathed out a prayer of thanks. "You're alive, *aknasha*. I will never ask for anything else."

Alaric shimmered into shape beside him, scanning the room even as he crouched down next to Denal. "What happened here? Why are they unconscious? There are no wounds that I can see."

"Bring me a blanket," Conlan demanded. "I need to cover her. Take her to a bed."

Alaric shook his head. "Do not move her yet. Let me check for internal injuries." He moved closer, held a hand over Riley's shoulder.

Conlan fought against his urge to snarl at the priest. His primal instincts had gone savage with the need to defend and protect, like an animal with its mate.

"I'm not touching her, Conlan. You need to—oh!" The priest yanked his hand away as if he'd been burned. Then he stared up at Conlan, shock widening his eyes.

"Move your shirt away from her back, Conlan. I must see her shoulder." The utter bewilderment in Alaric's voice persuaded Conlan to comply. He gently moved a corner of the fabric covering her.

And they both stared at the mark of the Trident, still smoking around the edges, branded into her skin.

"This is a mark I cannot heal, Conlan," Alaric murmured.

As they stared at each other, then back at the blackened skin, Riley's eyelashes fluttered open.

"Conlan? Alaric? Am I dead?"

⚮

Before he could answer her, she'd lapsed back into a deep level of unconsciousness. Alaric had been unable to bring her around from it and had suggested sleep. Conlan carried her to the bedroom and gently cleansed her legs and hands of the blood and gore that streaked them.

His hands trembled as he stroked the curve of her ankle, and he wanted to scream. Wanted to rage, destroy, murder someone or something.

Wanted to cry.

Did none of those things. Didn't deserve to cry for her. He'd left her to be attacked. She could have been killed.

He wasn't only worthless as a prince. He was worthless as a man.

She deserved better.

He paused, warm washcloth clenched in his hand, and gazed at her pale skin. Even now, his mind rebelled at the thought of anybody harming her. Someone was going to die.

Why had she been nude? What had they done to her?

Who was *they*?

The thought of any man—or, worse, any *creature*—attacking her spiked a soul-annihilating rage through him.

But why the Trident? Alaric had said it was the priest's mark, would say no more until Riley was awake.

But the priest had been shaken. Unsure. Almost afraid, if the harsh lines of his face were any indicator.

"Riley," Conlan whispered, pulling the blanket over her now-clean form. "Please come back to me."

A knock sounded at the door. He positioned himself between the door and the bed, hands on his daggers. "Enter."

Ven opened the door. "We're ready to go. I have another place, way outside of town. No houses around it for miles. Nobody but me knows about it, since I only bought it a few months ago."

Ven crossed to his brother. Looked down at the sleeping form on the bed. "Is she going to be okay?"

Conlan knelt beside her, gently moved the hair back from her face. "She has to be," he replied simply. "Or I will end with her."

Ven started to speak, stopped, laid a hand on Conlan's shoulder. "Then we'll make sure she's okay. Let's go."

Conlan tucked the blanket more securely around Riley and swept her into his arms. He followed Ven down the hall, where the others stood waiting, loosely circling Alaric, who was as pale as death.

"Brennan and Denal are in the back of the Hummer," Bastien said. "Alaric told us they are only sleeping, and will wake soon."

"A sleep like I've never seen," muttered Justice. "They didn't even flinch when we carried them out to the vehicles. Makes you wonder what happened to them."

Alexios pointed to an umbrella, lying on the floor. "Why the umbrella? There were weapons all over the floor when we entered behind you. I counted an axe, several daggers, and both of their swords. But no weapons from any intruders, nor any sign of them, except for their blood on our weapons."

Christophe held his hands out, palms raised. "Not that this is my thing, but since Alaric is out of commission, I can try to feel what power might have been used."

He closed his eyes and lifted his head, muscles in his neck straining. Then his body jerked, as if struck. "Somebody called power here. Huge power. On the level of what hit us at that warehouse, Alaric. What could do that?"

Christophe turned to Alaric. "Neither Denal nor Brennan can channel the elements on this level. What could have called this power?"

"It was the Trident," the priest said flatly. "Poseidon delivered his staff to Riley and ordained her."

Alaric's laughter was tinged with dark wildness. "It appears Poseidon has claimed your *aknasha*, Conlan. Now she belongs to him."

~~~

They drove to the new safe house, Alaric refusing to speculate further on what might have happened. Or even discuss what he'd meant about Riley. The house was a rambling farmhouse type, set well back from what Ven said was a sparsely traveled country road. Conlan had noticed signs for various horse-related businesses and seen a few horses in fields as they passed. He waited in the car with Riley while the others cleared the building. Nobody was taking any more chances.

"It's not set up like a bunker now, but it has great potential to be refurbished. Plus, it has the advantage of being way the hell out in the boonies," Ven said when he returned.

"I don't care what it takes. Put *everyone* on watch," Conlan said flatly. "Well, all but Denal and Brennan. Let them rest."

"Are you kidding? I couldn't make them rest if I tied them down," Ven said. "Ever since they came to, they're hell-bent on protecting Lady Sunshine. They appear to have one helluva story to tell."

Conlan scowled at his brother, but Ven simply shook his

head, his face solemn. "I'm right there with them, bro. They said she dove into the middle of the vamps. That's way beyond the call, man."

He glanced at the motionless shape in Conlan's arms as they walked into the house. "She's quite a woman. She deserves better than what we've gotten her into."

Ice spread through Conlan's veins. When he spoke, a barely controlled ferocity underscored his words. "She does. But I can't . . . I *won't* let her go. Not ever, Ven."

Ven shrugged. "It's not me you have to convince. Alaric seems to have some thoughts on the matter. I'd be glad to get out of the 'do not pass Go, marry an eleven-thousand-year-old virgin' rules myself. But smarter men than me are going to have to figure that one out."

He showed Conlan to a spacious room at the end of the hall on the second floor and excused himself. Conlan gently laid Riley on the bed and covered her with the quilt, wishing her breathing weren't so shallow.

Her skin weren't so pale.

Then he dragged a chair across the carpet, right up next to the bed, and took one of her hands in both of his. And prayed to the god who had left him to suffer for seven years.

∾⸺⸲

Some hours later, Ven came back to let him know that Denal and Brennan were asking to see him.

Conlan sat in his chair, still holding Riley's hand. He needed to touch at least her skin, since her mind and emotions were closed to him.

He forced himself to breathe past the rock in his throat that threatened to choke him. Alaric had said she'd be fine. He had to hold on to that.

Poseidon's silence had been deafening.

"Bring them," Conlan demanded. "I won't leave her."

Ven nodded. "I figured as much. They're here."

Conlan watched as Denal and Brennan walked into the room, their gaze focused on Riley. Brennan gave him a cursory nod, then returned his attention to the bed.

Denal threw back his head and howled a cry of such anguish that the hair on Conlan's arms stood at attention, and an icy shiver shot down his spine.

"She's dead?" Denal stumbled closer to the bed. "That wasn't a dream, then?"

"She lives," Conlan said. Denal's attention finally turned to his prince.

"Alaric says she'll be fine. She's sleeping the same peculiar deep sleep as the two of you were."

"Thank the gods," Brennan said, voice low and reverent, as he, too, approached. "Thank Poseidon, for it truly was him in the room with us, was it not?"

Conlan's hand shot out and caught Brennan's arm in a steel grasp. "Tell me. What happened? Was there a battle? Why was Riley unprotected?"

Brennan dropped to one knee before him, head bowed. "We failed you, my prince. We failed to protect her."

Denal knelt also, lifted a hand to touch Riley's hair. Conlan allowed the gesture, somehow knowing that the warrior needed to prove to himself that she lived.

Then Denal dropped his face to the edge of the bed and began to sob. Great wracking sobs that shook his entire body with the force of them. Riley's name was in there, and other, wordless, sorrow.

Conlan released Brennan and put a hand on Denal's shoulder. "Tell me, Denal. Pull yourself together and tell me."

He looked up, saw Alaric had joined Ven at the doorway. The others crowded the hall behind them. "Come in, all of you. Find seats. We need to hear this."

Alaric, moving as one old and exhausted, took the room's remaining chair. Ven and the others filed in and found perches on the floor or leaning against walls.

Denal's shoulders stopped heaving, and he took a deep breath. "Brennan should tell it. Having no emotion would be a blessing beyond all reckoning at this moment. I can't—" His voice trembled, and he stopped, shaking his head.

Brennan stood straight before them. "If only I could feel the pain that should be burned into my soul. Lady Riley deserves no less."

Slowly, and ascribing all fault to himself, Brennan relayed

the night's events, his gaze continually returning to Riley as he spoke.

Denal interrupted several times, trying to shoulder the blame.

Brennan shook his head at the younger warrior and concluded. "And then I pulled the sword out of Denal's body, and the poison from the vampire bites overwhelmed me. I was dying, my lord."

Conlan listened, silent, shaking with rage. When Brennan paused, Conlan leaned forward. "We have acted as protectors and only stepped in when the vamps attacked humans in the past. But they brought this to our doorstep. They hurt Riley. Now they die."

He looked around at his men and Alaric, all of whom nodded, grim faces echoing his own determination. "They all die," he repeated.

Alaric spoke up, voice quiet. "But we need to know what happened after that. Riley must wake up and tell us her part of the story. Clearly Denal is alive, and Brennan is no longer infected with the vamps' poison. And there are . . . other matters."

None but Conlan had seen the brand seared into Riley's back. He nodded, appreciating the priest's discretion.

Denal raised his head to stare at the priest, eyes reddened from the tears that still fell. "I know what happened after that. Somehow, I saw it all. I was in a beautiful place, filled with the sweet scent of the ocean. Nothing hurt, not even the sword wound that ended my life. But as I rested and welcomed the peace, I saw Riley on the floor of that room, holding my body.

"I, too, saw and heard everything that happened. Lady Riley bargained with the sea god himself. She offered her own life for ours."

The voice from the bed was so thin and hoarse that Conlan thought he was imagining it. "He told me you do not bargain with a god," Riley whispered. "So why am I still alive?"

Conlan was out of the chair, thrusting Denal to the side, in an instant. Riley looked up at him, her eyes huge in her pale face.

"Riley! You're awake."

He touched her hair, her face, leaned forward to press the

gentlest of kisses to her mouth. Thank the gods.

Thank the *gods*.

She smiled at him, tears glistening in her eyes. "What's more amazing is that I'm *alive*, I'm guessing. Especially after that crack about Poseidon frolicking with a Nereid. I hear gods have had people hanged for less."

She shifted in the bed, grimaced. "My shoulder really hurts, though. I'm not sure what happened to it."

Conlan felt the tears running down his face, didn't care. "It's okay. We'll take care of it. You're alive, and that's all that matters. If you had gone from me—"

He heard a throat clear behind him. Alaric put a hand on his shoulder. "Perhaps we should leave Riley to rest now. There is much we need to discuss."

Conlan shook off the hand. "Yes, you should all leave. I'll stay here while she rests."

Denal stood, happiness and shame warring on his expression. "There are no words for my joy that you live, my lady. I will spend the rest of my life repaying you for your sacrifice."

He bowed to her, and tears spilled over Riley's lashes. Brennan also bowed, then knelt beside the bed. "Your sacrifice for one as worthless as myself is beyond anything I can comprehend. Should you ever have need of me, you have but to call."

She smiled at them, pulled herself up on the pillow a little. "You put your lives on the line for me. For me to do the same for you was not a sacrifice. I am so glad you're alive!"

She held her arms out to Denal, who quickly looked to Conlan. Conlan nodded his head, and Denal leaned down so Riley could hug him. When he pulled away she did the same to Brennan.

If Conlan had held any hope of protecting even the furthest dark corners of his soul from his love from her, that moment crushed those illusions. The sight of her reaching out to his warriors, and the knowledge of the sacrifice she had made for them, honored him—honored them all—beyond the greatest gift.

He gently grasped her hands in his own and bowed his head, spoke the words forcing themselves up and out of his soul in ancient Atlantean:

I offer my sword, my heart, and my life to protect your own.

From now until the last drop of ocean has vanished from the earth.

You are my soul.

She smiled, of course not understanding a word of it, and her eyelids drifted closed.

He never even heard the others leave the room.

Chapter 31

Death came for Riley, shriveling her skin and burning acid into her flesh, again and again as she slept, until she finally screamed her way through to wakefulness. Except the screaming was confined to the dreams. The only sound coming from her throat was a husky gasp.

Even that small sound was enough to wake the man lying next to her on the bed. A different bed than the one she'd slept in the night before, she noticed.

A different room.

Conlan tightened the arm that lay protectively across her waist. "Riley? Are you awake? Are you well?"

She looked up into his eyes, saw the familiar blue-green flame burning in his pupils. The sign of his passion for her.

His love.

"They're really okay? I didn't dream that, too?"

He nodded. "You saved them both. Your sacrifice—" His voice broke.

She lifted a hand to stroke his hair back from his face. "Shhh," she soothed. "It's all right. I'm here."

His entire body shuddered. "If I'd lost you—don't *ever* risk your life like that again."

Riley smiled, feeling weaker than she'd ever been. And yet stronger, at the same time. "There you go ordering me around, again. We have to work on this royalty complex you've got."

Conlan's lips curved at the corners. "Get used to it. I'm going to be ordering you around for a very long time."

He bent and gently kissed her forehead, her nose, and then her lips. "I'm never letting you get away from me. You understand that, don't you?"

He pulled her closer to him in a fierce hug. "Never."

She opened her shields, felt the full extent of his passion, and her own body shuddered in response. "Conlan? I need to feel you now. I need to feel your warmth."

"I'll hold you all night long, *mi amara*. I'll hold you forever," he murmured into her hair, gently caressing her arms.

"No." She pushed him away, sat up. Tried to escape the boulder that crushed her lungs. "I need to feel *alive*. I need to tell you—I need to show you—"

She rolled over so that she lay half on top of his body, put her hands on his face. "I *need*," she whispered.

And then she kissed him like she was dying of thirst, and his lips held the last drop of water.

Conlan moaned at the feel of her. He'd tried so hard to be gentle. To give her the comfort and safety he'd been so sure she'd want, instead of overwhelming her with his hunger.

But she was kissing him like she wanted to devour him. The passion in her touch unleashed the floodgates of desire he'd fought to keep barred. The terror that he'd lived through at the sight of her limp body lying there on the floor.

The relief that she lived.

"Riley, my *aknasha*, I love you. I need you. I need to be inside you right now, right now, right now," he groaned into her mouth.

She smiled, opening her mind and heart to allow him to feel her own heat and need. Without thought, beyond reason, he ripped at his clothes, desperately needing to feel his skin against hers.

Riley trembled with wanting him. Needing him. Needing to feel him inside her, so she could know she was alive. His big body shook as he yanked and tore at his clothes until he was as nude as she. He swept the quilt off her and replaced it with his body, pushing her legs apart and driving his fingers inside her to feel her, test her, learn that she was ready for him.

He made a low sound deep in his throat and centered himself over her. She felt the thickness of him straining at her, and she arched up to help him. He was so fiercely aroused he had to work himself inside her, and she stretched to a point just short of pain as the length and the breadth of his erection pushed steadily into her.

She cried out with the wanting, with the *hunger*, and kissed and bit at his mouth as if she were consuming him. He pulled out a little and she whimpered, and then he drove into her as far as he could go.

And she screamed. Screamed and clawed at him, dug her nails into his shoulders, into his back. Begged him for more, more, harder, harder. Reaffirming that she lived, that he lived, that he was there with her.

At least for now.

Saw the ferocious predator she'd unleashed in his face. Reveled in it.

"You're mine, Riley. Mine, *mi amara aknasha*, my beloved empath. I'm going to take you now, fuck you, sear myself into your soul," he growled, jaw clenching with the shreds of self-control he seemed to have left. She could feel the burning drive to possess her that shook him, heart and soul.

She arched her neck, heat and desire burning through her, and gasped. Then she slowly smiled at him, the warmth of certain knowledge in her eyes. "No, Conlan. You're going to *make love* to me. Because you love me."

She touched his face. "And I love you, too."

He went completely still, hands trembling on her skin. "Say it again," he demanded hoarsely. "Tell me again."

"I love you, Conlan. And you're mine."

He closed his eyes, but she felt the starburst of his emotions explode through her. Ecstasy, brightly burning joy. Wonder. *Awe*.

Then he opened his eyes again and he kissed her. And he *made love* to her for a very long time.

Barrabas gazed at the cloth-wrapped Trident, unwilling to touch it with his bare hands. Sure that the penalty for daring to rob a god would be hideous beyond imagining.

Easily enough gotten. Seeing the human and the Atlanteans dying on the floor, he'd snaked a tree branch into the house and pulled the Trident across the threshold. He'd been unable to enter, since he hadn't been in the first wave that the stupid human had unwittingly invited in.

Supreme commanders were never on the front lines, after all.

The Trident. Poseidon's instrument of true power, according to the scrolls. Deeded to the seated high priest of Atlantis for use in sacred rites. Such as the rite of ascension for their brat prince.

Too bad, that.

Guess the little boy wouldn't be king after all.

Drakos materialized in the concrete-walled chamber a dozen paces in front of him, curiosity plain on his face. "Did you try to use it?" he asked.

Barrabas sneered. "Would you so brazenly try to play with the toy of the sea god? There is good reason why I am the master vampire, and you are merely my servant."

Drakos didn't have the sense to even pretend to be cowed. "Is a general a servant, then? And what of Anubisa? Have you told her of your new toy?"

"No! And you will not, either. I'm not quite ready to give up my new possession, and she will surely claim it."

Barrabas soared around the table to confront his general, pushing hard with his mind. Drakos did not crumple to the floor, but the strain on his face showed what it cost him to remain upright.

"Ah, a petty defiance, *general*? What brings this about? Do you seek to rise in my esteem now that Terminus is destroyed?"

Drakos inclined his head. "If you will it so, my lord. I have strategies in mind to deal with these Atlanteans. Strategies that will help you consolidate your power until it is unshakable."

Barrabas couldn't help a certain level of interest. He'd seen the results of Drakos's exceptionally brilliant battle planning before.

Perhaps he wouldn't kill his impertinent general just yet.

His gaze returned to the Trident. "We need to consult the

scrolls again. See if we can find any hint of how to control the power this weapon must wield."

Drakos bowed. "A wise plan, my lord."

Barrabas held out a hand, nearly touched it, then withdrew. "And bring me several of my blood pride. I think we'll try a few *experiments* to see what vengeance Poseidon wreaks on any vampire who tries to play with his toy."

"Remember that we have several of the Atlanteans that we captured. Surely they know something of its power," Drakos pointed out. "There are easy enough ways to get humans to talk. These cannot be so different."

Barrabas smiled. "We'll find out, won't we?"

~~~

Riley stumbled into the shower, exhausted but happy. When the steaming hot spray hit her, she all but purred in relief. She'd taken a shower during the night, a quick clean-off one, but this one was going to be all about luxury and relief for her various muscle aches.

Fighting vampires was tiring business.

The thought sobered her. She, Denal, and Brennan had all come so close to dying. Denal actually *had* died. And Conlan still hadn't told her yet what had happened with Reisen and the Trident.

As she washed her back, her fingers touched an odd raised ridge on her shoulder. Her memory flashed back to the searing pain she'd felt when Poseidon accepted her offer.

Surely he hadn't cut her open?

But then again, what did she know about what a god might do?

She pushed open the shower door and hurried to the mirror, grabbing a towel to wipe the steam off the surface. Then she turned her back to the glass and awkwardly contorted her neck so she could look back over her shoulder.

At the scar—no, the *brand*—that marked her.

"Oh, my God! He branded me!"

She didn't realize she'd shrieked the words until Conlan yanked the door open and ran into the room, daggers in his hands. "What is it?"

She looked up at him, then back in the mirror at the six-inch-long image burned into the flesh on her shoulder blade. "He marked me, Conlan. That's a . . . that's a—"

"That's the Trident." He sighed, wrapped a towel around her, and held her for a long moment. "We have to talk to Alaric to find out exactly what it means."

Riley wasn't sure she wanted to know.

They dressed silently and went downstairs to find breakfast. The smell of frying bacon had persuaded her to leave the room and venture out, in spite of her reluctance. Riley knew that the room had been an oasis—a mirage of peace.

"It's over now, isn't it? The illusion of safety we created last night. Back to reality," Riley said, reaching for his hand.

"I will protect you with everything I have and everything I am, *aknasha.*" Conlan stopped on the stair landing to draw her close for a quick hug. "Never doubt it."

She smiled, but it was more of a gesture for his benefit than a real reflection of any happiness. It might be a long time before she had any reason to smile again.

Bastien reigned in the cheerful red-and-white kitchen, flipping omelets and frying bacon with the skill of long practice. "What can I get for you, Lady Riley?"

She closed her eyes and inhaled, deciding to bliss out and enjoy the moment. A girl couldn't fight a battle on an empty stomach. "I'll have some of everything. I'm starved, and it smells great! And just Riley, please, Bastien."

He grinned at her. "Everything it is."

As she poured herself a cup of coffee from the fresh pot on the counter, she studied the men in the room. Ven and Christophe were finishing up their own breakfasts and, after quick smiles and nods to her and Conlan, they resumed their argument about the relative merits of Italian versus German automotive engineering.

Conlan put his hand on hers, but what she'd taken for a romantic gesture was really a sneaky way to get his hands on her coffee mug. She scowled at him, trying not to grin and ruin the effect. "Hey! Get your own coffee, prince boy."

He laughed, took a sip, and handed the cup back to her, then dropped a kiss on the top of her head. "No respect for my royal self at all."

"Not a bit."

Ven looked up at them, speculation in his gaze. "Well, you gotta love that in a woman, bro. It must make for a nice change from all that sucking up you get from the women back home."

Riley's happiness fizzled out like air from a pricked balloon. The women back home. His intended queen.

She sat down at the enormous wooden farmhouse table, her appetite suddenly gone, and stared at her mug. Ven seemed to realize he'd stuck his foot in his mouth and groaned. "Hey, sorry, I didn't mean—I just was digging on the fact that you two look so happy and teasing Conlan a little, and—oh, shit. I mean, excuse me, Lady Sunshine."

His remorse was painfully evident, and she tried to smile reassuringly. "No worries. I'm just tired."

Conlan leaned over and smacked his brother upside the head, then sat down beside Riley and put an arm around her shoulder. She could feel his concern, but she didn't have the energy to reassure him, too.

Just as they were finishing their breakfast, the energy in the room changed abruptly, almost as if a frigid wind iced through the kitchen. Riley looked up, hands clenching into fists, ready to defend.

To attack.

Even as a tiny part of her wondered what she was turning into.

It was Alaric, spreading the *warmth* of his personality in front of him.

"We need to talk," he said, gaze arrowing in on Riley.

"Hello to you, too. Yes, I'm fine, thank you for asking," she returned, heavy on the sarcasm.

Jerk.

He inclined his head, a tacit acknowledgment of her point. "How are you, Riley? More to the point, how is your shoulder?"

"You knew about that? What is it?"

Conlan stirred in his chair. "Perhaps we should discuss this more privately."

Ven shoved his chair back, stood up. "Yeah, well, it sounds like something I need to know about, too. Christophe, you're on KP duty since Bastien cooked."

Christophe groaned. "Man, somehow I always get sucked into—" He looked up, met Riley's gaze, subsided. "Yeah. I got it."

As Alaric led the way out of the room, Bastien put out a hand to lightly touch Riley's arm. "We've got your back, okay? Don't stress about any of this stuff. We'll take care of you."

She opened her shields and sent a wave of warmth and gratitude to him. Watched his eyes widen as he received it.

"Wow. You really—hey, this *aknasha* stuff is pretty cool," he said, grinning. "And you're welcome, but no thanks were necessary."

"Good manners are the last bastion of a civilized society," she murmured.

"What?"

"Oh, something my mother used to say a long time ago. Your name reminded me of it. Thank you for the wonderful breakfast, too."

Conlan called out to her from the hallway, and she sighed. Squared her shoulders. "On my way."

Chapter 32

Conlan watched Alaric pace the large room—some kind of a den, all leather and wood—and the repetitive motion pissed him off. "Cut it out. Just let us have the bad news, already. Trying to be diplomatic is wasting our time, and it's not your style, anyway."

Alaric's eyes flashed bright green briefly, but at least he stopped the damn pacing. "I have facts, and I have speculation. I'm going to give you both, and identify which is which. Then we must decide how to proceed."

Riley spoke up, her voice small and quiet. "This is about me, I'm guessing?"

Alaric said nothing. He didn't have to. The look on his face said it all.

She tried to smile, tightened her grip on Conlan's hand. "Okay, fire away. And I meant that figuratively, in case you were wondering."

"First, the facts. You offered yourself to Poseidon for Denal and Brennan. He chose to let you live. However, he branded you with the mark of the Trident that only priests bear." Alaric ticked off items on his fingers as he spoke.

"Second—"

"What do you mean, that only priests bear?" Riley interrupted. "I don't even really believe in him. I mean, clearly I believe he exists, after what happened, and I know he has some pretty amazing powers, but I'm strictly a 'Jesus loves me' kind of girl. I can't be his priest! Or priestess, or whatever."

Conlan felt her rising panic, sent calm and reassurance to her. "Let Alaric explain. I don't think he really meant priest in the literal sense. Poseidon doesn't have priestesses."

"You mean, he doesn't have priestesses *now*. Thousands of years ago, the high priest was just as likely to be a high priestess," Alaric said.

"What? But I've never heard that."

"There are certain things the temple has kept to ourselves over the past few millennia. Like the existence of *aknasha'an* among the ones chosen to leave Atlantis at the time of the Cataclysm." Alaric started pacing again, as if his body couldn't remain still.

"Hello? Still not a priest or a priestess or *whatever*, here," Riley said, curling her legs under her on the couch. "Plus, aren't priests supposed to be celibate?"

She laughed, her cheeks turning pink. "I mean, oh. Um, well, never mind."

Alaric stared at her, eyes icy green. "Yes, there is a vow of celibacy. Another fact we may wish to discuss."

"Are you kidding? No sex for hundreds of years? That sucks!" She blinked. "No offense, but no wonder you're in such a crappy mood all the time, Alaric. I may have to rethink my entire viewpoint on you."

In spite of the deadly nature of the conversation, Conlan had to stifle a grin. She was the most spontaneous person he'd ever known. Whatever she thought . . .

"Comes right out of my mouth, I know," she said, rolling her eyes at Conlan. "Quit thinking so loudly. I'm sorry, Alaric. That was thoughtless and tactless of me. I think the idea of an unplanned priesthood caught me off guard."

The temperature in the room warmed a couple of degrees as Alaric's normally impervious expression thawed a fraction. "Believe me, I understand. But Poseidon has marked you with the sign of the ordained priest or, in your case, priestess.

I must consult with the ancient temple scrolls to determine what this might mean."

Conlan shoved a hand through his hair. "Can't you ask Poseidon? I mean, you are his high priest."

"The high priest who let the Trident slip through his grasp yet again," Alaric said flatly. "I don't get a response when I try to speak to the sea god these days. Believe me, I've tried."

"But—"

"It's worse than even that," Alaric interrupted. "The portal does not respond to my call. I attempted to return to Atlantis during the night to consult the scrolls, and the magic of the portal refused my summons. I fear we may be stranded up here until the matter of the Trident is resolved."

Ven finally spoke up from where he leaned against the far wall near the unused fireplace. "We've all tried. No dice. Which means we can't call for help, either," he said. "But let's go back a ways. You said there are more of these *aknashas* in our history? Who were Atlantean?"

"Yes. Several of the *aknasha'an* were among those of our people chosen to scatter to the high grounds of the earth at the time of the Cataclysm. Empaths were much more common then. Still maybe only one in one hundred babies were born with the gift, but since Riley and—" The pause was barely perceptible. "Riley and her *sister* are the first we have encountered in thousands of years, you can see how the numbers diminished."

"And what function did we . . . did *they* serve?" Riley asked.

"They were among the most valued of the royal counselors, naturally, given the nature of their talents. They were essential to trade negotiations and the like. Also, they would often choose to serve Poseidon in his Temple and were very popular in the priesthood."

"I can see how the ability to sense emotion would make someone pretty awesome in the confessional," Ven said. "You did what? *Buzz!* Wrong answer! You really did something much worse!"

"Shut up, Ven. You're not helping," Conlan snapped.

"Back off. I'm trying to lighten up the mood. You're both scaring Riley to death," Ven growled.

They all turned to look at Riley, who lifted her chin. "Hey, I'm the one who used an axe against a vampire last night, remember? Talking about the old days doesn't really compare with having brains on my legs." She shuddered. "So don't worry about scaring poor little Riley."

"Back to the point, here is my speculation," Alaric said. "I believe that Riley and Quinn are descendants of those ancient Atlanteans and have our DNA in their blood. Furthermore, I believe that they manifest these ancient gifts in fulfillment of one of the most secret prophecies in the Temple scrolls."

He drew a deep breath. "I believe that they herald the time when Atlantis must intermarry with the humans to bring a new and better generation to the world."

Ven whistled. "That's blasphemy, dude."

Alaric nodded. "Not only that, but it is in direct contradiction to the teaching of the Council that any person of royal lineage who violates the royal marriage strictures will bring a second Cataclysm upon Atlantis."

"What?" Riley could only follow the formal speak for so long before her tired and scared brain cells glazed over.

"No stud farm, end of Atlantis," Ven put in tersely.

"Not just Atlantis. End of the whole damn *world*, is what I've had drummed into my head for my entire life," Conlan said slowly.

"How do we know which it is?" Riley asked. "I mean, not to jump the gun here, Conlan, since we've known each other for less than a week, but I'd rather go with the intermarry thing than option B: cause the world to end."

Conlan felt her trepidation and admired her courage all the more for it. By the gods, she was beautiful. And brave.

And she loved him.

The wonder of it nearly brought him to his knees.

He put his arms around her and hugged her tightly. "In case you didn't hear me the dozen or so times I said it last night, I love you. We'll figure this out."

She hugged him back, but he felt her trembling. "How do we figure this out?" she repeated.

"That's the problem. We can't get back to Atlantis, and Poseidon isn't answering his phone," Ven said, face grim.

Alaric and Riley spoke at the same time. "The Trident."

Then they stared at each other, eyes widening.

"Tell me," Alaric demanded.

"I don't know. Just a feeling I had when he was talking to me last night. He was so arrogant—all 'you do not bargain with a god.' I get the feeling that he can be capricious—"

"You have no idea," Alaric replied.

"Yeah. So maybe this whole thing has been about 'the best man wins.' You know? If Conlan and you get the Trident, you deserve to win the throne, Atlantis, the free stay at a beach resort of your choice, whatever."

Alaric nodded. "That has a decidedly correct feel to it. The gods are ever changeable, and Poseidon has often demonstrated his admiration for the champion in any challenge."

Conlan tightened his arms around Riley. "So. We recover the Trident, or Atlantis may be lost to us forever?"

Ven laughed, but he didn't sound the least bit amused. "Damn gods and their games. Well, that's a sound enough theory to get us going on, then. Now all we have to do is find the Trident. Alaric?"

Alaric closed his eyes, held out his arms to channel power. Several moments passed, then he shook his head. "Nothing. But I felt it only in flashes the other day. I will continue to try."

Footsteps sounded in the hall, and Christophe rounded the corner, holding something out in his head. "Sorry to interrupt, but Riley's cell phone kept ringing."

He held it out to her. "It's your sister, and she says there's trouble."

Nobody but Conlan noticed Alaric flinch.

Chapter 33

Riley snapped her phone closed, noting that the batteries were going to die any minute if she didn't charge it. "You didn't happen to bring my tote bag with us from the other house, did you? My purse and cell charger were in it."

The four men in the room looked at her like she'd just asked them to go shoe shopping.

She narrowed her eyes. "This is important, okay? Quinn's only way to contact us is my phone, since you don't exactly carry phones around in your water particle state."

"Your bag is in the front hallway on a table," Ven said. "Now maybe you could fill us in on the other half of that phone call."

"Bear with me, because this is kind of crazy. But Quinn says that Senator Barnes is really an ancient vampire named Barrabas, and that he's the same Barrabas—"

"Freed by Pontius Pilate instead of Jesus Christ. Yeah. We know," Conlan said.

She blinked. "Are you kidding me? You knew this? You might have mentioned it sometime. 'Oh, hey, earthlings, your new *Senate leader* is one of the *worst criminals in history*,' for example." She heard the anger and sarcasm in her voice, but didn't care.

"Really? As if a people who allowed *bloodsuckers* to take over their government were going to listen to us about Barnes?" Ven snapped, his anger matching hers.

"Focus, people. This doesn't help now. What did Quinn want?" Conlan asked.

"She found your people. Well, Reisen and his people. She says she had a meeting with a high-level vamp who is working with the revolution undercover. Somebody named Daniel. He is going to help her get them out tonight."

Alaric stepped forward, eyes gone savage and glowing a fiery green. "Help her? Help *Quinn*? Is she insane? She's going to storm the fucking Primus?"

"Daniel says Barrabas has the Trident. Plans to torture the Atlanteans until he figures out how to use it. So my *insane sister* is helping to save your *ass*, priest." Riley didn't understand what board Alaric had up his butt about Quinn, but she wasn't going to put up with it.

Quinn might not be as fragile as Riley'd thought, but it was still Riley's job to protect her. She thought of Bastien and smiled grimly. *I've got your back, Quinn.*

Conlan stepped forward and effortlessly took command of the room. Whatever X factor it was that made a man into a king, Conlan had it in a big way.

Her insecurities mocked her. *So what makes you think you're fit to marry a king?*

I love him. That's all. That's enough.

"An hour max to get loaded up. We're on our way to D.C.," Conlan ordered. "Riley, you—"

"No way am I staying behind, so get that out of your mind," she interrupted.

"But I need to know you're safe," he said in what must have been his "reason with the peasants" voice.

She folded her arms, sent a big wave of stubborn through their bond. "Not. Happening. Besides, look how well that turned out last night."

She felt the capitulation in his mind before he nodded. "All right. But you stay out of the line of fire, do you understand? If anything happens to you . . ."

She went to him, put her arms around his waist. "I know. I get it. I feel the same way about you."

Alaric stalked to the doorway, paused to look back at them. Riley saw the wildness in his eyes. "I'm leaving now. I'll meet you there."

"You can sense the Trident now?" she asked him.

"No. But I can feel Quinn." She caught the flash of pain before he slammed shut his own mental shields. Wondered at the cause.

What exactly had happened between Quinn and Alaric during that healing?

She added it to her mental list of "things to officially worry about later" and headed after him to the hallway to get her bag. She had an hour to charge her phone.

Oh. Yeah. And to prepare for the end of the world.

～～⌇

Less than four hours and fifty or so broken traffic laws later, they were on the outskirts of D.C. in a neighborhood so bad even the police didn't like to hang out there.

Riley could feel Quinn long before they arrived. She sent out a push to try to communicate in words instead of just emotions. Somehow she felt like her talents in that area had increased a little bit since she'd had a chat with a god.

Quinn! Can you hear me?

Riley? How are you—oh, you've changed. The power emanating from you is lighting up my corner of the world. What the hell have you been up to?

I had a heart-to-heart with a sea god, who apparently claimed me for his own. Life is . . . interesting.

There was a silence, as if Quinn were choosing her words carefully.

Riley, what is this? Is this big and bad on an apocalyptic level?

Yeah. Yes, it is. I'll explain as much as I can as soon as we get there.

Another silence. Finally Quinn spoke in Riley's mind again.

Okay, get here soon. And, Riley?

Yes?

He's here. Alaric. I can feel him in my blood. He's . . . near.

I know. We need to talk about that, too.

She cut off the communication, feeling a headache center

itself over her eyes from the strain. She may have become more powerful, but unused muscles needed to be trained.

If she lived long enough.

She shook her head, put her hand out to rest it on Conlan's leg as he drove. He glanced at her, eyebrows drawn together. "Are you all right? Was that Quinn?"

"Yes. We're almost there."

He nodded, concentrating on the road and the always hideous D.C. traffic.

Almost there. And tonight the shit hits the proverbial fan. What have I gotten myself into this time?

But she looked at his strong profile and knew there was nowhere she'd rather be.

~~~

Conlan took point going into the abandoned building that Riley assured him was Quinn's headquarters and base of operations for the East Coast cell of her freedom fighters. He couldn't persuade Riley to stay behind, but he could damn well protect her from at least the front wave of any ambush.

Ven and the rest of the Seven fanned around and behind her, weapons at the ready. "I wonder how long the hubcaps on the Hummer will last?" Ven said under his breath, probably trying to get Riley to smile.

"Oh, they're already gone, I bet," Bastien said. "Never liked that car anyway."

Christophe laughed. "I put a little zinger on the cars. If anybody goes after them, they're in for a surprise."

Conlan ignored the banter, led the way down a battered and graffiti-covered staircase at Riley's direction. Didn't like it one bit.

They hit the bottom step and found a dozen armed guards waiting for them, all dressed in old jeans and leather jackets. They looked like hoodlums or homeless people, until you noticed the very new, very shiny guns in their hands.

Conlan and the Seven immediately drew their weapons and aimed them. Riley pushed her way through to stand next to Conlan and shook her head. "Nice show, Quinn. Now call them off."

The man in front, huge and built like a warrior, slowly

bared his teeth in what he probably thought was a smile. Civilization was a bare veneer over the savagery in the man.

Conlan knew instantly that this was the leader. Nodded his head to the man. "I am Conlan of Atlantis. This is Riley, Quinn's sister. If you're not the people we seek, we'll walk out of here. Try to hinder us, and you'll die for your trouble."

The man gave an almost-imperceptible signal, and the men with him lowered their weapons. "Quinn! Looks like it's family reunion week," he called out.

He held out his hand to Conlan. "Jack Shepherd. I help out."

Quinn walked out of a small door behind Jack, arguing with somebody on the telephone. "No, it's now or never. I need that stuff tonight. Or by morning at the latest."

She held her hand over the receiver, nodded to Riley, looked at Jack. "Dawn?"

He nodded, body radiating a fierce tension. "Dawn. If your friends agree that it's better to hit the bloodsuckers at daylight?"

Conlan inhaled deeply, subtly called power. The elements sang to him, but the earth's song was the most piercing. He looked at Jack. "And how about you? Is it better for you and the other shape-shifters to hit at dawn, too?"

Chapter 34

While Ven and the Seven made nice with Quinn's strike force, Conlan, Riley, and Quinn and her buddy the alpha werewolf sat around a scarred metal table on chipped and battered wooden chairs.

Quinn looked at Conlan. "He's not."

"He's not what?"

"He's not a werewolf, if that's what you were thinking. He's . . . Jack, is it okay if I tell them?"

Jack shot a hard, measuring stare at Conlan. Oh, yeah. The man was definitely a warrior, no matter what kind of animal he turned into under the moon's pull.

"Fine. I guess knowing about Atlantis is about as tit for tat as we can get on this op," he said.

Quinn smiled briefly. "He's a weretiger. Not indigenous to North America. But when the vamps—"

"When the bloodsuckers destroyed my entire streak—my family group—I decided they were going to die. And the best way to take them down was to come to the source," Jack said, voice bleak.

Riley sent an affirmation through the bond. The man was telling the truth. That was good enough for Conlan. "We need to recover the Trident. Its power in the hands of Barrabas or— gods help us—Anubisa could well signal the beginning of the next Cataclysm."

Quinn nodded. "They have your people, too. Daniel told us he's planning a coup, and we—"

"Daniel?" Riley interrupted. "Who is he, and why do we trust him?"

"Good question," Jack growled. "He's one of Barrabas's top generals, and I *don't* trust him. Ask your crazy sister what the hell she's thinking."

A dark, swirling shadow swept through the room, driving an icy wind before it. Before he'd even materialized, Quinn stood up, hands outstretched. "Alaric."

He swept down, took her hands, and pushed her back and away from the shape-shifter.

Jack obviously didn't care for that at all. He was on his feet, gun in hand, in the blink of an eye. Conlan had nearly forgotten how fast shape-shifters could move.

From the look of it, maybe weretigers were the fastest of the bunch.

"Step away from the lady, magic boy," he growled, in a low, rumbling roar.

Next to him, Riley shivered at the jungle sound resonating through the small room. Conlan jumped up, flashed across the table to face Jack. "Calm down, he's with us."

"I don't care who he is, he needs to keep his hands off my partner, or he's going to be fertilizer." Jack's eyes glowed an eerie yellow-green shade and the pupils lengthened to slits.

Quinn's voice came from behind Conlan. "Jack, stop it. This is Alaric, and he healed me from that gunshot wound. He has . . . civility issues."

Heat and light shot through the room, and Conlan didn't have to turn around to know who was generating it. "Alaric! A little control, if you please. We've got a lot to deal with, here."

Alaric's voice was rusty, strained. "A word, if you would, my lady. I need—I need—" He broke off, breathing harshly.

Riley started to go to Quinn, but Conlan stopped her with a hand on her arm. This was something Quinn and Alaric had to figure out before they could all work as a team to storm the

Primus. Riley glared at him, then felt his emotions and signaled that she understood. Nodded and sat back down.

Quinn finally spoke, her voice unbearably weary. "Yes. We need to talk. Especially since that's all we will ever do with each other. Come with me. The rest of you, please just wait. Get to know each other."

She laughed. "Eat a cookie."

As Quinn and Alaric left the room, Conlan achieved a moment of clarity. The realization that Quinn had trapped Alaric in her empathic net as surely as Riley had done to Conlan.

But certain sea creatures founder and drown in nets.

And Alaric was looking like one of them.

Then they were gone, leaving him alone with a creature that everything in his heritage told him he should destroy.

Riley watched them leave, then heaved out a sigh. She leaned forward, elbows on the table, and smiled at Jack. "So. Tell us about being a tiger. Where are you from?"

∾⟶∾

Alaric faced Quinn on the roof of the building. Fighting desperately for self-control. For calm.

For the courage not to fall on his knees in front of this human female and beg for her touch.

How Poseidon must be laughing at his high priest now.

She watched him, wariness in every line of her body. "You're the most powerful with the magic, aren't you? I can feel it singing in your veins, thrumming underneath my skin. What did you do to me when you healed me? And thank you for that, by the way."

He stalked her, paced in an ever-diminishing circle around her position. Knowing he should stop.

Unable to do so.

"I did nothing unusual, although current events suggest that Riley may have aided in your healing," he said roughly. "What was unusual was what you did to me."

She wasn't even beautiful. He'd always thought he'd fall someday, into grand and gloriously unrequited love with an amazing beauty. A goddess among women.

Among *Atlantean* women.

Yet this scruffy human—this *rebel*—wasn't anything like

what he'd imagined. She was so thin as to look starved, all huge eyes with black circles under them over hollow cheeks. Her short hair looked like she'd cut it with that knife she kept in her pocket. Her clothes were no better than what he'd seen on beggars on the streets.

He wanted her so badly it was an actual physical pain squeezing his balls.

"I don't know what you think you see, but I'm not like my sister," she said, voice and emotions filled with sorrow. The heat and colors of her emotions swirled around him, tortured him. Wine red, dusky gray, and the blue of the sea at twilight danced into him, through him, piercing him with poignancy.

Bringing tears to his eyes.

He fought them back. Fought against the silken net she so effortlessly wove around his heart. Around his soul.

The woman who could tame a sea monster.

And he, the monster.

"You're nothing like your sister," he agreed. "And yet you're exactly like her. Foolishly idealistic, the both of you. She saves crack babies, and you save the world."

Feint, attack. "Did you know that Riley gave up her life for two of our warriors?"

She paled even beyond the marble whiteness that was her skin. Her perfect skin.

The skin he wanted to taste.

"What?" she gasped. "But, wait. You said 'gave up her life.' She was pretty clearly alive in that room."

"Yes. Poseidon plays with semantics as easily as he plays with destinies and lives. He took her for his own."

She scowled. Took a step closer to him. "What the hell does that mean? Is some ancient pervert of a mythological god going to try to rape my sister? Because I'll kick his fishy-tailed ass for him."

Alaric flinched at the blasphemy, then a thunderbolt of epiphany smashed into him. He'd fight Poseidon himself to protect Quinn.

He was ruined.

Strange that the word she'd used to describe herself flowed so easily into his mind. *Ruined.*

"Why are you ruined?" he asked abruptly. "What were you talking about?"

It was her turn to flinch. She whirled on her heel to stare out at the view. Abandoned buildings and junked cars held nothing to capture her attention, but something in her memories evidently did.

He silently moved until he was immediately behind her. Could feel her body heat warming the iciness of his skin. The frozen tundra of his heart.

Knew he had to get away or get burned.

Before he could move, she turned back again and nearly ended up in his arms. They were so close a mere breath separated them.

A breath and eleven thousand years of dogma.

"The rebel and the priest," he rasped. "What a pair we are."

Her eyes were huge in her starved face. "But a *pair* is what we could never be. I've done things . . . black and unforgivable things. In the name of freedom."

He put a hand up to touch her face, stopped with his fingers an inch away from her skin. "And I've done nothing. In the name of a god."

He flashed back a dozen or so paces, stood staring at her. Letting the full impact of his hunger and his wanting thunder toward her. *Into* her.

She bent at the waist, wrapping her arms around herself. Started to cry. "I have no right to ask it, but please go now," she said, a fractured dignity in her voice. "We'll work together tonight, and then we'll never see each other again. But go now. Don't torture me with visions of what I can never have."

He bowed to her, and then somehow he found the strength to walk away. Knew that facing Barrabas would be as nothing to the courage he called upon now.

Chapter 35

Riley stumbled, grabbed the edge of the counter where she'd been looking for the cookies Quinn had mentioned. The blast of pain sheared through her, nearly driving her to the ground.

"Quinn. Oh, Quinn," she moaned.

Instantly, Conlan was at her side, putting his arms around her and growling at Jack, who'd moved to help her. "Riley? Are you okay?"

"Yes. No. I don't know. It's Quinn, she—" The flow of torment abruptly stopped. Quinn had slammed shut her shields.

Riley sent sympathy and love to her sister.

Quinn, I'm here for you. I love you. I'm not sure what's going on with you, but I'm here for you.

But the only response was silence.

Ven walked into the room. "Hey, we're going to scout out the area now that it's getting dark. We'll pick up some food while we're out. Justice is pretty familiar with D.C. and of course Quinn's men . . ."

His voice trailed off and his focus zoomed in on Jack. "What the hell are you? I've never smelled *that* before."

Jack scowled at him. "Great manners, asswipe. Go around sniffing people all the time, do you?"

Ven smiled. "You wanna go? 'Cause I'm sitting on a shit-load of tension, and I'd be happy to rearrange your face just for fun. So let's go."

Jack's mouth was suddenly crowded with teeth. "Maybe you want to check the state of the moon before you go challenging the alpha of my streak, water boy."

Riley pulled away from Conlan, stepped between the two men. "Do we have a measuring tape in the room?"

Ven blinked, shot her a puzzled look. "What?"

She put on her best sweetness-and-innocence smile, and Conlan fought to keep from laughing. He knew what was coming.

"Well, I figured you two could whip them out, and we'd measure them and get it over with," she said, voice lilting.

It took a beat, but then both Ven and Jack roared with laughter, and they held their hands out to each other to shake.

"Ven. Want to show us the lay of the land, jungle boy?"

"Jack Shepherd. And it's jungle *man* to you."

Ven looked to Conlan, who nodded, and Ven and the tiger left the room. The plan was a good one. Although they had no reason not to trust Quinn, her judgment in the people around her was a question mark until proven otherwise.

Doing surveillance in advance was a no-brainer.

Riley snorted, shaking her head. "Boys will be boys, right?"

A dark shadow twisted through the room and materialized into Alaric. "What is the plan?"

"Where's my sister?"

"She's on her way. She wanted . . . a moment alone."

"If you hurt my sister, I'll—"

Conlan put a hand on her shoulder and sent his thoughts to her.

Riley. Look at him. Look with your heart. He'd die before he'd hurt her.

She paused, turned her focus to Alaric, then glanced back at Conlan.

Perhaps. But there are more ways to hurt than only one.

"The plan is that we wait and attack at dawn, when the vamp strength is at its nadir," Conlan replied to Alaric.

"Then I will return just before dawn," Alaric said, voice

rough. "Guard her for me, Conlan." His gaze flicked to Riley. "Guard them both."

Alaric lifted his arms and vanished.

Riley shook her head. "I'm never going to get used to that, am I?"

Conlan moved to the door, checking to be sure that Ven had left sufficient guard. Knowing that his brother would have it covered, but needing to move. Needing to *do* something.

"Sitting and waiting sucks," he said.

"You think?" Riley's voice was more than a little sarcastic. "And yet that's what you want me to do, right?"

"That's different. You're . . ."

"A woman? Oh, you *so* do not want to go there, mister," she warned.

He pulled her close to him again, rested his forehead against hers. "You are the heart that beats within my body. If you were to die, my existence would end with yours," he murmured.

She shivered in his arms, then raised her face for his kiss. "You're *gooood.*"

"I know."

Riley laughed. "Enough with the smug, fish boy. You're also way too old for me, by about four hundred and fifty years or so. Remember that when you're getting all full of yourself."

"That's *prince* fish boy to you," he teased.

Slowly, the smile faded from her face. "Is this what they call laughing in the face of death? Because I don't feel all that amused."

Quinn's voice sounded from the door. "Welcome to the club, baby sister."

～～～～

Ven and Jack brought back enough sandwiches for a small army, but Riley hadn't been able to manage more than a few bites.

Small army. Yeah, well, that's exactly what we are. Very small army.

She shivered and pulled her jacket tighter, even though she figured that this was the kind of cold that came from the inside. The idea of death wasn't a warm and cheerful one.

Her gaze followed Quinn as she walked around the room,

talking to her band of freedom fighters. Who would have believed that her fragile sister would grow up to be a rebel leader? Or that Riley herself would fall in love with the heir to the throne of a mythological land?

The entire experience was like being written into the script of an urban fantasy where the boundaries of prosaic reality blurred into fantastical images.

Either that, or a seriously bad trip. I picked a bad time not to be a drug addict.

The thought surprised a laugh out of her, causing Conlan, who stood across the room talking to Jack, to glance over at her, one of his dark eyebrows raised. The man's awareness of her was almost viscerally intense; she felt his presence in her blood, under her skin, racing across her nerve endings.

She shivered again, but from a wholly different cause. Decided to have a little fun. Sent a very specific emotion winging over to him.

Desire.

So I hear that "life is in jeopardy, might be the end of the world" sex is pretty hot.

She focused all of her concentration on the image of the two of them together, limbs twining. Her mouth on him. Her hands on him.

She watched as it hit him. Saw the sharply indrawn breath, the muscles in his jaw clench. Seconds later he was standing in front of her, crowding her back against the wall.

"Interesting talent, *aknasha*. Care to take this somewhere private and show me more?"

She smiled up at him. "Oh, yeah."

She waved to catch Quinn's attention, nodded her head toward the door. "We're going to get some rest," she said, knowing she wasn't fooling her sister.

Probably wasn't fooling anybody. In a room full of shape-shifters, they could almost certainly smell her heightened desire. The thought made her face go red, but didn't stop her.

Quinn nodded once and looked away. She hadn't told Riley anything about Alaric. Had merely looked at her, pain beyond measure in her eyes, and said there was nothing to tell.

The memory stopped her. "Conlan, maybe we should—"

He understood instantly; she could feel it in him. "Yes, we can stay if you want. But does Quinn really want us to?"

She gazed at her sister again. Quinn sat nearly head to head with Jack, both of them poring over the blueprints to the Primus yet again.

Jack was yet another issue. Riley had watched his oddly feral eyes track Quinn wherever she moved. The weretiger had deep feelings for her sister, it was pretty obvious. But Riley didn't think they were lovers. And what about Alaric?

"She's a grown woman, love. You cannot solve her problems for her," Conlan murmured in her ear.

"That doesn't mean I won't try," she said ruefully.

"Come with me now. Let me hold you for a little while until the dawn."

She sighed. Nodded. "Yes. Quinn showed me a room where we can sleep. It's cramped, but—"

He took her face in his hands, searched her eyes. "Wherever you are is as paradise come to earth for me."

Her breath caught in her throat. In what world was it fair that she'd finally found the other half to her soul, and it was unlikely either of them would survive another day?

"But we have tonight," she whispered. "Let's make it enough to last forever."

And she led him out of the room.

∽⌒∾

Barrabas snapped the neck of the Atlantean in front of him and watched the dead warrior fall to the floor. Then he threw his head back and howled his rage out to the stone walls of the chamber.

Drakos stood well back from the carnage, probably afraid that he'd be next. With the mood Barrabas was in, it was surely possible.

"How is it possible that these puny sacks of flesh can withstand my mind-control powers?" he hissed, kicking one of the bodies so hard he heard the ribs snap like kindling.

It would have been so much more satisfactory if the man had yet lived. Barrabas so enjoyed it when they screamed.

"But they did scream before they died, didn't they, Drakos?"

He walked through the gritty residue of the three vamps from his blood pride.

Point taken. Poseidon didn't approve of vampires touching his precious toy.

They'd died spectacularly, though. A waterfall of flaming death. Barrabas had to admit the sea god had style. One had to admire such creative methods of murder and annihilation.

His vampires had died screaming, too.

The Atlantean leader, Reisen, hung from one of the manacles on the wall, bloody and near death. But that one had never screamed. Not even when Barrabas hacked his hand off with a sword.

One had to admire such courage, too. Except when it obstructed his plans. Then one had to torture it mercilessly to death.

"Reisen thinks the others will come for the Trident. The prince and the priest," he mused, carefully rubbing his boot on one of the dead bodies to remove the blood. He watched as the thing's shirt turned reddish black, then deliberately stepped on its face as he strode over it.

"They wouldn't dare confront you, my lord," Drakos responded. He even looked outraged on Barrabas's behalf. A nice touch, that, genuine or not.

"A prince and a priest," Barrabas repeated. "Haven't these Atlanteans ever heard of the separation of church and state?"

He laughed and watched Reisen flinch, lifting his handless arm toward his chest. "Maybe we'll have to introduce you to the new and improved Bill of Rights when we take over your precious Seven Isles, what do you think?"

Reisen lifted his head and glared at Barrabas. "Conlan will obliterate you, and Alaric channels more power than you ever dreamed of, bloodsucker." He coughed, spat out a glob of blood.

Then the Atlantean smiled, blood running down his chin. "And I will dance on your salted grave."

Barrabas roared out his outrage, and the lights in the chamber flickered. "You will never live to see it, worm."

But before he could rip the warrior's head from his body, Drakos was in front of him, back of his hand smashing into the man. Reisen's head snapped back and cracked against the wall, then he collapsed, unconscious or dead.

Drakos bowed. "Perhaps he might prove useful later, my lord. Once he is sufficiently persuaded, he may be key to our learning more of the Trident."

Barrabas narrowed his eyes, wishing yet again that he could scan his general's mind. "Do you offer good strategy or defiance, Drakos? Why do you always seem to walk the razor edge between the two?"

"Would you want a weakling as your second?"

Barrabas waited several minutes before responding. Let Drakos worry. "No. But do not take that as leave to defy me, General Drakos."

Drakos bowed again. "Shall I bring the last of them? The one they call Micah?"

"Oh, yes. We still have a few hours until dawn. Let us see if we can make this one sing for us." Barrabas walked back across the bodies of the dead, enjoying the snap of bones as he crushed limbs.

"I do so love the sound of music."

Chapter 36

Conlan made it nearly two entire steps inside the dim room behind Riley before his control snapped. He slammed the door shut behind him and yanked her back against him, nearly crushing her in his arms. "I can't do this, Riley. I can't go into this battle tomorrow with you anywhere near danger. Please don't ask it of me."

She turned in his arms, put her arms around his neck. "I don't think it's up to us. I get the feeling that this is some kind of proving ground, and Poseidon is making all the rules. When he put this mark on my back, he put my game piece in play."

Conlan laughed, the sound of it ringing bitter and hard in his ears. "Because that's all we are to him. Pawns in some insane chess match."

Riley touched his face, traced the edge of his lips with one finger. "Doesn't history teach us that we are only pawns to all of them? My God, your gods, everybody's gods? We play the best game we can, and then we die. Match over. And all we have to show for it is how well we played the game."

She smiled. "I think I stretched that metaphor completely out of shape. But you get my meaning."

He closed his eyes. Focused on the feel of her breath on his skin. The heat exploding up through his body at her touch.

"I don't care about games or gods. Not tonight. All I want is to hold you and burn this moment into my memory for all time," he said roughly, tightening his arms around her.

"Yes," she said. Simple and direct. Just *yes*. And then she lifted her face to kiss him, and his world caught fire.

He lifted her, and her legs came up and around his waist. He cried out at the fierce pleasure that pounded through him at her touch. His body hardened, muscles clenching, and he walked, carrying her, until her back was pressed against the wall.

She moaned into his mouth and twined her fingers in his hair, pulling his head toward her as she plunged into his kiss. He shifted his hands until he felt her rounded ass in his palms, and he squeezed and caressed her, pulling her forward so her skirt rode up her thighs and nothing but his pants and the thin silk of her underwear was between them.

It was still too much. He propped her up on one of his thighs and shifted his hands to rip the lace in two and yank the pieces off her. Then he pushed his leg up so that the hardness of his leg rubbed against her wetness.

She moaned and writhed against him, her fingers digging into his shoulders. "Yes, touch me. Take me, Conlan. I need you."

He bent to bury his face in her neck, needing to shout out his triumph but wanting to muffle the sound from everyone gathered so near. With a muted growl, he bit at her neck where it curved into her shoulder, then caressed the spot with his tongue, soothing the tiny scrape.

She moaned again and arched into him, frantically pulling at his shirt, trying to get her hands on his skin. He ripped his shirt up out of his pants with one hand, unbuckled his belt and unzipped in seconds. Before he could do anything else, she put her hands on his shoulders and used them to lift up a little.

Then, looking into his eyes the entire time, she centered herself and slid down on his erection, wrapping him in her heat and wetness. He couldn't help it, he shouted out her name. Grabbed her delicious ass again and squeezed. Lifting her and driving into her again and again, watching pleasure glaze her eyes until they fluttered closed.

Then he stopped. She whimpered, blinked at him. "Why did you stop?"

Slowly, inch by inch, he lowered her onto his shaft again, watching her face. "Because I need to see you while I take you. I need to look into your eyes and see into your soul, my Riley, *mi amara aknasha*. I need to know that you are mine, now and forever."

He pulled back out of her, drove in again to the hilt, loving the sound of her gasp. "I want you to take me and know that I am yours as well."

She lifted up, feminine muscles clinging to his cock even as she pulled away from him. Torturing him with her deliberateness. "Now and forever, Conlan. No matter what the gods may have in mind for us, there will never be another for me. You are my only. My happily ever after. My love. My soul."

With the words, she seated herself on him, pushing against him until she could take no more.

There was no more to take.

Then stopped, surrounding him, tightening around him, his hardness entirely sheathed in her heat. His heart sheathed in hers.

Simultaneously, they swept aside any remaining barriers between their two souls.

And light and color blasted through his world—her world—their world. They stood trembling in a maelstrom of cerulean and aqua and silvery green. The music of rainbows lilted through them, around them, piercing them as they stood. A fountain of need, of longing, of utter fulfillment cascaded around them and into them until he could not tell where he ended and she began.

Worlds trembled on the verge of awakening, and stars burst into firestorms of radiance. Riley's soul opened to him, and he claimed it for his own.

She did the same with his.

And the fire, fury, and raging power of the elements soared through him and out of him into her, and he had a microsecond of time to wonder how such passion could explode without creating new life, but then she was screaming in his mind and the universe went supernova around them.

He fell to his knees, still cradling her in his arms, too weak to stand. She gasped for air, her breathing in time with his.

When she finally lifted her head, her face was almost too beautiful for his vision to bear. "What happened? Did the world end?" she whispered.

"That, I think, was the soul-melding," he replied, barely able to form words. "According to legend, it only grows more intense as time passes."

She blinked. "We're never going to survive it."

It was a long time before he could quit laughing enough to catch his breath and carry her to the cot in the corner. There he held her throughout the hours until dawn and watched her sleep. Thanking the gods for the gift of her love. Vowing his life to protect her.

Hear me, Poseidon, for I vow this with everything I am or will be. This woman is mine.

Light flashed through the room, a lightning strike of energy that scorched across his vision.

Poseidon's answer, perhaps. Now if Conlan only knew what in the nine hells it meant.

～～～

A few too-short hours later, Riley sat in a corner of Quinn's war room, hands cradling a mug of coffee. She couldn't stop watching Conlan. Her fierce warrior had so easily taken command of the planning and dominated the room. Even in a roomful of alpha males, he would always be the one who dominated.

For a man who didn't believe he had what it took to rule, he had the look of a king stamped into every hard line of his face.

And he wanted her to be his queen. The thought was too enormous to wrap her mind around, especially now. On the eve of a full-out assault of the vampire lair. She'd think about it later. She was getting damn good at denial.

Jack was pointing something out on the map. "These are concrete walls, it's not like we can blast through them. If Quinn's contact doesn't come through for us, we're fucked."

Quinn, looking like a stiff wind would knock her down,

merely nodded, face grim. "He'll be there. Don't you think I've tested his information on smaller issues before trusting him with something like this? He believes that Barrabas's way is wrong, and that the undead should return to the old ways."

"Eating people in the shadows?" Ven asked, voice flat.

"No, coexisting with humans without trying to conquer us," Quinn replied. "He has existed on animal blood for centuries, except for the rare voluntary donation."

"So he claims," Conlan pointed out. "No matter. We are committed to proceed on this information. May the gods have mercy on him if he has betrayed us."

The icy wind that seemed to be Alaric's calling card swirled through the room, coalesced into his dark form near Conlan. "There are no gods that heed the call of such vermin, save for Anubisa. And I would wish that she would come to his aid, so that I might end her existence."

"Oh, I'm down with that," Ven snarled.

Conlan's voice was calm and utterly lacking in emotion. "If Anubisa should appear, she is mine. Consider this my first royal decree."

Ven slowly nodded, but Riley noticed that Alaric made no sign of agreement. He simply stared at Quinn with the air of a predator examining its prey.

Or a man sentenced to die regarding his executioner.

She couldn't quite determine which.

Bastien broke the silence. "I'm not picky. If I have to take them down one by one, the bloodsuckers are going to die."

"You know the human police and soldiers will protect the Primus, as well. It's an official house of Congress," Justice said from a dark corner of the room. Riley hadn't even known he was back there. She had a sudden insight that he lived much of his life in dark corners.

Another thing to think about later.

"That's why Daniel is taking us in through the underground passage," Quinn replied, looking anywhere but at Alaric. "We may have to fight our way through some of Barrabas's blood pride to get to him, though. Daniel did warn us of that."

"To the Primus, then. We will retrieve the Trident, and teach these vampires a lesson in interfering with humanity or with the Warriors of Poseidon," Conlan said, voice ringing through the room. "A lesson that is some two thousand years overdue."

"Amen to that," Riley said fervently. Then she put her mug down and touched one hand to the silver cross around her neck. "And may God watch over us."

Then she thought of the mark on her back. "All of the gods."

Chapter 37

"It's unlocked. Just like he promised," Quinn whispered, as she opened the door that had been hidden behind a wall of cleaning products in the basement janitorial closet of a shabby office building. Conlan nodded, gestured to Ven that the two brothers would take point down the dark corridor.

From behind him, Jack let out a low rumbling roar. "I don't think so. I'm not putting my men in danger—I'm not putting *Quinn* in danger—unless I'm in the front row at the party, boys."

Conlan paused, nodded. "Join us, then, tiger. But this mission is under my command, as the future of my realm depends upon it. If you cannot agree to that, you will remain behind."

The shape-shifter's eyes glowed a fierce golden color. "Who's gonna stop me?"

Alaric waved a hand, almost nonchalant. "That would be me." The priest walked to stand in front of the shape-shifter, who was frozen in place, unable even to speak.

"Even at the dawning of the full moon's eve, my power exceeds yours. Do you challenge me, or do you work with us?" His voice was bored, as if the enormous weretiger were of no consequence.

But Jack must have made some kind of signal, because Alaric spoke a single word and released him.

Jack rolled his shoulders, not looking at all pleased. But he acquiesced. "Yeah, I'll go along with your command, Conlan. As long as nothing you do puts Quinn in danger, I'm your man. For this one mission, at least."

Conlan bared his teeth in a grimace. "If you think that I would allow either Riley or her sister to be harmed, you seriously underestimate me," he snarled. "And nobody who underestimates me usually lives long enough to regret it."

"If we're done with the pissing contest, let's go," Quinn said, reaching out for Riley with one hand and pulling a very deadly looking gun out of her pocket with the other. "People to meet, vamps to blow away, et cetera, et cetera . . ."

Conlan stopped, stepped close to Riley. "You stay behind us, do you hear me? You point that gun at anything undead that moves, and you stay out of danger. Promise me that."

"But—"

"*Promise* me, or I call it off now, and we'll go live on a farm in Iowa or something. Atlantis be damned."

She managed a shaky smile. "I'm allergic to cow poop. I promise."

He nodded, and took the first step down the corridor. The first step leading Riley into danger. The hardest step he'd ever taken.

As Quinn had predicted, three vamps guarded the corridor at about the midway point. Conlan channeled water and shot a horizontal wall of ice at them, decapitating them before they had time to sound any alarm.

Jack let out a low whistle. "Nice trick, prince. I'm glad to have you on my team. This is going to be a cakewalk."

"There will be more than three, tiger. Don't grow too complacent." Conlan moved further along the dark corridor, searching for any crack of light that would indicate an opening. Another hundred or so yards down the tunnel, they came across a more heavily guarded passageway.

This time, Alaric called the electric power of lightning and shot bolts of pure energy at them, incinerating five of the six. Ven's dagger caught the sixth in the heart, and it collapsed, sizzling down into nothingness.

"Holy water on the blades. Works every damn time," Ven observed with satisfaction. He retrieved his dagger and wiped it off on a rag he drew from his pocket, then tossed the rag on the ground. "Somehow don't mind littering in the vamp's backyard."

Conlan held up a hand for silence. "I think it may be the vamps' front yard, in fact, if the sound of screaming is any indication."

He waited while they all strained to pick up on what his Atlantean hearing had already caught. Someone was being tortured.

And somebody else was doing a damn thorough job of it.

~~~~

The instincts that had served him well for nearly three thousand years were telling Barrabas that something was wrong. He just couldn't figure out *what*.

He should have been well content. The Atlantean called Micah was bleeding on the floor in front of him, near death, and Barrabas could still taste Micah's blood in his mouth. Reisen hadn't found his way back to consciousness since Drakos had smashed his head into the wall.

And yet, a tiny niggling tremor of doubt snaked through him. He stared at Drakos, who gazed implacably back at him. The general had outlived his usefulness. No battle strategy, no matter how brilliant, was worth this constant suspicion.

Especially for one who was not even of his blood pride. Thinking of them made him reach out to them with his mind. Reassurance from his guards would go a long way toward . . .

There was no response.

Nothing in his mind but a blank space where his vanguard should be. He whipped his head around to find Drakos.

Who stood near the chamber door, smiling.

"Your reign is over, damned one," Drakos said. "Prepare to meet the future."

Before Barrabas could utter a sound, Drakos yanked the door open, and a swarm of warriors poured through. The one in front had hair and eyes as black as the deepest hell, and death was written on his face.

"I am Conlan of Atlantis, Barrabas," the warrior shouted out. "Prepare for your death!"

No, no mere warrior. Not with that regal air of command.

This must be the prince. Barrabas hissed, called out with every ounce of his being to Anubisa.

Come to me, my goddess! Your Atlanteans are here to recover the Trident I captured for you—I beg for your assistance.

With that, he sent another mental command, and every one of his blood pride asleep in their coffins in the room below him rose and began the rush to his aid.

"You think attacking at dawn is any detriment to a master vampire of my power, princeling? We are deep under the earth, blocked from the sun by tons of concrete!" he screamed. Then he dematerialized, laughing, right from under their Atlantean noses.

Chapter 38

Conlan watched as Barrabas did exactly what he'd expected, and he slashed a hand down in a signal to Alaric. Alaric threw his arms into the air and called water with such torrential force that the walls themselves seemed to reel under the power of it.

Barrabas rematerialized, bouncing off one of the walls.

And Conlan laughed. "Didn't your goddess mention that Poseidon's power over the element of water is the light to your dark? We cannot kill you with the *mortus desicana*, for your undead tissues have no living fluid to surrender."

He unsheathed his sword. "But we can block you from the use of your power. Prepare to die, bloodsucker."

Barrabas pulled a sword of his own. "I don't think so, little boy. Didn't you take a moment to see what I did to your friends?"

He pointed to the far wall, and Conlan glanced over to the shadowy corner. Reisen hung by one wrist from a manacle chained to the wall, bloody and broken. Another warrior lay near him, in similar condition.

"Ven! To Reisen!"

As Ven, daggers unsheathed, ran across the room, a grinding noise in the floor underneath warned Conlan in time to leap to the side. A panel in the floor opened up, and a black wave of vampires rushed up and into the room.

Justice and Denal ran up to flank him, swords at the ready, and he heard Jack's full-throated roar from behind him. Then he was too busy to notice anything else, as five vamps headed straight for him, fangs and claws bared.

Riley! Get out! Get to safety!

Her voice came back to him immediately.

I think Poseidon promoted one of his pawns.

He tried to see over the warriors and vampires battling all around him, but couldn't see her. Desperation tore at the last shreds of his sanity. "To me, Warriors! For Atlantis!"

And he sliced the head off the vamp in front of him, trying to work his way through to Barrabas. "For Atlantis!"

Riley watched while the floor opened up a doorway from hell and devils came pouring through to attack Conlan. She held the gun out in front of her, but couldn't shoot. Everywhere she looked, vamps and warriors and freedom fighters were locked so closely in battle that she had no chance of a clear shot.

A second wave of vamps broke through from the corridor. Quinn had been right about Daniel, at least. He was fighting against the vamps, using their own tricks against them. She shuddered at the sight of his bloodied fangs ripping into yet another of them.

Alaric flashed into the space in front of her, pushing her and Quinn behind him and against the wall, as more of the vamps headed for them. Alaric threw out wave after wave of the energy bolts, but the vamps kept coming as fast as he could mow them down. One of them threw a dagger and Alaric leaned over to snatch it out of the air.

But it must have been a ploy of misdirection, because the vamp whipped a second dagger through the air on Alaric's other side, and it pierced Quinn in the thigh. Quinn screamed, and Alaric's attention jerked around to her, the sound distracting him.

Useless, trembling, Riley saw the vamp aim his sword at Alaric. She fired the gun, but missed him completely. Almost in slow motion, she watched the point of the blade drive deeply through Alaric's chest. He fell forward, onto Quinn, and Riley screamed again as the point of the sword, driven clear through Alaric's body, impaled her sister.

Heard Quinn's voice, weak, in her mind.

It's burning like acid, Riley. Poisoned, probably. If you've been touched by a god, now would be a good time to page him.

In front of her, she saw Jack transform in a roaring frenzy from man to tiger and tear into the vampires with teeth and claws. Conlan and Ven fought side by side in the midst of a dozen or more of them.

She didn't know what to do. Didn't know how to call a god. Didn't know magic or have powers or *anything*. She was a social worker, damnit. She stood there, sobbing, anguish and fury searing through her, and heat and power climbed through her, raged through her, until she thought she might detonate from it.

That was when the hand wrapped around her throat.

～～～

The pure evil of the voice rang through the room. "I have your woman, Atlantean. What value do you place on her life?"

All sound and motion stopped as if the world had frozen around him, and Conlan zoomed in on the source of the voice he most despised.

It was Anubisa, and she had her fingers on Riley's throat. Conlan's vision sheared a brilliant blue-green, then grayed out to almost black. As the vampires groveled and cringed their way to the sides of the room, genuflecting to their goddess, he saw Alaric lying on the floor on top of Quinn. A sword run through their bodies.

Their blood pooling on the floor.

He fought the howl of utter despair rising from his soul at the sight of Riley held helpless in the hands of a creature who could kill her with a breath.

"Leave her," he commanded. "She is nothing to me. Are you so weak you make war on human females now?"

She laughed, and the sound rang with pure malice, so dark and twisted that Riley moaned and tried to put her hands over her ears.

As Conlan watched, trickles of blood began to drip from

Riley's nostrils and the corners of her eyes. A killing rage swept through him. A memory, a vow, burned through him.

Anubisa will beg, before I'm done with her.

"Let her go, and you can take me back to your happy little love nest with you, Anubisa."

She turned her head to the side, as if entranced. "Oh, look at the precious kitty!"

Jack, in his tiger form, shot through the air, five hundred pounds of lethal killing machine headed for her head. She waved at him with two fingers, and his body slammed backward, tumbling end over end until he crashed into a line of groveling vampires, knocking them down like a row of dominoes.

None of them moved after that.

Conlan took another step closer to Anubisa, and her fingers tightened on Riley's fragile neck, a clear warning.

"Oh, I think not, princeling. I can smell your cock on her. So this is the slut you would have *willingly*, when I had to take you by force?"

She flicked a contemptuous glance up and down her captive, then almost negligently tossed Riley across the room so hard that he heard her head smash against the wall. "You know I don't share my toys."

He tried to run to Riley as she slid down the wall into a broken heap on the ground, but Anubisa caught him in a firebolt of power, chaining him in place with invisible bands of her dark magic.

Barrabas crawled toward Anubisa on his hands and knees, babbling. "My queen, my goddess, thank you, thank you. You came, you are here, and all will be saved."

She curled her index finger, beckoning Barrabas to her. Conlan fought to channel the elements, call any power at all, but he was as helpless under her control as he'd been during his captivity. All he could do was watch as she called her minion to her.

Anubisa smiled, delicately stepping over the body of a fallen shape-shifter. "You are my first, Barrabas. My oldest child, my precious one. Of course I would come when you called."

Her eyes glowed red, and she parted her lips to show

Barrabas a mouth crowded with razor-sharp fangs. Punishing, ripping, and tearing fangs.

Conlan knew all about those fangs, would have shuddered if his body hadn't been held in a vise grip of power.

Barrabas swayed, trapped hypnotically in his master's deadly pull. "Yes, your first, my goddess."

She gracefully lifted a hand to touch him, ripped the shirt from his body. "Then *why*?" she screamed, rage suddenly lighting her face into incandescence.

"Why did you not tell me you had the Trident?" she roared, and the sound of it smashed all the glass in the room. Burst eardrums. Curdled the blood of anyone still conscious.

Gave Conlan hope. If rage overwhelmed her, there was a chance he could defeat her. If Riley still lived—and he refused to believe that she did not—Poseidon would find a way to heal her.

If Riley is dead, not one undead creature will leave this room, except as ash.

Barrabas shrieked, and the sound pierced Conlan's skull. He jerked his gaze back to the vamps in time to see Anubisa lift her head from Barrabas's shoulder.

What was left of Barrabas's shoulder.

A chunk of it was in her mouth.

She smiled at him again, blood and pieces of flesh trapped in her fangs. "You have failed me. Worse, you tried to deceive me, fool."

She flicked out a hand, ripped his pants from him. The vampire knelt naked and bleeding in front of her, sobbing and shrieking in a hideous cacophony of pleading and apology.

"We have to set an example, don't we, my dear?" she murmured, voice almost gentle. Then she curled her hand into a claw and it shot out toward Barrabas's groin.

A tortured shriek beyond any Conlan had ever heard since leaving her lair ricocheted through the room, and he watched in utter horror as she opened her fingers to show Barrabas the bloody spectacle of his own balls in her hand.

"Yes," she repeated, delicately sucking the meat out of her hand. "We have to set an example."

As Barrabas fell over, still screaming, her hand shot forward again.

This time, she came back with his heart.

Barrabas never uttered another sound.

~~~~~

Riley felt consciousness coming back to her in ripples, as muted waves of sound and light washed into her mind. Conlan's horror, unshielded, nearly made her vomit, but some instinct told her to play dead.

She damn near was, if the pain crashing through her head was any clue.

She opened her heart and her mind, opened her *soul*, and begged for help.

I believe. I came to you in defiance before, now I come to you in abject humility, Poseidon. You are the sea god. You have power over these, your subjects.

Utter silence flooded her brain. She'd failed.

She traded humility for defiance.

Will you really let this bitch win the day?

Still silence. Hopelessness devastated her. If even the god who'd marked her deserted her, what hope did she have against the goddess of death?

THERE IS ALWAYS HOPE, DISRESPECTFUL ONE. ABJECT HUMILITY? MORE LIKE A PETULANT CHILD.

She nearly shuddered in relief, remembering at the last second to remain perfectly still.

Tell me what to do, your royal seaworthiness, and I'm your woman.

I THINK NOT. YOU ARE CONLAN'S WOMAN, AND A FINE QUEEN YOU'LL MAKE. YOU MAY MAKE USE OF MY TRIDENT ONE LAST TIME, GREAT-GRANDDAUGHTER OF MY SEED. USE IT WELL.

With that, his thundering presence was gone from her mind. But something hard and sharp was poking her in the butt.

Guess you've got a sense of humor after all. And thanks.

She felt the unmistakable shape of the Trident warming beneath her bent and broken body, filling her with heat and light and healing. With a single, silent blast, every injury was repaired, and she was filled with a sense of enormous power.

The mark on her shoulder burned, reminding her of her duty.

Oh, it will be my pleasure.

With one smooth motion, she grasped the shaft of the Trident and jumped to her feet. "Hey, bitch! Wanna play?"

Anubisa, hand full of some disgustingly bloody-looking thing, swung her attention to Riley, hissing. Conlan stood in the center of the room, muscles quivering, clearly unable to move.

"You're not dead yet, little whore? And you think to play with the toys of the gods? Oh, please. This might be fun," Anubisa said, voice purring with smug superiority.

Riley took a deep breath and pointed the Trident at her. "Hell, I don't even know how to work this thing, but let's go with modified light-saber," she muttered.

Then she screamed out her own defiance. "Take this, you evil, ugly, bloodsucking fiend!"

And she called on the power with everything in her. *Now! Now! Let's take her down, now!*

The Trident sang with a sweet, clear sound of soaring power, and it vibrated in her hands. As Anubisa's expression changed from a sneer to shocked surprise, a silvery torrent of pure energy shot out of the point of the Trident and arrowed directly into the vampire goddess, blasting her off her feet.

The shock wave of power spread through the room, and Conlan broke free of whatever magic had held him and ran to Riley. "You're alive! Thank the gods, *aknasha*."

He grasped the shaft of the Trident with his hands over Riley's and they aimed it at Anubisa again, as she tried to stand up.

"Die, you foul hell spawn!" Conlan roared.

"Stay away from my boyfriend!" Riley yelled.

This time, the powerful surge of energy shot into Anubisa and lifted her up into the air, smashing her into the ceiling and holding her there. Her head fell back and her mouth opened, and the energy poured through her mouth and nose and eyes, and then—with a thunderclap of sound—she disintegrated.

The stream of energy shut off like a faucet, and Riley and Conlan fell against each other. He put his hands on her face, turning it back and forth. "You're not hurt? How are you not hurt? I saw—"

"Poseidon. He healed me with the Trident," she said, laughing and sobbing at the same time.

They both thought it at the same time. "The others!"

They ran to Alaric and Quinn first, and Riley dropped to her knees next to her sister, crying harder at the sight of Quinn lying in such a huge pool of blood. Conlan yanked the sword out of their bodies, then knelt beside Riley, putting his hands over hers on the Trident again.

They both focused, channeled the power again. Watched as the healing silvery-green light spread over Alaric and Quinn. Saw the color come back to their faces. Heard the gasps of air sucked into their lungs.

Quinn opened her eyes. "Riley?"

"You're going to be fine, Quinn. Everybody is going to be fine."

Chapter 39

Conlan and Riley blinked at the light as they walked out of the door and into the bright sunshine. Quinn and Alaric, Jack, back in human form, and the rest of the Seven and the shape-shifters followed them into the bright noontime sun. Reisen came last, cradling his wounded arm, with Micah. The Trident had healed him, but Poseidon had not gifted him with the re-turn of his hand.

The sea god's vengeance would be served its pound of flesh.

The band crossed the street and walked, content to be alive and free, down the sidewalk to where it bordered a tree-lined park. A fountain sparkled in the chill autumn air.

"So this is good-bye, Atlantean," Jack said.

Conlan, arm tight around Riley's waist, shook his head. "No, I have a feeling that we'll be seeing more of each other. This fight is far from over."

Jack grinned, saluted, and strode off, melting into the trees with the rest of the freedom fighters.

Quinn remained behind, still clutching her sister's hand. "What will you do now, Riley? Want a job? You're pretty handy to have around in a fight."

Riley smiled, but then looked up at Conlan, her gaze troubled. "I don't know, actually. We have kind of a problem. Conlan can't date a human without the world ending, and I'm kind of opposed to destroying all of humanity, Atlantis, and the shape-shifters in one fell swoop."

Ven laughed. "Hell, I never thought I'd say this, but one of those bloodsuckers wasn't all that bad. I never thought I'd see Drakos turn on Barrabas."

"Who's Drakos?" Quinn asked.

"You call him Daniel," Conlan replied absently, gaze fixed on Riley. "And he disappeared after the battle, though he gave no quarter during it. I think we will have to learn more of this Daniel."

Conlan pulled Riley into his arms and, right there in the park, in front of his men, Quinn, and half of D.C., he kissed Riley with all the passion inside him. All of the terror, all of the relief. Then, still holding her in his arms, he sought out the priest.

"Alaric. I choose *her*. Over my duty, over my kingship, and even over my *life*. Begin the ritual of divestiture—aid me to renounce the throne and gain my future."

He grinned at his brother. "Ven will make a wonderful king."

"Oh, *hell*, no," Ven said, backing away.

Alaric opened his mouth to answer, but the voice of the sea god issued forth instead. Pure power blazed out of the priest's eyes.

"YOU WILL NOT RENOUNCE THE THRONE, CONLAN OF ATLANTIS."

Conlan prepared to defy his god. "Wanna bet?"

"YOU WILL NOT RENOUNCE THE THRONE," the voice thundered, shaking the ground they stood on.

"YOU WILL MAKE THIS FEMALE WHO BEARS MY MARK YOUR QUEEN. I COMMAND IT. YOUR CHILD WHOM SHE CARRIES IN HER WOMB WILL RISE TO BE A KING LIKE THE WORLD HAS NEVER BEFORE SEEN."

Conlan's mouth fell open. He looked down at Riley, who was also gaping in shock.

"BETWEEN THE TWO OF YOU, THERE IS ENOUGH DEFIANCE TO RULE THE WORLD. AS THE GOD OF ATLANTIS, I WOULD HOPE YOU WOULD TEACH YOUR SON SOME RESPECT FOR MY AUTHORITY."

Alaric's mouth snapped shut, and he fell against Quinn, who put her arms around his waist to support him. "What the hell was that?" she asked.

"Oh, that was nobody of the nine hells," Riley answered, grinning. "That was Poseidon, and I guess we have his okay."

Conlan swept her up in his arms and swung her around and around, whooping with joy. "My lady, my wife, my queen. What more could I ask?"

When he put her down, she folded her arms. "I don't know, but there's a lot more that I could ask."

He felt his heart shrivel inside him. "What are you saying?"

She smiled at him, eyes sparkling. Her heart shone fiercely with the love that she sent flowing out to him. To *all* of them, he guessed, when he heard the startled gasps of his warriors. "I could ask for an actual proposal, for starters."

He opened his mouth. Closed it. Dropped to one knee. "I, Conlan, high prince and heir to the throne of the Seven Isles of Atlantis, do ask you, Riley Elisabeth Dawson, owner of my heart and soul and body, to be my lady wife and queen. Do you accept me?"

She put her hands out to him. Pulled him up to stand in front of her. "I accept with all of my heart, Conlan. I will love you until the end of time."

Even as he caught her lips with his own, Conlan heard his brother's relieved words.

"Whew! Dodged that bullet!"

Conlan kissed Riley with all the joy in his heart, until he even imagined he heard the music of rushing water dancing around them.

Then it splashed on his face.

Lifting his head, he saw the water in the pond shoot into the air in a firework of sparkling color, splashing a mist of droplets onto all of them. The wind whipped the airborne water into streams of beautiful shapes and phantom images. The earth joined in, trembling under their feet.

Alaric spoke in his own voice, holding the Trident up in the air. "My prince, Poseidon has decreed that you have found your true queen. Hail to King Conlan and Queen Riley."

As one, the Seven all knelt, holding daggers and swords up in the air and shouting. "Hail to King Conlan and Queen Riley."

Reisen and Micah were on their knees as fast as the rest. The face Reisen raised to Conlan was somber with devotion and apology. Conlan nodded. Healing would come faster with forgiveness than punishment.

Quinn laughed and hugged Riley and Conlan both. "You'd better invite me to the wedding, is all I have to say."

She put a hand on Riley's stomach. "Do you think it's true? That you're pregnant?"

Wonder swept through Riley's emotions, and she looked down at her sister's hand on her belly. "Oh, my God! Or, oh, sea god! I guess he might know what he's talking about."

Conlan held his hand out to Quinn, pulled her close to himself and Riley. "You will never fight alone again, my new sister."

He looked to Alaric and Ven, saw the grim determination side by side with their joy. "War is coming, and it is time to fulfill our sacred duty to protect mankind."

Conlan looked around at his brother, his new family, his priest, and his men. "Atlantis must rise."

Turn the page for a special preview
of the next book in the
Warriors of Poseidon series

ATLANTIS AWAKENING

by Alyssa Day.

Coming in November 2007 from Berkley Sensation!

Ven wanted to smash something. Bad. Preferably the face of the jerk he'd been supposed to meet forty-five minutes ago.

He scanned the losers slouching on the barstools of the dive where they'd set up the meet. Professional drinkers, all. Professional losers. Although who else hung out in a place like this at midnight on a Tuesday night? Stale beer and desperation hung in the air in a foul cloud.

Well, losers except for one highly pissed off Atlantean warrior. Prince, even. Second in line to the throne, at least until Conlan and Riley started popping out babies. Which had better be soon, because no way did Ven ever want *that* little obligation. King of the Seven Isles of Atlantis.

He shuddered, downed his beer at the thought. Nope. He was much better as head of the warrior training academy. The King's Vengeance, whose sworn duty it was to protect his brother, the king.

Ven was the ultimate warrior. Feared by all.

He glanced up at the cracked face of the Budweiser clock on the wall. Except, of course, by the asshole he was supposed to be meeting to discuss a human-Atlantean alliance. The asshole who was now fifty-two minutes late.

The squeak of the hinges on the bar's door alerted him, and he looked up into the mirror behind the bar, gaze trained on the person walking in.

His eyes widened, and then narrowed in appreciation. If he had to waste time waiting for the jerk Quinn had sent, at least now he had something worth looking at. All curves and attitude in a small package, the blonde came striding into the place as if she owned it.

High-heeled leather boots worn under snug jeans, hips he'd love to get his hands on, and a tight-fitting black leather jacket. Oh, yeah. She was exactly his type of woman.

And he must have been dreaming, because she walked right past the lowlife scum who were drooling at the sight of her and stopped in front of him.

Ven was used to the reactions of human women to him. Hell, after several centuries, he knew that they considered him attractive. Not a lot of six-foot-seven-inch muscled warrior types running around with *human* DNA these days.

This one flicked her icy-blue gaze down, then up him and curled her lips back a little. He'd looked at steaming piles of peacock shit on the palace grounds with more enthusiasm.

"So," she drawled, disgust dripping from her voice. "*You're* the pride of Atlantis?"

She stalked around him and leaned back on the vacant barstool on his left, glanced his way again.

Then she rolled her freaking eyes.

Ven had seen and heard way more than enough. He rose to his full height, which gave him more than a foot on her, and stared down his nose. "You're late."

Okay, *that* was lame. Sadly, it was all he could think of, considering his brain cells had gone south at the sight of the creamy cleavage nestled in the gap between the lapels of her jacket and some lacy thing she wore underneath it.

For some reason, he wanted to lick it.

And her.

Oh, boy, she was trouble with a capital *bitch*.

"Make that a capital W, warrior," she said. "And you can sit down now and leave your Intimidation 101 tactics for somebody who is impressed with them."

He sat down, feeling like a damn fool, gaping at her. "Capital *W*? How did you—"

She smiled slowly, sensual lips curving over a gorgeous set of teeth. God, even her *teeth* turned him on. Suddenly he was a horny fucking dentist.

He shifted on the stool, hoping she hadn't noticed the sudden bulge in his leather pants.

"Capital W is for *witch*, warrior," she said. "Welcome to the revolution."

GLOSSARY OF TERMS

Aknasha—empath; one who can feel the emotions of others and, usually, send her own emotions into the minds and hearts of others, as well. There have been no *aknasha'an* in the recorded history of Atlantis for more than ten thousand years.

Atlanteans—a race separate from humans, descended directly from a mating between Poseidon and one of the Nereids, whose name is lost in time. Atlanteans inherited some of the gifts of their ancestors: the ability to control all elements except fire—especially water; the ability to transform to mist and travel in that manner; and superhuman strength and agility. Ancient scrolls hint at other powers, as well, but these are either lost to the passage of time or dormant in present-day Atlanteans.

Atlantis—the Seven Isles of Atlantis were driven beneath the sea during a mighty cataclysm of earthquakes and volcanic activity that shifted the tectonic plates of the Earth more than eleven thousand years ago. The ruling prince of the largest isle, also called Atlantis, ascends to serve as high king to all seven isles, though each are ruled by the lords of the individual isle's ruling house.

Blood pride—a master vampire's created vampires.

Landwalkers—Atlantean term for humans.

The Seven—the elite guard of the high prince or king of Atlantis. Many of the rulers of the other six isles have formed their own guard of seven in imitation of this tradition.

Shape-shifters—a species who started off as humans, but were cursed to transform into animals each full moon. Many shape-shifters can control the change during other times of the month, but newly initiated shape-shifters cannot. Shape-shifters have superhuman strength and speed and can live for more than three hundred years, if not injured or killed. They have a long-standing blood feud against the vampires, but old alliances and enemies are shifting.

Thought-mining—the Atlantean ability, long lost, to sift through another's mind and memories to gather information.

Vampires—an ancient race descended from the incestuous mating of the god Chaos and his daughter, Anubisa, goddess of the night. They are voracious for political intrigue and the amassing of power and are extremely long-lived. Vampires have the ability to dematerialize and teleport themselves long distances, but not over large bodies of water.

Warriors of Poseidon—warriors sworn to the service of Poseidon and the protection of humanity. They all bear Poseidon's mark on their bodies.

Penguin Group (USA) Online

What will you be reading tomorrow?

Tom Clancy, Patricia Cornwell, W.E.B. Griffin,
Nora Roberts, William Gibson, Robin Cook,
Brian Jacques, Catherine Coulter, Stephen King,
Dean Koontz, Ken Follett, Clive Cussler,
Eric Jerome Dickey, John Sandford,
Terry McMillan, Sue Monk Kidd, Amy Tan,
John Berendt…

You'll find them all at
penguin.com

*Read excerpts and newsletters,
find tour schedules and reading group guides,
and enter contests.*

Subscribe to Penguin Group (USA) newsletters
and get an exclusive inside look
at exciting new titles and the authors you love
long before everyone else does.

PENGUIN GROUP (USA)
us.penguingroup.com